The Lost Prince

The Frances Hodgson Burnett
Essential Collection

The Secret Garden
A Little Princess
Little Lord Fauntleroy
The Lost Prince

THE

FRANCES HODGSON BURNETT
ESSENTIAL COLLECTION

The Lost Prince

Frances Hodgson Burnett

ALADDIN

New York   London   Toronto   Sydney   New Delhi

ALADDIN

An imprint of Simon & Schuster Children's Publishing Division
1230 Avenue of the Americas, New York, New York 10020
First Aladdin hardcover edition December 2022
Jacket illustration copyright © 2022 by Bethany Stancliffe
This edition includes editorial revisions.
Also available in an Aladdin paperback edition.
All rights reserved, including the right of reproduction in whole or in part in any form.
ALADDIN and related logo are registered trademarks of Simon & Schuster, Inc.
For information about special discounts for bulk purchases, please contact Simon & Schuster
Special Sales at 1-866-506-1949 or business@simonandschuster.com.
The Simon & Schuster Speakers Bureau can bring authors to your live event.
For more information or to book an event contact the Simon & Schuster Speakers Bureau
at 1-866-248-3049 or visit our website at www.simonspeakers.com.
Jacket designed by Heather Palisi and Ginny Kemmerer
Interior designed by Mike Rosamilia
The text of this book was set in Bembo Std.
Manufactured in China 0822 SCP
2 4 6 8 10 9 7 5 3 1
Library of Congress Control Number 2022935531
ISBN 9781665931632 (hc)
ISBN 9781665931625 (pbk)
ISBN 9781665931649 (ebook)

Contents

The Lost Prince

The New Lodgers at No. 7 Philibert Place

There are many dreary and dingy rows of ugly houses in certain parts of London, but there certainly could not be any row more ugly or dingier than Philibert Place. There were stories that it had once been more attractive, but that had been so long ago that no one remembered the time. It stood back in its gloomy, narrow strips of uncared-for, smoky gardens, whose broken iron railings were supposed to protect it from the surging traffic of a road which was always roaring with the rattle of busses, cabs, drays, and vans, and the passing of people who were shabbily dressed and looked as if they were either going to hard work or coming from it, or hurrying to see if they could find some of it to do to keep themselves from going hungry. The brick fronts of the houses were blackened with smoke, their windows were nearly all dirty and hung with dingy curtains, or had no curtains at all; the strips of ground, which had once been intended to grow flowers in, had been trodden down into bare earth in which even weeds had forgotten to grow. One of them was used as a stone-cutter's yard, and cheap monuments, crosses, and slates were set out for sale, bearing inscriptions beginning with "Sacred to the Memory of." Another had piles of old lumber in it, another exhibited second-hand furniture, chairs with unsteady legs, sofas with horsehair stuffing bulging out of holes in their covering, mirrors with blotches or cracks in them. The insides of the houses were as gloomy as the outside. They were all exactly alike. In each a dark entrance passage led to narrow stairs going up to bedrooms, and to narrow steps going down to a basement kitchen. The back bedroom looked out on small, sooty, flagged yards, where thin cats quarreled, or sat on the coping of the brick walls hoping that some-time they might feel the sun; the front rooms looked over the noisy road, and through their windows came the roar and rattle of it. It was shabby and cheerless on the brightest days, and on foggy or rainy ones it was the most forlorn place in London.

At least that was what one boy thought as he stood near the iron railings watching the passers-by on the morning on which this story begins, which was also the morning after he had been brought by his father to live as a lodger in the back sitting-room of the house No. 7.

He was a boy about twelve years old, his name was Marco Loristan, and he was the kind of boy people look at a second time when they have looked at him once. In the first place, he was a very big boy—tall for his years, and with a particularly strong frame. His shoulders were broad and his arms and legs were long and powerful. He was quite used to hearing people say, as they glanced at him, "What a fine, big lad!" And then they always looked again at his face. It was not an English face or an American one, and was very dark in coloring. His features were strong, his black hair grew on his head like a mat, his eyes were large and deep set, and looked out between thick, straight, black lashes. He was as un-English a boy as one could imagine, and an observing person would have been struck at once by a sort of SILENT look expressed by his whole face, a look which suggested that he was not a boy who talked much.

This look was specially noticeable this morning as he stood before the iron railings. The things he was thinking of were of a kind likely to bring to the face of a twelve-year-old boy an unboyish expression.

He was thinking of the long, hurried journey he and his father and their old soldier servant, Lazarus, had made during the last few days—the journey from Russia. Cramped in a close third-class railway carriage, they had dashed across the Continent as if something important or terrible were driving them, and here they were, settled in London as if they were going to live forever at No. 7 Philibert Place. He knew, however, that though they might stay a year, it was just as probable that, in the middle of some night, his father or Lazarus might waken him from his sleep and say, "Get up—

dress yourself quickly. We must go at once." A few days later, he might be in St. Petersburg, Berlin, Vienna, or Budapest, huddled away in some poor little house as shabby and comfortless as No. 7 Philibert Place.

He passed his hand over his forehead as he thought of it and watched the busses. His strange life and his close association with his father had made him much older than his years, but he was only a boy, after all, and the mystery of things sometimes weighed heavily upon him, and set him to deep wondering.

In not one of the many countries he knew had he ever met a boy whose life was in the least like his own. Other boys had homes in which they spent year after year; they went to school regularly, and played with other boys, and talked openly of the things which happened to them, and the journeys they made. When he remained in a place long enough to make a few boy-friends, he knew he must never forget that his whole existence was a sort of secret whose safety depended upon his own silence and discretion.

This was because of the promises he had made to his father, and they had been the first thing he remembered.

Not that he had ever regretted anything connected with his father. He threw his black head up as he thought of that. None of the other boys had such a father, not one of them. His father was his idol and his chief. He had scarcely ever seen him when his clothes had not been poor and shabby, but he had also never seen him when, despite his worn coat and frayed linen, he had not stood out among all others as more distinguished than the most noticeable of them. When he walked down a street, people turned to look at him even oftener than they turned to look at Marco, and the boy felt as if it was not merely because he was a big man with a handsome, dark face, but because he looked, somehow, as if he had been born to command armies, and as if no one would think of disobeying him. Yet Marco had never seen him command anyone, and they had always been poor, and shabbily dressed, and often enough ill-fed. But whether they were in one country or another, and whatsoever dark place they seemed to be hiding in, the few people they saw treated him with a sort of deference, and nearly always stood when they were in his presence, unless he bade them sit down.

"It is because they know he is a patriot, and patriots are respected," the boy had told himself.

He himself wished to be a patriot, though he had never seen his own country of Samavia. He knew it well, however. His father had talked to him about it ever since that day when he had made the promises. He had taught him to know it by helping him to study curious detailed maps of it—maps of its cities, maps of its mountains, maps of its roads. He had told him stories of the wrongs done its people, of their sufferings and struggles for liberty, and, above all, of their unconquerable courage. When they talked together of its history, Marco's boy-blood burned and leaped in his veins, and he always knew, by the look in his father's eyes, that his blood burned also. His countrymen had been killed, they had been robbed, they had died by thousands of cruelties and starvation, but their souls had never been conquered, and, through all the years during which more powerful nations crushed and enslaved them, they never ceased to struggle to free themselves and stand unfettered as Samavians had stood centuries before.

"Why do we not live there," Marco had cried on the

day the promises were made. "Why do we not go back and fight? When I am a man, I will be a soldier and die for Samavia."

"We are of those who must LIVE for Samavia—working day and night," his father had answered; "denying ourselves, training our bodies and souls, using our brains, learning the things which are best to be done for our people and our country. Even exiles may be Samavian soldiers—I am one, you must be one."

"Are we exiles?" asked Marco.

"Yes," was the answer. "But even if we never set foot on Samavian soil, we must give our lives to it. I have given mine since I was sixteen. I shall give it until I die."

"Have you never lived there?" said Marco.

A strange look shot across his father's face.

"No," he answered, and said no more. Marco, watching him, knew he must not ask the question again.

The next words his father said were about the promises. Marco was quite a little fellow at the time, but he understood the solemnity of them, and felt that he was being honored as if he were a man.

"When you are a man, you shall know all you wish

to know," Loristan said. "Now you are a child, and your mind must not be burdened. But you must do your part. A child sometimes forgets that words may be dangerous. You must promise never to forget this. Wheresoever you are; if you have playmates, you must remember to be silent about many things. You must not speak of what I do, or of the people who come to see me. You must not mention the things in your life which make it different from the lives of other boys. You must keep in your mind that a secret exists which a chance foolish word might betray. You are a Samavian, and there have been Samavians who have died a thousand deaths rather than betray a secret. You must learn to obey without question, as if you were a soldier. Now you must take your oath of allegiance."

He rose from his seat and went to a corner of the room. He knelt down, turned back the carpet, lifted a plank, and took something from beneath it. It was a sword, and, as he came back to Marco, he drew it out from its sheath. The child's strong, little body stiffened and drew itself up, his large, deep eyes flashed. He was to take his oath of allegiance upon a sword as if he were a man. He did not know that his small hand opened and shut with a fierce understanding grip because those of his blood had for long centuries past carried swords and fought with them.

Loristan gave him the big bared weapon, and stood erect before him.

"Repeat these words after me sentence by sentence!" he commanded.

And as he spoke them Marco echoed each one loudly and clearly.

"The sword in my hand—for Samavia!

"The heart in my breast—for Samavia!

"The swiftness of my sight, the thought of my brain, the life of my life—for Samavia.

"Here grows a man for Samavia.

"God be thanked!"

Then Loristan put his hand on the child's shoulder, and his dark face looked almost fiercely proud.

"From this hour," he said, "you and I are comrades at arms."

And from that day to the one on which he stood beside the broken iron railings of No. 7 Philibert Place, Marco had not forgotten for one hour.

❧ 2 ❧
A Young Citizen of the World

He had been in London more than once before, but not to the lodgings in Philibert Place. When he was brought a second or third time to a town or city, he always knew that the house he was taken to would be in a quarter new to him, and he should not see again the people he had seen before. Such slight links of acquaintance as sometimes formed themselves between him and other children as shabby and poor as himself were easily broken. His father, however, had never forbidden him to make chance acquaintances. He had, in fact, told him that he had reasons for not wishing him to hold himself aloof from other boys. The only barrier which must exist between them must be the barrier of silence concerning his wanderings from country to country. Other boys as poor as he was did not make constant journeys, therefore they would miss nothing from his boyish talk when he omitted all mention of his. When he was in Russia, he must speak only of Russian places and Russian people and customs. When he was in France, Germany, Austria, or England, he must do the same thing. When he had learned English, French, German, Italian, and Russian he did not know. He had seemed to grow up in the midst of changing tongues which all seemed familiar to him, as languages are familiar to children who have lived with them until one scarcely seems less familiar than another. He did remember, however, that his father had always been unswerving in his attention to his pronunciation and method of speaking the language of any country they chanced to be living in.

"You must not seem a foreigner in any country," he had said to him. "It is necessary that you should not. But when you are in England, you must not know French, or German, or anything but English."

Once, when he was seven or eight years old, a boy had asked him what his father's work was.

"His own father is a carpenter, and he asked me if my father was one," Marco brought the story to Loristan. "I said you were not. Then he asked if you were a shoemaker, and another one said you might be a bricklayer or a tailor—and I didn't know what to tell them." He had been out playing in a London street, and he put a grubby little hand on his father's arm, and clutched and almost fiercely shook it. "I wanted to say that you were not like their fathers, not at all. I knew you were not, though you were quite as poor. You are not a bricklayer or a shoemaker, but a patriot—you could not be only a bricklayer—you!" He said it grandly and with a strange indignation, his black head held up and his eyes angry.

Loristan laid his hand against his mouth.

"Hush! Hush!" he said. "Is it an insult to a man to think he may be a carpenter or make a good suit of clothes? If I could make our clothes, we should go better dressed. If I were a shoemaker, your toes would not be making their way into the world as they are now." He was smiling, but Marco saw his head held itself high, too, and his eyes were glowing as he touched his shoulder. "I know you did not tell them I was a patriot," he ended. "What was it you said to them?"

"I remembered that you were nearly always writing and drawing maps, and I said you were a writer, but I did not know what you wrote—and that you said it was a poor trade. I heard you say that once to Lazarus. Was that a right thing to tell them?"

"Yes. You may always say it if you are asked. There are poor fellows enough who write a thousand different things which bring them little money. There is nothing strange in my being a writer."

So Loristan answered him, and from that time if, by any chance, his father's means of livelihood were inquired into, it was simple enough and true enough to say that he wrote to earn his bread.

In the first days of strangeness to a new place, Marco often walked a great deal. He was strong and untiring, and it amused him to wander through unknown streets, and look at shops, and houses, and people. He did not confine himself to the great thoroughfares, but liked to branch off into the side streets and odd, deserted-looking squares, and even courts and alleyways. He often stopped to watch workmen and talk to them if they were friendly. In this way he made stray acquaintances in his strollings, and learned a good many things. He had a fondness for wandering musicians, and, from an old Italian who had in his youth been a singer in opera, he had learned to sing a number of songs in his strong, musical boy-voice. He knew well many of the songs of the people in several countries.

It was very dull this first morning, and he wished that he had something to do or someone to speak to. To do nothing whatever is a depressing thing at all times, but perhaps it is more especially so when one is a big, healthy boy twelve years old. London as he saw it in the Marylebone Road seemed to him a hideous place. It was murky and shabby-looking, and full of dreary-faced people. It was not the first time he had seen the same things, and they always made him feel that he wished he had something to do.

Suddenly he turned away from the gate and went

into the house to speak to Lazarus. He found him in his dingy closet of a room on the fourth floor at the back of the house.

"I am going for a walk," he announced to him. "Please tell my father if he asks for me. He is busy, and I must not disturb him."

Lazarus was patching an old coat as he often patched things—even shoes sometimes. When Marco spoke, he stood up at once to answer him. He was very obstinate and particular about certain forms of manner. Nothing would have obliged him to remain seated when Loristan or Marco was near him. Marco thought it was because he had been so strictly trained as a soldier. He knew that his father had had great trouble to make him lay aside his habit of saluting when they spoke to him.

"Perhaps," Marco had heard Loristan say to him almost severely, once when he had forgotten himself and had stood at salute while his master passed through a broken-down iron gate before an equally broken-down-looking lodging-house—"perhaps you can force yourself to remember when I tell you that it is not safe—IT IS NOT SAFE! You put us in danger!"

It was evident that this helped the good fellow to control himself. Marco remembered that at the time he had actually turned pale, and had struck his forehead and poured forth a torrent of Samavian dialect in penitence and terror. But, though he no longer saluted them in public, he omitted no other form of reverence and ceremony, and the boy had become accustomed to being treated as if he were anything but the shabby lad whose very coat was patched by the old soldier who stood "at attention" before him.

"Yes, sir," Lazarus answered. "Where was it your wish to go?"

Marco knitted his black brows a little in trying to recall distinct memories of the last time he had been in London.

"I have been to so many places, and have seen so many things since I was here before, that I must begin to learn again about the streets and buildings I do not quite remember."

"Yes, sir," said Lazarus. "There HAVE been so many. I also forget. You were but eight years old when you were last here."

"I think I will go and find the royal palace, and then I will walk about and learn the names of the streets," Marco said.

"Yes, sir," answered Lazarus, and this time he made his military salute.

Marco lifted his right hand in recognition, as if he had been a young officer. Most boys might have looked awkward or theatrical in making the gesture, but he made it with naturalness and ease, because he had been familiar with the form since his babyhood. He had seen officers returning the salutes of their men when they encountered each other by chance in the streets, he had seen princes passing sentries on their way to their carriages, more august personages raising the quiet, recognizing hand to their helmets as they rode through applauding crowds. He had seen many royal persons and many royal pageants, but always only as an ill-clad boy standing on the edge of the crowd of common people. An energetic lad, however poor, cannot spend his days in going from one country to another without, by mere everyday chance, becoming familiar with the outer life of royalties and courts. Marco had stood in Continental thoroughfares when visiting emperors rode by with glittering soldiery before and behind them, and a populace shouting courteous welcomes. He knew where in various great capitals the sentries stood before kingly or princely palaces. He had seen certain royal faces often enough to know them well, and to be ready to make his salute when particular quiet and unattended carriages passed him by.

"It is well to know them. It is well to observe everything and to train one's self to remember faces and circumstances," his father had said. "If you were a young prince or a young man training for a diplomatic career, you would be taught to notice and remember people and things as you would be taught to speak your own language with elegance. Such observation would be your most practical accomplishment and greatest power. It is as practical for one man as another—for a poor lad in a patched coat as for one whose place is to be in courts. As you cannot be educated in the ordinary way, you must learn from travel and the world. You must lose nothing—forget nothing."

It was his father who had taught him everything, and he had learned a great deal. Loristan had the power of making all things interesting to fascination. To Marco it seemed that he knew everything in the world. They were not rich enough to buy many books, but Loristan knew the treasures of all great cities, the resources of the smallest towns. Together he and his boy walked through the endless galleries filled with the wonders of the world, the pictures before which through centuries an unbroken procession of almost worshipping eyes had passed uplifted. Because his father made the pictures seem the glowing, burning work of still-living men whom the centuries could not turn to dust, because he could tell the stories of their living and laboring to triumph, stories of what they felt and suffered and were, the boy became as familiar with the old masters—Italian, German, French, Dutch, English, Spanish—as he was with most of the countries they had lived in. They were not merely old masters to him, but men who were great, men who seemed to him to have wielded beautiful swords and held high, splendid lights. His father could not go often with him, but he always took him for the first time to the galleries, museums, libraries, and historical places which were richest in treasures of art, beauty, or story. Then, having seen them once through his eyes, Marco went again and again alone, and so grew intimate with the wonders of the world. He knew that he was gratifying a wish of his father's when he tried to train himself to observe all things and forget nothing. These palaces of marvels were his schoolrooms, and his strange but rich education was the most interesting part of his life. In time, he knew exactly the places where the great Rembrandts, Van Dycks, Rubens, Raphaels, Tintorettos, or Frans Hals hung; he knew whether this masterpiece or that was in Vienna, in Paris, in Venice, or Munich, or Rome. He knew stories of splendid crown jewels, of old armor, of ancient crafts, and of Roman relics dug up from beneath the foundations of old German cities. Any boy wandering to amuse himself through museums and palaces on "free days" could see what he saw, but boys living fuller and less lonely lives would have been less likely to concentrate their entire minds on what they looked at, and also less likely to store away facts with the determination to be able to recall at any moment the mental shelf on which they were laid. Having no playmates and nothing to play with, he began when he was a very little fellow to make a sort of game out of his rambles through picture-galleries, and the places which, whether they called themselves museums or not, were storehouses or relics of antiquity. There were always the blessed "free days," when he could climb any marble steps, and enter any great portal without paying an entrance fee. Once inside, there were plenty of plainly and poorly dressed people to be seen, but there were not often boys as young as himself who were not attended by older companions. Quiet and orderly as he was, he often found himself stared at. The game he had created for himself was as simple as it was absorbing. It was to try how much he could remember and clearly describe to his father when they sat together at night and talked of what he had seen. These night talks filled his happiest hours. He never felt lonely then, and when his father sat and watched him with a certain curious and deep attention in his dark, reflective eyes, the boy was utterly comforted and content. Sometimes he brought back rough and crude sketches of objects he wished to ask questions about, and Loristan could always relate to him the full, rich story of the thing he wanted to know. They were stories made so splendid and full of color in the telling that Marco could not forget them.

↶ 3 ↷
The Legend of the Lost Prince

As he walked through the streets, he was thinking of one of these stories. It was one he had heard first when he was very young, and it had so seized upon his imagination that he had asked often for it. It was, indeed, a part of the long-past history of Samavia, and he had loved it for that reason. Lazarus had often told it to him, sometimes adding much detail, but he had always liked best his father's version, which seemed a thrilling and living thing. On their journey from Russia, during an hour when they had been forced to wait in a cold wayside station and had found the time long, Loristan had discussed it with him. He always found some such way of making hard and comfortless hours easier to live through.

"Fine, big lad—for a foreigner," Marco heard a man say to his companion as he passed them this morning. "Looks like a Pole or a Russian."

It was this which had led his thoughts back to the story of the Lost Prince. He knew that most of the people who looked at him and called him a "foreigner" had not even heard of Samavia. Those who chanced to recall its existence knew of it only as a small fierce country, so placed upon the map that the larger countries which were its neighbors felt they must control and keep it in order, and therefore made incursions into it, and fought its people and each other for possession. But it had not been always so. It was an old, old country, and hundreds of years ago it had been as celebrated for its peaceful happiness and wealth as for its beauty. It was often said that it was one of the most beautiful places in the world. A favorite Samavian legend was that it had been the site of the Garden of Eden. In those past centuries, its people had been of such great stature, physical beauty, and strength, that they had been like a race of noble giants. They were in those days a pastoral people, whose rich crops and splendid flocks and herds were the envy of less fertile countries. Among the shepherds and herdsmen there were poets who sang their own songs when they piped among their sheep upon the mountain sides and in the flower-thick valleys. Their songs had been about patriotism and bravery, and faithfulness to their chieftains and their country. The simple courtesy of the poorest peasant was as stately as the manner of a noble. But that, as Loristan had said with a tired smile, had been before they had had time to outlive and forget the Garden of Eden. Five hundred years ago, there had succeeded to the throne a king who was bad and weak. His father had lived to be ninety years old, and his son had grown tired of waiting in Samavia for his crown. He had gone out into the world, and visited other countries and their courts. When he returned and became king, he lived as no Samavian king had lived before. He was an extravagant, vicious man of furious temper and bitter jealousies. He was jealous of the larger courts and countries he had seen, and tried to introduce their customs and their ambitions. He ended by introducing their worst faults and vices. There arose political quarrels and savage new factions. Money was squandered until poverty began for the first time to stare the country in the face. The big Samavians, after their first stupefaction, broke forth into furious rage. There were mobs and riots, then bloody battles. Since it was the king who had worked this wrong, they would have none of him. They would depose him and make his son king in his place. It was at this part of the story that Marco was always most deeply interested. The young prince was totally unlike his father. He was a true royal Samavian. He was bigger and stronger for his age than any man in the country, and he was as handsome as a young Viking god. More than this, he had a lion's heart, and before he was sixteen, the shepherds and herdsmen had already begun to make songs about his young valor, and his kingly courtesy, and generous kindness. Not only the shepherds and herds- men sang them, but the people in the streets. The king, his father, had always been jealous of him, even when he was only a beautiful, stately child whom the people roared with joy to see as he rode through the streets. When he returned from his journeyings and found him a splendid youth, he detested him. When the people began to clamor and demand that he himself should abdicate, he became insane with rage, and committed such cruelties that the people ran mad themselves. One day they stormed the palace, killed and overpowered the guards, and, rushing into the royal apartments, burst in upon the king as he shuddered green with terror and fury in his private room. He was king no more, and must leave the country, they vowed, as they closed round him with bared weapons and shook them in his face. Where was the prince? They must see him and tell him their ultimatum. It was he whom they wanted for a king. They trusted him and would obey him. They began to shout aloud his name, calling him in a sort of chant in unison, "Prince Ivor—Prince Ivor—Prince Ivor!" But no answer came. The people of the palace had hidden themselves, and the place was utterly silent.

The king, despite his terror, could not help but sneer.

"Call him again," he said. "He is afraid to come out of his hole!"

A savage fellow from the mountain fastnesses struck him on the mouth.

"He afraid!" he shouted. "If he does not come, it

is because thou hast killed him—and thou art a dead man!"

This set them aflame with hotter burning. They broke away, leaving three on guard, and ran about the empty palace rooms shouting the prince's name. But there was no answer. They sought him in a frenzy, bursting open doors and flinging down every obstacle in their way. A page, found hidden in a closet, owned that he had seen His Royal Highness pass through a corridor early in the morning. He had been softly singing to himself one of the shepherd's songs.

And in this strange way out of the history of Samavia, five hundred years before Marco's day, the young prince had walked—singing softly to himself the old song of Samavia's beauty and happiness. For he was never seen again.

In every nook and cranny, high and low, they sought for him, believing that the king himself had made him prisoner in some secret place, or had privately had him killed. The fury of the people grew to frenzy. There were new risings, and every few days the palace was attacked and searched again. But no trace of the prince was found. He had vanished as a star vanishes when it drops from its place in the sky. During a riot in the palace, when a last fruitless search was made, the king himself was killed. A powerful noble who had headed one of the uprisings made himself king in his place. From that time, the once splendid little kingdom was like a bone fought for by dogs. Its pastoral peace was forgotten. It was torn and worried and shaken by stronger countries. It tore and worried itself with internal fights. It assassinated kings and created new ones. No man was sure in his youth what ruler his maturity would live under, or whether his children would die in useless fights, or through stress of poverty and cruel, useless laws. There were no more shepherds and herdsmen who were poets, but on the mountain sides and in the valleys sometimes some of the old songs were sung. Those most beloved were songs about a Lost Prince whose name had been Ivor. If he had been king, he would have saved Samavia, the verses said, and all brave hearts believed that he would still return. In the modern cities, one of the jocular cynical sayings was, "Yes, that will happen when Prince Ivor comes again."

In his more childish days, Marco had been bitterly troubled by the unsolved mystery. Where had he gone—the Lost Prince? Had he been killed, or had he been hidden away in a dungeon? But he was so big and brave, he would have broken out of any dungeon. The boy had invented for himself a dozen endings to the story.

"Did no one ever find his sword or his cap—or hear anything or guess anything about him ever—ever— ever?" he would say restlessly again and again.

One winter's night, as they sat together before a small fire in a cold room in a cold city in Austria, he had been so eager and asked so many searching questions, that his father gave him an answer he had never given him before, and which was a sort of ending to the story, though not a satisfying one:

"Everybody guessed as you are guessing. A few very old shepherds in the mountains who like to believe ancient histories relate a story which most people consider a kind of legend. It is that almost a hundred years after the prince was lost, an old shepherd told a story his long-dead father had confided to him in secret just before he died. The father had said that, going out in the early morning on the mountain side, he had found in the forest what he at first thought to be the dead body of a beautiful, boyish, young huntsman. Some enemy had plainly attacked him from behind and believed he had killed him. He was, however, not quite dead, and the shepherd dragged him into a cave where he himself often took refuge from storms with his flocks. Since there was such riot and disorder in the city, he was afraid to speak of what he had found; and, by the time he discovered that he was harboring the prince, the king had already been killed, and an even worse man had taken possession of his throne, and ruled Samavia with a bloodstained, iron hand. To the terrified and simple peasant the safest thing seemed to get the wounded youth out of the country before there was any chance of his being discovered and murdered outright, as he would surely be. The cave in which he was hidden was not far from the frontier, and while he was still so weak that he was hardly conscious of what befell him, he was smuggled across it in a cart loaded with sheepskins, and left with some kind monks who did not know his rank or name. The shepherd went back to his flocks and his mountains, and lived and died among them, always in terror of the changing rulers and their savage battles with each other. The mountaineers said among them-selves, as the generations succeeded each other, that the Lost Prince must have died young, because otherwise he would have come back to his country and tried to restore its good, bygone days."

"Yes, he would have come," Marco said.

"He would have come if he had seen that he could help his people," Loristan answered, as if he were not reflecting on a story which was probably only a kind of legend. "But he was very young, and Samavia was in the hands of the new dynasty, and filled with his ene-mies. He could not have crossed the frontier without an army. Still, I think he died young."

It was of this story that Marco was thinking as he walked, and perhaps the thoughts that filled his mind expressed themselves in his face in some way which attracted attention. As he was nearing Buckingham Palace, a distinguished-looking well-dressed man with clever eyes caught sight of him, and, after looking at him keenly, slackened his pace as he approached him from the opposite direction. An observer might have thought he saw something which puzzled and surprised him. Marco didn't see him at all, and still moved forward, thinking of the shepherds and the prince. The well-dressed man began to walk still more slowly. When he was quite close to Marco, he stopped and spoke to him—in the Samavian language.

"What is your name?" he asked.

Marco's training from his earliest childhood had been an extraordinary thing. His love for his father had made it simple and natural to him, and he had never questioned the reason for it. As he had been taught to keep silence, he had been taught to control the expression of his face and the sound of his voice, and, above all, never to allow himself to look startled. But for this he might have started at the extraordinary sound of the Samavian words suddenly uttered in a London street by an English gentleman. He might even have answered the question in Samavian himself. But he did not. He courteously lifted his cap and replied in English:

"Excuse me?"

The gentleman's clever eyes scrutinized him keenly. Then he also spoke in English.

"Perhaps you do not understand? I asked your name because you are very like a Samavian I know," he said.

"I am Marco Loristan," the boy answered him.

The man looked straight into his eyes and smiled.

"That is not the name," he said. "I beg your pardon, my boy."

He was about to go on, and had indeed taken a couple of steps away, when he paused and turned to him again.

"You may tell your father that you are a very well-trained lad. I wanted to find out for myself." And he went on.

Marco felt that his heart beat a little quickly. This was one of several incidents which had happened during the last three years, and made him feel that he was living among things so mysterious that their very mystery hinted at danger. But he himself had never before seemed involved in them. Why should it matter that he was well-behaved? Then he remembered something. The man had not said "well-behaved," he had said "well-TRAINED." Well-trained in what way? He felt his forehead prickle slightly as he thought of the smiling, keen look which set itself so straight upon him. Had he spoken to him in Samavian for an experiment, to see if he would be startled into forgetting that he had been trained to seem to know only the language of the country he was temporarily living in? But he had not forgotten. He had remembered well, and was thankful that he had betrayed nothing. "Even exiles may be Samavian soldiers. I am one. You must be one," his father had said on that day long ago when he had made him take his oath. Perhaps remembering his training was being a soldier. Never had Samavia needed help as she needed it today. Two years before, a rival claimant to the throne had assassinated the then reigning king and his sons, and since then, bloody war and tumult had raged. The new king was a powerful man, and had a great following of the worst and most self-seeking of the people. Neighboring countries had interfered for their own welfare's sake, and the newspapers had been full of stories of savage fighting and atrocities, and of starving peasants.

Marco had late one evening entered their lodgings to find Loristan walking to and fro like a lion in a cage, a paper crushed and torn in his hands, and his eyes blazing. He had been reading of cruelties wrought upon innocent peasants and women and children. Lazarus was standing staring at him with huge tears running down his cheeks. When Marco opened the door, the old soldier strode over to him, turned him about, and led him out of the room.

"Pardon, sir, pardon!" he sobbed. "No one must see him, not even you. He suffers so horribly."

He stood by a chair in Marco's own small bedroom, where he half pushed, half led him. He bent his grizzled head, and wept like a beaten child.

"Dear God of those who are in pain, assuredly it is now the time to give back to us our Lost Prince!" he said, and Marco knew the words were a prayer, and wondered at the frenzied intensity of it, because it seemed so wild a thing to pray for the return of a youth who had died five hundred years before.

When he reached the palace, he was still thinking of the man who had spoken to him. He was thinking of

him even as he looked at the majestic gray stone build-
ing and counted the number of its stories and windows.
He walked round it that he might make a note in his
memory of its size and form and its entrances, and guess
at the size of its gardens. This he did because it was part
of his game, and part of his strange training.

When he came back to the front, he saw that in the
great entrance court within the high iron railings an
elegant but quiet-looking closed carriage was drawing
up before the doorway. Marco stood and watched with
interest to see who would come out and enter it. He
knew that kings and emperors who were not on parade
looked merely like well-dressed private gentlemen, and
often chose to go out as simply and quietly as other men.
So he thought that, perhaps, if he waited, he might see
one of those well-known faces which represent the
highest rank and power in a monarchical country, and
which in times gone by had also represented the power
over human life and death and liberty.

"I should like to be able to tell my father that I have
seen the King and know his face, as I know the faces of
the czar and the two emperors."

There was a little movement among the tall men-servants in the royal scarlet liveries, and an elderly man descended the steps attended by another who walked behind him. He entered the carriage, the other man followed him, the door was closed, and the carriage drove through the entrance gates, where the sentries saluted.

Marco was near enough to see distinctly. The two men were talking as if interested. The face of the one farthest from him was the face he had often seen in shop-windows and newspapers. The boy made his quick, formal salute. It was the King; and, as he smiled and acknowledged his greeting, he spoke to his companion.

"That fine lad salutes as if he belonged to the army," was what he said, though Marco could not hear him.

His companion leaned forward to look through the window. When he caught sight of Marco, a singular expression crossed his face.

"He does belong to an army, sir," he answered, "though he does not know it. His name is Marco Loristan."

Then Marco saw him plainly for the first time. He was the man with the keen eyes who had spoken to him in Samavian.

The Rat

Marco would have wondered very much if he had heard the words, but, as he did not hear them, he turned toward home wondering at something else. A man who was in intimate attendance on a king must be a person of importance. He no doubt knew many things not only of his own ruler's country, but of the countries of other kings. But so few had really known anything of poor little Samavia until the newspapers had begun to tell them of the horrors of its war—and who but a Samavian could speak its language? It would be an interesting thing to tell his father—that a man who knew the King had spoken to him in Samavian, and had sent that curious message.

Later he found himself passing a side street and looked up it. It was so narrow, and on either side of it were such old, tall, and sloping-walled houses that it attracted his attention. It looked as if a bit of old London had been left to stand while newer places grew up and hid it from view. This was the kind of street he liked to pass through for curiosity's sake. He knew many of them in the old quarters of many cities. He had lived in some of them. He could find his way home from the other end of it. Another thing than its strangeness attracted him. He heard a clamor of boys' voices, and he wanted to see what they were doing. Sometimes, when he had reached a new place and had had that lonely feeling, he had followed some boyish clamor of play or wrangling, and had found a temporary friend or so.

Halfway to the street's end there was an arched brick passage. The sound of the voices came from there—one of them high, and thinner and shriller than the rest.

Marco tramped up to the arch and looked down through the passage. It opened onto a gray flagged space, shut in by the railings of a black, deserted, and ancient grave-yard behind a venerable church which turned its face toward some other street. The boys were not playing, but listening to one of their number who was reading to them from a newspaper.

Marco walked down the passage and listened also, standing in the dark arched outlet at its end and watching the boy who read. He was a strange little creature with a big forehead, and deep eyes which were curiously sharp. But this was not all. He had a hunched back, his legs seemed small and crooked. He sat with them crossed before him on a rough wooden platform set on low wheels, on which he evidently pushed himself about. Near him were a number of sticks stacked together as if they were rifles. One of the first things that Marco noticed was that he had a savage little face marked with lines as if he had been angry all his life.

"Hold your tongues, you fools!" he shrilled out to some boys who interrupted him. "Don't you want to know anything, you ignorant swine?"

He was as ill-dressed as the rest of them, but he did not speak in the Cockney dialect. If he was of the riff-raff of the streets, as his companions were, he was somehow different.

Then he, by chance, saw Marco, who was standing in the arched end of the passage.

"What are you doing there listening?" he shouted, and at once stooped to pick up a stone and threw it at him. The stone hit Marco's shoulder, but it did not hurt him much. What he did not like was that another lad should want to throw something at him before they had even exchanged boy-signs. He also did not like the fact that two other boys promptly took the matter up by bending down to pick up stones also.

He walked forward straight into the group and stopped close to the boy with the hunched back.

"What did you do that for?" he asked, in his rather deep young voice.

He was big and strong-looking enough to suggest that he was not a boy it would be easy to dispose of, but it was not that which made the group stand still a moment to stare at him. It was something in himself—half of it a kind of impartial lack of anything like irritation at the stone-throwing. It was as if it had not mattered to him in the least. It had not made him feel angry or insulted. He was only rather curious about it. Because he was clean, and his hair and his shabby clothes were brushed, the first impression given by his appearance as he stood in the archway was that he was a young "toff" poking his nose where it was not wanted; but, as he drew near, they saw that the well-brushed clothes were worn, and there were patches on his shoes.

"What did you do that for?" he asked, and he asked it merely as if he wanted to find out the reason.

"I'm not going to have you swells dropping in to my club as if it was your own," said the boy.

"I'm not a swell, and I didn't know it was a club," Marco answered. "I heard boys, and I thought I'd come and look. When I heard you reading about Samavia, I wanted to hear."

He looked at the reader with his silent-expressioned eyes.

"You needn't have thrown a stone," he added. "They don't do it at men's clubs. I'll go away."

He turned about as if he were going, but, before he had taken three steps, the boy hailed him unceremoniously.

"Hi!" he called out. "Hi, you!"

"What do you want?" said Marco.

"I bet you don't know where Samavia is, or what they're fighting about." The boy threw the words at him.

"Yes, I do. It's north of Beltrazo and east of Jiardasia, and they are fighting because one party has assassinated King Maran, and the other will not let them crown Nicola Iarovitch. And why should they? He's a brigand, and hasn't a drop of royal blood in him."

"Oh!" reluctantly admitted the boy. "You do know that much, do you? Come back here."

Marco turned back, while the other boys still stared. It was as if two leaders or generals were meeting for the first time, and the rabble, looking on, wondered what would come of their encounter.

"The Samavians of the Iarovitch party are a bad lot and want only bad things," said Marco, speaking first. "They care nothing for Samavia. They only care for money and the power to make laws which will serve them and crush everybody else. They know Nicola is a weak man, and that, if they can crown him king, they can make him do what they like."

The fact that he spoke first, and that, though he spoke in a steady boyish voice without swagger, he somehow seemed to take it for granted that they would listen, made his place for him at once. Boys are impressionable creatures, and they know a leader when they see him. The boy with the hunched back fixed glittering eyes on him. The rabble began to murmur.

"Rat! Rat!" several voices cried at once in good strong Cockney. "Arst 'im some more, Rat!"

"Is that what they call you?" Marco asked the boy with the hunched back.

"It's what I called myself," he answered resentfully. "'The Rat.' Look at me! Crawling round on the ground like this! Look at me!"

He made a gesture ordering his followers to move aside, and began to push himself rapidly, with strange darts this side and that round the inclosure. He bent his head and body, and twisted his face, and made strange animal-like movements. He even uttered sharp squeaks as he rushed here and there—as a rat might have done when it was being hunted. He did it as if he were displaying an accomplishment, and his followers' laughter was applause.

"Wasn't I like a rat?" he demanded, when he suddenly stopped.

"You made yourself like one on purpose," Marco answered. "You do it for fun."

"Not so much fun," said The Rat. "I feel like one. Everyone's my enemy. I'm vermin. I can't fight or defend myself unless I bite. I can bite, though." And he showed two rows of fierce, strong, white teeth, sharper at the points than human teeth usually are. "I bite my father when he gets drunk and beats me. I've bitten him till he's learned to remember." He laughed a shrill, squeaking laugh. "He hasn't tried it for three months—even when he was drunk—and he's always drunk." Then he laughed again still more shrilly. "He's a gentleman," he said. "I'm a gentleman's son. He was a Master at a big school until he was kicked out—that was when I was four and my mother died. I'm thirteen now. How old are you?"

"I'm twelve," answered Marco.

The Rat twisted his face enviously.

"I wish I was your size! Are you a gentleman's son? You look as if you were."

"I'm a very poor man's son," was Marco's answer. "My father is a writer."

"Then, ten to one, he's a sort of gentleman," said The Rat. Then quite suddenly he threw another question at him. "What's the name of the other Samavian party?"

"The Maranovitch. The Maranovitch and the Iarovitch have been fighting with each other for five hundred years. First one dynasty rules, and then the other gets in when it has killed somebody as it killed King Maran," Marco answered without hesitation.

"What was the name of the dynasty that ruled before they began fighting? The first Maranovitch assassinated the last of them," The Rat asked him.

"The Fedorovitch," said Marco. "The last one was a bad king."

"His son was the one they never found again," said The Rat. "The one they call the Lost Prince."

Marco would have started but for his long training in exterior self-control. It was so strange to hear his dream-hero spoken of in this back alley in a slum, and just after he had been thinking of him.

"What do you know about him?" he asked, and, as he did so, he saw the group of vagabond lads draw nearer.

"Not much. I only read something about him in a torn magazine I found in the street," The Rat answered. "The man that wrote about him said he was only part of a legend, and he laughed at people for believing in him. He said it was about time that he should turn up again if he intended to. I've invented things about him because these chaps like to hear me tell them. They're only stories."

"We likes 'im," a voice called out, "becos 'e wos the right sort; 'e'd fight, 'e would, if 'e was in Samavia now."

Marco rapidly asked himself how much he might say. He decided and spoke to them all.

"He is not part of a legend. He's part of Samavian history," he said. "I know something about him too."

"How did you find it out?" asked The Rat.

"Because my father's a writer, he's obliged to have books and papers, and he knows things. I like to read, and I go into the free libraries. You can always get books and papers there. Then I ask my father questions. All the newspapers are full of things about Samavia just now." Marco felt that this was an explanation which betrayed nothing. It was true that no one could open a newspaper at this period without seeing news and stories of Samavia.

The Rat saw possible vistas of information opening up before him.

"Sit down here," he said, "and tell us what you know about him. Sit down, you fellows."

There was nothing to sit on but the broken flagged pavement, but that was a small matter. Marco himself had sat on flags or bare ground often enough before, and so had the rest of the lads. He took his place near The Rat, and the others made a semicircle in front of them. The two leaders had joined forces, so to speak, and the followers fell into line at "attention."

Then the newcomer began to talk. It was a good

story, that of the Lost Prince, and Marco told it in a way which gave it reality. How could he help it? He knew, as they could not, that it was real. He who had pored over maps of little Samavia since his seventh year, who had studied them with his father, knew it as a country he could have found his way to any part of if he had been dropped in any forest or any mountain of it. He knew every highway and byway, and in the capital city of Melzarr could almost have made his way blindfolded. He knew the palaces and the forts, the churches, the poor streets and the rich ones. His father had once shown him a plan of the royal palace which they had studied together until the boy knew each apartment and corridor in it by heart. But this he did not speak of. He knew it was one of the things to be silent about. But of the mountains and the emerald velvet meadows climbing their sides and only ending where huge bare crags and peaks began, he could speak. He could make pictures of the wide fertile plains where herds of wild horses fed, or raced and sniffed the air; he could describe the fertile valleys where clear rivers ran and flocks of sheep pastured on deep sweet grass. He could speak of them because he could offer a good enough reason for his knowledge of them. It was not the only reason he had for his knowledge, but it was one which would serve well enough.

"That torn magazine you found had more than one article about Samavia in it," he said to The Rat. "The same man wrote four. I read them all in a free library. He had been to Samavia, and knew a great deal about it. He said it was one of the most beautiful countries he had ever traveled in—and the most fertile. That's what they all say of it."

The group before him knew nothing of fertility or open country. They only knew London back streets and courts. Most of them had never traveled as far as the public parks, and in fact scarcely believed in their existence. They were a rough lot, and as they had stared at Marco at first sight of him, so they continued to stare at him as he talked. When he told of the tall Samavians who had been like giants centuries ago, and who had hunted the wild horses and captured and trained them to obedience by a sort of strong and gentle magic, their mouths fell open. This was the sort of thing to allure any boy's imagination.

"Blimme, if I wouldn't 'ave liked ketchin' one o' them 'orses," broke in one of the audience, and his exclamation was followed by a dozen of like nature from the others. Who wouldn't have liked "ketchin' one"?

When he told of the deep endless-seeming forests, and of the herdsmen and shepherds who played on their pipes and made songs about high deeds and bravery, they grinned with pleasure without knowing they were grinning. They did not really know that in this neglected, broken-flagged inclosure, shut in on one side by smoke-blackened, poverty-stricken houses, and on the other by a deserted and forgotten sunken graveyard, they heard the rustle of green forest boughs where birds nested close, the swish of the summer wind in the river reeds, and the tinkle and laughter and rush of brooks running.

They heard more or less of it all through the Lost Prince story, because Prince Ivor had loved lowland woods and mountain forests and all out-of-door life. When Marco pictured him tall and strong-limbed and young, winning all the people when he rode smiling among them, the boys grinned again with unconscious pleasure.

"Wisht 'e 'adn't got lost!" someone cried out.

When they heard of the unrest and dissatisfaction of the Samavians, they began to get restless themselves. When Marco reached the part of the story in which the mob rushed into the palace and demanded their prince from the king, they ejaculated scraps of bad language. "The old geezer had got him hidden somewhere in some dungeon, or he'd killed him out an' out—that's what he'd been up to!" they clamored. "Wisht the lot of us had been there then—wisht we 'ad. We'd 'ave give' 'im wot for, anyway!"

"An' 'im walkin' out o' the place so early in the mornin' just singin' like that! 'E 'ad 'im follered an' done for!" they decided with various exclamations of boyish wrath. Somehow, the fact that the handsome royal lad had strolled into the morning sunshine singing made them more savage. Their language was extremely bad at this point.

But if it was bad here, it became worse when the old shepherd found the young huntsman's half-dead body in the forest. He HAD "bin 'done for' IN THE BACK! 'E'd bin give' no charnst. G-r-r-r!" they groaned in chorus. "Wisht THEY'D bin there when 'e'd bin 'it! They'd 'ave done fur somebody" themselves. It was a story which had a strange effect on them. It made them think they saw things; it fired their blood; it set them wanting to fight for ideals they knew nothing about—adventurous things, for instance, and high and noble young princes who were full of the possibility of great and good deeds. Sitting upon the broken flag-stones of the bit of ground behind the deserted grave-yard, they were suddenly dragged into the world of romance, and noble young princes and great and good deeds became as real as the sunken gravestones, and far more interesting.

And then the smuggling across the frontier of the unconscious prince in the bullock cart loaded with sheepskins! They held their breaths. Would the old shepherd get him past the line! Marco, who was lost in the recital himself, told it as if he had been present. He felt as if he had, and as this was the first time he had ever told it to thrilled listeners, his imagination got him in its grip, and his heart jumped in his breast as he was sure the old man's must have done when the guard stopped his cart and asked him what he was carrying out of the country. He knew he must have had to call up all his strength to force his voice into steadiness.

And then the good monks! He had to stop to explain what a monk was, and when he described the solitude of the ancient monastery, and its walled gardens full of flowers and old simples to be used for healing, and the wise monks walking in the silence and the sun, the boys stared a little helplessly, but still as if they were vaguely pleased by the picture.

And then there was no more to tell—no more. There it broke off, and something like a low howl of dismay broke from the semicircle.

"Aw!" they protested, "it 'adn't ought to stop there! Ain't there no more? Is that all there is?"

"It's all that was ever known really. And that last part might only be a sort of story made up by somebody. But I believe it myself."

The Rat had listened with burning eyes. He had sat biting his fingernails, as was a trick of his when he was excited or angry.

"Tell you what!" he exclaimed suddenly. "This was

what happened. It was some of the Maranovitch fellows that tried to kill him. They meant to kill his father and make their own man king, and they knew the people wouldn't stand it if young Ivor was alive. They just stabbed him in the back, the fiends! I dare say they heard the old shepherd coming, and left him for dead and ran."

"Right, oh! That was it!" the lads agreed. "Yer right there, Rat!"

"When he got well," The Rat went on feverishly, still biting his nails, "he couldn't go back. He was only a boy. The other fellow had been crowned, and his followers felt strong because they'd just conquered the country. He could have done nothing without an army, and he was too young to raise one. Perhaps he thought he'd wait till he was old enough to know what to do. I dare say he went away and had to work for his living as if he'd never been a prince at all. Then perhaps sometime he married somebody and had a son, and told him as a secret who he was and all about Samavia." The Rat began to look vengeful. "If I'd bin him I'd have told him not to forget what the Maranovitch had done to me. I'd have told him that if I couldn't get back the throne, he must see what he could do when he grew to be a man. And I'd have made him swear, if he got it back, to take it out of them or their children or their children's children in torture and killing. I'd have made him swear not to leave a Maranovitch alive. And I'd have told him that, if he couldn't do it in his life, he must pass the oath on to his son and his son's son, as long as there was a Fedorovitch on earth. Wouldn't you?" he demanded hotly of Marco.

Marco's blood was also hot, but it was a different kind of blood, and he had talked too much to a very sane man.

"No," he said slowly. "What would have been the use? It wouldn't have done Samavia any good, and it wouldn't have done him any good to torture and kill people. Better keep them alive and make them do things for the country. If you're a patriot, you think of the country." He wanted to add "That's what my father says," but he did not.

"Torture 'em first and then attend to the country," snapped The Rat. "What would you have told your son if you'd been Ivor?"

"I'd have told him to learn everything about Samavia—and all the things kings have to know—and study things about laws and other countries—and about keeping silent—and about governing himself as if he were a general commanding soldiers in battle—so that he would never do anything he did not mean to do or could be ashamed of doing after it was over. And I'd have asked him to tell his son's sons to tell their sons to learn the same things. So, you see, however long the time was, there would always be a king getting ready for Samavia—when Samavia really wanted him. And he would be a real king."

He stopped himself suddenly and looked at the staring semicircle.

"I didn't make that up myself," he said. "I have heard a man who reads and knows things say it. I believe the Lost Prince would have had the same thoughts. If he had, and told them to his son, there has been a line of kings in training for Samavia for five hundred years, and perhaps one is walking about the streets of Vienna, or Budapest, or Paris, or London now, and he'd be ready if the people found out about him and called him."

"Wisht they would!" someone yelled.

"It would be a strange secret to know all the time when no one else knew it," The Rat communed with himself as it were, "that you were a king and you ought to be on a throne wearing a crown. I wonder if it would make a chap look different?"

He laughed his squeaky laugh, and then turned in his sudden way to Marco:

"But he'd be a fool to give up the vengeance. What is your name?"

"Marco Loristan. What's yours? It isn't The Rat really."

"It's Jem RATcliffe. That's pretty near. Where do you live?"

"No. 7 Philibert Place."

"This club is a soldiers' club," said The Rat. "It's called the Squad. I'm the captain. 'Tention, you fellows! Let's show him."

The semicircle sprang to its feet. There were about twelve lads altogether, and, when they stood upright, Marco saw at once that for some reason they were accustomed to obeying the word of command with military precision.

"Form in line!" ordered The Rat.

They did it at once, and held their backs and legs straight and their heads up amazingly well. Each had seized one of the sticks which had been stacked together like guns.

The Rat himself sat up straight on his platform. There was actually something military in the bearing of his lean body. His voice lost its squeak and its sharpness became commanding.

He put the dozen lads through the drill as if he had been a smart young officer. And the drill itself was prompt and smart enough to have done credit to practiced soldiers in barracks. It made Marco involuntarily stand very straight himself, and watch with surprised interest.

"That's good!" he exclaimed when it was at an end. "How did you learn that?"

The Rat made a savage gesture.

"If I'd had legs to stand on, I'd have been a soldier!" he said. "I'd have enlisted in any regiment that would take me. I don't care for anything else."

Suddenly his face changed, and he shouted a command to his followers.

"Turn your backs!" he ordered.

And they did turn their backs and looked through the railings of the old churchyard. Marco saw that they were obeying an order which was not new to them. The Rat had thrown his arm up over his eyes and covered them. He held it there for several moments, as if he did not want to be seen. Marco turned his back as the rest had done. All at once he understood that, though The Rat was not crying, yet he was feeling something which another boy would possibly have broken down under.

"All right!" he shouted presently, and dropped his ragged-sleeved arm and sat up straight again.

"I want to go to war!" he said hoarsely. "I want to fight! I want to lead a lot of men into battle! And I haven't got any legs. Sometimes it takes the pluck out of me."

"You've not grown up yet!" said Marco. "You might get strong. No one knows what is going to happen. How did you learn to drill the club?"

"I hang about barracks. I watch and listen. I follow soldiers. If I could get books, I'd read about wars. I can't go to libraries as you can. I can do nothing but scuffle about like a rat."

"I can take you to some libraries," said Marco. "There are places where boys can get in. And I can get some papers from my father."

"Can you?" said The Rat. "Do you want to join the club?"

"Yes!" Marco answered. "I'll speak to my father about it."

He said it because the hungry longing for companionship in his own mind had found a sort of response in the odd hungry look in The Rat's eyes. He wanted to see him again. Strange creature as he was, there was attraction in him. Scuffling about on his low wheeled platform, he had drawn this group of rough lads to him and made himself their commander. They obeyed him; they listened to his stories and harangues about war and soldiering; they let him drill them and give them orders. Marco knew that, when he told his father about him, he would be interested. The boy wanted to hear what Loristan would say.

"I'm going home now," he said. "If you're going to be here tomorrow, I will try to come."

"We shall be here," The Rat answered. "It's our barracks."

Marco drew himself up smartly and made his salute as if to a superior officer. Then he wheeled about and marched through the brick archway, and the sound of his boyish tread was as regular and decided as if he had been a man keeping time with his regiment.

"He's been drilled himself," said The Rat. "He knows as much as I do."

And he sat up and stared down the passage with new interest.

❧ 5 ❧
"Silence Is Still the Order"

They were even poorer than usual just now, and the supper Marco and his father sat down to was scant enough. Lazarus stood upright behind his master's chair and served him with strictest ceremony. Their poor lodgings were always kept with a soldierly cleanliness and order. When an object could be polished it was forced to shine, no grain of dust was allowed to lie undisturbed. Lazarus made himself extremely popular by taking the work of caring for his master's rooms entirely out of the hands of the overburdened maids of all work. He had learned to do many things in his young days in barracks. He carried about with him coarse bits of tablecloths and towels, which he laundered as if they had been the finest linen. He mended, he patched, he darned, and in the hardest fight the poor must face—the fight with dirt and dinginess—he always held his own. They had nothing but dry bread and coffee this evening, but Lazarus had made the coffee and the bread was good.

As Marco ate, he told his father the story of The Rat and his followers. Loristan listened, as the boy had known he would, with the far-off, intently-thinking smile in his dark eyes. It was a look which always fascinated Marco because it meant that he was thinking so many things. Perhaps he would tell some of them and perhaps he would not. His spell over the boy lay in the fact that to him he seemed like a wonderful book of which one had only glimpses. It was full of pictures and adventures which were true, and one could not help continually making guesses about them. Yes, the feeling that Marco had was that his father's attraction was for him a sort of spell, and that others felt the same thing.

When he stood and talked to commoner people, he held his tall body with singular quiet grace which was like power. He never stirred or moved himself as if he were nervous or uncertain. He could hold his hands (he had beautiful slender and strong hands) quite still; he could stand on his fine arched feet without shuffling them. He could sit without any ungrace or restlessness. His mind knew what his body should do, and gave it orders without speaking, and his fine limbs and muscles and nerves obeyed. So he could stand still and at ease and look at the people he was talking to, and they always looked at him and listened to what he said, and somehow, courteous and uncondescending as his manner unfailingly was, it used always to seem to Marco as if he were "giving an audience" as kings gave them.

He had often seen people bow very low when they went away from him, and more than once it had happened that some humble person had stepped out of his presence backward, as people do when retiring before a sovereign. And yet his bearing was the quietest and least assuming in the world.

"And they were talking about Samavia? And he

knew the story of the Lost Prince?" he said ponderingly. "Even in that place!"

"He wants to hear about wars—he wants to talk about them," Marco answered. "If he could stand and were old enough, he would go and fight for Samavia himself."

"It is a blood-drenched and sad place now!" said Loristan. "The people are mad when they are not heart-broken and terrified."

Suddenly Marco struck the table with a sounding slap of his boy's hand. He did it before he realized any intention in his own mind.

"Why should either one of the Iarovitch or one of the Maranovitch be king!" he cried. "They were only savage peasants when they first fought for the crown hundreds of years ago. The most savage one got it, and they have been fighting ever since. Only the Fedorovitch were born kings. There is only one man in the world who has the right to the throne— and I don't know whether he is in the world or not. But I believe he is! I do!"

Loristan looked at his hot twelve-year-old face with

a reflective curiousness. He saw that the flame which had leaped up in him had leaped without warning—just as a fierce heartbeat might have shaken him.

"You mean—?" he suggested softly.

"Ivor Fedorovitch. King Ivor he ought to be. And the people would obey him, and the good days would come again."

"It is five hundred years since Ivor Fedorovitch left the good monks." Loristan still spoke softly.

"But, Father," Marco protested, "even The Rat said what you said—that he was too young to be able to come back while the Maranovitch were in power. And he would have to work and have a home, and perhaps he is as poor as we are. But when he had a son he would call him Ivor and TELL him—and his son would call HIS son Ivor and tell HIM—and it would go on and on. They could never call their eldest sons anything but Ivor. And what you said about the training would be true. There would always be a king being trained for Samavia, and ready to be called." In the fire of his feelings he sprang from his chair and stood upright. "Why! There may be a king of Samavia in some city now who knows he is king, and, when he reads about the fighting among his people, his blood gets red-hot. They're his own people—his very own! He ought to go to them—he ought to go and tell them who he is! Don't you think he ought, Father?"

"It would not be as easy as it seems to a boy," Loristan answered. "There are many countries which would have something to say—Russia would have her word, and Austria, and Germany; and England never is silent. But, if he were a strong man and knew how to make strong friends in silence, he might sometime be able to declare himself openly."

"But if he is anywhere, someone—some Samavian—ought to go and look for him. It ought to be a Samavian who is very clever and a patriot—" He stopped at a flash of recognition. "Father!" he cried out. "Father! You—you are the one who could find him if anyone in the world could. But perhaps—" and he stopped a moment again because new thoughts rushed through his mind. "Have YOU ever looked for him?" he asked hesitating.

Perhaps he had asked a stupid question—perhaps his father had always been looking for him, perhaps that was his secret and his work.

But Loristan did not look as if he thought him stupid. Quite the contrary. He kept his handsome eyes fixed on him still in that curious way, as if he were studying him—as if he were much more than twelve years old, and he were deciding to tell him something.

"Comrade at arms," he said, with the smile which always gladdened Marco's heart, "you have kept your oath of allegiance like a man. You were not seven years old when you took it. You are growing older. Silence is still the order, but you are man enough to be told more." He paused and looked down, and then looked up again, speaking in a low tone. "I have not looked for him," he said, "because—I believe I know where he is."

Marco caught his breath.

"Father!" He said only that word. He could say no more. He knew he must not ask questions. "Silence is still the order." But as they faced each other in their dingy room at the back of the shabby house on the side of the roaring common road—as Lazarus stood stock-still behind his father's chair and kept his eyes fixed on the empty coffee cups and the dry bread plate, and everything looked as poor as things always did—there was a king of Samavia—an Ivor Fedorovitch with the blood of the Lost Prince in his veins—alive in some town or city this moment! And Marco's own father knew where he was!

He glanced at Lazarus, but, though the old soldier's face looked as expressionless as if it were cut out of wood, Marco realized that he knew this thing and had always known it. He had been a comrade at arms all his life. He continued to stare at the bread plate.

Loristan spoke again and in an even lower voice. "The Samavians who are patriots and thinkers," he said, "formed themselves into a secret party about eighty years ago. They formed it when they had no reason for hope, but they formed it because one of them discovered that an Ivor Fedorovitch was living. He was head forester on a great estate in the Austrian Alps. The nobleman he served had always thought him a mystery because he had the bearing and speech of a man who had not been born a servant, and his methods in caring for the forests and game were those of a man who was educated and had studied his subject. But he never was familiar or assuming, and never professed superiority over any of his fellows. He was a man of great stature, and was extraordinarily brave and silent. The nobleman who was his master made a sort of companion of him when they hunted together. Once he took him with him when he traveled to Samavia to hunt wild horses. He found that he knew the country strangely well, and that he was familiar with Samavian hunting and customs. Before he returned to Austria, the man obtained permission to go to the mountains alone. He went among the shepherds and made friends among them, asking many questions.

"One night around a forest fire he heard the songs about the Lost Prince which had not been forgotten even after nearly five hundred years had passed. The shepherds and herdsmen talked about Prince Ivor, and told old stories about him, and related the prophecy that he would come back and bring again Samavia's good days. He might come only in the body of one of his descendants, but it would be his spirit which came, because his spirit would never cease to love Samavia. One very old shepherd tottered to his feet and lifted his face to the myriad stars bestrewn like jewels in the blue sky above the forest trees, and he wept and prayed aloud that the great God would send their king to them. And the stranger huntsman stood upright also and lifted his face to the stars. And, though he said no word, the herdsman nearest to him saw tears on his cheeks—great, heavy tears. The next day, the stranger went to the monastery where the order of good monks lived who had taken care of the Lost Prince. When he had left Samavia, the secret society was formed, and the members of it knew that an Ivor Fedorovitch had passed through his ancestors' country as the servant of another man. But the secret society was only a small one, and, though it has been growing ever since and it has done good deeds and good work in secret, the huntsman died an old man before it was strong enough even to dare to tell Samavia what it knew."

"Had he a son?" cried Marco. "Had he a son?"

"Yes. He had a son. His name was Ivor. And he was trained as I told you. That part I knew to be true, though I should have believed it was true even if I had not known. There has ALWAYS been a king ready for Samavia—even when he has labored with his hands and served others. Each one took the oath of allegiance."

"As I did?" said Marco, breathless with excitement. When one is twelve years old, to be so near a Lost Prince who might end wars is a thrilling thing.

"The same," answered Loristan.

Marco threw up his hand in salute.

"'Here grows a man for Samavia! God be thanked!'" he quoted. "And HE is somewhere? And you know?"

Loristan bent his head in acquiescence.

"For years much secret work has been done, and the Fedorovitch party has grown until it is much greater and more powerful than the other parties dream. The larger countries are tired of the constant war and disorder in Samavia. Their interests are disturbed by them, and they are deciding that they must have peace and laws which can be counted on. There have been Samavian patriots who have spent their lives in trying to bring this about by making friends in the most powerful capitals, and working secretly for the future good of their own land. Because Samavia is so small and uninfluential, it has taken a long time but when King Maran and his family were assassinated and the war broke out, there were great powers which began to say that if some king of good blood and reliable characteristics were given the crown, he should be upheld."

"HIS blood"—Marco's intensity made his voice drop almost to a whisper—"HIS blood has been trained for five hundred years, Father! If it comes true"— though he laughed a little, he was obliged to wink his eyes hard because suddenly he felt tears rush into them, which no boy likes—"the shepherds will have to make a new song—it will have to be a shouting one about a prince going away and a king coming back!"

"They are a devout people and observe many an ancient rite and ceremony. They will chant prayers and burn altar-fires on their mountain sides," Loristan said. "But the end is not yet—the end is not yet. Sometimes it seems that perhaps it is near—but God knows!"

Then there leaped back upon Marco the story he had to tell, but which he had held back for the last—the story of the man who spoke Samavian and drove in the carriage with the King. He knew now that it might mean some important thing which he could not have before suspected.

"There is something I must tell you," he said.

He had learned to relate incidents in few but clear

words when he related them to his father. It had been part of his training. Loristan had said that he might sometime have a story to tell when he had but few moments to tell it in—some story which meant life or death to someone. He told this one quickly and well. He made Loristan see the well-dressed man with the deliberate manner and the keen eyes, and he made him hear his voice when he said, "Tell your father that you are a very well-trained lad."

"I am glad he said that. He is a man who knows what training is," said Loristan. "He is a person who knows what all Europe is doing, and almost all that it will do. He is an ambassador from a powerful and great country. If he saw that you are a well-trained and fine lad, it might—it might even be good for Samavia."

"Would it matter that *I* was well-trained? COULD it matter to Samavia?" Marco cried out.

Loristan paused for a moment—watching him gravely—looking him over—his big, well-built boy's frame, his shabby clothes, and his eagerly burning eyes.

He smiled one of his slow wonderful smiles.

"Yes. It might even matter to Samavia!" he answered.

❧ 6 ❧
The Drill and the Secret Party

Loristan did not forbid Marco to pursue his acquaintance with The Rat and his followers.

"You will find out for yourself whether they are friends for you or not," he said. "You will know in a few days, and then you can make your own decision. You have known lads in various countries, and you are a good judge of them, I think. You will soon see whether they are going to be MEN or mere rabble. The Rat now—how does he strike you?"

And the handsome eyes held their keen look of questioning.

"He'd be a brave soldier if he could stand," said Marco, thinking him over. "But he might be cruel."

"A lad who might make a brave soldier cannot be disdained, but a man who is cruel is a fool. Tell him that from me," Loristan answered. "He wastes force—his own and the force of the one he treats cruelly. Only a fool wastes force."

"May I speak of you sometimes?" asked Marco.

"Yes. You will know how. You will remember the things about which silence is the order."

"I never forget them," said Marco. "I have been trying not to, for such a long time."

"You have succeeded well, Comrade!" returned Loristan, from his writing-table, to which he had gone and where he was turning over papers.

A strong impulse overpowered the boy. He marched over to the table and stood very straight, making his soldierly young salute, his whole body glowing.

"Father!" he said. "You don't know how I love you! I wish you were a general and I might die in battle for you.

When I look at you, I long and long to do something for you a boy could not do. I would die of a thousand wounds rather than disobey you—or Samavia!"

He seized Loristan's hand, and knelt on one knee and kissed it.

"I took my oath of allegiance to you, Father, when I took it to Samavia. It seems as if you were Samavia, too," he said, and kissed his hand again.

Loristan had turned toward him with one of the movements which were full of dignity and grace. Marco, looking up at him, felt that there was always a certain remote stateliness in him which made it seem quite natural that anyone should bend the knee and kiss his hand.

A sudden great tenderness glowed in his father's face as he raised the boy and put his hand on his shoulder.

"Comrade," he said, "you don't know how much I love you—and what reason there is that we should love each other! You don't know how I have been watching you, and thanking God each year that here grew a man for Samavia. That I know you are—a MAN, though you have lived but twelve years. Twelve years may grow a man—or prove that a man will never grow, though a human thing he may remain for ninety years. This year may be full of strange things for both of us. We cannot know WHAT I may have to ask you to do for me—and for Samavia. Perhaps such a thing as no twelve-year-old boy has ever done before."

"Every night and every morning," said Marco, "I shall pray that I may be called to do it, and that I may do it well."

"You will do it well, Comrade, if you are called. That I could make oath," Loristan answered him.

The Squad had collected in the inclosure behind the church when Marco appeared at the arched end of the passage. The boys were drawn up with their rifles, but they all wore a rather dogged and sullen look. The explanation which darted into Marco's mind was that this was because The Rat was in a bad humor. He sat crouched together on his platform biting his nails fiercely, his elbows on his updrawn knees, his face twisted into a hideous scowl. He did not look around, or even look up from the cracked flagstone of the pavement on which his eyes were fixed.

Marco went forward with military step and stopped opposite to him with prompt salute.

"Sorry to be late, sir," he said, as if he had been a private speaking to his colonel.

"It's 'im, Rat! 'E's come, Rat!" the Squad shouted. "Look at 'im!"

But The Rat would not look, and did not even move.

"What's the matter?" said Marco, with less ceremony than a private would have shown. "There's no use in my coming here if you don't want me."

"'E's got a grouch on 'cos you're late!" called out the head of the line. "No doin' nothin' when 'e's got a grouch on."

"I shan't try to do anything," said Marco, his boy-face setting itself into good stubborn lines. "That's not what I came here for. I came to drill. I've been with my father. He comes first. I can't join the Squad if he doesn't come first. We're not on active service, and we're not in barracks."

Then The Rat moved sharply and turned to look at him.

"I thought you weren't coming at all!" he snapped and growled at once. "My father said you wouldn't. He said you were a young swell for all your patched clothes. He said your father would think he was a swell, even if he was only a penny-a-liner on newspapers, and he wouldn't let you have anything to do with a vagabond and a nuisance. Nobody begged you to join. Your father can go to blazes!"

"Don't you speak in that way about my father," said Marco, quite quietly, "because I can't knock you down."

"I'll get up and let you!" began The Rat, immediately white and raging. "I can stand up with two sticks. I'll get up and let you!"

"No, you won't," said Marco. "If you want to know what my father said, I can tell you. He said I could come as often as I liked—till I found out whether we should be friends or not. He says I shall find that out for myself."

It was a strange thing The Rat did. It must always be remembered of him that his wretched father, who had each year sunk lower and lower in the underworld, had been a gentleman once, a man who had been familiar with good manners and had been educated in the customs of good breeding. Sometimes when he was drunk, and sometimes when he was partly sober, he talked to The Rat of many things the boy would otherwise never have heard of. That was why the lad was different from the other vagabonds. This, also, was why he suddenly altered the whole situation by doing this strange and unexpected thing. He utterly changed his expression and voice, fixing his sharp eyes shrewdly on Marco's. It was almost as if he were asking him a conundrum. He knew it would have been one to most boys of the class he appeared outwardly to belong to. He would either know the answer or he wouldn't.

"I beg your pardon," The Rat said.

That was the conundrum. It was what a gentleman and an officer would have said, if he felt he had been mistaken or rude. He had heard that from his drunken father.

"I beg yours—for being late," said Marco.

That was the right answer. It was the one another officer and gentleman would have made. It settled the matter at once, and it settled more than was apparent at the moment. It decided that Marco was one of those who knew the things The Rat's father had once known—the things gentlemen do and say and think. Not another word was said. It was all right. Marco slipped into line with the Squad, and The Rat sat erect with his military bearing and began his drill:

"Squad!

"'Tention!

"Number!

"Slope arms!

"Form fours!

"Right!

"Quick march!

"Halt!

"Left turn!

"Order arms!

"Stand at ease!

"Stand easy!"

They did it so well that it was quite wonderful when one considered the limited space at their disposal. They had evidently done it often, and The Rat had been not only a smart, but a severe, officer. This morning they repeated the exercise a number of times, and even varied it with Review Drill, with which they seemed just as familiar.

"Where did you learn it?" The Rat asked, when the arms were stacked again and Marco was sitting by him as he had sat the previous day.

"From an old soldier. And I like to watch it, as you do."

"If you were a young swell in the Guards, you couldn't be smarter at it," The Rat said. "The way you hold yourself! The way you stand! You've got it! Wish I was you! It comes natural to you."

"I've always liked to watch it and try to do it myself. I did when I was a little fellow," answered Marco.

"I've been trying to kick it into these chaps for more than a year," said The Rat. "A nice job I had of it! It nearly made me sick at first."

The semicircle in front of him only giggled or laughed outright. The members of it seemed to take very little offense at his cavalier treatment of them. He had evidently something to give them which was entertaining enough to make up for his tyranny and indifference. He thrust his hand into one of the pockets of his ragged coat, and drew out a piece of newspaper.

"My father brought home this, wrapped round a loaf of bread," he said. "See what it says there!"

He handed it to Marco, pointing to some words printed in large letters at the head of a column. Marco looked at it and sat very still.

The words he read were: "The Lost Prince."

"Silence is still the order," was the first thought which flashed through his mind. "Silence is still the order."

"What does it mean?" he said aloud.

"There isn't much of it. I wish there was more," The Rat said fretfully. "Read and see. Of course they say it mayn't be true—but I believe it is. They say that people think someone knows where he is—at least where one of his descendants is. It'd be the same thing. He'd be the real king. If he'd just show himself, it might stop all the fighting. Just read."

Marco read, and his skin prickled as the blood went racing through his body. But his face did not change. There was a sketch of the story of the Lost Prince to begin with. It had been regarded by most people, the article said, as a sort of legend. Now there was a definite rumor that it was not a legend at all, but a part of the long past history of Samavia. It was said that through the centuries there had always been a party secretly loyal to the memory of this worshipped and lost Fedorovitch. It was even said that from father to son, generation after generation after generation, had descended the oath of fealty to him and his descendants. The people had made a god of him, and now, romantic as it seemed, it was beginning to be an open secret that some persons believed that a descendant had been found—a Fedorovitch worthy of his young ancestor— and that a certain Secret Party also held that, if he were called back to the throne of Samavia, the interminable wars and bloodshed would reach an end.

The Rat had begun to bite his nails fast.

"Do you believe he's found?" he asked feverishly. "DON'T YOU? I do!"

"I wonder where he is, if it's true? I wonder! Where?" exclaimed Marco. He could say that, and he might seem as eager as he felt.

The Squad all began to jabber at once. "Yus, where wos'e? There is no knowin'. England'd be too far from

Samavia. 'Ow far off wos Samavia? Wos it in Roosha, or where the French were, or the Germans? But wherever 'e wos, 'e'd be the sort a chap'd turn and look at in the street."

The Rat continued to bite his nails.

"He might be anywhere," he said, his small fierce face glowing. "That's what I like to think about. He might be passing in the street outside there; he might be up in one of those houses," jerking his head over his shoulder toward the backs of the inclosing dwellings. "Perhaps he knows he's a king, and perhaps he doesn't. He'd know if what you said yesterday was true—about the king always being made ready for Samavia."

"Yes, he'd know," put in Marco.

"Well, it'd be finer if he did," went on The Rat. "However poor and shabby he was, he'd know the secret all the time. And if people sneered at him, he'd sneer at them and laugh to himself. I dare say he'd walk tremendously straight and hold his head up. If I was him, I'd like to make people suspect a bit that I wasn't like the common lot o' them." He put out his hand and pushed Marco excitedly. "Let's work out plots for him!"

he said. "That'd be a splendid game! Let's pretend we're the Secret Party!"

He was tremendously excited. Out of the ragged pocket he fished a piece of chalk. Then he leaned forward and began to draw something quickly on the flagstones closest to his platform. The Squad leaned forward also, quite breathlessly, and Marco leaned forward. The chalk was sketching a roughly outlined map, and he knew what map it was, before The Rat spoke.

"That's a map of Samavia," he said. "It was in that piece of magazine I told you about—the one where I read about Prince Ivor. I studied it until it fell to pieces. But I could draw it myself by that time, so it didn't matter. I could draw it with my eyes shut. That's the capital city," pointing to a spot. "It's called Melzarr. The palace is there. It's the place where the first of the Maranovitch killed the last of the Fedorovitch— the bad chap that was Ivor's father. It's the palace Ivor wandered out of singing the shepherds' song that early morning. It's where the throne is that his descendant would sit upon to be crowned—that he's GOING to sit upon. I believe he is! Let's swear he shall!" He flung down his piece of chalk and sat up. "Give me two sticks. Help me to get up."

Two of the Squad sprang to their feet and came to him. Each snatched one of the sticks from the stacked rifles, evidently knowing what he wanted. Marco rose too, and watched with sudden, keen curiosity. He had thought that The Rat could not stand up, but it seemed that he could, in a fashion of his own, and he was going to do it. The boys lifted him by his arms, set him against the stone coping of the iron railings of the churchyard, and put a stick in each of his hands. They stood at his side, but he supported himself.

"'E could get about if 'e 'ad the money to buy crutches!" said one whose name was Cad, and he said it quite proudly. The strange thing that Marco had noticed was that the ragamuffins were proud of The Rat, and regarded him as their lord and master. "—'E could get about an' stand as well as anyone," added the other, and he said it in the tone of one who boasts. His name was Ben.

"I'm going to stand now, and so are the rest of you," said The Rat. "Squad! 'Tention! You at the head of the line," to Marco. They were in line in a moment—straight, shoulders back, chins up. And Marco stood at the head.

"We're going to take an oath," said The Rat. "It's an oath of allegiance. Allegiance means faithfulness to a thing—a king or a country. Ours means allegiance to the King of Samavia. We don't know where he is, but we swear to be faithful to him, to fight for him, to plot for him, to DIE for him, and to bring him back to his throne!" The way in which he flung up his head when he said the word "die" was very fine indeed. "We are the Secret Party. We will work in the dark and find out things—and run risks—and collect an army no one will know anything about until it is strong enough to suddenly rise at a secret signal, and overwhelm the Maranovitch and Iarovitch, and seize their forts and citadels. No one even knows we are alive. We are a silent, secret thing that never speaks aloud!"

Silent and secret as they were, however, they spoke aloud at this juncture. It was such a grand idea for a game, and so full of possible larks, that the Squad broke into a howl of an exultant cheer.

"Hooray!" they yelled. "Hooray for the oath of 'legiance! 'Ray! 'Ray! 'Ray!"

"Shut up, you swine!" shouted The Rat. "Is that the way you keep yourself secret? You'll call the police in, you fools! Look at HIM!" He pointed to Marco. "He's got some sense."

Marco, in fact, had not made any sound.

"Come here, you—Cad and Ben—and put me back on my wheels," raged the Squad's commander. "I'll not make up the game at all. It's no use with a lot of fathead, raw recruits like you."

The line broke and surrounded him in a moment, pleading and urging.

"Aw, Rat! We forgot. It's the primest game you've ever thought out! Rat! Rat! Don't get a grouch on! We'll keep still, Rat! Primest lark of all 'll be the sneakin' about an' keepin' quiet. Aw, Rat! Keep it up!"

"Keep it up yourselves!" snarled The Rat.

"Not another cove of us could do it but you! Not one! There's no other cove could think it out. You're the only chap that can think out things. You thought out the Squad! That's why you're captain!"

This was true. He was the one who could invent entertainment for them, these street lads who had nothing. Out of that nothing he could create what excited them, and give them something to fill empty, useless, often cold or wet or foggy, hours. That made him their captain and their pride.

The Rat began to yield, though grudgingly. He pointed again to Marco, who had not moved, but stood still at attention.

"Look at HIM!" he said. "He knows enough to stand where he's put until he's ordered to break line. He's a soldier, he is—not a raw recruit that don't know the goose-step. He's been in barracks before."

But after this outburst, he deigned to go on.

"Here's the oath," he said. "We swear to stand any torture and submit in silence to any death rather than betray our secret and our king. We will obey in silence and in secret. We will swim through seas of blood and fight our way through lakes of fire, if we are ordered. Nothing shall bar our way. All we do and say and think is for our country and our king. If any of you have anything to say, speak out before you take the oath."

He saw Marco move a little, and he made a sign to him.

"You," he said. "Have you something to say?"

Marco turned to him and saluted.

"Here stand ten men for Samavia. God be thanked!" he said. He dared say that much, and he felt as if his father himself would have told him that they were the right words.

The Rat thought they were. Somehow he felt that they struck home. He reddened with a sudden emotion.

"Squad!" he said. "I'll let you give three cheers on that. It's for the last time. We'll begin to be quiet afterwards."

And to the Squad's exultant relief he led the cheer, and they were allowed to make as much uproar as they liked. They liked to make a great deal, and when it was at an end, it had done them good and made them ready for business.

The Rat opened the drama at once. Never surely had there ever before been heard a conspirator's whisper as hollow as his.

"Secret Ones," he said, "it is midnight. We meet in

the depths of darkness. We dare not meet by day. When we meet in the daytime, we pretend not to know each other. We are meeting now in a Samavian city where there is a fortress. We shall have to take it when the secret sign is given and we make our rising. We are getting everything ready, so that, when we find the king, the secret sign can be given."

"What is the name of the city we are in?" whispered Cad.

"It is called Larrina. It is an important seaport. We must take it as soon as we rise. The next time we meet I will bring a dark lantern and draw a map and show it to you."

It would have been a great advantage to the game if Marco could have drawn for them the map he could have made, a map which would have shown every fortress—every stronghold and every weak place. Being a boy, he knew what excitement would have thrilled each breast, how they would lean forward and pile question on question, pointing to this place and to that. He had learned to draw the map before he was ten, and he had drawn it again and again because there had been times when his father had told him that changes had taken place. Oh, yes! He could have drawn a map which would have moved them to a frenzy of joy. But he sat silent and listened, only speaking when he asked a question, as if he knew nothing more about Samavia than The Rat did. What a Secret Party they were! They drew themselves together in the closest of circles; they spoke in unearthly whispers.

"A sentinel ought to be posted at the end of the passage," Marco whispered.

"Ben, take your gun!" commanded The Rat.

Ben rose stealthily, and, shouldering his weapon, crept on tiptoe to the opening. There he stood on guard.

"My father says there's been a Secret Party in Samavia for a hundred years," The Rat whispered.

"Who told him?" asked Marco.

"A man who has been in Samavia," answered The Rat. "He said it was the most wonderful Secret Party in the world, because it has worked and waited so long, and never given up, though it has had no reason for hoping. It began among some shepherds and charcoal-burners who bound themselves by an oath to find the Lost Prince and bring him back to the throne. There were too few of them to do anything against the Maranovitch, and when the first lot found they were growing old, they made their sons take the same oath. It has been passed on from generation to generation, and in each generation the band has grown. No one really knows how large it is now, but they say that there are people in nearly all the countries in Europe who belong to it in dead secret, and are sworn to help it when they are called. They are only waiting. Some are rich people who will give money, and some are poor ones who will slip across the frontier to fight or to help to smuggle in arms. They even say that for all these years there have been arms made in caves in the mountains, and hidden there year after year. There are men who are called Forgers of the Sword, and they, and their fathers, and grandfathers, and great-grandfathers have always made swords and stored them in caverns no one knows of, hidden caverns underground."

Marco spoke aloud the thought which had come into his mind as he listened, a thought which brought fear to him. "If the people in the streets talk about it, they won't be hidden long."

"It isn't common talk, my father says. Only very few have guessed, and most of them think it is part of the Lost Prince legend," said The Rat. "The Maranovitch and Iarovitch laugh at it. They have always been great fools. They're too full of their own swagger to think anything can interfere with them."

"Do you talk much to your father?" Marco asked him.

The Rat showed his sharp white teeth in a grin.

"I know what you're thinking of," he said. "You're remembering that I said he was always drunk. So he is, except when he's only HALF drunk. And when he's HALF drunk, he's the most splendid talker in London. He remembers everything he has ever learned or read or heard since he was born. I get him going and listen. He wants to talk and I want to hear. I found out almost everything I know in that way. He didn't know he was teaching me, but he was. He goes back into being a gentleman when he's half drunk."

"If—if you care about the Samavians, you'd better ask him not to tell people about the Secret Party and the Forgers of the Sword," suggested Marco.

The Rat started a little.

"That's true!" he said. "You're sharper than I am. It oughtn't to be blabbed about, or the Maranovitch might hear enough to make them stop and listen. I'll get him to promise. There's one strange thing about him," he added very slowly, as if he were thinking it over, "I suppose it's part of the gentleman that's left in him. If he makes a promise, he never breaks it, drunk or sober."

"Ask him to make one," said Marco. The next moment he changed the subject because it seemed the best thing to do. "Go on and tell us what our own Secret Party is to do. We're forgetting," he whispered.

The Rat took up his game with renewed keenness. It was a game which attracted him immensely because it called upon his imagination and held his audience spellbound, besides plunging him into war and strategy.

"We're preparing for the rising," he said. "It must come soon. We've waited so long. The caverns are stacked with arms. The Maranovitch and the Iarovitch are fighting and using all their soldiers, and now is our time." He stopped and thought, his elbows on his knees. He began to bite his nails again.

"The Secret Signal must be given," he said. Then he stopped again, and the Squad held its breath and pressed nearer with a softly shuffling sound. "Two of the Secret Ones must be chosen by lot and sent forth," he went on; and the Squad almost brought ruin and disgrace upon itself by wanting to cheer again, and only just stopping itself in time. "Must be chosen BY LOT," The Rat repeated, looking from one face to another. "Each one will take his life in his hand when he goes forth. He may have to die a thousand deaths, but he must go. He must steal in silence and disguise from one country to another. Wherever there is one of the Secret Party, whether he is in a hovel or on a throne, the messengers must go to him in darkness and stealth and give him the sign. It will mean, 'The hour has come. God save Samavia!'"

"God save Samavia!" whispered the Squad, excitedly. And, because they saw Marco raise his hand to his forehead, every one of them saluted.

They all began to whisper at once.

"Let's draw lots now. Let's draw lots, Rat. Don't let's 'ave no waitin'."

The Rat began to look about him with dread anxiety. He seemed to be examining the sky.

"The darkness is not as thick as it was," he whispered. "Midnight has passed. The dawn of day will be upon us. If anyone has a piece of paper or a string, we will draw the lots before we part."

Cad had a piece of string, and Marco had a knife which could be used to cut it into lengths. This The Rat did himself. Then, after shutting his eyes and mixing them, he held them in his hand ready for the drawing.

"The Secret One who draws the longest lot is chosen. The Secret One who draws the shortest is chosen," he said solemnly.

The drawing was as solemn as his tone. Each boy wanted to draw either the shortest lot or the longest one. The heart of each thumped somewhat as he drew his piece of string.

When the drawing was at an end, each showed his lot. The Rat had drawn the shortest piece of string, and Marco had drawn the longest one.

"Comrade!" said The Rat, taking his hand. "We will face death and danger together!"

"God save Samavia!" answered Marco.

And the game was at an end for the day. The primest thing, the Squad said, The Rat had ever made up for them. "'E wos a wonder, he wos!"

7
"The Lamp Is Lighted!"

On his way home, Marco thought of nothing but the story he must tell his father, the story the stranger who had been to Samavia had told The Rat's father. He felt that it must be a true story and not merely an invention. The Forgers of the Sword must be real men, and the hidden subterranean caverns stacked through the centuries with arms must be real, too. And if they were real, surely his father was one of those who knew the secret. His thoughts ran very fast. The Rat's boyish invention of the rising was only part of a game, but how natural it would be that sometime—perhaps before long—there would be a real rising! Surely there would be one if the Secret Party had grown so strong, and if many weapons and secret friends in other countries were ready and waiting. During all these years, hidden work and preparation would have been going on continually, even though it was preparation for an unknown day. A party which had lasted so long—which passed its oath on from generation to generation—must be of a deadly determination.

What might it not have made ready in its caverns and secret meeting-places! He longed to reach home and tell his father, at once, all he had heard. He recalled to mind, word for word, all that The Rat had been told, and even all he had added in his game, because—well, because that seemed so real too, so real that it actually might be useful.

But when he reached No. 7 Philibert Place, he found Loristan and Lazarus very much absorbed in work. The door of the back sitting-room was locked when he first knocked on it, and locked again as soon as he had entered. There were many papers on the table, and they were evidently studying them. Several of them were maps. Some were road-maps, some maps of towns and cities, and some of fortifications; but they were all maps of places in Samavia. They were usually kept in a strong box, and when they were taken out to be studied, the door was always kept locked.

Before they had their evening meal, these were all returned to the strong box, which was pushed into a corner and had newspapers piled upon it.

"When he arrives," Marco heard Loristan say to Lazarus, "we can show him clearly what has been planned. He can see for himself."

His father spoke scarcely at all during the meal, and, though it was not the habit of Lazarus to speak at such times unless spoken to, this evening it seemed to Marco that he LOOKED more silent than he had ever seen him look before. They were plainly both thinking anxiously of deeply serious things. The story of the stranger who had been to Samavia must not be told yet. But it was one which would keep.

Loristan did not say anything until Lazarus had removed the things from the table and made the room as neat as possible. While that was being done, he sat with his forehead resting on his hand, as if absorbed in thought. Then he made a gesture to Marco.

"Come here, Comrade," he said.

Marco went to him.

"Tonight someone may come to talk with me about grave things," he said. "I think he will come, but I cannot be quite sure. It is important that he should know that, when he comes, he will find me quite alone. He will come at a late hour, and Lazarus will open the door quietly that no one may hear. It is important that no one should see him. Someone must go and walk on the opposite side of the street until he appears. Then the one who goes to give warning must cross the pavement before him and say in a low voice, 'The Lamp is lighted!' and at once turn quietly away."

What boy's heart would not have leaped with joy at the mystery of it! Even a common and dull boy who knew nothing of Samavia would have felt jerky. Marco's voice almost shook with the thrill of his feeling.

"How shall I know him?" he said at once. Without asking at all, he knew he was the "someone" who was to go.

"You have seen him before," Loristan answered. "He is the man who drove in the carriage with the King."

"I shall know him," said Marco. "When shall I go?"

"Not until it is half-past one o'clock. Go to bed and sleep until Lazarus calls you." Then he added, "Look well at his face before you speak. He will probably not be dressed as well as he was when you saw him first."

Marco went upstairs to his room and went to bed as he was told, but it was hard to go to sleep. The rattle and roaring of the road did not usually keep him awake, because he had lived in the poorer quarter of too many big capital cities not to be accustomed to noise. But tonight it seemed to him that, as he lay and looked out at the lamplight, he heard every bus and cab which went past. He could not help thinking of the people who were in them, and on top of them, and of the people who were hurrying along on the pavement outside the broken iron railings. He was wondering what they would think if they knew that things connected with the battles they read of in the daily papers were going on in one of the shabby houses they scarcely gave a glance to as they went by them. It must be something connected with the war, if a man who was a great diplomat and the companion of kings came in secret to talk alone with a patriot who was a Samavian. Whatever his father was doing was for the good of Samavia, and perhaps the Secret Party knew he was doing it. His heart almost beat aloud under his shirt as he lay on the lumpy mattress thinking it over. He must indeed look well at the stranger before he even moved toward him. He must be sure he was the right man. The game he had amused himself with so long—the game of trying to remember pictures and people and places clearly and in detail—had been a wonderful training. If he could draw, he knew he could have made a sketch of the keen-eyed, clever, aquiline face with the well-cut and delicately close mouth, which looked as if it had been shut upon secrets always—always. If he could draw, he found himself saying again. He COULD draw, though perhaps only roughly. He had often amused himself by making sketches of things he wanted to ask questions about. He had even drawn people's faces in his untrained way, and his father had said that he had a crude gift for catching a likeness. Perhaps he could make a sketch of this face which would show his father that he knew and would recognize it.

He jumped out of bed and went to a table near the window. There was paper and a pencil lying on it. A street lamp exactly opposite threw into the room quite light enough for him to see by. He half knelt by the table and began to draw. He worked for about twenty minutes steadily, and he tore up two or three unsatisfactory sketches. The poor drawing would not matter if he could catch that subtle look which was not slyness but something more dignified and important. It was not difficult to get the marked, aristocratic outline of the features. A common-looking man with less pronounced profile would have been less easy to draw in one sense. He gave his mind wholly to the recalling of every detail which had photographed itself on his memory through its trained habit. Gradually he saw that the likeness was becoming clearer. It was not long before it was clear enough to be a striking one. Anyone who knew the man would recognize it. He got up, drawing a long and joyful breath.

He did not put on his shoes, but crossed his room

as noiselessly as possible, and as noiselessly opened the door. He made no ghost of a sound when he went down the stairs. The woman who kept the lodging-house had gone to bed, and so had the other lodgers and the maid of all work. All the lights were out except the one he saw a glimmer of under the door of his father's room. When he had been a mere baby, he had been taught to make a special sign on the door when he wished to speak to Loristan. He stood still outside the back sitting-room and made it now. It was a low scratching sound—two scratches and a soft tap. Lazarus opened the door and looked troubled.

"It is not yet time, sir," he said very low.

"I know," Marco answered. "But I must show something to my father." Lazarus let him in, and Loristan turned round from his writing-table questioningly.

Marco went forward and laid the sketch down before him.

"Look at it," he said. "I remember him well enough to draw that. I thought of it all at once—that I could make a sort of picture. Do you think it is like him?" Loristan examined it closely.

"It is very like him," he answered. "You have made me feel entirely safe. Thanks, Comrade. It was a good idea."

There was relief in the grip he gave the boy's hand, and Marco turned away with an exultant feeling. Just as he reached the door, Loristan said to him:

"Make the most of this gift. It is a gift. And it is true your mind has had good training. The more you draw, the better. Draw everything you can."

Neither the street lamps, nor the noises, nor his thoughts kept Marco awake when he went back to bed. But before he settled himself upon his pillow he gave himself certain orders. He had both read, and heard Loristan say, that the mind can control the body when people once find out that it can do so. He had tried experiments himself, and had found out some curious things. One was that if he told himself to remember a certain thing at a certain time, he usually found that he DID remember it. Something in his brain seemed to remind him. He had often tried the experiment of telling himself to awaken at a particular hour, and had awakened almost exactly at the moment by the clock.

"I will sleep until one o'clock," he said as he shut his eyes. "Then I will awaken and feel quite fresh. I shall not be sleepy at all."

He slept as soundly as a boy can sleep. And at one o'clock exactly he awakened, and found the street lamp still throwing its light through the window. He knew it was one o'clock, because there was a cheap little round clock on the table, and he could see the time. He was quite fresh and not at all sleepy. His experiment had succeeded again.

He got up and dressed. Then he went downstairs as noiselessly as before. He carried his shoes in his hands, as he meant to put them on only when he reached the street. He made his sign at his father's door, and it was Loristan who opened it.

"Shall I go now?" Marco asked.

"Yes. Walk slowly to the other side of the street. Look in every direction. We do not know where he will come from. After you have given him the sign, then come in and go to bed again."

Marco saluted as a soldier would have done on receiving an order.

Then, without a second's delay, he passed noiselessly out of the house.

Loristan turned back into the room and stood silently in the center of it. The long lines of his handsome body looked particularly erect and stately, and his eyes were glowing as if something deeply moved him.

"There grows a man for Samavia," he said to Lazarus, who watched him. "God be thanked!"

Lazarus's voice was low and hoarse, and he saluted quite reverently.

"Your—sir!" he said. "God save the Prince!"

"Yes," Loristan answered, after a moment's hesitation, "when he is found." And he went back to his table smiling his beautiful smile.

The wonder of silence in the deserted streets of a great city, after midnight has hushed all the roar and tumult to rest, is an almost unbelievable thing. The stillness in the depths of a forest or on a mountain-top is not so strange. A few hours ago, the tumult was rushing past; in a few hours more, it will be rushing past again.

But now the street is a naked thing; a distant

policeman's tramp on the bare pavement has a hollow and almost fearsome sound. It seemed especially so to Marco as he crossed the road. Had it ever been so empty and deadly silent before? Was it so every night? Perhaps it was, when he was fast asleep on his lumpy mattress with the light from a street lamp streaming into the room. He listened for the step of the policeman on night-watch, because he did not wish to be seen. There was a jutting wall where he could stand in the shadow while the man passed. A policeman would stop to look questioningly at a boy who walked up and down the pavement at half-past one in the morning. Marco could wait until he had gone by, and then come out into the light and look up and down the road and the cross streets.

He heard his approaching footsteps in a few minutes, and was safely in the shadows before he could be seen. When the policeman passed, he came out and walked slowly down the road, looking on each side, and now and then looking back. At first no one was in sight. Then a late hansom-cab came tinkling along. But the people in it were returning from some festivity, and were laughing and talking, and noticed nothing but their own joking. Then there was silence again, and for a long time, as it seemed to Marco, no one was to be seen. It was not really so long as it appeared, because he was anxious. Then a very early vegetable-wagon on the way from the country to Covent Garden Market came slowly lumbering by with its driver almost asleep on his piles of potatoes and cabbages. After it had passed, there was stillness and emptiness once more, until the policeman showed himself again on his beat, and Marco slipped into the shadow of the wall as he had done before.

When he came out into the light, he had begun to hope that the time would not seem long to his father. It had not really been long, he told himself, it had only seemed so. But his father's anxiousness would be greater than his own could be. Loristan knew all that depended on the coming of this great man who sat side by side with a king in his carriage and talked to him as if he knew him well.

"It might be something which all Samavia is waiting to know—at least all the Secret Party," Marco thought. "The Secret Party is Samavia"—he started at the sound of footsteps. "Someone is coming!" he said. "It is a man."

It was a man who was walking up the road on the same side of the pavement as his own. Marco began to walk toward him quietly but rather rapidly. He thought it might be best to appear as if he were some boy sent on a midnight errand—perhaps to call a doctor. Then, if it was a stranger he passed, no suspicion would be aroused. Was this man as tall as the one who had driven with the King? Yes, he was about the same height, but he was too far away to be recognizable otherwise. He drew nearer, and Marco noticed that he also seemed slightly to hasten his footsteps. Marco went on. A little nearer, and he would be able to make sure. Yes, now he was near enough. Yes, this man was the same height and not unlike in figure, but he was much younger. He was not the one who had been in the carriage with His Majesty. He was not more than thirty years old. He began swinging his cane and whistling a music-hall song softly as Marco passed him without changing his pace.

It was after the policeman had walked round his beat and disappeared for the third time, that Marco heard footsteps echoing at some distance down a cross street. After listening to make sure that they were approaching instead of receding in another direction, he placed himself at a point where he could watch the length of the thoroughfare. Yes, someone was coming. It was a man's figure again. He was able to place himself rather in the shadow so that the person approaching would not see that he was being watched. The solitary walker reached a recognizable distance in about two minutes' time. He was dressed in an ordinary shop-made suit of clothes which was rather shabby and quite unnoticeable in its appearance. His common hat was worn so that it rather shaded his face. But even before he had crossed to Marco's side of the road, the boy had clearly recognized him. It was the man who had driven with the King!

Chance was with Marco. The man crossed at exactly the place which made it easy for the boy to step lightly from behind him, walk a few paces by his side, and then pass directly before him across the pavement, glancing quietly up into his face as he said in a low voice but distinctly, the words "The Lamp is lighted," and without pausing a second walk on his way down the road. He did not slacken his pace or look back until he was some distance away. Then he glanced over his shoulder, and saw that the figure had crossed the street and was inside the railings. It was all right. His father would not be disappointed. The great man had come.

He walked for about ten minutes, and then went home and to bed. But he was obliged to tell himself to go to sleep several times before his eyes closed for the rest of the night.

~ 8 ~
An Exciting Game

Loristan referred only once during the next day to what had happened.

"You did your errand well. You were not hurried or nervous," he said. "The Prince was pleased with your calmness."

No more was said. Marco knew that the quiet mention of the stranger's title had been made merely as a designation. If it was necessary to mention him again in the future, he could be referred to as "the Prince." In various Continental countries there were many princes who were not royal or even serene highnesses—who were merely princes as other nobles were dukes or barons. Nothing special was revealed when a man was spoken of as a prince. But though nothing was said on the subject of the incident, it was plain that much work was being done by Loristan and Lazarus. The sitting-room door was locked, and the maps and documents, usually kept in the iron box, were being used.

Marco went to the Tower of London and spent part of the day in living again the stories which, centuries past, had been inclosed within its massive and ancient stone walls. In this way, he had throughout boyhood become intimate with people who to most boys seemed only the unreal creatures who professed to be alive in school-books of history. He had learned to know them as men and women because he had stood in the palaces they had been born in and had played in as children, had died in at the end. He had seen the dungeons they had been imprisoned in, the blocks on which they had laid their heads, the battlements on which they had fought to defend their fortressed towers, the thrones they had sat upon, the crowns they had worn, and the jeweled scepters they had held. He had stood before their portraits and had gazed curiously at their "Robes of Investiture," sewn with tens of thousands of seed-pearls. To look at a man's face and feel his pictured eyes follow you as you move away from him, to see the strangely splendid garments he once warmed with his living flesh, is to realize that history is not a mere lesson in a school-book, but is a relation of the life stories of men and women who saw strange and splendid days, and sometimes suffered strange and terrible things.

There were only a few people who were being led about sight-seeing. The man in the ancient Beef-eaters' costume, who was their guide, was good-natured, and evidently fond of talking. He was a big and stout man, with a large face and a small, merry eye. He was rather like pictures of Henry the Eighth, himself, which Marco remembered having seen. He was specially talkative when he stood by the tablet that marks the spot where stood the block on which Lady Jane Grey had laid her young head. One of the sight-seers who knew little of English history had asked some questions about the reasons for her execution.

"If her father-in-law, the Duke of Northumberland, had left that young couple alone—her and her husband, Lord Guildford Dudley—they'd have kept their heads on. He was bound to make her a queen, and Mary Tudor was bound to be queen herself. The duke wasn't clever enough to manage a conspiracy and work up the people. These Samavians we're reading about in the papers would have done it better."

"They had a big battle outside Melzarr yesterday," the sight-seer standing next to Marco said to the young woman who was his companion. "Thousands of 'em killed. I saw it in big letters on the boards as I rode on the top of the bus. They're just slaughtering each other, that's what they're doing."

The talkative Beef-eater heard him.

"They can't even bury their dead fast enough," he said. "There'll be some sort of plague breaking out and sweeping into the countries nearest them. It'll end by spreading all over Europe as it did in the Middle Ages. They have got to choose a decent king."

"I'll tell my father that too," Marco thought. "It shows that everybody is thinking and talking of

Samavia, and that even the common people know it must have a real king. This must be THE TIME!" And what he meant was that this must be the time for which the Secret Party had waited and worked so long—the time for the rising. But his father was out when he went back to Philibert Place, and Lazarus looked more silent than ever as he stood behind his chair and waited on him through his insignificant meal. However plain and scant the food they had to eat, it was always served with as much care and ceremony as if it had been a banquet.

"A man can eat dry bread and drink cold water as if he were a gentleman," his father had said long ago. "And it is easy to form careless habits. Even if one is hungry enough to feel ravenous, a man who has been well bred will not allow himself to look so. A dog may, a man may not. Just as a dog may howl when he is angry or in pain and a man may not."

It was only one of the small parts of the training which had quietly made the boy, even as a child, self-controlled and courteous, had taught him ease and grace of boyish carriage, the habit of holding his body well and his head erect, and had given him a certain look of young distinction which, though it assumed nothing, set him apart from boys of carelessly awkward bearing.

"Is there a newspaper here which tells of the battle, Lazarus?" he asked, after he had left the table.

"Yes, sir," was the answer. "Your father said that you might read it. It is a black tale!" he added, as he handed him the paper.

It was a black tale. As he read, Marco felt as if he could scarcely bear it. It was as if Samavia swam in blood, and as if the other countries must stand aghast before such furious cruelties.

"Lazarus," he said, springing to his feet at last, his eyes burning, "something must stop it! There must be something strong enough. The time has come. The time has come." And he walked up and down the room because he was too excited to stand still.

How Lazarus watched him! What a strong and glowing feeling there was in his own restrained face!

"Yes, sir. Surely the time has come," he answered. But that was all he said, and he turned and went out of the shabby back sitting-room at once. It was as if he felt it were wiser to go before he lost power over himself and said more.

Marco made his way to the meeting-place of the Squad, to which The Rat had in the past given the name of the Barracks. The Rat was sitting among his followers, and he had been reading the morning paper to them, the one which contained the account of the battle of Melzarr. The Squad had become the Secret Party, and each member of it was thrilled with the spirit of dark plot and adventure. They all whispered when they spoke.

"This is not the Barracks now," The Rat said. "It is a subterranean cavern. Under the floor of it thousands of swords and guns are buried, and it is piled to the roof with them. There is only a small place left for us to sit and plot in. We crawl in through a hole, and the hole is hidden by bushes."

To the rest of the boys this was only an exciting game, but Marco knew that to The Rat it was more. Though The Rat knew none of the things he knew, he saw that the whole story seemed to him a real thing. The struggles of Samavia, as he had heard and read of them in the newspapers, had taken possession of him. His passion for soldiering and warfare and his curiously mature brain had led him into following every detail he could lay hold of. He had listened to all he had heard with remarkable results. He remembered things older people forgot after they had mentioned them. He forgot nothing. He had drawn on the flagstones a map of Samavia which Marco saw was actually correct, and he had made a rough sketch of Melzarr and the battle which had had such disastrous results.

"The Maranovitch had possession of Melzarr," he explained with feverish eagerness. "And the Iarovitch attacked them from here," pointing with his finger. "That was a mistake. I should have attacked them from a place where they would not have been expecting it. They expected attack on their fortifications, and they were ready to defend them. I believe the enemy could have stolen up in the night and rushed in here," pointing again. Marco thought he was right. The Rat had argued it all out, and had studied Melzarr as he might have studied a puzzle or an arithmetical problem. He was very clever, and as sharp as his strange face looked.

"I believe you would make a good general if you were grown up," said Marco. "I'd like to show your maps to my father and ask him if he doesn't think your stratagem would have been a good one."

"Does he know much about Samavia?" asked The Rat.

"He has to read the newspapers because he writes things," Marco answered. "And everyone is thinking about the war. No one can help it."

The Rat drew a dingy, folded paper out of his pocket and looked it over with an air of reflection.

"I'll make a clean one," he said. "I'd like a grown-up man to look at it and see if it's all right. My father was more than half-drunk when I was drawing this, so I couldn't ask him questions. He'll kill himself before long. He had a sort of fit last night."

"Tell us, Rat, wot you an' Marco'll 'ave ter do. Let's 'ear wot you've made up," suggested Cad. He drew closer, and so did the rest of the circle, hugging their knees with their arms.

"This is what we shall have to do," began The Rat, in the hollow whisper of a Secret Party. "THE HOUR

HAS COME. To all the Secret Ones in Samavia, and to the friends of the Secret Party in every country, the sign must be carried. It must be carried by someone who could not be suspected. Who would suspect two boys? The best thing of all for us is that I am crippled. Who would suspect me? When my father is drunk and beats me, he does it because I won't go out and beg in the streets and bring him the money I get. He says that people will nearly always give money to a crippled boy. I won't be a beggar for him—the swine—but I will be one for Samavia and the Lost Prince. Marco shall pretend to be my brother and take care of me. I say," speaking to Marco with a sudden change of voice, "can you sing anything? It doesn't matter how you do it."

"Yes, I can sing," Marco replied.

"Then Marco will pretend he is singing to make people give him money. I'll get a pair of crutches somewhere, and part of the time I will go on crutches and part of the time on my platform. We'll live like beggars and go wherever we want to. I can whiz past a man and give the sign and no one will know. Sometimes Marco can give it when people are dropping money into his cap. We can pass from one country to another and rouse everybody who is of the Secret Party. We'll work our way into Samavia, and we'll be only two boys—and one crippled—and nobody will think we could be doing anything. We'll beg in great cities and on the high road."

"Where'll you get the money to travel?" said Cad.

"The Secret Party will give it to us, and we shan't need much. We could beg enough, for that matter. We'll sleep under the stars, or under bridges, or archways, or in dark corners of streets. I've done it myself many a time when my father drove me out of doors. If it's cold weather, it's bad enough but if it's fine weather, it's better than sleeping in the kind of place I'm used to. Comrade," to Marco, "are you ready?"

He said "Comrade" as Loristan did, and somehow Marco did not resent it, because he was ready to labor for Samavia. It was only a game, but it made them comrades—and was it really only a game, after all? His excited voice and his strange, lined face made it singularly unlike one.

"Yes, Comrade, I am ready," Marco answered him.

"We shall be in Samavia when the fighting for the Lost Prince begins." The Rat carried on his story with fire. "We may see a battle. We might do something to help. We might carry messages under a rain of bullets—a rain of bullets!" The thought so elated him that he forgot his whisper and his voice rang out fiercely. "Boys have been in battles before. We might find the Lost King—no, the Found King—and ask him to let us be his servants. He could send us where he couldn't send bigger people. I could say to him, 'Your Majesty, I am called "The Rat," because I can creep through holes and into corners and dart about. Order me into any danger and I will obey you. Let me die like a soldier if I can't live like one.'"

Suddenly he threw his ragged coat sleeve up across his eyes. He had wrought himself up tremendously with the picture of the rain of bullets. And he felt as if he saw the King who had at last been found. The next moment he uncovered his face.

"That's what we've got to do," he said. "Just that, if you want to know. And a lot more. There's no end to it!"

Marco's thoughts were in a whirl. It ought not to be

nothing but a game. He grew quite hot all over. If the Secret Party wanted to send messengers no one would think of suspecting, who could be more harmless-looking than two vagabond boys wandering about picking up their living as best they could, not seeming to belong to anyone? And one crippled. It was true—yes, it was true, as The Rat said, that his being crippled made him look safer than anyone else. Marco actually put his forehead in his hands and pressed his temples.

"What's the matter?" exclaimed The Rat. "What are you thinking about?"

"I'm thinking what a general you would make. I'm thinking that it might all be real—every word of it. It mightn't be a game at all," said Marco.

"No, it mightn't," The Rat answered. "If I knew where the Secret Party was, I'd like to go and tell them about it. What's that!" he said, suddenly turning his head toward the street. "What are they calling out?"

Some newsboy with a particularly shrill voice was shouting out something at the topmost of his lungs.

Tense and excited, no member of the circle stirred or spoke for a few seconds. The Rat listened, Marco listened, the whole Squad listened, pricking up their ears.

"Startling news from Samavia," the newsboy was shrilling out. "Amazing story! Descendant of the Lost Prince found! Descendant of the Lost Prince found!"

"Any chap got a penny?" snapped The Rat, beginning to shuffle toward the arched passage.

"I have!" answered Marco, following him.

"Come on!" The Rat yelled. "Let's go and get a paper!" And he whizzed down the passage with his swiftest rat-like dart, while the Squad followed him, shouting and tumbling over each other.

ᕦ 9 ᕤ
"It Is Not a Game"

Loristan walked slowly up and down the back sitting-room and listened to Marco, who sat by the small fire and talked.

"Go on," he said, whenever the boy stopped. "I want to hear it all. He's a strange lad, and it's a splendid game."

Marco was telling him the story of his second and third visits to the inclosure behind the deserted churchyard. He had begun at the beginning, and his father had listened with a deep interest.

A year later, Marco recalled this evening as a thrilling memory, and as one which would never pass away from him throughout his life. He would always be able to call it all back. The small and dingy back room, the dimness of the one poor gas-burner, which was all they could afford to light, the iron box pushed into the corner with its maps and plans locked safely in it, the erect bearing and actual beauty of the tall form, which the shabbiness of worn and mended clothes could not hide or dim. Not even rags and tatters could have made Loristan seem insignificant or undistinguished. He was always the same. His eyes seemed darker and more wonderful than ever in their remote thoughtfulness and interest as he spoke.

"Go on," he said. "It is a splendid game. And it is curious. He has thought it out well. The lad is a born soldier."

"It is not a game to him," Marco said. "And it is not a game to me. The Squad is only playing, but with him it's quite different. He knows he'll never really get what he wants, but he feels as if this was something near it. He said I might show you the map he made. Father, look at it."

He gave Loristan the clean copy of The Rat's map of

Samavia. The city of Melzarr was marked with certain signs. They were to show at what points The Rat—if he had been a Samavian general—would have attacked the capital. As Marco pointed them out, he explained The Rat's reasons for his planning.

Loristan held the paper for some minutes. He fixed his eyes on it curiously, and his black brows drew themselves together.

"This is very wonderful!" he said at last. "He is quite right. They might have got in there, and for the very reasons he hit on. How did he learn all this?"

"He thinks of nothing else now," answered Marco. "He has always thought of wars and made plans for battles. He's not like the rest of the Squad. His father is nearly always drunk, but he is very well educated, and, when he is only half drunk, he likes to talk.

"The Rat asks him questions then, and leads him on until he finds out a great deal. Then he begs old newspapers, and he hides himself in corners and listens to what people are saying. He says he lies awake at night thinking it out, and he thinks about it all the day. That was why he got up the Squad."

Loristan had continued examining the paper.

"Tell him," he said, when he refolded and handed it back, "that I studied his map, and he may be proud of it. You may also tell him"—and he smiled quietly as he spoke—"that in my opinion he is right. The Iarovitch would have held Melzarr today if he had led them."

Marco was full of exultation.

"I thought you would say he was right. I felt sure you would. That is what makes me want to tell you the rest," he hurried on.

"If you think he is right about the rest too—" He stopped awkwardly because of a sudden wild thought which rushed upon him. "I don't know what you will think," he stammered. "Perhaps it will seem to you as if the game—as if that part of it could—could only be a game."

He was so fervent in spite of his hesitation that Loristan began to watch him with sympathetic respect, as he always did when the boy was trying to express something he was not sure of. One of the great bonds between them was that Loristan was always interested in his boyish mental processes—in the way in which his thoughts led him to any conclusion.

"Go on," he said again. "I am like The Rat and I am like you. It has not seemed quite like a game to me, so far."

He sat down at the writing-table and Marco, in his eagerness, drew nearer and leaned against it, resting on his arms and lowering his voice, though it was always their habit to speak at such a pitch that no one outside the room they were in could distinguish what they said.

"It is The Rat's plan for giving the signal for a rising," he said.

Loristan made a slight movement.

"Does he think there will be a rising?" he asked.

"He says that must be what the Secret Party has been preparing for all these years. And it must come soon. The other nations see that the fighting must be put an end to even if they have to stop it themselves. And if the real King is found—but when The Rat bought the newspaper there was nothing in it about where he was. It was only a sort of rumor. Nobody seemed to know anything." He stopped a few seconds, but he did not utter the words which were in his mind. He did not say: "But YOU know."

"And The Rat has a plan for giving the signal?" Loristan said.

Marco forgot his first feeling of hesitation. He began to see the plan again as he had seen it when The Rat talked. He began to speak as The Rat had spoken, forgetting that it was a game. He made even a clearer picture than The Rat had made of the two vagabond boys making their way from one place to another, quite free to carry messages or warnings where they chose, because they were so insignificant and poor-looking that no one could think of them as anything but waifs and strays, belonging to nobody and blown about by the wind of poverty and chance. He felt as if he wanted to convince his father that the plan was a possible one. He did not quite know why he felt so anxious to win his approval of the scheme—as if it were real—as if it could actually be done. But this feeling was what inspired him to enter into new details and suggest possibilities.

"A boy who was crippled and one who was only a street singer and a sort of beggar could get almost anywhere," he said. "Soldiers would listen to a singer if he sang good songs—and they might not be afraid to talk before him. A strolling singer and crippled boy would perhaps hear a great many things it might be useful for the Secret Party to know. They might even hear important things. Don't you think so?"

Before he had gone far with his story, the faraway look had fallen upon Loristan's face—the look Marco had known so well all his life. He sat turned a little side-wise from the boy, his elbow resting on the table and his forehead on his hand. He looked down at the worn carpet at his feet, and so he looked as he listened to the end. It was as if some new thought were slowly growing in his mind as Marco went on talking and enlarging on The Rat's plan. He did not even look up or change his position as he answered, "Yes. I think so."

But, because of the deep and growing thought in his face, Marco's courage increased. His first fear that this part of the planning might seem so bold and reckless that it would only appear to belong to a boyish game, gradually faded away for some strange reason. His father had said that the first part of The Rat's imaginings had not seemed quite like a game to him, and now—even now—he was not listening as if he were listening to the details of mere exaggerated fancies. It was as if the thing he was hearing was not wildly impossible. Marco's knowledge of Continental countries and of methods of journeying helped him to enter into much detail and give realism to his plans.

"Sometimes we could pretend we knew nothing but English," he said. "Then, though The Rat could not understand, I could. I should always understand in each country. I know the cities and the places we should want to go to. I know how boys like us live, and so we should not do anything which would make the police angry or make people notice us. If anyone asked questions, I would let them believe that I had met The Rat by chance, and we had made up our minds to travel together because people gave more money to a boy who sang if he was with a crippled boy. There was a boy who used to play the guitar in the streets of Rome, and he always had a lame girl with him, and everyone knew it was for that reason. When he played, people looked at the girl and were sorry for her and gave her soldi. You remember."

"Yes, I remember. And what you say is true," Loristan answered.

Marco leaned forward across the table so that he came closer to him. The tone in which the words were said made his courage leap like a flame. To be allowed to go on with this boldness was to feel that he was being treated almost as if he were a man. If his father had wished to stop him, he could have done it with one quiet glance, without uttering a word. For some wonderful reason he did not wish him to cease talking. He was willing to hear what he had to say—he was even interested.

"You are growing older," he had said the night he had revealed the marvelous secret. "Silence is still the order, but you are man enough to be told more."

Was he man enough to be thought worthy to help Samavia in any small way—even with boyish fancies which might contain a germ of some thought which older and wiser minds might make useful? Was he being listened to because the plan, made as part of a game, was not an impossible one—if two boys who could be trusted could be found? He caught a deep breath as he went on, drawing still nearer and speaking so low that his tone was almost a whisper.

"If the men of the Secret Party have been working and thinking for so many years—they have prepared everything. They know by this time exactly what must be done by the messengers who are to give the signal. They can tell them where to go and how to know the secret friends who must be warned. If the orders could be written and given to—to someone who has—who has learned to remember things!" He had begun to breathe so quickly that he stopped for a moment.

Loristan looked up. He looked directly into his eyes.

"Someone who has been TRAINED to remember things?" he said.

"Someone who has been trained," Marco went on, catching his breath again. "Someone who does not forget—who would never forget—never! That one, even if he were only twelve—even if he were only ten—could go and do as he was told."

Loristan put his hand on his shoulder.

"Comrade," he said, "you are speaking as if you were ready to go yourself."

Marco's eyes looked bravely straight into his, but he said not one word.

"Do you know what it would mean, Comrade?" his father went on. "You are right. It is not a game. And you are not thinking of it as one. But have you thought how it would be if something betrayed you—and you were set up against a wall to be SHOT?"

Marco stood up quite straight. He tried to believe he felt the wall against his back.

"If I were shot, I should be shot for Samavia," he said. "And for YOU, Father."

Even as he was speaking, the front-door bell rang and Lazarus evidently opened it. He spoke to someone, and then they heard his footsteps approaching the back sitting-room.

"Open the door," said Loristan, and Marco opened it.

"There is a boy who is crippled here, sir," the old soldier said. "He asked to see Master Marco."

"If it is The Rat," said Loristan, "bring him in here. I wish to see him."

Marco went down the passage to the front door. The Rat was there, but he was not upon his platform. He was leaning upon an old pair of crutches, and Marco thought he looked wild and strange. He was white, and somehow the lines of his face seemed twisted in a new way. Marco wondered if something had frightened him, or if he felt ill.

"Rat," he began, "my father—"

"I've come to tell you about MY father," The Rat broke in without waiting to hear the rest, and his voice was as strange as his pale face. "I don't know why I've come, but I—I just wanted to. He's dead!"

"Your father?" Marco stammered. "He's—"

"He's dead," The Rat answered shakily. "I told you he'd kill himself. He had another fit and he died in it. I knew he would, one of these days. I told him so. He knew he would himself. I stayed with him till he was dead—and then I got a bursting headache and I felt sick—and I thought about you."

Marco made a jump at him because he saw he was suddenly shaking as if he were going to fall. He was just in time, and Lazarus, who had been looking on from the back of the passage, came forward. Together they held him up.

"I'm not going to faint," he said weakly, "but I felt as if I was. It was a bad fit, and I had to try and hold him. I was all by myself. The people in the other attic thought he was only drunk, and they wouldn't come in. He's lying on the floor there, dead."

"Come and see my father," Marco said. "He'll tell us what to do. Lazarus, help him."

"I can get on by myself," said The Rat. "Do you see my crutches? I did something for a pawnbroker last night, and he gave them to me for pay."

But though he tried to speak carelessly, he had plainly been horribly shaken and overwrought. His face was yellowish white still, and he was trembling a little.

Marco led the way into the back sitting-room. In the midst of its shabby gloom and under the dim light Loristan was standing in one of his still, attentive attitudes. He was waiting for them.

"Father, this is The Rat," the boy began. The Rat stopped short and rested on his crutches, staring at the tall, reposeful figure with widened eyes.

"Is that your father?" he said to Marco. And then added, with a jerky half-laugh, "He's not much like mine, is he?"

ᔈ 10 ᔈ
The Rat—and Samavia

What The Rat thought when Loristan began to speak to him, Marco wondered. Suddenly he stood in an unknown world, and it was Loristan who made it so because its poverty and shabbiness had no power to touch him. He looked at the boy with calm and clear eyes, he asked him practical questions gently, and it was plain that he understood many things without asking questions at all. Marco thought that perhaps he had, at some time, seen drunken men die, in his life in strange places. He seemed to know the terribleness of the night through which The Rat had passed. He made him sit down, and he ordered Lazarus to bring him some hot coffee and simple food.

"Haven't had a bite since yesterday," The Rat said, still staring at him. "How did you know I hadn't?"

"You have not had time," Loristan answered.

Afterwards he made him lie down on the sofa.

"Look at my clothes," said The Rat.

"Lie down and sleep," Loristan replied, putting his hand on his shoulder and gently forcing him toward the sofa. "You will sleep a long time. You must tell me how to find the place where your father died, and I will see that the proper authorities are notified."

"What are you doing it for?" The Rat asked, and then he added, "sir."

"Because I am a man and you are a boy. And this is a terrible thing," Loristan answered him.

He went away without saying more, and The Rat lay on the sofa staring at the wall and thinking about it until he fell asleep. But, before this happened, Marco had quietly left him alone. So, as Loristan had told him he would, he slept deeply and long; in fact, he slept through all the night.

When he awakened it was morning, and Lazarus was standing by the side of the sofa looking down at him.

"You will want to make yourself clean," he said. "It must be done."

"Clean!" said The Rat, with his squeaky laugh. "I couldn't keep clean when I had a room to live in, and now where am I to wash myself?" He sat up and looked about him.

"Give me my crutches," he said. "I've got to go. They've let me sleep here all night. They didn't turn me into the street. I don't know why they didn't. Marco's father—he's the right sort. He looks like a swell."

"The Master," said Lazarus, with a rigid manner, "the Master is a great gentleman. He would turn no tired creature into the street. He and his son are poor, but they are of those who give. He desires to see and talk to you again. You are to have bread and coffee with him and the young Master. But it is I who tell you that you cannot sit at table with them until you are clean.

Come with me," and he handed him his crutches. His manner was authoritative, but it was the manner of a soldier; his somewhat stiff and erect movements were those of a soldier, also, and The Rat liked them because they made him feel as if he were in barracks. He did not know what was going to happen, but he got up and followed him on his crutches.

Lazarus took him to a closet under the stairs where a battered tin bath was already full of hot water, which the old soldier himself had brought in pails. There were soap and coarse, clean towels on a wooden chair, and also there was a much worn but clean suit of clothes.

"Put these on when you have bathed," Lazarus ordered, pointing to them. "They belong to the young Master and will be large for you, but they will be better than your own." And then he went out of the closet and shut the door.

It was a new experience for The Rat. So long as he remembered, he had washed his face and hands—when he had washed them at all—at an iron tap set in the wall of a back street or court in some slum. His father and himself had long ago sunk into the world where to wash one's self is not a part of everyday life. They had lived amid dirt and foulness, and when his father had been in a maudlin state, he had sometimes cried and talked of the long-past days when he had shaved every morning and put on a clean shirt.

To stand even in the most battered of tin baths full of clean hot water and to splash and scrub with a big piece of flannel and plenty of soap was a marvelous thing. The Rat's tired body responded to the novelty with a curious feeling of freshness and comfort.

"I dare say swells do this every day," he muttered. "I'd do it myself if I was a swell. Soldiers have to keep themselves so clean they shine."

When, after making the most of his soap and water, he came out of the closet under the stairs, he was as fresh as Marco himself; and, though his clothes had been built for a more stalwart body, his recognition of their cleanliness filled him with pleasure. He wondered if by any effort he could keep himself clean when he went out into the world again and had to sleep in any hole the police did not order him out of.

He wanted to see Marco again, but he wanted

more to see the tall man with the soft dark eyes and that strange look of being a swell in spite of his shabby clothes and the dingy place he lived in. There was something about him which made you keep on looking at him, and wanting to know what he was thinking of, and why you felt as if you'd take orders from him as you'd take orders from your general, if you were a soldier. He looked, somehow, like a soldier, but as if he were something more—as if people had taken orders from him all his life, and always would take orders from him. And yet he had that quiet voice and those fine, easy movements, and he was not a soldier at all, but only a poor man who wrote things for papers which did not pay him well enough to give him and his son a comfortable living. Through all the time of his seclusion with the battered bath and the soap and water, The Rat thought of him, and longed to have another look at him and hear him speak again. He did not see any reason why he should have let him sleep on his sofa or why he should give him a breakfast before he turned him out to face the world. It was first-rate of him to do it. The Rat felt that when he was turned out, after he had had the coffee, he should want to hang about the neighborhood just on the chance of seeing him pass by sometimes. He did not know what he was going to do. The parish officials would by this time have taken his dead father, and he would not see him again. He did not want to see him again. He had never seemed like a father. They had never cared anything for each other. He had only been a wretched outcast whose best hours had been when he had drunk too much to be violent and brutal. Perhaps, The Rat thought, he would be driven to going about on his platform on the pavements and begging, as his father had tried to force him to do. Could he sell newspapers? What else could he do?

Lazarus was waiting for him in the passage. The Rat held back a little.

"Perhaps they'd rather not eat their breakfast with me," he hesitated. "I'm not—I'm not the kind they are. I could swallow the coffee out here and carry the bread away with me. And you could thank him for me. I'd want him to know I thanked him."

Lazarus also had a steady eye. The Rat realized that he was looking him over as if he were summing him up.

"You may not be the kind they are, but you may be of a kind the Master sees good in. If he did not see something, he would not ask you to sit at his table. You are to come with me."

The Squad had seen good in The Rat, but no one else had. Policemen had moved him on whenever they set eyes on him, the wretched women of the slums had regarded him as they regarded his darting, thieving namesake; loafing or busy men had seen in him a young nuisance to be kicked or pushed out of the way. The Squad had not called "good" what they saw in him. They would have yelled with laughter if they had heard anyone else call it so. "Goodness" was not considered an attraction in their world.

The Rat grinned a little and wondered what was meant, as he followed Lazarus into the back sitting-room.

It was as dingy and gloomy as it had looked the night before, but by the daylight The Rat saw how rigidly neat it was, how well swept and free from any speck of dust, how the poor windows had been cleaned and polished, and how everything was set in order. The coarse linen cloth on the table was fresh and spotless, so was the cheap crockery, the spoons shone with brightness.

Loristan was standing on the hearth and Marco was near him. They were waiting for their vagabond guest as if he had been a gentleman.

The Rat hesitated and shuffled at the door for a moment, and then it suddenly occurred to him to stand as straight as he could and salute. When he found himself in the presence of Loristan, he felt as if he ought to do something, but he did not know what.

Loristan's recognition of his gesture and his expression as he moved forward lifted from The Rat's shoulders a load which he himself had not known lay there. Somehow he felt as if something new had happened to him, as if he were not mere "vermin," after all, as if he need not be on the defensive—even as if he need not feel so much in the dark, and like a thing there was no place in the world for. The mere straight and far-seeing look of this man's eyes seemed to make a place somewhere for what he looked at. And yet what he said was quite simple.

"This is well," he said. "You have rested. We will have some food, and then we will talk together." He made a slight gesture in the direction of the chair at the right hand of his own place.

The Rat hesitated again. What a swell he was! With that wave of the hand he made you feel as if you were a fellow like himself, and he was doing you some honor.

"I'm not—" The Rat broke off and jerked his head toward Marco. "He knows—" He ended, "I've never sat at a table like this before."

"There is not much on it." Loristan made the slight gesture toward the righthand seat again and smiled. "Let us sit down."

The Rat obeyed him and the meal began. There were only bread and coffee and a little butter before them. But Lazarus presented the cups and plates on a small japanned tray as if it were a golden salver. When he was not serving, he stood upright behind his master's chair, as though he wore royal livery of scarlet and gold. To the boy who had gnawed a bone or munched a crust wheresoever he found them, and with no thought but of the appeasing of his own wolfish hunger, to watch the two with whom he sat eat their simple food was a new thing. He knew nothing of the everyday decencies of civilized people. The Rat liked to look at them, and he found himself trying to hold his cup as Loristan did, and to sit and move as Marco was sitting and moving— taking his bread or butter, when it was held at his side by Lazarus, as if it were a simple thing to be waited upon. Marco had had things handed to him all his life, and it did not make him feel awkward. The Rat knew that his own father had once lived like this. He himself would have been at ease if chance had treated him fairly. It made him scowl to think of it. But in a few minutes Loristan began to talk about the copy of the map of Samavia. Then The Rat forgot everything else and was ill at ease no more. He did not know that Loristan was leading him on to explain his theories about the country and the people and the war. He found himself telling all that he had read, or overheard, or THOUGHT as he lay awake in his garret. He had thought out a great many things in a way not at all like a boy's. His strangely con-centrated and over-mature mind had been full of mil-itary schemes which Loristan listened to with curiosity and also with amazement. He had become extraor-dinarily clever in one direction because he had fixed all his mental powers on one thing. It seemed scarcely natural that an untaught vagabond lad should know so much and reason so clearly. It was at least extraordinarily interesting. There had been no skirmish, no attack, no battle which he had not led and fought in his own imagination, and he had made scores of rough strange plans of all that had been or should have been done. Lazarus listened as attentively as his master, and once Marco saw him exchange a startled, rapid glance with Loristan. It was at a moment when The Rat was sketching with his finger on the cloth an attack which OUGHT to have been made but was not. And Marco knew at once that the quickly exchanged look meant "He is right! If it had been done, there would have been victory instead of disaster!"

It was a wonderful meal, though it was only of bread and coffee. The Rat knew he should never be able to forget it.

Afterwards, Loristan told him of what he had done the night before. He had seen the parish authorities and all had been done which a city government provides in the case of a pauper's death.

His father would be buried in the usual manner. "We will follow him," Loristan said in the end. "You and I and Marco and Lazarus."

The Rat's mouth fell open.

"You—and Marco—and Lazarus!" he exclaimed, staring. "And me! Why should any of us go? I don't want to. He wouldn't have followed me if I'd been the one."

Loristan remained silent for a few moments.

"When a life has counted for nothing, the end of it is a lonely thing," he said at last. "If it has forgotten all respect for itself, pity is all that one has left to give. One would like to give SOMETHING to anything so lonely." He said the last brief sentence after a pause.

"Let us go," Marco said suddenly; and he caught The Rat's hand.

The Rat's own movement was sudden. He slipped from his crutches to a chair, and sat and gazed at the worn carpet as if he were not looking at it at all, but at something a long way off. After a while he looked up at Loristan.

"Do you know what I thought of, all at once?" he

said in a shaky voice. "I thought of that 'Lost Prince' one. He only lived once. Perhaps he didn't live a long time. Nobody knows. But it's five hundred years ago, and, just because he was the kind he was, everyone that remembers him thinks of something fine. It's strange, but it does you good just to hear his name. And if he has been training kings for Samavia all these centuries—they may have been poor and nobody may have known about them, but they've been KINGS. That's what HE did—just by being alive a few years. When I think of him and then think of—the other—there's such an awful difference that—yes—I'm sorry. For the first time. I'm his son and I can't care about him; but he's too lonely—I want to go."

So it was that when the forlorn derelict was carried to the graveyard where nameless burdens on the city were given to the earth, a curious funeral procession followed him. There were two tall and soldierly looking men and two boys, one of whom walked on crutches, and behind them were ten other boys who walked two by two. These ten were a strange, ragged lot; but they had respectfully sober faces, held their heads and their shoulders well, and walked with a remarkably regular marching step.

It was the Squad; but they had left their "rifles" at home.

☜ 11 ☞
"Come with Me"

When they came back from the graveyard, The Rat was silent all the way. He was thinking of what had happened and of what lay before him. He was, in fact, thinking chiefly that nothing lay before him—nothing. The certainty of that gave his sharp, lined face new lines and sharpness which made it look pinched and hard.

He had nothing before but a corner in a bare garret in which he could find little more than a leaking roof over his head—when he was not turned out into the street. But, if policemen asked him where he lived, he could say he lived in Bone Court with his father. Now he couldn't say it.

He got along very well on his crutches, but he was rather tired when they reached the turn in the street which led in the direction of his old haunts. At any rate, they were haunts he knew, and he belonged to them more than he belonged elsewhere. The Squad stopped at this particular corner because it led to such homes as they possessed. They stopped in a body and looked at The Rat, and The Rat stopped also. He swung himself to Loristan's side, touching his hand to his forehead.

"Thank you, sir," he said. "Line and salute, you chaps!" And the Squad stood in line and raised their hands also. "Thank you, sir. Thank you, Marco. Good-bye."

"Where are you going?" Loristan asked.

"I don't know yet," The Rat answered, biting his lips.

He and Loristan looked at each other a few moments in silence. Both of them were thinking very hard. In The Rat's eyes there was a kind of desperate adoration. He did not know what he should do when this man turned and walked away from him. It would be as if the sun itself had dropped out of the heavens—and The Rat had not thought of what the sun meant before.

But Loristan did not turn and walk away. He looked deep into the lad's eyes as if he were searching to find some certainty. Then he said in a low voice, "You know how poor I am."

"I—I don't care!" said The Rat. "You—you're like a king to me. I'd stand up and be shot to bits if you told me to do it."

"I am so poor that I am not sure I can give you enough dry bread to eat—always. Marco and Lazarus and I are often hungry. Sometimes you might have nothing to sleep on but the floor. But I can find a PLACE for you if I take you with me," said Loristan. "Do you know what I mean by a PLACE?"

"Yes, I do," answered The Rat. "It's what I've never had before—sir."

What he knew was that it meant some bit of space, out of all the world, where he would have a sort of right to stand, howsoever poor and bare it might be.

"I'm not used to beds or to food enough," he said.

But he did not dare to insist too much on that "place." It seemed too great a thing to be true.

Loristan took his arm.

"Come with me," he said. "We won't part. I believe you are to be trusted."

The Rat turned quite white in a sort of anguish of joy. He had never cared for anyone in his life. He had been a sort of young Cain, his hand against every man and every man's hand against him. And during the last twelve hours he had plunged into a tumultuous ocean of boyish hero-worship. This man seemed like a sort of god to him. What he had said and done the day before, in what had been really The Rat's hours of extremity, after that appalling night—the way he had looked into his face and understood it all, the talk at the table when he had listened to him seriously, comprehending and actually respecting his plans and rough maps; his silent companionship as they followed the pauper hearse together—these things were enough to make the lad longingly ready to be any sort of servant to him if he might see and be spoken to by him even once or twice a day.

The Squad wore a look of dismay for a moment, and Loristan saw it.

"I am going to take your captain with me," he said. "But he will come back to Barracks. So will Marco."

"Will yer go on with the game?" asked Cad, as eager spokesman. "We want to go on being the 'Secret Party.'"

"Yes, I'll go on," The Rat answered. "I won't give it up. There's a lot in the papers today."

So they were pacified and went on their way, and Loristan and Lazarus and Marco and The Rat went on theirs also.

"Strange thing is," The Rat thought as they walked together, "I'm a bit afraid to speak to him unless he speaks to me first. Never felt that way before with anyone."

He had jeered at policemen and had impudently chaffed "swells," but he felt a sort of secret awe of this man, and actually liked the feeling.

"It's as if I was a private and he was commander-in-chief," he thought. "That's it."

Loristan talked to him as they went. He was simple enough in his statements of the situation. There was an old sofa in Marco's bedroom. It was narrow and hard, as Marco's bed itself was, but The Rat could sleep upon it. They would share what food they had. There were newspapers and magazines to be read. There were papers and pencils to draw new maps and plans of battles. There was even an old map of Samavia of Marco's which the two boys could study together as an aid to their game. The Rat's eyes began to have points of fire in them.

"If I could see the papers every morning, I could fight the battles on paper by night," he said, quite panting at the incredible vision of splendor. Were all the kingdoms of the earth going to be given to him? Was he going to sleep without a drunken father near him?

Was he going to have a chance to wash himself and to sit at a table and hear people say "Thank you," and "I beg pardon," as if they were using the most ordinary fashion of speech? His own father, before he had sunk into the depths, had lived and spoken in this way.

"When I have time, we will see who can draw up the best plans," Loristan said.

"Do you mean that you'll look at mine then—

when you have time?" asked The Rat, hesitatingly. "I wasn't expecting that."

"Yes," answered Loristan, "I'll look at them, and we'll talk them over."

As they went on, he told him that he and Marco could do many things together. They could go to museums and galleries, and Marco could show him what he himself was familiar with.

"My father said you wouldn't let him come back to Barracks when you found out about it," The Rat said, hesitating again and growing hot because he remembered so many ugly past days. "But—but I swear I won't do him any harm, sir. I won't!"

"When I said I believed you could be trusted, I meant several things," Loristan answered him. "That was one of them. You're a new recruit. You and Marco are both under a commanding officer." He said the words because he knew they would elate him and stir his blood.

ᴥ 12 ᴥ
"Only Two Boys"

The words did elate him, and his blood was stirred by them every time they returned to his mind. He remembered them through the days and nights that followed. He sometimes, indeed, awakened from his deep sleep on the hard and narrow sofa in Marco's room, and found that he was saying them half aloud to himself. The hardness of the sofa did not prevent his resting as he had never rested before in his life. By contrast with the past he had known, this poor existence was comfort which verged on luxury.

He got into the battered tin bath every morning, he sat at the clean table, and could look at Loristan and speak to him and hear his voice. His chief trouble was that he could hardly keep his eyes off him, and he was a little afraid he might be annoyed. But he could not bear to lose a look or a movement.

At the end of the second day, he found his way, at some trouble, to Lazarus's small back room at the top of the house.

"Will you let me come in and talk a bit?" he said.

When he went in, he was obliged to sit on the top of Lazarus's wooden box because there was nothing else for him.

"I want to ask you," he plunged into his talk at once, "do you think he minds me looking at him so much? I can't help it—but if he hates it—well—I'll try and keep my eyes on the table."

"The Master is used to being looked at," Lazarus made answer. "But it would be well to ask himself. He likes open speech."

"I want to find out everything he likes and everything he doesn't like," The Rat said. "I want—isn't there anything—anything you'd let me do for him? It wouldn't matter what it was. And he needn't know you are not doing it. I know you wouldn't be willing to give up anything particular. But you wait on him night and day. Couldn't you give up something to me?"

Lazarus pierced him with keen eyes. He did not answer for several seconds.

"Now and then," he said gruffly at last, "I'll let you brush his boots. But not every day—perhaps once a week."

"When will you let me have my first turn?" The Rat asked.

Lazarus reflected. His shaggy eyebrows drew themselves down over his eyes as if this were a question of state.

"Next Saturday," he conceded. "Not before. I'll tell him when you brush them."

"You needn't," said The Rat. "It's not that I want him to know. I want to know myself that I'm doing something for him. I'll find out things that I can do without interfering with you. I'll think them out."

"Anything anyone else did for him would be interfering with me," said Lazarus.

It was The Rat's turn to reflect now, and his face twisted itself into new lines and wrinkles.

"I'll tell you before I do anything," he said, after he had thought it over. "You served him first."

"I have served him ever since he was born," said Lazarus.

"He's—he's yours," said The Rat, still thinking deeply.

"I am his," was Lazarus's stern answer. "I am his—and the young Master's."

"That's it," The Rat said. Then a squeak of a half-laugh broke from him. "I've never been anybody's," he added.

His sharp eyes caught a passing look on Lazarus's face. Such a strange, disturbed, sudden look. Could he be rather sorry for him?

Perhaps the look meant something like that.

"If you stay near him long enough—and it needn't be long—you will be his too. Everybody is."

The Rat sat up as straight as he could. "When it comes to that," he blurted out, "I'm his now, in my way. I was his two minutes after he looked at me with his strange, handsome eyes. They're strange because they get you, and you want to follow him. I'm going to follow."

That night Lazarus recounted to his master the story of the scene. He simply repeated word for word what had been said, and Loristan listened gravely.

"We have not had time to learn much of him yet," he commented. "But that is a faithful soul, I think."

A few days later, Marco missed The Rat soon after their breakfast hour. He had gone out without saying anything to the household. He did not return for several hours, and when he came back he looked tired. In the afternoon he fell asleep on his sofa in Marco's room and slept heavily. No one asked him any questions as he volunteered no explanation. The next day he went out again in the same mysterious manner, and the next and the next. For an entire week he went out and returned with the tired look; but he did not explain until one morning, as he lay on his sofa before getting up, he said to Marco:

"I'm practicing walking with my crutches. I don't want to go about like a rat anymore. I mean to be as near like other people as I can. I walk farther every morning. I began with two miles. If I practice every day, my crutches will be like legs."

"Shall I walk with you?" asked Marco.

"Wouldn't you mind walking with a cripple?"

"Don't call yourself that," said Marco. "We can talk together, and try to remember everything we see as we go along."

"I want to learn to remember things. I'd like to train myself in that way too," The Rat answered. "I'd give anything to know some of the things your father taught you. I've got a good memory. I remember a lot of things I don't want to remember. Will you go this morning?"

That morning they went, and Loristan was told the reason for their walk. But though he knew one reason, he did not know all about it. When The Rat was allowed his "turn" of the boot-brushing, he told more to Lazarus.

"What I want to do," he said, "is not only walk as fast as other people do, but faster. Acrobats train themselves to do anything. It's training that does it. There might come a time when he might need someone to go on an errand quickly, and I'm going to be ready. I'm going to train myself until he needn't think of me as if I were only a cripple who can't do things and has to be taken care of. I want him to know that I'm really as strong as Marco, and where Marco can go I can go."

"He" was what he always said, and Lazarus always understood without explanation.

"'The Master' is your name for him," he had explained at the beginning. "And I can't call him just 'Mister' Loristan. It sounds like cheek. If he was called 'General' or 'Colonel' I could stand it—though it wouldn't be quite right. Someday I shall find a name. When I speak to him, I say 'Sir.'"

The walks were taken every day, and each day were longer. Marco found himself silently watching The Rat with amazement at his determination and endurance. He knew that he must not speak of what he could not fail to see as they walked. He must not tell him that he looked tired and pale and sometimes desperately fatigued. He had inherited from his father the tact which sees what people do not wish to be reminded of. He knew that for some reason of his own The Rat had determined to do this thing at any cost to himself. Sometimes his face grew white and worn and he breathed hard, but he never rested more than a few minutes, and never turned back or shortened a walk they had planned.

"Tell me something about Samavia, something to remember," he would say, when he looked his worst. "When I begin to try to remember, I forget—other things."

So, as they went on their way, they talked, and The Rat committed things to memory. He was quick at it, and grew quicker every day. They invented a game of remembering faces they passed. Both would learn them by heart, and on their return home Marco would draw them. They went to the museums and galleries and learned things there, making from memory lists and descriptions which at night they showed to Loristan, when he was not too busy to talk to them.

As the days passed, Marco saw that The Rat was gaining strength. This exhilarated him greatly. They often went to Hampstead Heath and walked in the wind and sun. There The Rat would go through curious exercises which he believed would develop his muscles.

He began to look less tired during and after his journey. There were even fewer wrinkles on his face, and his sharp eyes looked less fierce. The talks between the two boys were long and curious. Marco soon realized that The Rat wanted to learn—learn—learn.

"Your father can talk to you almost as if you were twenty years old," he said once. "He knows you can understand what he's saying. If he were to talk to me, he'd always have to remember that I was only a rat that had lived in gutters and seen nothing else."

They were talking in their room, as they nearly always did after they went to bed and the street lamp shone in and lighted their bare little room. They often sat up clasping their knees, Marco on his poor bed, The Rat on his hard sofa, but neither of them conscious either of the poorness or hardness, because to each one the long unknown sense of companionship was such a satisfying thing. Neither of them had ever talked intimately to another boy, and now they were together day and night. They revealed their thoughts to each other; they told each other things it had never before occurred to either to think of telling anyone. In fact, they found out about themselves, as they talked, things they had not quite known before. Marco had gradually discovered that the admiration The Rat had for his father was an impassioned and curious feeling which possessed him entirely. It seemed to Marco that it was beginning to be like a sort of religion. He evidently thought of him every moment. So when he spoke of Loristan's knowing him to be only a rat of the gutter, Marco felt he himself was fortunate in remembering something he could say.

"My father said yesterday that you had a big brain and a strong will," he answered from his bed. "He said that you had a wonderful memory which only needed exercising. He said it after he looked over the list you made of the things you had seen in the Tower."

The Rat shuffled on his sofa and clasped his knees tighter.

"Did he? Did he?" he said.

He rested his chin upon his knees for a few minutes and stared straight before him. Then he turned to the bed.

"Marco," he said, in a rather hoarse voice, a strange voice; "are you jealous?"

"Jealous," said Marco; "why?"

"I mean, have you ever been jealous? Do you know what it is like?"

"I don't think I do," answered Marco, staring a little.

"Are you ever jealous of Lazarus because he's always with your father—because he's with him oftener than you are—and knows about his work—and can do things for him you can't? I mean, are you jealous of—your father?"

Marco loosed his arms from his knees and lay down flat on his pillow.

"No, I'm not. The more people love and serve him, the better," he said. "The only thing I care for is—is him. I just care for HIM. Lazarus does too. Don't you?"

The Rat was greatly excited internally. He had been thinking of this thing a great deal. The thought had sometimes terrified him. He might as well have it out now if he could. If he could get at the truth, everything would be easier. But would Marco really tell him?

"Don't you mind?" he said, still hoarse and eager—"don't you mind how much I care for him? Could it ever make you feel savage? Could it ever set you thinking I was nothing but—what I am—and that it was cheek of me to push myself in and fasten on to a gentleman who only took me up for charity? Here's the living truth," he ended in an outburst; "if I were you and you were me, that's what I should be thinking. I know it is. I couldn't help it. I should see every low thing there was in you, in your manners and your voice and your looks. I should see nothing but the contrast between you and me and between you and him. I should be so jealous that I should just rage. I should HATE you—and I should DESPISE you!"

He had wrought himself up to such a passion of feeling that he set Marco thinking that what he was hearing meant strange and strong emotions such as he himself had never experienced. The Rat had been thinking over all this in secret for some time, it was evident. Marco lay still a few minutes and thought it over. Then he found something to say, just as he had found something before.

"You might, if you were with other people who thought in the same way," he said, "and if you hadn't found out that it is such a mistake to think in that way, that it's even stupid. But, you see, if you were I, you would have lived with my father, and he'd have told you what he knows—what he's been finding out all his life."

"What's he found out?"

"Oh!" Marco answered, quite casually, "just that you can't set savage thoughts loose in the world, any more than you can let loose savage beasts with hydrophobia. They spread a sort of rabies, and they always tear and worry you first of all."

"What do you mean?" The Rat gasped out.

"It's like this," said Marco, lying flat and cool on his hard pillow and looking at the reflection of the street lamp on the ceiling. "That day I turned into your Barracks, without knowing that you'd think I was spying, it made you feel savage, and you threw the stone at me. If it had made me feel savage and I'd rushed in and fought, what would have happened to all of us?"

The Rat's spirit of generalship gave the answer.

"I should have called on the Squad to charge with fixed bayonets. They'd have half killed you. You're a strong chap, and you'd have hurt a lot of them."

A note of terror broke into his voice. "What a fool I should have been!" he cried out. "I should never have come here! I should never have known HIM!" Even by the light of the street lamp Marco could see him begin to look almost ghastly.

"The Squad could easily have half killed me," Marco added. "They could have quite killed me, if they had wanted to do it. And who would have got any good out of it? It would only have been a street-lads' row—with the police and prison at the end of it."

"But because you'd lived with him," The Rat pondered, "you walked in as if you didn't mind, and just asked why we did it, and looked like a stronger chap than any of us—and different—different. I wondered what was the matter with you, you were so cool and steady. I know now. It was because you were like him. He'd taught you. He's like a wizard."

"He knows things that wizards think they know, but he knows them better," Marco said. "He says they're not strange and unnatural. They're just simple laws of nature. You have to be either on one side or the other, like an army. You choose your side. You either build up or tear down. You either keep in the light where you can see, or you stand in the dark and fight everything that comes near you, because you can't see and you think it's an enemy. No, you wouldn't have been jealous if you'd been I and I'd been you."

"And you're NOT?" The Rat's sharp voice was almost hollow. "You'll swear you're not?"

"I'm not," said Marco.

The Rat's excitement even increased a shade as he poured forth his confession.

"I was afraid," he said. "I've been afraid every day since I came here. I'll tell you straight out. It seemed just natural that you and Lazarus wouldn't stand me, just as I wouldn't have stood you. It seemed just natural that you'd work together to throw me out. I knew how I should have worked myself. Marco—I said I'd tell you straight out—I'm jealous of you. I'm jealous of Lazarus. It makes me wild when I see you both knowing all about him, and fit and ready to do anything he wants done. I'm not ready and I'm not fit."

"You'd do anything he wanted done, whether you were fit and ready or not," said Marco. "He knows that."

"Does he? Do you think he does?" cried The Rat. "I wish he'd try me. I wish he would."

Marco turned over on his bed and rose up on his elbow so that he faced The Rat on his sofa.

"Let us WAIT," he said in a whisper. "Let us WAIT."

There was a pause, and then The Rat whispered also. "For what?"

"For him to find out that we're fit to be tried. Don't you see what fools we should be if we spent our time in being jealous, either of us. We're only two boys. Suppose he saw we were only two silly fools. When you are jealous of me or of Lazarus, just go and sit down in a still place and think of HIM. Don't think about yourself or about us. He's so quiet that to think about him makes you quiet yourself. When things go wrong or when I'm lonely, he's taught me to sit down and make myself think of things I like— pictures, books, monuments, splendid places. It pushes the other things out and sets your mind going properly. He doesn't know I nearly always think of him. He's the best thought himself. You try it. You're not really jealous. You only THINK you are. You'll find that out if you always stop yourself in time. Anyone can be such a fool if he lets himself. And he can always stop it if he makes up his mind. I'm not jealous. You must let that thought alone. You're not jealous yourself. Kick that thought into the street."

The Rat caught his breath and threw his arms up over his eyes. "Oh, Lord! Oh, Lord!" he said; "if I'd lived near him always as you have. If I just had."

"We're both living near him now," said Marco. "And here's something to think of," leaning more forward on his elbow. "The kings who were being made ready for Samavia have waited all these years; WE can make ourselves ready and wait so that, if just two boys are wanted to do something—just two boys—we can step out of the ranks when the call comes and say 'Here!' Now let's lie down and think of it until we go to sleep."

Loristan Attends a Drill of the Squad, and Marco Meets a Samavian

The Squad was not forgotten. It found that Loristan himself would have regarded neglect as a breach of military duty.

"You must remember your men," he said, two or three days after The Rat became a member of his household. "You must keep up their drill. Marco tells me it was very smart. Don't let them get slack."

"His men!" The Rat felt what he could not have put into words.

He knew he had worked, and that the Squad had worked, in their hidden holes and corners. Only hidden holes and corners had been possible for them because they had existed in spite of the protest of their world and the vigilance of its policemen. They had tried many refuges before they found the Barracks. No one but resented the existence of a troop of noisy vagabonds. But somehow this man knew that there had evolved from it something more than mere noisy play, that he, The Rat, had MEANT order and discipline.

"His men!" It made him feel as if he had had the Victoria Cross fastened on his coat. He had brain enough to see many things, and he knew that it was in this way that Loristan was finding him his "place." He knew how.

When they went to the Barracks, the Squad greeted them with a tumultuous welcome which expressed a great sense of relief. Privately the members had been filled with fears which they had talked over together in deep gloom. Marco's father, they decided, was too big a swell to let the two come back after he had seen the sort the Squad was made up of. He might be poor just now, toffs sometimes lost their money for a bit, but you could see what he was, and fathers like him weren't going to let their sons make friends with "such as us." He'd stop the drill and the "Secret Society" game. That's what he'd do!

But The Rat came swinging in on his secondhand crutches looking as if he had been made a general, and Marco came with him; and the drill the Squad was put through was stricter and finer than any drill they had ever known.

"I wish my father could have seen that," Marco said to The Rat.

The Rat turned red and white and then red again, but he said not a single word. The mere thought was like a flash of fire passing through him. But no fellow could hope for a thing as big as that. The Secret Party, in its subterranean cavern, surrounded by its piled arms, sat down to read the morning paper.

The war news was bad to read. The Maranovitch held the day for the moment, and while they suffered and wrought cruelties in the capital city, the Iarovitch suffered and wrought cruelties in the country outside.

So fierce and dark was the record that Europe stood aghast.

The Rat folded his paper when he had finished, and sat biting his nails. Having done this for a few minutes, he began to speak in his dramatic and hollow Secret Party whisper.

"The hour has come," he said to his followers. "The messengers must go forth. They know nothing of what they go for; they only know that they must obey. If they were caught and tortured, they could betray nothing because they know nothing but that, at certain places, they must utter a certain word. They carry no papers. All commands they must learn by heart. When the sign is given, the Secret Party will know what to do—where to meet and where to attack."

He drew plans of the battle on the flagstones, and he sketched an imaginary route which the two messengers were to follow. But his knowledge of the map of Europe was not worth much, and he turned to Marco.

"You know more about geography than I do. You know more about everything," he said. "I only know Italy is at the bottom and Russia is at one side and England's at the other. How would the Secret Messengers go to Samavia? Can you draw the countries they'd have to pass through?"

Because any school-boy who knew the map could have done the same thing, Marco drew them. He also knew the stations the Secret Two would arrive at and leave by when they entered a city, the streets they would walk through and the very uniforms they would see; but of these things he said nothing. The reality his knowledge gave to the game was, however, a thrilling thing. He wished he could have been free to explain to The Rat the things he knew. Together they could have worked out so many details of travel and possible adventure that it would have been almost as if they had set out on their journey in fact.

As it was, the mere sketching of the route fired The Rat's imagination. He forged ahead with the story of adventure, and filled it with such mysterious purport and design that the Squad at times gasped for breath. In his glowing version the Secret Two entered cities by midnight and sang and begged at palace gates where kings driving outward paused to listen and were given the Sign.

"Though it would not always be kings," he said. "Sometimes it would be the poorest people. Sometimes they might seem to be beggars like ourselves, when they were only Secret Ones disguised. A great lord might wear poor clothes and pretend to be a workman, and we should only know him by the signs we had learned by heart. When we were sent to Samavia, we should be obliged to creep in through some back part of the country where no fighting was being done and where no one would attack. Their generals are not clever enough to protect the parts which are joined to friendly countries, and they have not forces enough. Two boys could find a way in if they thought it out."

He became possessed by the idea of thinking it out on the spot. He drew his rough map of Samavia on the flagstones with his chalk.

"Look here," he said to Marco, who, with the elated and thrilled Squad, bent over it in a close circle of heads. "Beltrazo is here and Carnolitz is here—and here is Jiardasia. Beltrazo and Jiardasia are friendly, though they don't take sides. All the fighting is going on in the country about Melzarr. There is no reason why they should prevent single travelers from coming in across the frontiers of friendly neighbors. They're not fighting with the countries outside, they are fighting with themselves." He paused a moment and thought.

"The article in that magazine said something about a huge forest on the eastern frontier. That's here. We could wander into a forest and stay there until we'd planned all we wanted to do. Even the people who had seen us would forget about us. What we have to do is to make people feel as if we were nothing—nothing."

They were in the very midst of it, crowded together, leaning over, stretching necks and breathing quickly with excitement, when Marco lifted his head. Some mysterious impulse made him do it in spite of himself.

"There's my father!" he said.

The chalk dropped, everything dropped, even Samavia. The Rat was up and on his crutches as if some magic force had swung him there. How he gave the command, or if he gave it at all, not even he himself knew. But the Squad stood at salute.

Loristan was standing at the opening of the archway as Marco had stood that first day. He raised his right hand in return salute and came forward.

"I was passing the end of the street and remembered the Barracks was here," he explained. "I thought I should like to look at your men, Captain."

He smiled, but it was not a smile which made his words really a joke. He looked down at the chalk map drawn on the flagstones.

"You know that map well," he said. "Even I can see that it is Samavia. What is the Secret Party doing?"

"The messengers are trying to find a way in," answered Marco.

"We can get in there," said The Rat, pointing with a crutch. "There's a forest where we could hide and find out things."

"Reconnoiter," said Loristan, looking down. "Yes. Two stray boys could be very safe in a forest. It's a good game."

That he should be there! That he should, in his own wonderful way, have given them such a thing as this. That he should have cared enough even to look up the Barracks, was what The Rat was thinking. A batch of ragamuffins they were and nothing else, and he standing looking at them with his fine smile. There was something about him which made him seem even splendid. The Rat's heart thumped with startled joy.

"Father," said Marco, "will you watch The Rat drill us? I want you to see how well it is done."

"Captain, will you do me that honor?" Loristan said to The Rat, and to even these words he gave the right tone, neither jesting nor too serious. Because it was so right a tone, The Rat's pulses beat only with exultation. This god of his had looked at his maps, he had talked of his plans, he had come to see the soldiers who were his work! The Rat began his drill as if he had been reviewing an army.

What Loristan saw done was wonderful in its mechanical exactness.

The Squad moved like the perfect parts of a perfect machine. That they could so do it in such space, and that they should have accomplished such precision, was an extraordinary testimonial to the military efficiency and curious qualities of this one hunchbacked, vagabond officer.

"That is magnificent!" the spectator said, when it

was over. "It could not be better done. Allow me to congratulate you."

He shook The Rat's hand as if it had been a man's, and, after he had shaken it, he put his own hand lightly on the boy's shoulder and let it rest there as he talked a few minutes to them all.

He kept his talk within the game, and his clear comprehension of it added a flavor which even the dullest member of the Squad was elated by. Sometimes you couldn't understand toffs when they made a shy at being friendly, but you could understand him, and he stirred up your spirits. He didn't make jokes with you, either, as if a chap had to be kept grinning. After the few minutes were over, he went away. Then they sat down again in their circle and talked about him, because they could talk and think about nothing else. They stared at Marco furtively, feeling as if he were a creature of another world because he had lived with this man. They stared at The Rat in a new way also. The wonderful-looking hand had rested on his shoulder, and he had been told that what he had done was magnificent.

"When you said you wished your father could have seen the drill," said The Rat, "you took my breath away. I'd never have had the cheek to think of it myself—and I'd never have dared to let you ask him, even if you wanted to do it. And he came himself! It struck me dumb."

"If he came," said Marco, "it was because he wanted to see it."

When they had finished talking, it was time for Marco and The Rat to go on their way. Loristan had given The Rat an errand. At a certain hour he was to present himself at a certain shop and receive a package.

"Let him do it alone," Loristan said to Marco. "He will be better pleased. His desire is to feel that he is trusted to do things alone."

So they parted at a street corner, Marco to walk back to No. 7 Philibert Place, The Rat to execute his commission. Marco turned into one of the better streets, through which he often passed on his way home. It was not a fashionable quarter, but it contained some respectable houses in whose windows here and there were to be seen neat cards bearing the word "Apartments," which meant that the owner of the house would let to lodgers his drawing-room or sitting-room suite.

As Marco walked up the street, he saw someone come out of the door of one of the houses and walk quickly and lightly down the pavement. It was a young woman wearing an elegant though quiet dress, and a hat which looked as if it had been bought in Paris or Vienna. She had, in fact, a slightly foreign air, and it was this, indeed, which made Marco look at her long enough to see that she was also a graceful and lovely person. He wondered what her nationality was. Even at some yards' distance he could see that she had long dark eyes and a curved mouth which seemed to be smiling to itself. He thought she might be Spanish or Italian.

He was trying to decide which of the two countries she belonged to, as she drew near to him, but quite suddenly the curved mouth ceased smiling as her foot seemed to catch in a break in the pavement, and she so lost her balance that she would have fallen if he had not leaped forward and caught her.

She was light and slender, and he was a strong lad

and managed to steady her. An expression of sharp momentary anguish crossed her face.

"I hope you are not hurt," Marco said.

She bit her lip and clutched his shoulder very hard with her slim hand.

"I have twisted my ankle," she answered. "I am afraid I have twisted it badly. Thank you for saving me. I should have had a bad fall."

Her long, dark eyes were very sweet and grateful. She tried to smile, but there was such distress under the effort that Marco was afraid she must have hurt herself very much.

"Can you stand on your foot at all?" he asked.

"I can stand a little now," she said, "but I might not be able to stand in a few minutes. I must get back to the house while I can bear to touch the ground with it. I am so sorry. I am afraid I shall have to ask you to go with me. Fortunately it is only a few yards away."

"Yes," Marco answered. "I saw you come out of the house. If you will lean on my shoulder, I can soon help you back. I am glad to do it. Shall we try now?"

She had a gentle and soft manner which would have

appealed to any boy. Her voice was musical and her enunciation exquisite.

Whether she was Spanish or Italian, it was easy to imagine her a person who did not always live in London lodgings, even of the upper class.

"If you please," she answered him. "It is very kind of you. You are very strong, I see. But I am glad to have only a few steps to go."

She rested on his shoulder as well as on her umbrella, but it was plain that every movement gave her intense pain. She caught her lip with her teeth, and Marco thought she turned white. He could not help liking her. She was so lovely and gracious and brave. He could not bear to see the suffering in her face.

"I am so sorry!" he said, as he helped her, and his boy's voice had something of the wonderful sympathetic tone of Loristan's. The beautiful lady herself remarked it, and thought how unlike it was to the ordinary boy-voice.

"I have a latch-key," she said, when they stood on the low step.

She found the latch-key in her purse and opened the

door. Marco helped her into the entrance-hall. She sat down at once in a chair near the hat-stand. The place was quite plain and old-fashioned inside.

"Shall I ring the front-door bell to call someone?" Marco inquired.

"I am afraid that the servants are out," she answered. "They had a holiday. Will you kindly close the door? I shall be obliged to ask you to help me into the sitting-room at the end of the hall. I shall find all I want there—if you will kindly hand me a few things. Someone may come in presently—perhaps one of the other lodgers—and, even if I am alone for an hour or so, it will not really matter."

"Perhaps I can find the landlady," Marco suggested. The beautiful person smiled.

"She has gone to her sister's wedding. That is why I was going out to spend the day myself. I arranged the plan to accommodate her. How good you are! I shall be quite comfortable directly, really. I can get to my easy-chair in the sitting-room now I have rested a little."

Marco helped her to her feet, and her sharp, involuntary exclamation of pain made him wince internally.

Perhaps it was a worse sprain than she knew.

The house was of the early-Victorian London order. A "front lobby" with a dining-room on the right hand, and a "back lobby," after the foot of the stairs was passed, out of which opened the basement kitchen staircase and a sitting-room looking out on a gloomy flagged back yard inclosed by high walls. The sitting-room was rather gloomy itself, but there were a few luxurious things among the ordinary furnishings. There was an easy-chair with a small table near it, and on the table were a silver lamp and some rather elegant trifles. Marco helped his charge to the easy-chair and put a cushion from the sofa under her foot. He did it very gently, and, as he rose after doing it, he saw that the long, soft dark eyes were looking at him in a curious way.

"I must go away now," he said, "but I do not like to leave you. May I go for a doctor?"

"How dear you are!" she exclaimed. "But I do not want one, thank you. I know exactly what to do for a sprained ankle. And perhaps mine is not really a sprain. I am going to take off my shoe and see."

"May I help you?" Marco asked, and he kneeled

down again and carefully unfastened her shoe and withdrew it from her foot. It was a slender and delicate foot in a silk stocking, and she bent and gently touched and rubbed it.

"No," she said, when she raised herself, "I do not think it is a sprain. Now that the shoe is off and the foot rests on the cushion, it is much more comfortable, much more. Thank you, thank you. If you had not been passing I might have had a dangerous fall."

"I am very glad to have been able to help you," Marco answered, with an air of relief. "Now I must go, if you think you will be all right."

"Don't go yet," she said, holding out her hand. "I should like to know you a little better, if I may. I am so grateful. I should like to talk to you. You have such beautiful manners for a boy," she ended, with a pretty, kind laugh, "and I believe I know where you got them from."

"You are very kind to me," Marco answered, wondering if he did not redden a little. "But I must go because my father will—"

"Your father would let you stay and talk to me,"

she said, with even a prettier kindliness than before. "It is from him you have inherited your beautiful manner. He was once a friend of mine. I hope he is my friend still, though perhaps he has forgotten me."

All that Marco had ever learned and all that he had ever trained himself to remember, quickly rushed back upon him now, because he had a clear and rapidly working brain, and had not lived the ordinary boy's life. Here was a beautiful lady of whom he knew nothing at all but that she had twisted her foot in the street and he had helped her back into her house. If silence was still the order, it was not for him to know things or ask questions or answer them. She might be the loveliest lady in the world and his father her dearest friend, but, even if this were so, he could best serve them both by obeying her friend's commands with all courtesy, and forgetting no instruction he had given.

"I do not think my father ever forgets anyone," he answered.

"No, I am sure he does not," she said softly. "Has he been to Samavia during the last three years?"

Marco paused a moment.

"Perhaps I am not the boy you think I am," he said. "My father has never been to Samavia."

"He has not? But—you are Marco Loristan?"

"Yes. That is my name."

Suddenly she leaned forward and her long lovely eyes filled with fire.

"Then you are a Samavian, and you know of the disasters overwhelming us. You know all the hideousness and barbarity of what is being done. Your father's son must know it all!"

"Everyone knows it," said Marco.

"But it is your country—your own! Your blood must burn in your veins!"

Marco stood quite still and looked at her. His eyes told whether his blood burned or not, but he did not speak. His look was answer enough, since he did not wish to say anything.

"What does your father think? I am a Samavian myself, and I think night and day. What does he think of the rumor about the descendant of the Lost Prince? Does he believe it?"

Marco was thinking very rapidly. Her beautiful

face was glowing with emotion, her beautiful voice trembled. That she should be a Samavian, and love Samavia, and pour her feeling forth even to a boy, was deeply moving to him. But howsoever one was moved, one must remember that silence was still the order. When one was very young, one must remember orders first of all.

"It might be only a newspaper story," he said. "He says one cannot trust such things. If you know him, you know he is very calm."

"Has he taught you to be calm too?" she said pathetically. "You are only a boy. Boys are not calm. Neither are women when their hearts are wrung. Oh, my Samavia! Oh, my poor little country! My brave, tortured country!" and with a sudden sob she covered her face with her hands.

A great lump mounted to Marco's throat. Boys could not cry, but he knew what she meant when she said her heart was wrung.

When she lifted her head, the tears in her eyes made them softer than ever.

"If I were a million Samavians instead of one

woman, I should know what to do!" she cried. "If your father were a million Samavians, he would know, too. He would find Ivor's descendant, if he is on the earth, and he would end all this horror!"

"Who would not end it if they could?" cried Marco, quite fiercely.

"But men like your father, men who are Samavians, must think night and day about it as I do," she impetuously insisted. "You see, I cannot help pouring my thoughts out even to a boy—because he is a Samavian. Only Samavians care. Samavia seems so little and unimportant to other people. They don't even seem to know that the blood she is pouring forth pours from human veins and beating human hearts. Men like your father must think, and plan, and feel that they must—must find a way. A woman feels it. Even a boy must. Stefan Loristan cannot be sitting quietly at home, knowing that Samavian hearts are being shot through and Samavian blood poured forth. He cannot think and say NOTHING!"

Marco started in spite of himself. He felt as if his father had been struck in the face. How dare she say such words! Big as he was, suddenly he looked bigger, and the beautiful lady saw that he did.

"He is my father," he said slowly.

She was a clever, beautiful person, and saw that she had made a great mistake.

"You must forgive me," she exclaimed. "I used the wrong words because I was excited. You must see that I meant that I knew he was giving his heart and strength, his whole being, to Samavia, even though he must stay in London."

She started and turned her head to listen to the sound of someone using the latch-key and opening the front door. The someone came in with the heavy step of a man.

"It is one of the lodgers," she said. "I think it is the one who lives in the third floor sitting-room."

"Then you won't be alone when I go," said Marco. "I am glad someone has come. I will say good morning. May I tell my father your name?"

"Tell me that you are not angry with me for expressing myself so awkwardly," she said.

"You couldn't have meant it. I know that," Marco answered boyishly. "You couldn't."

"No, I couldn't," she repeated, with the same emphasis on the words.

She took a card from a silver case on the table and gave it to him.

"Your father will remember my name," she said. "I hope he will let me see him and tell him how you took care of me."

She shook his hand warmly and let him go. But just as he reached the door she spoke again.

"Oh, may I ask you to do one thing more before you leave me?" she said suddenly. "I hope you won't mind. Will you run upstairs into the drawing-room and bring me the purple book from the small table? I shall not mind being alone if I have something to read."

"A purple book? On a small table?" said Marco.

"Between the two long windows," she smiled back at him.

The drawing-room of such houses as these is always to be reached by one short flight of stairs.

Marco ran up lightly.

❧ 14 ❧
Marco Does Not Answer

B y the time he turned the corner of the stairs, the beautiful lady had risen from her seat in the back room and walked into the dining-room at the front. A heavily-built, dark-bearded man was standing inside the door as if waiting for her.

"I could do nothing with him," she said at once, in her soft voice, speaking quite prettily and gently, as if what she said was the most natural thing in the world. "I managed the little trick of the sprained foot really well, and got him into the house. He is an amiable boy with perfect manners, and I thought it might be easy to surprise him into saying more than he knew he was saying. You can generally do that with children and young things. But he either knows nothing or has been trained to hold his tongue. He's not stupid, and he's of a high spirit. I made a pathetic little scene about Samavia, because I saw he could be worked up. It did work him up. I tried him with the Lost Prince rumor; but, if there is truth in it, he does not or will not know. I tried to make him lose his temper and betray something in defending his father, whom he thinks a god, by the way. But I made a mistake. I saw that. It's a pity. Boys can sometimes be made to tell anything." She spoke very quickly under her breath. The man spoke quickly too.

"Where is he?" he asked.

"I sent him up to the drawing-room to look for a book. He will look for a few minutes. Listen. He's an innocent boy. He sees me only as a gentle angel. Nothing will SHAKE him so much as to hear me tell him the truth suddenly. It will be such a shock to him that perhaps you can do something with him then. He may lose his hold on himself. He's only a boy."

"You're right," said the bearded man. "And when he finds out he is not free to go, it may alarm him and we may get something worth while."

"If we could find out what is true, or what Loristan thinks is true, we should have a clue to work from," she said.

"We have not much time," the man whispered. "We are ordered to Bosnia at once. Before midnight we must be on the way."

"Let us go into the other room. He is coming."

When Marco entered the room, the heavily-built man with the pointed dark beard was standing by the easy-chair.

"I am sorry I could not find the book," he apologized. "I looked on all the tables."

"I shall be obliged to go and search for it myself," said the Lovely Person.

She rose from her chair and stood up smiling. And at her first movement Marco saw that she was not disabled in the least.

"Your foot!" he exclaimed. "It's better?"

"It wasn't hurt," she answered, in her softly pretty

voice and with her softly pretty smile. "I only made you think so."

It was part of her plan to spare him nothing of shock in her sudden transformation. Marco felt his breath leave him for a moment.

"I made you believe I was hurt because I wanted you to come into the house with me," she added. "I wished to find out certain things I am sure you know."

"They were things about Samavia," said the man. "Your father knows them, and you must know something of them at least. It is necessary that we should hear what you can tell us. We shall not allow you to leave the house until you have answered certain questions I shall ask you."

Then Marco began to understand. He had heard his father speak of political spies, men and women who were paid to trace the people that certain governments or political parties desired to have followed and observed. He knew it was their work to search out secrets, to disguise themselves and live among innocent people as if they were merely ordinary neighbors.

They must be spies who were paid to follow his

father because he was a Samavian and a patriot. He did not know that they had taken the house two months before, and had accomplished several things during their apparently innocent stay in it. They had discovered Loristan and had learned to know his outgoings and incomings, and also the outgoings and incomings of Lazarus, Marco, and The Rat. But they meant, if possible, to learn other things. If the boy could be startled and terrified into unconscious revelations, it might prove well worth their while to have played this bit of melodrama before they locked the front door behind them and hastily crossed the Channel, leaving their landlord to discover for himself that the house had been vacated.

In Marco's mind strange things were happening. They were spies! But that was not all. The Lovely Person had been right when she said that he would receive a shock. His strong young chest swelled. In all his life, he had never come face to face with black treachery before. He could not grasp it. This gentle and friendly being with the grateful soft voice and grateful soft eyes had betrayed—BETRAYED him! It seemed impossible to believe it, and yet the smile on her curved mouth told him that it was true. When he had sprung to help her, she had been playing a trick! When he had been sorry for her pain and had winced at the sound of her low exclamation, she had been deliberately laying a trap to harm him. For a few seconds he was stunned—perhaps, if he had not been his father's son, he might have been stunned only. But he was more. When the first seconds had passed, there arose slowly within him a sense of something like high, remote disdain. It grew in his deep boy's eyes as he gazed directly into the pupils of the long soft dark ones. His body felt as if it were growing taller.

"You are very clever," he said slowly. Then, after a second's pause, he added, "I was too young to know that there was anyone so—clever—in the world."

The Lovely Person laughed, but she did not laugh easily. She spoke to her companion.

"A grand seigneur!" she said. "As one looks at him, one half believes it is true."

The man with the beard was looking very angry. His eyes were savage and his dark skin reddened. Marco thought that he looked at him as if he hated him, and was made fierce by the mere sight of him, for some mysterious reason.

"Two days before you left Moscow," he said, "three men came to see your father. They looked like peasants. They talked to him for more than an hour. They brought with them a roll of parchment. Is that not true?"

"I know nothing," said Marco.

"Before you went to Moscow, you were in Budapest. You went there from Vienna. You were there for three months, and your father saw many people. Some of them came in the middle of the night."

"I know nothing," said Marco.

"You have spent your life in traveling from one country to another," persisted the man. "You know the European languages as if you were a courier, or the *portier* in a Viennese hotel. Do you not?"

Marco did not answer.

The Lovely Person began to speak to the man rapidly in Russian.

"A spy and an adventurer Stefan Loristan has always been and always will be," she said. "We know what he is. The police in every capital in Europe know him as a sharper and a vagabond, as well as a spy. And yet, with all his cleverness, he does not seem to have money. What did he do with the bribe the Maranovitch gave him for betraying what he knew of the old fortress? The boy doesn't even suspect him. Perhaps it's true that he knows nothing. Or perhaps it is true that he has been so ill-treated and flogged from his babyhood that he dare not speak. There is a cowed look in his eyes in spite of his childish swagger. He's been both starved and beaten."

The outburst was well done. She did not look at Marco as she poured forth her words. She spoke with abruptness and impetuosity. If Marco was sensitive about his father, she felt sure that his youth would make his face reveal something if his tongue did not—if he understood Russian, which was one of the things it would be useful to find out, because it was a fact which would verify many other things.

Marco's face disappointed her. No change took place in it, and the blood did not rise to the surface of his skin. He listened with an uninterested air, blank and cold and polite. Let them say what they chose.

The man twisted his pointed beard and shrugged his shoulders.

"We have a good little wine-cellar downstairs," he said. "You are going down into it, and you will probably stay there for some time if you do not make up your mind to answer my questions. You think that nothing can happen to you in a house in a London street where policemen walk up and down. But you are mistaken. If you yelled now, even if anyone chanced to hear you, they would only think you were a lad getting a thrashing he deserved. You can yell as much as you like in the black little wine-cellar, and no one will hear at all. We only took this house for three months, and we shall leave it tonight without mentioning the fact to anyone. If we choose to leave you in the wine-cellar, you will wait there until somebody begins to notice that no one goes in and out, and chances to mention it to the landlord—which few people would take the trouble to do. Did you come here from Moscow?"

"I know nothing," said Marco.

"You might remain in the good little black cellar an unpleasantly long time before you were found," the man went on, quite coolly. "Do you remember the peasants who came to see your father two nights before you left?"

"I know nothing," said Marco.

"By the time it was discovered that the house was empty and people came in to make sure, you might be too weak to call out and attract their attention. Did you go to Budapest from Vienna, and were you there for three months?" asked the inquisitor.

"I know nothing," said Marco.

"You are too good for the little black cellar," put in the Lovely Person. "I like you. Don't go into it!"

"I know nothing," Marco answered, but the eyes which were like Loristan's gave her just such a look as Loristan would have given her, and she felt it. It made her uncomfortable.

"I don't believe you were ever ill-treated or beaten," she said. "I tell you, the little black cellar will be a hard thing. Don't go there!"

And this time Marco said nothing, but looked at her still as if he were some great young noble who was very proud.

He knew that every word the bearded man had

spoken was true. To cry out would be of no use. If they went away and left him behind them, there was no knowing how many days would pass before the people of the neighborhood would begin to suspect that the place had been deserted, or how long it would be before it occurred to someone to give warning to the owner. And in the meantime, neither his father nor Lazarus nor The Rat would have the faintest reason for guessing where he was. And he would be sitting alone in the dark in the wine-cellar. He did not know in the least what to do about this thing. He only knew that silence was still the order.

"It is a jet-black little hole," the man said. "You might crack your throat in it, and no one would hear. Did men come to talk with your father in the middle of the night when you were in Vienna?"

"I know nothing," said Marco.

"He won't tell," said the Lovely Person. "I am sorry for this boy."

"He may tell after he has sat in the good little black wine-cellar for a few hours," said the man with the pointed beard. "Come with me!"

He put his powerful hand on Marco's shoulder and pushed him before him. Marco made no struggle. He remembered what his father had said about the game not being a game. It wasn't a game now, but somehow he had a strong haughty feeling of not being afraid.

He was taken through the hallway, toward the rear, and down the commonplace flagged steps which led to the basement. Then he was marched through a narrow, ill-lighted, flagged passage to a door in the wall. The door was not locked and stood a trifle ajar. His companion pushed it farther open and showed part of a wine-cellar which was so dark that it was only the shelves nearest the door that Marco could faintly see. His captor pushed him in and shut the door. It was as black a hole as he had described. Marco stood still in the midst of darkness like black velvet. His guard turned the key.

"The peasants who came to your father in Moscow spoke Samavian and were big men. Do you remember them?" he asked from outside.

"I know nothing," answered Marco.

"You are a young fool," the voice replied. "And I

believe you know even more than we thought. Your father will be greatly troubled when you do not come home. I will come back to see you in a few hours, if it is possible. I will tell you, however, that I have had disturbing news which might make it necessary for us to leave the house in a hurry. I might not have time to come down here again before leaving."

Marco stood with his back against a bit of wall and remained silent.

There was stillness for a few minutes, and then there was to be heard the sound of footsteps marching away.

When the last distant echo died all was quite silent, and Marco drew a long breath. Unbelievable as it may appear, it was in one sense almost a breath of relief. In the rush of strange feeling which had swept over him when he found himself facing the astounding situation upstairs, it had not been easy to realize what his thoughts really were; there were so many of them and they came so fast. How could he quite believe the evidence of his eyes and ears? A few minutes, only a few minutes, had changed his prettily grateful and kindly acquaintance into a subtle and cunning creature whose love for Samavia had been part of a plot to harm it and to harm his father.

What did she and her companion want to do—what could they do if they knew the things they were trying to force him to tell?

Marco braced his back against the wall stoutly.

"What will it be best to think about first?"

This he said because one of the most absorbingly fascinating things he and his father talked about together was the power of the thoughts which human beings allow to pass through their minds—the strange strength of them. When they talked of this, Marco felt as if he were listening to some marvelous Eastern story of magic which was true. In Loristan's travels, he had visited many countries, and he had seen and learned many things which seemed marvels, and they had taught him deep thinking. He had known, and reasoned through days with men who believed that when they desired a thing, clear and exalted thought would bring it to them. He had discovered why they believed this, and had learned to understand their profound arguments. What he himself believed, he had taught Marco quite simply from his childhood. It was this: he himself—Marco, with the strong boy-body, the thick mat of black hair, and the patched clothes—was the magician. He held and waved his wand himself—and his wand was his own Thought. When special privation or anxiety beset them, it was their rule to say, "What will it be best to think about first?" which was Marco's reason for saying it to himself now as he stood in the darkness which was like black velvet.

He waited a few minutes for the right thing to come to him.

"I will think of the very old hermit who lived on the ledge of the mountains in India and who let my father talk to him through all one night," he said at last. This had been a wonderful story and one of his favorites. Loristan had traveled far to see this ancient man, and what he had seen and heard during that one night had made changes in his life. The part of the story which came back to Marco now was these words:

"Let pass through thy mind, my son, only the image thou wouldst desire to see a truth. Meditate only upon the wish of thy heart, seeing first that it can injure no man and is not ignoble. Then will it take earthly form and draw near to thee. This is the law of that which creates."

"I am not afraid," Marco said aloud. "I shall not be afraid. In some way I shall get out."

This was the image he wanted most to keep steadily in his mind—that nothing could make him afraid, and that in some way he would get out of the wine-cellar.

He thought of this for some minutes, and said the words over several times. He felt more like himself when he had done it.

"When my eyes are accustomed to the darkness, I shall see if there is any little glimmer of light anywhere," he said next.

He waited with patience, and it seemed for some time that he saw no glimmer at all. He put out his hands on either side of him, and found that, on the side of the wall against which he stood, there seemed to be no shelves. Perhaps the cellar had been used for other purposes than the storing of wine, and, if that was true, there might be somewhere some opening for ventilation. The air was not bad, but then the door had not been shut tightly when the man opened it.

"I am not afraid," he repeated. "I shall not be afraid. In some way I shall get out."

He would not allow himself to stop and think about his father waiting for his return. He knew that would only rouse his emotions and weaken his courage. He began to feel his way carefully along the wall. It reached farther than he had thought it would.

The cellar was not so very small. He crept round it gradually, and, when he had crept round it, he made his way across it, keeping his hands extended before him and setting down each foot cautiously. Then he sat down on the stone floor and thought again, and what he thought was of the things the old man had told his father, and that there was a way out of this place for him, and he should somehow find it, and, before too long a time had passed, be walking in the street again.

It was while he was thinking in this way that he felt a startling thing. It seemed almost as if something touched him. It made him jump, though the touch was so light and soft that it was scarcely a touch at all, in fact he could not be sure that he had not imagined it. He stood up and leaned against the wall again. Perhaps the suddenness of his movement placed him at some angle he had not reached before, or perhaps his eyes had become more completely accustomed to the darkness, for, as he turned his head to listen, he made a discovery: above the door there was a place where the velvet blackness was not so dense. There was something like a slit in the wall, though, as it did not open upon daylight but upon the dark passage, it was not light it admitted so much as a lesser shade of darkness. But even that was better than nothing, and Marco drew another long breath.

"That is only the beginning. I shall find a way out," he said.

"I SHALL."

He remembered reading a story of a man who, being shut by accident in a safety vault, passed through such terrors before his release that he believed he had spent two days and nights in the place when he had been there only a few hours.

"His thoughts did that. I must remember. I will sit

down again and begin thinking of all the pictures in the cabinet rooms of the Art History Museum in Vienna. It will take some time, and then there are the others," he said.

It was a good plan. While he could keep his mind upon the game which had helped him to pass so many dull hours, he could think of nothing else, as it required close attention—and perhaps, as the day went on, his captors would begin to feel that it was not safe to run the risk of doing a thing as desperate as this would be. They might think better of it before they left the house at least. In any case, he had learned enough from Loristan to realize that only harm could come from letting one's mind run wild.

"A mind is either an engine with broken and flying gear, or a giant power under control," was the thing they knew.

He had walked in imagination through three of the cabinet rooms and was turning mentally into a fourth, when he found himself starting again quite violently. This time it was not at a touch but at a sound. Surely it was a sound. And it was in the cellar with him. But it was the tiniest possible noise, a ghost of a squeak and a suggestion of a movement. It came from the opposite side of the cellar, the side where the shelves were. He looked across in the darkness, and in the darkness saw a light which there could be no mistake about. It WAS a light, two lights indeed, two round phosphorescent greenish balls. They were two eyes staring at him. And then he heard another sound. Not a squeak this time, but something so homely and comfortable that he actually burst out laughing. It was a cat purring, a nice warm cat! And she was curled up on one of the lower shelves purring to some new-born kittens. He knew there were kittens because it was plain now what the tiny squeak had been, and it was made plainer by the fact that he heard another much more distinct one and then another. They had all been asleep when he had come into the cellar. If the mother had been awake, she had probably been very much afraid. Afterwards she had perhaps come down from her shelf to investigate, and had passed close to him. The feeling of relief which came upon him at this strange and simple discovery was wonderful. It was so natural and comfortable an everyday thing that it seemed to make spies and criminals unreal, and only natural things possible. With a mother cat purring away among her kittens, even a dark wine-cellar was not so black. He got up and kneeled by the shelf. The greenish eyes did not shine in an unfriendly way. He could feel that the owner of them was a nice big cat, and he counted four round little balls of kittens. It was a curious delight to stroke the soft fur and talk to the mother cat. She answered with purring, as if she liked the sense of friendly human nearness. Marco laughed to himself.

"It's strange what a difference it makes!" he said. "It is almost like finding a window."

The mere presence of these harmless living things was companionship. He sat down close to the low shelf and listened to the motherly purring, now and then speaking and putting out his hand to touch the warm fur. The phosphorescent light in the green eyes was a comfort in itself.

"We shall get out of this—both of us," he said. "We shall not be here very long, Puss-cat."

He was not troubled by the fear of being really hungry for some time. He was so used to eating scantily from necessity, and to passing long hours without food during his journeys, that he had proved to himself that fasting is not, after all, such a desperate ordeal as most people imagine. If you begin by expecting to feel famished and by counting the hours between your meals, you will begin to be ravenous. But he knew better.

The time passed slowly; but he had known it would pass slowly, and he had made up his mind not to watch it nor ask himself questions about it. He was not a restless boy, but, like his father, could stand or sit or lie still. Now and then he could hear distant rumblings of carts and vans passing in the street. There was a certain degree of companionship in these also. He kept his place near the cat and his hand where he could occasionally touch her. He could lift his eyes now and then to the place where the dim glimmer of something like light showed itself.

Perhaps the stillness, perhaps the darkness, perhaps the purring of the mother cat, probably all three, caused his thoughts to begin to travel through his mind slowly and more slowly. At last they ceased and he fell asleep. The mother cat purred for some time, and then fell asleep herself.

᭦ 15 ᭦
A Sound in a Dream

Marco slept peacefully for several hours. There was nothing to awaken him during that time. But at the end of it, his sleep was penetrated by a definite sound. He had dreamed of hearing a voice at a distance, and, as he tried in his dream to hear what it said, a brief metallic ringing sound awakened him outright. It was over by the time he was fully conscious, and at once he realized that the voice of his dream had been a real one, and was speaking still. It was the Lovely Person's voice, and she was speaking rapidly, as if she were in the greatest haste. She was speaking through the door.

"You will have to search for it," was all he heard. "I have not a moment!" And, as he listened to her hurriedly departing feet, there came to him with their hastening echoes the words, "You are too good for the cellar. I like you!"

He sprang to the door and tried it, but it was still locked. The feet ran up the cellar steps and through the upper hall, and the front door closed with a bang. The two people had gone away, as they had threatened. The voice had been excited as well as hurried. Something had happened to frighten them, and they had left the house in great haste.

Marco turned and stood with his back against the door. The cat had awakened and she was gazing at him with her green eyes. She began to purr encouragingly. She really helped Marco to think. He was thinking with all his might and trying to remember.

"What did she come for? She came for something," he said to himself. "What did she say? I only heard part of it, because I was asleep. The voice in the dream was part of it. The part I heard was, 'You will have to search for it. I have not a moment.' And as she ran down the passage, she called back, 'You are too good for the cellar. I like you.'" He said the words over and over again and tried to recall exactly how they had sounded, and also to recall the voice which had seemed to be part of a dream but had been a real thing. Then he began to try his favorite experiment. As he often tried the experiment of commanding his mind to go to sleep, so he frequently experimented on commanding it to work for him—to help him to remember, to understand, and to argue about things clearly.

"Reason this out for me," he said to it now, quite naturally and calmly. "Show me what it means."

What did she come for? It was certain that she was in too great a hurry to be able, without a reason, to spare the time to come. What was the reason? She had said she liked him. Then she came because she liked him. If she liked him, she came to do something which was not unfriendly. The only good thing she could do for him was something which would help him to get out of the cellar. She had said twice that he was too good for the cellar. If he had been awake, he would have heard all she said and have understood what she wanted him to do or meant to do for him. He must not stop even to think of that. The first words he had heard—what had they been? They had been less clear to him than her last because he had heard them only as he was awakening. But he thought he was sure that they had been, "You will have to search for it." Search for it. For what? He thought and thought. What must he search for?

He sat down on the floor of the cellar and held his head in his hands, pressing his eyes so hard that curious lights floated before them.

"Tell me! Tell me!" he said to that part of his being which the anchorite had said held all knowledge and could tell a man everything if he called upon it in the right spirit.

And in a few minutes, he recalled something which seemed so much a part of his sleep that he had not been sure that he had not dreamed it. The ringing sound! He sprang up on his feet with a little gasping shout. The ringing sound! It had been the ring of metal, striking as it fell. Anything made of metal might have sounded like that. She had thrown something made of metal into the cellar. She had thrown it through the slit in the bricks near the door. She liked him, and said he was too good for his prison. She had thrown to him the only thing which could set him free. She had thrown him the KEY of the cellar!

For a few minutes the feelings which surged through him were so full of strong excitement that they set his brain in a whirl. He knew what his father would say—that would not do. If he was to think, he must hold himself still and not let even joy overcome him. The key was in the black little cellar, and he must find it in the dark. Even the woman who liked him enough to give him a chance of freedom knew that she must not open the door and let him out. There must be a delay. He would have to find the key himself, and it would be sure to take time. The chances were that they would be at a safe enough distance before he could get out.

"I will kneel down and crawl on my hands and knees," he said. "I will crawl back and forth and go over every inch of the floor with my hands until I find it. If I go over every inch, I shall find it."

So he kneeled down and began to crawl, and the cat watched him and purred.

"We shall get out, Puss-cat," he said to her. "I told you we should."

He crawled from the door to the wall at the side of the shelves, and then he crawled back again. The key might be quite a small one, and it was necessary that he should pass his hands over every inch, as he had said. The difficulty was to be sure, in the darkness, that he did not miss an inch. Sometimes he was not sure enough, and then he went over the ground again. He crawled backward and forward, and he crawled forward and backward. He crawled crosswise and lengthwise, he crawled diagonally, and he crawled round and round. But he did not find the key. If he had had only a little light, but he had none. He was so absorbed in his search that he did not know he had been engaged in it for several hours, and that it was the middle of the night. But at last he realized that he must stop for a rest, because his knees were beginning to feel bruised, and the skin of his hands was sore as a result of the rubbing on the flags. The cat and her kittens had gone to sleep and awakened again two or three times.

"But it is somewhere!" he said obstinately. "It is inside the cellar. I heard something fall which was made of metal. That was the ringing sound which awakened me."

When he stood up, he found his body ached and he was very tired. He stretched himself and exercised his arms and legs.

"I wonder how long I have been crawling about," he thought. "But the key is in the cellar. It is in the cellar."

He sat down near the cat and her family, and, laying his arm on the shelf above her, rested his head on it. He began to think of another experiment.

"I am so tired, I believe I shall go to sleep again. 'Thought which Knows All'"—he was quoting something the hermit had said to Loristan in their midnight talk—"'Thought which Knows All! Show me this little thing. Lead me to it when I awake.'"

And he did fall asleep, sound and fast.

He did not know that he slept all the rest of the night. But he did. When he awakened, it was daylight in the streets, and the milk-carts were beginning to jingle about, and the early postmen were knocking big double-knocks at front doors. The cat may have heard the milk-carts, but the actual fact was that she herself was hungry and wanted to go in search of food. Just as Marco lifted his head from his arm and sat up, she jumped down from her shelf and went to the door. She had expected to find it ajar as it had been before. When she found it shut, she scratched at it and was disturbed to find this of no use. Because she knew Marco was in the cellar, she felt she had a friend who would assist her, and she miauled appealingly.

This reminded Marco of the key.

"I will when I have found it," he said. "It is inside the cellar."

The cat miauled again, this time very anxiously indeed. The kittens heard her and began to squirm and squeak piteously.

"Lead me to this little thing," said Marco, as if speaking to Something in the darkness about him, and he got up.

He put his hand out toward the kittens, and it touched something lying not far from them. It must have been lying near his elbow all night while he slept.

It was the key! It had fallen upon the shelf, and not on the floor at all.

Marco picked it up and then stood still a moment. He made the sign of the cross.

Then he found his way to the door and fumbled until he found the keyhole and got the key into it. Then he turned it and pushed the door open—and the cat ran out into the passage before him.

❧ 16 ❧
The Rat to the Rescue

Marco walked through the passage and into the kitchen part of the basement. The doors were all locked, and they were solid doors. He ran up the flagged steps and found the door at the top shut and bolted also, and that too was a solid door. His jailers had plainly made sure that it should take time enough for him to make his way into the world, even after he got out of the wine-cellar.

The cat had run away to some part of the place where mice were plentiful. Marco was by this time rather gnawingly hungry himself. If he could get into the kitchen, he might find some fragments of food left in a cupboard; but there was no moving the locked door. He tried the outlet into the area, but that was immovable. Then he saw near it a smaller door. It was evidently the entrance to the coal-cellar under the pavement. This was proved by the fact that trodden coal-dust marked the flagstones, and near it stood a scuttle with coal in it.

This coal-scuttle was the thing which might help him! Above the area door was a small window which was supposed to light the entry. He could not reach it, and, if he reached it, he could not open it. He could throw pieces of coal at the glass and break it, and then he could shout for help when people passed by. They might not notice or understand where the shouts came from at first, but, if he kept them up, someone's attention would be attracted in the end.

He picked a large-sized solid piece of coal out of the heap in the scuttle, and threw it with all his force against the grimy glass. It smashed through and left a big hole. He threw another, and the entire pane was splintered and fell outside into the area. Then he saw it was broad daylight, and guessed that he had been shut up a good many hours. There was plenty of coal in the scuttle, and he had a strong arm and a good aim. He smashed pane after pane, until only the framework remained. When he shouted, there would be nothing between his voice and the street. No one could see him, but if he could do something which would make people slacken their pace to listen, then he could call out that he was in the basement of the house with the broken window.

"Hallo!" he shouted. "Hallo! Hallo! Hallo! Hallo!"

But vehicles were passing in the street, and the passers-by were absorbed in their own business. If they heard a sound, they did not stop to inquire into it.

"Hallo! Hallo! I am locked in!" yelled Marco, at the topmost power of his lungs. "Hallo! Hallo!"

After half an hour's shouting, he began to think that he was wasting his strength.

"They only think it is a boy shouting," he said. "Some-one will notice in time. At night, when the streets are quiet, I might make a policeman hear. But my father does not know where I am. He will be trying to find me—so will Lazarus—so will The Rat. One of them might pass through this very street, as I did. What can I do!"

A new idea flashed light upon him.

"I will begin to sing a Samavian song, and I will sing it very loud. People nearly always stop a moment to listen to music and find out where it comes from. And if any of my own people came near, they would stop at once—and now and then I will shout for help."

Once when they had stopped to rest on Hampstead Heath, he had sung a valiant Samavian song for The Rat. The Rat had wanted to hear how he would sing when they went on their secret journey. He wanted him to sing for the Squad someday, to make the thing seem real. The Rat had been greatly excited, and had begged for the song often. It was a stirring martial thing with a sort of trumpet call of a chorus. Thousands of Samavians had sung it together on their way to the battlefield, hundreds of years ago.

He drew back a step or so, and, putting his hands on his hips, began to sing, throwing his voice upward that it might pass through the broken window. He had a splendid and vibrant young voice, though he knew nothing of its fine quality. Just now he wanted only to make it loud.

In the street outside very few people were passing. An irritable old gentleman who was taking an invalid walk quite jumped with annoyance when the song suddenly trumpeted forth. Boys had no right to yell in that manner. He hurried his step to get away from the sound. Two or three other people glanced over their shoulders, but had not time to loiter. A few others listened with pleasure as they drew near and passed on.

"There's a boy with a fine voice," said one.

"What's he singing?" said his companion. "It sounds foreign."

"Don't know," was the reply as they went by. But at last a young man who was a music-teacher, going to give a lesson, hesitated and looked about him. The song was very loud and spirited just at this moment. The music-teacher could not understand where it came from, and paused to find out. The fact that he stopped attracted the attention of the next comer, who also paused.

"Who's singing?" he asked. "Where is he singing?"

"I can't make out," the music-teacher laughed. "Sounds as if it came out of the ground."

And, because it was strange that a song should seem to be coming out of the ground, a costermonger stopped, and then a little boy, and then a workingwoman, and then a lady.

There was quite a little group when another person turned the corner of the street. He was a shabby boy on crutches, and he had a frantic look on his face.

And Marco actually heard, as he drew near to the group, the *tap-tap-tap* of crutches.

"It might be," he thought. "It might be!"

And he sang the trumpet-call of the chorus as if it were meant to reach the skies, and he sang it again and again. And at the end of it shouted, "Hallo! Hallo! Hallo! Hallo! Hallo!"

The Rat swung himself into the group and looked as if he had gone crazy. He hurled himself against the people.

"Where is he! Where is he!" he cried, and he poured out some breathless words; it was almost as if he sobbed them out.

"We've been looking for him all night!" he shouted. "Where is he! Marco! Marco! No one else sings it but him. Marco! Marco!" And out of the area, as it seemed, came a shout of answer.

"Rat! Rat! I'm here in the cellar—locked in. I'm here!" and a big piece of coal came hurtling through the broken window and fell crashing on the area flags. The Rat got down the steps into the area as if he had not been on crutches but on legs, and banged on the door, shouting back:

"Marco! Marco! Here I am! Who locked you in? How can I get the door open?"

Marco was close against the door inside. It was The Rat! It was The Rat! And he would be in the street again in a few minutes. "Call a policeman!" he shouted through the keyhole. "The people locked me in on purpose and took away the keys."

Then the group of lookers-on began to get excited and press against the area railings and ask questions. They could not understand what had happened to cause the boy with the crutches to look as if he were crazy with terror and relief at the same time.

And the little boy ran delightedly to fetch a police-man, and found one in the next street, and, with some difficulty, persuaded him that it was his business to come and get a door open in an empty house where a boy who was a street singer had got locked up in a cellar.

⌒ 17 ⌒
"It Is a Very Bad Sign"

The policeman was not so much excited as out of temper. He did not know what Marco knew or what The Rat knew. Some common lad had got himself locked up in a house, and someone would have to go to the landlord and get a key from him. He had no intention of laying himself open to the law by breaking into a private house with his truncheon, as The Rat expected him to do.

"He got himself in through some of his larks, and he'll have to wait till he's got out without smashing locks," he growled, shaking the area door. "How did you get in there?" he shouted.

It was not easy for Marco to explain through a keyhole that he had come in to help a lady who had met with an accident. The policeman thought this mere boy's talk. As to the rest of the story, Marco knew that it could not be related at all without saying things which could not be explained to anyone but his father. He quickly made up his mind that he must let it be believed that he had been locked in by some strange accident. It must be supposed that the people had not remembered, in their haste, that he had not yet left the house.

When the young clerk from the house agency came with the keys, he was much disturbed and bewildered after he got inside.

"They've made a bolt of it," he said. "That happens now and then, but there's something strange about this. What did they lock these doors in the basement for, and the one on the stairs? What did they say to you?" he asked Marco, staring at him suspiciously.

"They said they were obliged to go suddenly," Marco answered.

"What were you doing in the basement?"

"The man took me down."

"And left you there and bolted? He must have been in a hurry."

"The lady said they had not a moment's time."

"Her ankle must have got well in short order," said the young man.

"I knew nothing about them," answered Marco. "I had never seen them before."

"The police were after them," the young man said. "That's what I should say. They paid three months' rent in advance, and they have only been here two. Some of these foreign spies lurking about London; that's what they were."

The Rat had not waited until the keys arrived. He had swung himself at his swiftest pace back through the streets to No. 7 Philibert Place. People turned and stared at his wild pale face as he almost shot past them.

He had left himself barely breath enough to speak with when he reached the house and banged on the door with his crutch to save time.

Both Loristan and Lazarus came to answer.

The Rat leaned against the door gasping.

"He's found! He's all right!" he panted. "Someone had locked him in a house and left him. They've sent for the keys. I'm going back. Brandon Terrace, Number 10."

Loristan and Lazarus exchanged glances. Both of them were at the moment as pale as The Rat.

"Help him into the house," said Loristan to Lazarus. "He must stay here and rest. We will go." The Rat knew it was an order.

He did not like it, but he obeyed.

"This is a bad sign, Master," said Lazarus, as they went out together.

"It is a very bad one," answered Loristan.

"God of the Right, defend us!" Lazarus groaned.

"Amen!" said Loristan. "Amen!"

The group had become a small crowd by the time they reached Brandon Terrace. Marco had not found it easy to leave the place because he was being questioned. Neither the policeman nor the agent's clerk seemed willing to relinquish the idea that he could give them some information about the absconding pair.

The entrance of Loristan produced its usual effect.

The agent's clerk lifted his hat, and the policeman stood straight and made salute. Neither of them realized that the tall man's clothes were worn and threadbare. They felt only that a personage was before them, and that it was not possible to question his air of absolute and serene authority. He laid his hand on Marco's shoulder and held it there as he spoke. When Marco looked up at him and felt the closeness of his touch, it seemed as if it were an embrace—as if he had caught him to his breast.

"My boy knew nothing of these people," he said. "That I can guarantee. He had seen neither of them before. His entering the house was the result of no boyish trick. He has been shut up in this place for nearly twenty-four hours and has had no food. I must take him home. This is my address." He handed the young man a card.

Then they went home together, and all the way to Philibert Place, Loristan's firm hand held closely to his boy's shoulder as if he could not endure to let him go. But on the way they said very little.

"Father," Marco said, rather hoarsely, when they first got away from the house in the terrace, "I can't talk well in the street. For one thing, I am so glad to be with you again. It seemed as if—it might turn out badly."

"Beloved one," Loristan said the words in their own Samavian, "until you are fed and at rest, you shall not talk at all."

Afterwards, when he was himself again and was allowed to tell his strange story, Marco found that both his father and Lazarus had at once had suspicions when he had not returned. They knew no ordinary event could have kept him. They were sure that he must have been detained against his will, and they were also sure that, if he had been so detained, it could only have been for reasons they could guess at.

"This was the card that she gave me," Marco said, and he handed it to Loristan. "She said you would remember the name." Loristan looked at the lettering with an ironic half-smile.

"I never heard it before," he replied. "She would not send me a name I knew. Probably I have never seen either of them. But I know the work they do. They are spies of the Maranovitch, and suspect that I know something of the Lost Prince. They believed they could terrify you into saying things which would be a clue. Men and women of their class will use desperate means to gain their end."

"Might they—have left me as they threatened?" Marco asked him.

"They would scarcely have dared, I think. Too great a hue and cry would have been raised by the discovery of such a crime. Too many detectives would have been set at work to track them."

But the look in his father's eyes as he spoke, and the pressure of the hand he stretched out to touch him, made Marco's heart thrill. He had won a new love and trust from his father. When they sat together and talked that night, they were closer to each other's souls than they had ever been before.

They sat in the firelight, Marco upon the worn hearth-rug, and they talked about Samavia—about the war and its heart-rending struggles, and about how they might end.

"Do you think that sometime we might be exiles no longer?" the boy said wistfully. "Do you think we might go there together—and see it—you and I, Father?"

There was a silence for a while. Loristan looked into the sinking bed of red coal.

"For years—for years I have made for my soul that image," he said slowly. "When I think of my friend on the side of the Himalayan Mountains, I say, 'The Thought which Thought the World may give us that also!'"

❧ 18 ❧
"Cities and Faces"

The hours of Marco's unexplained absence had been terrible to Loristan and to Lazarus. They had reason for fears which it was not possible for them to express. As the night drew on, the fears took stronger form. They forgot the existence of The Rat, who sat biting his nails in the bedroom, afraid to go out lest he might lose the chance of being given some errand to do but also afraid to show himself lest he should seem in the way.

"I'll stay upstairs," he had said to Lazarus. "If you just whistle, I'll come."

The anguish he passed through as the day went by and Lazarus went out and came in and he himself received no orders, could not have been expressed in any ordinary words. He writhed in his chair, he bit his nails to the quick, he wrought himself into a frenzy of misery and terror by recalling one by one all the crimes his knowledge of London police-courts supplied him with. He was doing nothing, yet he dared not leave his post. It was his post after all, though they had not given it to him. He must do something.

In the middle of the night Loristan opened the door of the back sitting-room, because he knew he must at least go upstairs and throw himself upon his bed even if he could not sleep.

He started back as the door opened. The Rat was sitting huddled on the floor near it with his back against the wall. He had a piece of paper in his hand and his twisted face was a weird thing to see.

"Why are you here?" Loristan asked.

"I've been here three hours, sir. I knew you'd have to come out sometime and I thought you'd let me speak to you. Will you—will you?"

"Come into the room," said Loristan. "I will listen to anything you want to say. What have you been drawing on that paper?" as The Rat got up in the wonderful way he had taught himself. The paper was covered with lines which showed it to be another of his plans.

"Please look at it," he begged. "I daren't go out lest you might want to send me somewhere. I daren't sit doing nothing. I began remembering and thinking things out. I put down all the streets and squares he MIGHT have walked through on his way home. I've not missed one. If you'll let me start out and walk through every one of them and talk to the policemen on the beat and look at the houses—and think out things and work at them—I'll not miss an inch—I'll not miss a brick or a flagstone—I'll—" His voice had a hard sound but it shook, and he himself shook.

Loristan touched his arm gently.

"You are a good comrade," he said. "It is well for us that you are here. You have thought of a good thing."

"May I go now?" said The Rat.

"This moment, if you are ready," was the answer. The Rat swung himself to the door.

Loristan said to him a thing which was like the sudden lighting of a great light in the very center of his being.

"You are one of us. Now that I know you are doing this I may even sleep. You are one of us." And it was because he was following this plan that The Rat had turned into Brandon Terrace and heard the Samavian song ringing out from the locked basement of No. 10.

"Yes, he is one of us," Loristan said, when he told this part of the story to Marco as they sat by the fire. "I had not been sure before. I wanted to be very sure. Last night I saw into the depths of him and KNEW. He may be trusted."

From that day The Rat held a new place. Lazarus himself, strangely enough, did not resent his holding it. The boy was allowed to be near Loristan as he had never dared to hope to be near. It was not merely that he was allowed to serve him in many ways, but he was taken into the intimacy which had before enclosed only the three. Loristan talked to him as he talked to Marco, drawing him within the circle which held so much that was comprehended without speech. The Rat knew that he was being trained and observed and he realized it with exaltation. His idol had said that he was "one of them" and he was watching and putting him to tests so that he might find out how much he was one of them. And he was doing it for some grave reason of his own. This thought possessed The Rat's whole mind. Perhaps he was wondering if he should find out that he was to be trusted, as a rock is to be trusted. That he should even think that perhaps he might find that he was like a rock, was inspiration enough.

"Sir," he said one night when they were alone together, because The Rat had been copying a road-map. His voice was very low—"do you think that— sometime—you could trust me as you trust Marco? Could it ever be like that—ever?"

"The time has come," and Loristan's voice was almost as low as his own, though strong and deep feeling underlay its quiet—"the time has come when I can trust you with Marco—to be his companion—to care for him, to stand by his side at any moment. And Marco is—Marco is my son." That was enough to uplift The Rat to the skies. But there was more to follow.

"It may not be long before it may be his part to do work in which he will need a comrade who can be trusted—as a rock can be trusted."

He had said the very words The Rat's own mind had given to him.

"A Rock! A Rock!" the boy broke out. "Let me show you, sir. Send me with him for a servant. The crutches are nothing. You've seen that they're as good as legs, haven't you? I've trained myself."

"I know, I know, dear lad." Marco had told him all of it. He gave him a gracious smile which seemed as if it held a sort of fine secret. "You shall go as his aide-de-camp. It shall be part of the game."

He had always encouraged "the game," and during the last weeks had even found time to help them in their plannings for the mysterious journey of the Secret Two. He had been so interested that once or twice he had called on Lazarus as an old soldier and Samavian to give his opinions of certain routes—and of the customs and habits of people in towns and villages by the way. Here they would find simple pastoral folk who danced, sang after their day's work, and who would tell all they knew; here they would find those who served or feared the Maranovitch and who would not talk at all. In one place they would meet with hospitality, in another with unfriendly suspicion of all strangers. Through talk and stories The Rat began to know the country almost as Marco knew it. That was part of the game too—because it was always "the game," they called it. Another part was The Rat's training of his memory, and bringing home his proofs of advance at night when he returned from his walk and could describe, or recite, or roughly sketch all he had seen in his passage from one place to another. Marco's part was to recall and sketch faces. Loristan one night gave him a number of photographs of people to commit to memory. Under each face was written the name of a place.

"Learn these faces," he said, "until you would know each one of them at once wheresoever you met it. Fix them upon your mind, so that it will be impossible for you to forget them. You must be able to sketch any one of them and recall the city or town or neighborhood connected with it."

Even this was still called "the game," but Marco

began to know in his secret heart that it was so much more, that his hand sometimes trembled with excitement as he made his sketches over and over again. To make each one many times was the best way to imbed it in his memory. The Rat knew, too, though he had no reason for knowing, but mere instinct. He used to lie awake in the night and think it over and remember what Loristan had said of the time coming when Marco might need a comrade in his work. What was his work to be? It was to be something like "the game." And they were being prepared for it. And though Marco often lay awake on his bed when The Rat lay awake on his sofa, neither boy spoke to the other of the thing his mind dwelt on. And Marco worked as he had never worked before. The game was very exciting when he could prove his prowess. The four gathered together at night in the back sitting-room. Lazarus was obliged to be with them because a second judge was needed. Loristan would mention the name of a place, perhaps a street in Paris or a hotel in Vienna, and Marco would at once make a rapid sketch of the face under whose photograph the name of the locality had been written. It was not long before he could begin his sketch without more than a moment's hesitation. And yet even when this had become the case, they still played the game night after night. There was a great hotel near the Place de la Concorde in Paris, of which Marco felt he should never hear the name during all his life without there starting up before his mental vision a tall woman with fierce black eyes and a delicate high-bridged nose across which the strong eyebrows almost met. In Vienna there was a palace which would always bring back at once a pale cold-faced man with a heavy blonde lock which fell over his forehead. A certain street in Munich meant a stout genial old aristocrat with a sly smile; a village in Bavaria, a peasant with a vacant and simple countenance. A curled and smoothed man who looked like a hair-dresser brought up a place in an Austrian mountain town. He knew them all as he knew his own face and No. 7 Philibert Place.

But still night after night the game was played.

Then came a night when, out of a deep sleep, he was awakened by Lazarus touching him. He had so long been secretly ready to answer any call that he sat up straight in bed at the first touch.

"Dress quickly and come downstairs," Lazarus said. "The Prince is here and wishes to speak with you."

Marco made no answer but got out of bed and began to slip on his clothes.

Lazarus touched The Rat.

The Rat was as ready as Marco and sat upright as he had done.

"Come down with the young Master," he commanded. "It is necessary that you should be seen and spoken to." And having given the order he went away.

No one heard the shoeless feet of the two boys as they stole down the stairs.

An elderly man in ordinary clothes, but with an unmistakable face, was sitting quietly talking to Loristan who with a gesture called both forward.

"The Prince has been much interested in what I have told him of your game," he said in his lowest voice. "He wishes to see you make your sketches, Marco."

Marco looked very straight into the Prince's eyes which were fixed intently on him as he made his bow.

"His Highness does me honor," he said, as his father might have said it. He went to the table at once and took from a drawer his pencils and pieces of cardboard.

"I should know he was your son and a Samavian," the Prince remarked.

Then his keen and deep-set eyes turned themselves on the boy with the crutches.

"This," said Loristan, "is the one who calls himself The Rat. He is one of us."

The Rat saluted.

"Please tell him, sir," he whispered, "that the crutches don't matter."

"He has trained himself to an extraordinary activity," Loristan said. "He can do anything."

The keen eyes were still taking The Rat in.

"They are an advantage," said the Prince at last.

Lazarus had nailed together a light, rough easel which Marco used in making his sketches when the game was played. Lazarus was standing in state at the door, and he came forward, brought the easel from its corner, and arranged the necessary drawing materials upon it.

Marco stood near it and waited the pleasure of his father and his visitor. They were speaking together in low tones and he waited several minutes. What The Rat noticed was what he had noticed before—that the big boy could stand still in perfect ease and silence. It was not necessary for him to say things or to ask questions—to look at people as if he felt restless if they did not speak to or notice him. He did not seem to require notice, and The Rat felt vaguely that, young as he was, this very freedom from any anxiety to be looked at or addressed made him somehow look like a great gentleman.

Loristan and the Prince advanced to where he stood.

"L'Hôtel de Marigny," Loristan said.

Marco began to sketch rapidly. He began the portrait of the handsome woman with the delicate high-bridged nose and the black brows which almost met. As he did it, the Prince drew nearer and watched the work over his shoulder. It did not take very long and, when it was finished, the inspector turned, and after giving Loristan a long and strange look, nodded twice.

"It is a remarkable thing," he said. "In that rough sketch she is not to be mistaken."

Loristan bent his head.

Then he mentioned the name of another street in another place—and Marco sketched again. This time it was the peasant with the simple face. The Prince nodded again. Then Loristan gave another name, and after that another and another; and Marco did his work until it was at an end, and Lazarus stood near with a handful of sketches which he had silently taken charge of as each was laid aside.

"You would know these faces wheresoever you saw them?" said the Prince. "If you passed one in Bond Street or in the Marylebone Road, you would recognize it at once?"

"As I know yours, sir," Marco answered.

Then followed a number of questions. Loristan asked them as he had often asked them before. They were questions as to the height and build of the originals of the pictures, of the color of their hair and eyes, and the order of their complexions. Marco answered them all. He knew all but the names of these people, and it was plainly not necessary that he should know them, as his father had never uttered them.

After this questioning was at an end the Prince pointed to The Rat who had leaned on his crutches against the wall, his eyes fiercely eager like a ferret's.

"And he?" the Prince said. "What can he do?"

"Let me try," said The Rat. "Marco knows."

Marco looked at his father.

"May I help him to show you?" he asked.

"Yes," Loristan answered, and then, as he turned to the Prince, he said again in his low voice: "HE IS ONE OF US."

Then Marco began a new form of the game. He held up one of the pictured faces before The Rat, and The Rat named at once the city and place connected with it, he detailed the color of eyes and hair, the height, the build, all the personal details as Marco himself had detailed them. To these he added descriptions of the cities, and points concerning the police system, the palaces, the people. His face twisted itself, his eyes burned, his voice shook, but he was amazing in his readiness of reply and his exactness of memory.

"I can't draw," he said at the end. "But I can remember. I didn't want anyone to be bothered with thinking I was trying to learn it. So only Marco knew."

This he said to Loristan with appeal in his voice.

"It was he who invented 'the game,'" said Loristan. "I showed you his strange maps and plans."

"It is a good game," the Prince answered in the manner of a man extraordinarily interested and impressed. "They know it well. They can be trusted."

"No such thing has ever been done before," Loristan said. "It is as new as it is daring and simple."

"Therein lies its safety," the Prince answered.

"Perhaps only boyhood," said Loristan, "could have dared to imagine it."

"The Prince thanks you," he said after a few more words spoken aside to his visitor. "We both thank you. You may go back to your beds."

And the boys went.

❧ 19 ❧
"That Is One!"

Aweek had not passed before Marco brought to The Rat in their bedroom an envelope containing a number of slips of paper on each of which was written something.

"This is another part of the game," he said gravely. "Let us sit down together by the table and study it."

They sat down and examined what was written on the slips. At the head of each was the name of one of the places with which Marco had connected a face he had sketched. Below were clear and concise directions as to how it was to be reached and the words to be said when each individual was encountered.

"This person is to be found at his stall in the market," was written of the vacant-faced peasant. "You will first attract his attention by asking the price of something. When he is looking at you, touch your left thumb lightly with the forefinger of your right hand. Then utter in a low distinct tone the words 'The Lamp is lighted.' That is all you are to do."

Sometimes the directions were not quite so simple, but they were all instructions of the same order. The originals of the sketches were to be sought out—always with precaution which should conceal that they were being sought at all, and always in such a manner as would cause an encounter to appear to be mere chance. Then certain words were to be uttered, but always without attracting the attention of any bystander or passer-by.

The boys worked at their task through the entire day. They concentrated all their powers upon it. They wrote and re-wrote—they repeated to each other what they committed to memory as if it were a lesson. Marco worked with the greater ease and more rapidly, because exercise of this order had been his practice and entertainment from his babyhood. The Rat, however, almost kept pace with him, as he had been born with a phenomenal memory and his eagerness and desire were a fury.

But throughout the entire day neither of them once referred to what they were doing as anything but "the game."

At night, it is true, each found himself lying awake and thinking. It was The Rat who broke the silence from his sofa.

"It is what the messengers of the Secret Party would be ordered to do when they were sent out to give the Sign for the rising," he said. "I made that up the first day I invented the party, didn't I?"

"Yes," answered Marco.

After a third day's concentration they knew by heart everything given to them to learn. That night Loristan put them through an examination.

"Can you write these things?" he asked, after each had repeated them and emerged safely from all cross-questioning.

Each boy wrote them correctly from memory.

"Write yours in French—in German—in Russian—in Samavian," Loristan said to Marco.

"All you have told me to do and to learn is part of myself, Father," Marco said in the end. "It is part of me, as if it were my hand or my eyes—or my heart."

"I believe that is true," answered Loristan.

He was pale that night and there was a shadow on his face. His eyes held a great longing as they rested on Marco. It was a yearning which had a sort of dread in it.

Lazarus also did not seem quite himself. He was red instead of pale, and his movements were uncertain and restless. He cleared his throat nervously at intervals and more than once left his chair as if to look for something.

It was almost midnight when Loristan, standing near Marco, put his arm round his shoulders.

"The game"—he began, and then was silent a few moments while Marco felt his arm tighten its hold. Both Marco and The Rat felt a hard quick beat in their breasts, and, because of this and because the pause seemed long, Marco spoke.

"The game—yes, Father?" he said.

"The game is about to give you work to do—both of you," Loristan answered.

Lazarus cleared his throat and walked to the easel in the corner of the room. But he only changed the position of a piece of drawing-paper on it and then came back.

"In two days you are to go to Paris—as you," to The Rat, "planned in the game."

"As I planned?" The Rat barely breathed the words.

"Yes," answered Loristan. "The instructions you have learned you will carry out. There is no more to be done than to manage to approach certain persons closely enough to be able to utter certain words to them."

"Only two young strollers whom no man could suspect," put in Lazarus in an astonishingly rough and shaky voice. "They could pass near the Emperor himself without danger. The young Master"—his voice became so hoarse that he was obliged to clear it loudly—"the young Master must carry himself less finely. It would be well to shuffle a little and slouch as if he were of the common people."

"Yes," said The Rat hastily. "He must do that. I can

teach him. He holds his head and his shoulders like a gentleman. He must look like a street lad."

"I will look like one," said Marco, with determination.

"I will trust you to remind him," Loristan said to The Rat, and he said it with gravity. "That will be your charge."

As he lay upon his pillow that night, it seemed to Marco as if a load had lifted itself from his heart. It was the load of uncertainty and longing. He had so long borne the pain of feeling that he was too young to be allowed to serve in any way. His dreams had never been wild ones—they had in fact always been boyish and modest, howsoever romantic. But now no dream which could have passed through his brain would have seemed so wonderful as this—that the hour had come—the hour had come—and that he, Marco, was to be its messenger. He was to do no dramatic deed and be announced by no flourish of heralds. No one would know what he did. What he achieved could only be attained if he remained obscure and unknown and seemed to everyone only a common ordinary boy who knew nothing whatever of important things. But his father had given to him a gift so splendid that he trembled with awe and joy as he thought of it. The game had become real. He and The Rat were to carry with them the Sign, and it would be like carrying a tiny lamp to set aflame lights which would blaze from one mountain-top to another until half the world seemed on fire.

As he had awakened out of his sleep when Lazarus touched him, so he awakened in the middle of the night again. But he was not aroused by a touch. When he opened his eyes he knew it was a look which had penetrated his sleep—a look in the eyes of his father who was standing by his side. In the road outside there was the utter silence he had noticed the night of the Prince's first visit—the only light was that of the lamp in the street, but he could see Loristan's face clearly enough to know that the mere intensity of his gaze had awakened him. The Rat was sleeping profoundly. Loristan spoke in Samavian and under his breath.

"Beloved one," he said. "You are very young. Because I am your father—just at this hour I can feel nothing else. I have trained you for this through all the years of your life. I am proud of your young maturity and strength but—Beloved—you are a child! Can I do this thing!"

For the moment, his face and his voice were scarcely like his own.

He kneeled by the bedside, and, as he did it, Marco half sitting up caught his hand and held it hard against his breast.

"Father, I know!" he cried under his breath also. "It is true. I am a child but am I not a man also? You yourself said it. I always knew that you were teaching me to be one—for some reason. It was my secret that I knew it. I learned well because I never forgot it. And I learned. Did I not?"

He was so eager that he looked more like a boy than ever. But his young strength and courage were splendid to see. Loristan knew him through and through and read every boyish thought of his.

"Yes," he answered slowly. "You did your part—and now if I—drew back—you would feel that *I had failed you—failed you.*"

"You!" Marco breathed it proudly. "You *could* not fail even the weakest thing in the world."

There was a moment's silence in which the two pairs of eyes dwelt on each other with the deepest meaning, and then Loristan rose to his feet.

"The end will be all that our hearts most wish," he said. "Tomorrow you may begin the new part of 'the game.' You may go to Paris."

When the train which was to meet the boat that crossed from Dover to Calais steamed out of the noisy Charing Cross Station, it carried in a third-class carriage two shabby boys. One of them would have been a handsome lad if he had not carried himself slouchingly and walked with a street lad's careless shuffling gait. The other was crippled and moved slowly, and apparently with difficulty, on crutches. There was nothing remarkable or picturesque enough about them to attract attention. They sat in the corner of the carriage and neither talked much nor seemed to be particularly interested in the journey or each other. When they went on board the steamer, they were soon lost among the commoner passengers and in fact found for themselves a secluded place which was not advantageous enough to be wanted by anyone else.

"What can such a poor-looking pair of lads be going to Paris for?" someone asked his companion.

"Not for pleasure, certainly; perhaps to get work," was the casual answer.

In the evening they reached Paris, and Marco led the way to a small cafe in a side street where they got some cheap food. In the same side street they found a bed they could share for the night in a tiny room over a baker's shop.

The Rat was too much excited to be ready to go to bed early. He begged Marco to guide him about the brilliant streets. They went slowly along the broad Avenue des Champs-Élysées under the lights glittering among the horse-chestnut trees. The Rat's sharp eyes took it all in—the light of the cafes among the embowering trees, the many carriages rolling by, the people who loitered and laughed or sat at little tables drinking wine and listening to music, the broad stream of life which flowed on to the Arc de Triomphe and back again.

"It's brighter and clearer than London," he said to Marco. "The people look as if they were having more fun than they do in England."

The Place de la Concorde spreading its stately spaces—a world of illumination, movement, and majestic beauty—held him as though by a fascination. He wanted to stand and stare at it, first from one point of view and then from another. It was bigger and more wonderful than he had been able to picture it when Marco had described it to him and told him of the part it had played in the days of the French Revolution when the guillotine had stood in it and the tumbrils had emptied themselves at the foot of its steps.

He stood near the Obelisk a long time without speaking.

"I can see it all happening," he said at last, and he pulled Marco away.

Before they returned home, they found their way to a large house which stood in a courtyard. In the iron work of the handsome gates which shut it in was wrought a gilded coronet. The gates were closed and the house was not brightly lighted.

They walked past it and round it without speaking, but, when they neared the entrance for the second time, The Rat said in a low tone:

"She is five feet seven, has black hair, a nose with a high bridge, her eyebrows are black and almost meet across it, she has a pale olive skin and holds her head proudly."

"That is the one," Marco answered.

They were a week in Paris and each day passed this big house. There were certain hours when great ladies were more likely to go out and come in than they were at others. Marco knew this, and they managed to be within sight of the house or to pass it at these hours. For two days they saw no sign of the person they wished to see, but one morning the gates were thrown open and they saw flowers and palms being taken in.

"She has been away and is coming back," said Marco. The next day they passed three times—once at the hour when fashionable women drive out to do their shopping, once at the time when afternoon visiting is most likely to begin, and once when the streets were brilliant with lights and the carriages had begun to roll by to dinner-parties and theaters.

Then, as they stood at a little distance from the iron gates, a carriage drove through them and stopped before the big open door which was thrown open by two tall footmen in splendid livery.

"She is coming out," said The Rat.

They would be able to see her plainly when she came, because the lights over the entrance were so bright.

Marco slipped from under his coat sleeve a carefully made sketch.

He looked at it and The Rat looked at it.

A footman stood erect on each side of the open door. The footman who sat with the coachman had got down and was waiting by the carriage. Marco and The Rat glanced again with furtive haste at the sketch. A handsome woman appeared upon the threshold. She paused and gave some order to the footman who stood on the right. Then she came out in the full light and got into the carriage which drove out of the courtyard and quite near the place where the two boys waited.

When it was gone, Marco drew a long breath as he tore the sketch into very small pieces indeed. He did not throw them away but put them into his pocket.

The Rat drew a long breath also.

"Yes," he said positively.

"Yes," said Marco.

When they were safely shut up in their room over the baker's shop, they discussed the chances of their being able to pass her in such a way as would seem accidental. Two common boys could not enter the courtyard. There was a back entrance for tradespeople and messengers. When she drove, she would always enter her carriage from the same place. Unless she sometimes walked, they could not approach her. What should be done? The thing was difficult. After they had talked some time, The Rat sat and gnawed his nails.

"Tomorrow afternoon," he broke out at last, "we'll watch and see if her carriage drives in for her—then, when she comes to the door, I'll go in and begin to beg. The servant will think I'm a foreigner and don't know what I'm doing. You can come after me to tell me to come away, because you know better than I do that I shall be ordered out. She may be a good-natured woman and listen to us—and you might get near her."

"We might try it," Marco answered. "It might work. We will try it."

The Rat never failed to treat him as his leader. He

had begged Loristan to let him come with Marco as his servant, and his servant he had been more than willing to be. When Loristan had said he should be his aide-de-camp, he had felt his trust lifted to a military dignity which uplifted him with it. As his aide-de-camp he must serve him, watch him, obey his lightest wish, make everything easy for him. Sometimes, Marco was troubled by the way in which he insisted on serving him, this strange, once dictatorial and cantankerous lad who had begun by throwing stones at him.

"You must not wait on me," he said to him. "I must wait upon myself."

The Rat rather flushed.

"He told me that he would let me come with you as your aide-de-camp," he said. "It—it's part of the game. It makes things easier if we keep up the game."

It would have attracted attention if they had spent too much time in the vicinity of the big house. So it happened that the next afternoon the great lady evidently drove out at an hour when they were not watching for her. They were on their way to try if they could carry out their plan, when, as they walked together along the

Rue Royale, The Rat suddenly touched Marco's elbow.

"The carriage stands before the shop with lace in the windows," he whispered hurriedly.

Marco saw and recognized it at once. The owner had evidently gone into the shop to buy something. This was a better chance than they had hoped for, and, when they approached the carriage itself, they saw that there was another point in their favor. Inside were no less than three beautiful little Pekingese spaniels that looked exactly alike. They were all trying to look out of the window and were pushing against each other. They were so perfect and so pretty that few people passed by without looking at them. What better excuse could two boys have for lingering about a place?

They stopped and, standing a little distance away, began to look at and discuss them and laugh at their excited little antics. Through the shop-window Marco caught a glimpse of the great lady.

"She does not look much interested. She won't stay long," he whispered, and added aloud, "That little one is the master. See how he pushes the others aside! He is stronger than the other two, though he is so small."

"He can snap, too," said The Rat.

"She is coming now," warned Marco, and then laughed aloud as if at the Pekingese, which, catching sight of their mistress at the shop-door, began to leap and yelp for joy.

Their mistress herself smiled, and was smiling as Marco drew near her.

"May we look at them, Madame?" he said in French, and, as she made an amiable gesture of acquiescence and moved toward the carriage with him, he spoke a few words, very low but very distinctly, in Russian.

"The Lamp is lighted," he said.

The Rat was looking at her keenly, but he did not see her face change at all. What he noticed most throughout their journey was that each person to whom they gave the Sign had complete control over his or her countenance, if there were bystanders, and never betrayed by any change of expression that the words meant anything unusual.

The great lady merely went on smiling, and spoke only of the dogs, allowing Marco and himself to look at them through the window of the carriage as the foot-man opened the door for her to enter.

"They are beautiful little creatures," Marco said, lifting his cap, and, as the footman turned away, he uttered his few Russian words once more and moved off without even glancing at the lady again.

"That is ONE!" he said to The Rat that night before they went to sleep, and with a match he burned the scraps of the sketch he had torn and put into his pocket.

ༀ 20 ༀ
Marco Goes to the Opera

Their next journey was to Munich, but the night before they left Paris an unexpected thing happened.

To reach the narrow staircase which led to their bedroom it was necessary to pass through the baker's shop itself.

The baker's wife was a friendly woman who liked the two boy lodgers who were so quiet and gave no trouble. More than once she had given them a hot roll or so or a freshly baked little tartlet with fruit in the

ༀ **288** ༀ

center. When Marco came in this evening, she greeted him with a nod and handed him a small parcel as he passed through.

"This was left for you this afternoon," she said. "I see you are making purchases for your journey. My man and I are very sorry you are going."

"Thank you, Madame. We also are sorry," Marco answered, taking the parcel. "They are not large purchases, you see."

But neither he nor The Rat had bought anything at all, though the ordinary-looking little package was plainly addressed to him and bore the name of one of the big cheap shops. It felt as if it contained something soft.

When he reached their bedroom, The Rat was gazing out of the window watching every living thing which passed in the street below. He who had never seen anything but London was absorbed by the spell of Paris and was learning it by heart.

"Something has been sent to us. Look at this," said Marco.

The Rat was at his side at once. "What is it? Where did it come from?"

They opened the package and at first sight saw only several pairs of quite common woolen socks. As Marco took up the sock in the middle of the parcel, he felt that there was something inside it—something laid flat and carefully. He put his hand in and drew out a number of five-franc notes—not new ones, because new ones would have betrayed themselves by crackling. These were old enough to be soft. But there were enough of them to amount to a substantial sum.

"It is in small notes because poor boys would have only small ones. No one will be surprised when we change these," The Rat said.

Each of them believed the package had been sent by the great lady, but it had been done so carefully that not the slightest clue was furnished.

To The Rat, part of the deep excitement of "the game" was the working out of the plans and methods of each person concerned. He could not have slept without working out some scheme which might have been used in this case. It thrilled him to contemplate the difficulties the great lady might have found herself obliged to overcome.

"Perhaps," he said, after thinking it over for some time, "she went to a big common shop dressed as if she were an ordinary woman and bought the socks and pretended she was going to carry them home herself. She would do that so that she could take them into some corner and slip the money in. Then, as she wanted to have them sent from the shop, perhaps she bought some other things and asked the people to deliver the packages to different places. The socks were sent to us and the other things to someone else. She would go to a shop where no one knew her and no one would expect to see her and she would wear clothes which looked neither rich nor too poor."

He created the whole episode with all its details and explained them to Marco. It fascinated him for the entire evening and he felt relieved after it and slept well.

Even before they had left London, certain newspapers had swept out of existence the story of the descendant of the Lost Prince. This had been done by derision and light handling—by treating it as a romantic legend.

At first, The Rat had resented this bitterly, but one day at a meal, when he had been producing arguments to prove that the story must be a true one, Loristan somehow checked him by his own silence.

"If there is such a man," he said after a pause, "it is well for him that his existence should not be believed in—for some time at least."

The Rat came to a dead stop. He felt hot for a moment and then felt cold. He saw a new idea all at once. He had been making a mistake in tactics.

No more was said but, when they were alone afterwards, he poured himself forth to Marco.

"I was a fool!" he cried out. "Why couldn't I see it for myself! Shall I tell you what I believe has been done? There is someone who has influence in England and who is a friend to Samavia. They've got the newspapers to make fun of the story so that it won't be believed. If it was believed, both the Iarovitch and the Maranovitch would be on the lookout, and the Secret Party would lose their chances. What a fool I was not to think of it! There's someone watching and working here who is a friend to Samavia."

"But there is someone in Samavia who has begun to suspect that it might be true," Marco answered. "If there were not, I should not have been shut in the cellar. Someone thought my father knew something. The spies had orders to find out what it was."

"Yes. Yes. That's true, too!" The Rat answered anxiously. "We shall have to be very careful."

In the lining of the sleeve of Marco's coat there was a slit into which he could slip any small thing he wished to conceal and also wished to be able to reach without trouble. In this he had carried the sketch of the lady which he had torn up in Paris. When they walked in the streets of Munich, the morning after their arrival, he carried still another sketch. It was the one picturing the genial-looking old aristocrat with the sly smile.

One of the things they had learned about this one was that his chief characteristic was his passion for music. He was a patron of musicians and he spent much time in Munich because he loved its musical atmosphere and the earnestness of its opera-goers.

"The military band plays in the Feldherrnhalle at midday. When something very good is being played, sometimes people stop their carriages so that they can listen. We will go there," said Marco.

"It's a chance," said The Rat. "We mustn't lose anything like a chance."

The day was brilliant and sunny, the people passing through the streets looked comfortable and homely, the mixture of old streets and modern ones, of ancient corners and shops and houses of the day was picturesque and cheerful. The Rat swinging through the crowd on his crutches was full of interest and exhilaration. He had begun to grow, and the change in his face and expression which had begun in London had become more noticeable. He had been given his "place," and a work to do which entitled him to hold it.

No one could have suspected them of carrying a strange and vital secret with them as they strolled along together. They seemed only two ordinary boys who looked in at shop-windows and talked over their contents, and who loitered with upturned faces in the Marienplatz before the ornate Gothic Rathaus to hear the eleven o'clock chimes play and see the painted figures of the King and Queen watch from their balcony the passing before them of the automatic tournament procession with its trumpeters and tilting knights.

When the show was over and the automatic cock broke forth into his lusty farewell crow, they laughed just as any other boys would have laughed. Sometimes it would have been easy for The Rat to forget that there was anything graver in the world than the new places and new wonders he was seeing, as if he were a wandering minstrel in a story.

But in Samavia bloody battles were being fought, and bloody plans were being wrought out, and in anguished anxiety the Secret Party and the Forgers of the Sword waited breathlessly for the Sign for which they had waited so long. And inside the lining of Marco's coat was hidden the sketched face, as the two unnoticed lads made their way to the Feldherrnhalle to hear the band play and see who might chance to be among the audience.

Because the day was sunny, and also because the band was playing a specially fine program, the crowd in the square was larger than usual. Several vehicles had stopped, and among them were one or two which were not merely hired cabs but were the carriages of private persons.

One of them had evidently arrived early, as it was drawn up in a good position when the boys reached the corner. It was a big open carriage and a grand one, luxuriously upholstered in green. The footman and coachman wore green and silver liveries and seemed to know that people were looking at them and their master.

He was a stout, genial-looking old aristocrat with a sly smile, though, as he listened to the music, it almost forgot to be sly. In the carriage with him were a young officer and a little boy, and they also listened attentively. Standing near the carriage door were several people who were plainly friends or acquaintances, as they occasionally spoke to him. Marco touched The Rat's coat sleeve as the two boys approached.

"It would not be easy to get near him," he said. "Let us go and stand as close to the carriage as we can get without pushing. Perhaps we may hear someone say something about where he is going after the music is over."

Yes, there was no mistaking him. He was the right man. Each of them knew by heart the creases on his stout face and the sweep of his gray moustache. But there was nothing noticeable in a boy looking for a moment at a piece of paper, and Marco sauntered a few steps to a bit of space left bare by the crowd and took a last glance at his sketch. His rule was to make sure at the final moment. The music was very good and the group about the carriage was evidently enthusiastic. There was talk and praise and comment, and the old aristocrat nodded his head repeatedly in applause.

"The Chancellor is music mad," a looker-on near the boys said to another. "At the opera every night unless serious affairs keep him away! There you may see him nodding his old head and bursting his gloves with applauding when a good thing is done. He ought to have led an orchestra or played a 'cello. He is too big for first violin."

There was a group about the carriage to the last, when the music came to an end and it drove away. There had been no possible opportunity of passing close to it even had the presence of the young officer and the boy not presented an insurmountable obstacle.

Marco and The Rat went on their way and passed by the Hoftheater and read the bills. *Tristan and Isolde* was to be presented at night and a great singer would sing Isolde.

"He will go to hear that," both boys said at once. "He will be sure to go."

It was decided between them that Marco should go on his quest alone when night came. One boy who hung around the entrance of the Opera would be observed less than two.

"People notice crutches more than they notice legs," The Rat said. "I'd better keep out of the way unless you need me. My time hasn't come yet. Even if it doesn't come at all I've—I've been on duty. I've gone with you and I've been ready—that's what an aide-de-camp does."

He stayed at home and read such English papers as he could lay hands on and he drew plans and re-fought battles on paper.

Marco went to the opera. Even if he had not known his way to the square near the place where the Hoftheater stood, he could easily have found it by following the groups of people in the streets who all seemed walking in one direction. There were students in their odd caps walking three or four abreast, there were young couples and older ones, and here and there whole families; there were soldiers of all ages, officers and privates; and, when talk was to be heard in passing, it was always talk about music.

For some time Marco waited in the square and watched the carriages roll up and pass under the huge pillared portico to deposit their contents at the entrance and at once drive away in orderly sequence. He must make sure that the grand carriage with the green and silver liveries rolled up with the rest. If it came, he would buy a cheap ticket and go inside.

It was rather late when it arrived. People in Munich are not late for the opera if it can be helped, and the coachman drove up hurriedly. The green and silver footman leaped to the ground and opened the carriage door almost before it stopped. The Chancellor got out looking less genial than usual because he was afraid that he might lose some of the overture. A rosy-cheeked girl in a white frock was with him and she was evidently trying to soothe him.

"I do not think we are really late, Father," she said.

"Don't feel cross, dear. It will spoil the music for you."

This was not a time in which a man's attention could be attracted quietly. Marco ran to get the ticket which would give him a place among the rows of young soldiers, artists, male and female students, and musicians who were willing to stand four or five deep throughout the performance of even the longest opera. He knew that, unless they were in one of the few boxes which belonged only to the court, the Chancellor and his rosy-cheeked daughter would be in the best seats in the front curve of the balcony which were the most desirable of the house. He soon saw them. They had secured the central places directly below the large royal box where two quiet princesses and their attendants were already seated.

When he found he was not too late to hear the overture, the Chancellor's face become more genial than ever. He settled himself down to an evening of enjoyment and evidently forgot everything else in the world. Marco did not lose sight of him. When the audience went out between acts to promenade in the corridors, he might go also and there might be a chance to pass near to him in the crowd. He watched him closely.

Sometimes his fine old face saddened at the beautiful woe of the music, sometimes it looked enraptured, and it was always evident that every note reached his soul.

The pretty daughter who sat beside him was attentive but not so enthralled. After the first act two glittering young officers appeared and made elegant and low bows, drawing their heels together as they kissed her hand. They looked sorry when they were obliged to return to their seats again.

After the second act the Chancellor sat for a few minutes as if he were in a dream. The people in the seats near him began to rise from their seats and file out into the corridors. The young officers were to be seen rising also. The rosy daughter leaned forward and touched her father's arm gently.

"She wants him to take her out," Marco thought. "He will take her because he is good-natured."

He saw him recall himself from his dream with a smile, and then he rose and, after helping to arrange a silvery blue scarf round the girl's shoulders, gave her his arm just as Marco skipped out of his fourth-row standing-place.

It was a rather warm night and the corridors were full. By the time Marco had reached the balcony floor, the pair had issued from the little door and were temporarily lost in the moving numbers.

Marco quietly made his way among the crowd trying to look as if he belonged to somebody. Once or twice his strong body and his dense black eyes and lashes made people glance at him, but he was not the only boy who had been brought to the opera so he felt safe enough to stop at the foot of the stairs and watch those who went up and those who passed by. Such a miscellaneous crowd as it was made up of—good unfashionable music-lovers mixed here and there with grand people of the court and the merry world.

Suddenly he heard a low laugh and a moment later a hand lightly touched him.

"You DID get out, then?" a soft voice said.

When he turned he felt his muscles stiffen. He ceased to slouch and did not smile as he looked at the speaker. What he felt was a wave of fierce and haughty anger. It swept over him before he had time to control it.

A lovely person who seemed swathed in several

shades of soft violet drapery was smiling at him with long, lovely eyes.

It was the woman who had trapped him into No. 10 Brandon Terrace.

↬ 21 ↫
"Help!"

"id it take you so long to find it?" asked the Lovely Person with the smile. "Of course I knew you would find it in the end. But we had to give ourselves time. How long did it take?"

Marco removed himself from beneath the touch of her hand. It was quietly done, but there was a disdain in his young face which made her wince though she pretended to shrug her shoulders amusedly.

"You refuse to answer?" she laughed.

"I refuse."

At that very moment he saw at the curve of the corridor the Chancellor and his daughter approaching slowly. The two young officers were talking gaily to the girl. They were on their way back to their box. Was he going to lose them? Was he?

The delicate hand was laid on his shoulder again, but this time he felt that it grasped him firmly.

"Naughty boy!" the soft voice said. "I am going to take you home with me. If you struggle I shall tell these people that you are my bad boy who is here without permission. What will you answer? My escort is coming down the staircase and will help me. Do you see?" And in fact there appeared in the crowd at the head of the staircase the figure of the man he remembered.

He did see. A dampness broke out on the palms of his hands. If she did this bold thing, what could he say to those she told her lie to? How could he bring proof or explain who he was—and what story dare he tell? His protestations and struggles would merely amuse the lookers-on, who would see in them only the impotent rage of an insubordinate youngster.

There swept over him a wave of remembrance

which brought back, as if he were living through it again, the moment when he had stood in the darkness of the wine-cellar with his back against the door and heard the man walk away and leave him alone. He felt again as he had done then—but now he was in another land and far away from his father. He could do nothing to help himself unless Something showed him a way.

He made no sound, and the woman who held him saw only a flame leap under his dense black lashes.

But something within him called out. It was as if he heard it. It was that strong self—the self that was Marco, and it called—it called as if it shouted.

"Help!" it called—to that Unknown Stranger Thing which had made worlds and which he and his father so often talked of and in whose power they so believed. "Help!"

The Chancellor was drawing nearer. Perhaps! Should he—?

"You are too proud to kick and shout," the voice went on. "And people would only laugh. Do you see?"

The stairs were crowded and the man who was at

the head of them could only move slowly. But he had seen the boy.

Marco turned so that he could face his captor squarely as if he were going to say something in answer to her. But he was not.

Even as he made the movement of turning, the help he had called for came and he knew what he should do. And he could do two things at once—save himself and give his Sign—because, the Sign once given, the Chancellor would understand.

"He will be here in a moment. He has recognized you," the woman said.

As he glanced up the stairs, the delicate grip of her hand unconsciously slackened.

Marco whirled away from her. The bell rang which was to warn the audience that they must return to their seats and he saw the Chancellor hasten his pace.

A moment later, the old aristocrat found himself amazedly looking down at the pale face of a breathless lad who spoke to him in German and in such a manner that he could not but pause and listen.

"Sir," he was saying, "the woman in violet at the foot

of the stairs is a spy. She trapped me once and she threatens to do it again. Sir, may I beg you to protect me?"

He said it low and fast. No one else could hear his words.

"What! What!" the Chancellor exclaimed.

And then, drawing a step nearer and quite as low and rapidly but with perfect distinctness, Marco uttered four words:

"The Lamp is lighted."

The Help cry had been answered instantly. Marco saw it at once in the old man's eyes, notwithstanding that he turned to look at the woman at the foot of the staircase as if she only concerned him.

"What! What!" he said again, and made a movement toward her, pulling his large moustache with a fierce hand.

Then Marco recognized that a curious thing happened. The Lovely Person saw the movement and the gray moustache, and that instant her smile died away and she turned quite white—so white, that under the brilliant electric light she was almost green and scarcely looked lovely at all. She made a sign to the man on the staircase and slipped through the crowd like an eel. She was a slim flexible creature and never was a disappearance more wonderful in its rapidity. Between stout matrons and their thin or stout escorts and families she made her way and lost herself—but always making toward the exit. In two minutes there was no sight of her violet draperies to be seen. She was gone and so, evidently, was her male companion.

It was plain to Marco that to follow the profession of a spy was not by any means a safe thing. The Chancellor had recognized her—she had recognized the Chancellor who turned looking ferociously angry and spoke to one of the young officers.

"She and the man with her are two of the most dangerous spies in Europe. She is a Rumanian and he is a Russian. What they wanted of this innocent lad I don't pretend to know. What did she threaten?" to Marco.

Marco was feeling rather cold and sick and had lost his healthy color for the moment.

"She said she meant to take me home with her and would pretend I was her son who had come here without permission," he answered. "She believes I know something I do not." He made a hesitating but grateful bow. "The third act, sir—I must not keep you. Thank you! Thank you!"

The Chancellor moved toward the entrance door of the balcony seats, but he did it with his hand on Marco's shoulder.

"See that he gets home safely," he said to the younger of the two officers. "Send a messenger with him. He's young to be attacked by creatures of that kind."

Polite young officers naturally obey the commands of Chancellors and such dignitaries. This one found without trouble a young private who marched with Marco through the deserted streets to his lodgings. He was a stolid young Bavarian peasant and seemed to have no curiosity or even any interest in the reason for the command given him. He was in fact thinking of his sweetheart who lived near Königssee and who had skated with him on the frozen lake last winter. He scarcely gave a glance to the schoolboy he was to escort, he neither knew nor wondered why.

The Rat had fallen asleep over his papers and lay

with his head on his folded arms on the table. But he was awakened by Marco's coming into the room and sat up blinking his eyes in the effort to get them open.

"Did you see him? Did you get near enough?" he drowsed.

"Yes," Marco answered. "I got near enough."

The Rat sat upright suddenly.

"It's not been easy," he exclaimed. "I'm sure something happened—something went wrong."

"Something nearly went wrong—VERY nearly," answered Marco. But as he spoke he took the sketch of the Chancellor out of the slit in his sleeve and tore it and burned it with a match. "But I did get near enough. And that's TWO."

They talked long, before they went to sleep that night. The Rat grew pale as he listened to the story of the woman in violet.

"I ought to have gone with you!" he said. "I see now. An aide-de-camp must always be in attendance. It would have been harder for her to manage two than one. I must always be near to watch, even if I am not close by you. If you had not come back—if you had not come back!" He struck his clenched hands together fiercely. "What should I have done!"

When Marco turned toward him from the table near which he was standing, he looked like his father.

"You would have gone on with the game just as far as you could," he said. "You could not leave it. You remember the places, and the faces, and the Sign. There is some money; and when it was all gone, you could have begged, as we used to pretend we should. We have not had to do it yet; and it was best to save it for country places and villages. But you could have done it if you were obliged to. The game would have to go on."

The Rat caught at his thin chest as if he had been struck breathless.

"Without you?" he gasped. "Without you?"

"Yes," said Marco. "And we must think of it, and plan in case anything like that should happen."

He stopped himself quite suddenly, and sat down, looking straight before him, as if at some faraway thing he saw.

"Nothing will happen," he said. "Nothing can."

"What are you thinking of?" The Rat gulped, because his breath had not quite come back. "Why will nothing happen?"

"Because—" The boy spoke in an almost matter-of-fact tone—in quite an unexalted tone at all events, "You see I can always make a strong call, as I did tonight."

"Did you shout?" The Rat asked. "I didn't know you shouted."

"I didn't. I said nothing aloud. But I—the myself that is in me," Marco touched himself on the breast, "called out, 'Help! Help!' with all its strength. And help came."

The Rat regarded him dubiously.

"What did it call to?" he asked.

"To the Power—to the Strength-place—to the Thought that does things. The Buddhist hermit, who told my father about it, called it 'The Thought that thought the World.'"

A reluctant suspicion betrayed itself in The Rat's eyes.

"Do you mean you prayed?" he inquired, with a slight touch of disfavor.

Marco's eyes remained fixed upon him in vague thoughtfulness for a moment or so of pause.

"I don't know," he said at last. "Perhaps it's the same thing—when you need something so much that you cry out loud for it. But it's not words, it's a strong thing without a name. I called like that when I was shut in the wine-cellar. I remembered some of the things the old man told my father."

The Rat moved restlessly.

"The help came that time," he admitted. "How did it come tonight?"

"In that thought which flashed into my mind almost the next second. It came like lightning. All at once I knew if I ran to the Chancellor and said the woman was a spy, it would startle him into listening to me; and that then I could give him the Sign; and that when I gave him the Sign, he would know I was speaking the truth and would protect me."

"It was a splendid thought!" The Rat said. "And it was quick. But it was you who thought of it."

"All thinking is part of the Big Thought," said Marco slowly. "It KNOWS—It KNOWS. And the outside part of us somehow broke the chain that linked us to It. And we are always trying to mend the chain, without knowing it. That is what our thinking is—trying to mend the chain. But we shall find out how to do it sometime. The man told my father so—just as the sun was rising from behind a high peak of the Himalayas." Then he added hastily, "I am only telling you what my father told me, and he only told me what the old hermit told him."

"Does your father believe what he told him?" The Rat's bewilderment had become an eager and restless thing.

"Yes, he believes it. He always thought something like it, himself. That is why he is so calm and knows so well how to wait."

"Is THAT it!" breathed The Rat. "Is that why? Has—has he mended the chain?" And there was awe in his voice, because of this one man to whom he felt any achievement was possible.

"I believe he has," said Marco. "Don't you think so yourself?"

"He has done something," The Rat said.

He seemed to be thinking things over before he spoke again—and then even more slowly than Marco.

"If he could mend the chain," he said almost in a whisper, "he could find out where the descendant of the Lost Prince is. He would know what to do for Samavia!"

He ended the words with a start, and his whole face glowed with a new, amazed light.

"Perhaps he does know!" he cried. "If the help comes like thoughts—as yours did—perhaps his thought of letting us give the Sign was part of it. We—just we two everyday boys—are part of it!"

"The hermit said—" began Marco.

"Look here!" broke in The Rat. "Tell me the whole story. I want to hear it."

It was because Loristan had heard it, and listened and believed, that The Rat had taken fire. His imagination seized upon the idea, as it would have seized on some theory of necromancy proved true and workable.

With his elbows on the table and his hands in his hair, he leaned forward, twisting a lock with restless fingers. His breath quickened.

"Tell it," he said, "I want to hear it all!"

"I shall have to tell it in my own words," Marco said. "And it won't be as wonderful as it was when my father told it to me. This is what I remember:

"My father had gone through much pain and trouble. A great load was upon him, and he had been told he was going to die before his work was done. He had gone to India, because a man he was obliged to speak to had gone there to hunt, and no one knew when he would return. My father followed him for months from one wild place to another, and, when he found him, the man would not hear or believe what he had come so far to say. Then he had jungle-fever and almost died. Once his guides left him for dead in a bungalow in the forest, and he heard the jackals howling round him all the night. Through all the hours he was only alive enough to be conscious of two things—all the rest of him seemed gone from his body: his thought knew that his work was unfinished—and his body heard the jackals howl!"

"Was the work for Samavia?" The Rat put in quickly.

"If he had died that night, the descendant of the Lost

Prince never would have been found—never!" The Rat bit his lip so hard that a drop of blood started from it.

"When he was slowly coming alive again, an Indian man, who had gone back and stayed to wait upon him, told him that near the summit of a mountain, about fifty miles away, there was a ledge which jutted out into space and hung over the valley, which was thousands of feet below. On the ledge there was a hut in which there lived an ancient holy man, as they called him, and who had been there during time which had not been measured. They said that their grandparents and great-grandparents had known of him, though very few persons had ever seen him. It was told that the most savage beast was tame before him. They said that a man-eating tiger would stop to salute him, and that a thirsty lioness would bring her whelps to drink at the spring near his hut."

"That was a lie," said The Rat promptly.

Marco neither laughed nor frowned.

"How do we KNOW?" he said. "My father neither said it was true nor false. He listened to all that was told him by the locals. They said that the holy man was the brother of the stars. He knew all things past and to come, and could heal the sick. But most people, especially those who had sinful thoughts, were afraid to go near him."

"I'd like to have seen—" The Rat pondered aloud, but he did not finish.

"Before my father was well, he had made up his mind to travel to the ledge if he could. He felt as if he must go. He thought that if he were going to die, the hermit might tell him some wise thing to do for Samavia."

"He might have given him a message to leave to the Secret Ones," said The Rat.

"He was so weak when he set out on his journey that he wondered if he would reach the end of it. Part of the way he traveled by bullock cart, and part, he was carried. But at last the bearers came to a place more than halfway up the mountain, and would go no further. Then they went back and left him to climb the rest of the way himself. They had traveled slowly and he had got more strength, but he was weak yet. The forest was more wonderful than anything he had ever seen. There were tropical trees with foliage like lace, and some with huge leaves, and some of them seemed to reach the sky. Sometimes he could barely see gleams of blue through them. And vines swung down from their high branches, and caught each other, and matted together; and there were hot scents, and strange flowers, and dazzling birds darting about, and thick moss, and little cascades bursting out. The path grew narrower and steeper, and the flower scents and the sultriness made it like walking in a hothouse. He heard rustlings in the undergrowth, which might have been made by any kind of wild animal; once he stepped across a deadly snake without seeing it. But it was asleep and did not hurt him. He knew the locals had been convinced that he would not reach the ledge; but for some strange reason he believed he should. He stopped and rested many times, and he drank some milk he had brought in a canteen. The higher he climbed, the more wonderful everything was, and a strange feeling began to fill him. He said his body stopped being tired and began to feel very light. And his load lifted itself from his heart, as if it were not his load anymore but belonged to something stronger. Even Samavia seemed to be safe. As he went higher and higher, and looked down the abyss at the world below, it appeared as if it were not real but only a dream he had wakened from—only a dream."

The Rat moved restlessly.

"Perhaps he was light-headed with the fever," he suggested.

"The fever had left him, and the weakness had left him," Marco answered. "It seemed as if he had never really been ill at all—as if no one could be ill, because things like that were only dreams, just as the world was."

"I wish I'd been with him! Perhaps I could have thrown these away—down into the abyss!" And The Rat shook his crutches which rested against the table. "I feel as if I was climbing, too. Go on."

Marco had become more absorbed than The Rat. He had lost himself in the memory of the story.

"I felt that *I* was climbing, when he told me," he said. "I felt as if I were breathing in the hot flower-scents and pushing aside the big leaves and giant ferns. There had been a rain, and they were wet and shining with big drops, like jewels, that showered over him as he thrust his way through and under them. And the stillness and the height—the stillness and the height! I can't make it real to you as he made it to me! I can't! I was there. He took me. And it was so high—and so still—and so beautiful that I could scarcely bear it."

But the truth was, that with some vivid boy-touch he had carried his hearer far. The Rat was deadly quiet. Even his eyes had not moved. He spoke almost as if he were in a sort of trance. "It's real," he said. "I'm there now. As high as you—go on—go on. I want to climb higher."

And Marco, understanding, went on.

"The day was over and the stars were out when he reached the place were the ledge was. He said he thought that during the last part of the climb he never looked on the earth at all. The stars were so immense that he could not look away from them. They seemed to be drawing him up. And all overhead was like violet velvet, and they hung there like great lamps of radiance. Can you see them? You must see them. My father saw them all night long. They were part of the wonder."

"I see them," The Rat answered, still in his trance-like voice and without stirring, and Marco knew he did.

"And there, with the huge stars watching it, was the hut on the ledge. And there was no one there. The door was open. And outside it was a low bench and table of stone. And on the table was a meal of dates and rice, waiting. Not far from the hut was a deep spring, which ran away in a clear brook. My father drank and bathed his face there. Then he went out on the ledge, and sat down and waited, with his face turned up to the stars. He did not lie down, and he thought he saw the stars all the time he waited. He was sure he did not sleep. He did not know how long he sat there alone. But at last he drew his eyes from the stars, as if he had been commanded to do it. And he was not alone anymore. A yard or so away from him sat the holy man. He knew it was the hermit because his eyes were different from any human eyes he had ever beheld. They were as still as the night was, and as deep as the shadows covering the world thousands of feet below, and they had a far, far look, and a strange light was in them."

"What did he say?" asked The Rat hoarsely.

"He only said, 'Rise, my son. I awaited thee. Go and eat the food I prepared for thee, and then we will speak together.' He didn't move or speak again until my father had eaten the meal. He only sat on the moss and let his eyes rest on the shadows over the abyss. When my father went back, he made a gesture which meant that he should sit near him.

"Then he sat still for several minutes, and let his eyes rest on my father, until he felt as if the light in them were set in the midst of his own body and his soul. Then he said, 'I cannot tell thee all thou wouldst know. That I may not do.' He had a wonderful gentle voice, like a deep soft bell. 'But the work will be done. Thy life and thy son's life will set it on its way.'

"They sat through the whole night together. And the stars hung quite near, as if they listened. And there were sounds in the bushes of stealthy, padding feet which wandered about as if the owners of them listened too. And the wonderful, low, peaceful voice of the holy man went on and on, telling of wonders which seemed like miracles but which were to him only the 'working of the Law.'"

"What is the Law?" The Rat broke in.

"There were two my father wrote down, and I learned them. The first was the Law of the One. I'll try to say that," and he covered his eyes and waited through a moment of silence.

It seemed to The Rat as if the room held an extraordinary stillness.

"Listen!" came next. "This is it:

"'There are a myriad worlds. There is but One Thought out of which they grew. Its Law is Order which cannot swerve. Its creatures are free to choose. Only they can create Disorder, which in itself is Pain and Woe and Hate and Fear. These they alone can bring forth. The Great One is a Golden Light. It is not remote but near. Hold thyself within its glow and thou wilt behold all things clearly. First, with all thy breathing being, know one thing! That thine own thought—when so thou standest—is one with That which thought the Worlds!'"

"What?" gasped The Rat. "MY thought—the things *I* think!"

"Your thoughts—boys' thoughts—anybody's thoughts."

"You're giving me the jim-jams!"

"He said it," answered Marco. "And it was then he spoke about the broken Link—and about the greatest books in the world—that in all their different ways, they were only saying over and over again one thing thousands of times. Just this thing—'Hate not, Fear not, Love.' And he said that was Order. And when it was disturbed, suffering came—poverty and misery and catastrophe and wars."

"Wars!" The Rat said sharply. "The World couldn't do without war—and armies and defenses! What about Samavia?"

"My father asked him that. And this is what he answered. I learned that too. Let me think again," and he waited as he had waited before. Then he lifted his head. "Listen! This is it:

"'Out of the blackness of Disorder and its out-pouring of human misery, there will arise the Order which is Peace. When Man learns that he is one with the Thought which itself creates all beauty, all power, all splendor, and all repose, he will not fear that his brother can rob him of his heart's desire. He will stand in the Light and draw to himself his own.'"

"Draw to himself?" The Rat said. "Draw what he wants? I don't believe it!"

"Nobody does," said Marco. "We don't know. He said we stood in the dark of the night—without stars—and did not know that the broken chain swung just above us."

"I don't believe it!" said The Rat. "It's too big!"

Marco did not say whether he believed it or not. He only went on speaking.

"My father listened until he felt as if he had stopped breathing. Just at the stillest of the stillness the holy man stopped speaking. And there was a rustling of the undergrowth a few yards away, as if something big was pushing its way through—and there was the soft pad of feet. The man turned his head and my father heard him say softly: 'Come forth, Sister.'

"And a huge leopardess with two cubs walked out onto the ledge and came to him and threw herself down with a heavy lunge near his feet."

"Your father saw that!" cried out The Rat. "You mean the old fellow knew something that made wild beasts afraid to touch him or anyone near him?"

"Not afraid. They knew he was their brother, and that he was one with the Law. He had lived so long with the Great Thought that all darkness and fear had left him forever. He had mended the Chain."

The Rat had reached deep waters. He leaned forward—his hands burrowing in his hair, his face scowling and twisted, his eyes boring into space. He had climbed to the ledge at the mountain-top; he had seen the luminous immensity of the stars, and he had looked down into the shadows filling the world thousands of feet below. Was there some remote deep in him from whose darkness a slow light was rising? All that Loristan had said he knew must be true. But the rest of it—?

Marco got up and came over to him. He looked like his father again.

"If the descendant of the Lost Prince is brought back to rule Samavia, he will teach his people the Law of the One. It was for that the holy man taught my father until the dawn came."

"Who will—who will teach the Lost Prince—the new King—when he is found?" The Rat cried. "Who will teach him?"

"The hermit said my father would. He said he would also teach his son—and that son would teach his son—and he would teach his. And through such as they were, the whole world would come to know the Order and the Law."

Never had The Rat looked so strange and fierce a thing. A whole world at peace! No tactics—no battles—no slaughtered heroes—no clash of arms, and fame! It made him feel sick. And yet—something set his chest heaving.

"And your father would teach him that—when he was found! So that he could teach his sons. Your father BELIEVES in it?"

"Yes," Marco answered. He said nothing but "Yes." The Rat threw himself forward on the table, face downward.

"Then," he said, "he must make me believe it. He must teach me—if he can."

They heard a clumping step upon the staircase, and, when it reached the landing, it stopped at their door. Then there was a solid knock.

When Marco opened the door, the young soldier

who had escorted him from the Hoftheater was standing outside. He looked as uninterested and stolid as before, as he handed in a small flat package.

"You must have dropped it near your seat at the Opera," he said. "I was to give it into your own hands. It is your purse."

After he had clumped down the staircase again, Marco and The Rat drew a quick breath at one and the same time.

"I had no seat and I had no purse," Marco said. "Let us open it."

There was a flat limp leather note-holder inside. In it was a paper, at the head of which were photographs of the Lovely Person and her companion. Beneath were a few lines which stated that they were the well known spies, Eugenia Karovna and Paul Varel, and that the bearer must be protected against them. It was signed by the Chief of the Police. On a separate sheet was written the command: "Carry this with you as protection."

"That is help," The Rat said. "It would protect us, even in another country. The Chancellor sent it—but you made the strong call—and it's here!"

There was no street lamp to shine into their windows when they went at last to bed. When the blind was drawn up, they were nearer the sky than they had been in the Marylebone Road. The last thing each of them saw, as he went to sleep, was the stars—and in their dreams, they saw them grow larger and larger, and hang like lamps of radiance against the violet-velvet sky above a ledge of a Himalayan Mountain, where they listened to the sound of a low voice going on and on and on.

❧ 22 ❧
A Night Vigil

O n a hill in the midst of a great Austrian plain, around which high Alps wait watching through the ages, stands a venerable fortress, almost more beautiful than anything one has ever seen. Perhaps, if it were not for the great plain flowering broadly about it with its wide-spread beauties of meadow-land, and wood, and dim toned buildings gathered about farms, and its dream of a small ancient city at its feet, it might—though it is to be doubted—seem something less a marvel of medieval picturesqueness. But out of the plain rises the low hill, and surrounding it at a stately distance stands guard the giant majesty of Alps, with shoulders in the clouds and god-like heads above them, looking on—always looking on—sometimes themselves ethereal clouds of snow-whiteness, sometimes monster bare crags which pierce the blue, and whose unchanging silence seems to know the secret of the everlasting. And on the hill which this august circle holds in its embrace, as though it enclosed a treasure, stands the old, old, towered fortress built as a citadel for the Prince Archbishops, who were kings in their domain in the long past centuries when the splendor and power of ecclesiastical princes was among the greatest upon earth.

And as you approach the town—and as you leave it—and as you walk through its streets, the broad calm empty-looking ones, or the narrow thoroughfares whose houses seem so near to each other, whether you climb or descend—or cross bridges, or gaze at churches, or step out on your balcony at night to look at the mountains and the moon—always it seems that from some point you can see it gazing down at you—the citadel of Hohensalzburg.

It was to Salzburg they went next, because at Salzburg was to be found the man who looked like a hair-dresser and who worked in a barber's shop. Strange as it might seem, to him also must be carried the Sign.

"There may be people who come to him to be shaved—soldiers, or men who know things," The Rat worked it out, "and he can speak to them when he is standing close to them. It will be easy to get near him. You can go and have your hair cut."

The journey from Munich was not a long one, and during the latter part of it they had the wooden-seated third-class carriage to themselves. Even the drowsy old peasant who nodded and slept in one corner got out with his bundles at last. To Marco the mountains were long-known wonders which could never grow old. They had always and always been so old! Surely they had been the first of the world! Surely they had been standing there waiting when it was said "Let there be Light." The Light had known it would find them there. They were so silent, and yet it seemed as if they said some amazing thing—something which would take your breath from you if you could hear it. And they never changed. The clouds changed, they wreathed them, and hid them, and trailed down them, and poured out storm torrents on them, and thundered against them, and darted forked lightnings round them. But the mountains stood there afterwards as if such things had not been and were not in the world. Winds roared and tore at them, centuries passed over them—centuries of millions of lives, of changing of kingdoms and empires, of battles and world-wide fame which grew and died and passed away; and temples crumbled, and kings' tombs were forgotten, and cities were buried and others built over them after hundreds of years—and perhaps a few stones fell from a mountain side, or a fissure was worn, which the people below could not even see. And that was all. There they stood, and perhaps their secret was that they had been there forever and ever. That was what the mountains said to Marco, which was why he did not want to talk much, but sat and gazed out of the carriage window.

The Rat had been very silent all the morning. He had been silent when they got up, and he had scarcely spoken when they made their way to the station at Munich and sat waiting for their train. It seemed to

Marco that he was thinking so hard that he was like a person who was far away from the place he stood in. His brows were drawn together and his eyes did not seem to see the people who passed by. Usually he saw everything and made shrewd remarks on almost all he saw. But today he was somehow otherwise absorbed. He sat in the train with his forehead against the window and stared out. He moved and gasped when he found himself staring at the Alps, but afterwards he was even strangely still. It was not until after the sleepy old peasant had gathered his bundles and got out at a station that he spoke, and he did it without turning his head.

"You only told me one of the two Laws," he said. "What was the other one?"

Marco brought himself back from his dream of reaching the highest mountain-top and seeing clouds float beneath his feet in the sun. He had to come back a long way.

"Are you thinking of that? I wondered what you had been thinking of all the morning," he said.

"I couldn't stop thinking of it. What was the second one?" said The Rat, but he did not turn his head.

"It was called the Law of Earthly Living. It was for every day," said Marco. "It was for the ordering of common things—the small things we think don't matter, as well as the big ones. I always remember that one without any trouble. This was it:

"'Let pass through thy mind, my son, only the image thou wouldst desire to see become a truth. Meditate only upon the wish of thy heart—seeing first that it is such as can wrong no man and is not ignoble. Then will it take earthly form and draw near to thee.

"'This is the Law of That which Creates.'"

Then The Rat turned round. He had a shrewdly reasoning mind.

"That sounds as if you could get anything you wanted, if you think about it long enough and in the right way," he said. "But perhaps it only means that, if you do it, you'll be happy after you're dead. My father used to shout with laughing when he was drunk and talked about things like that and looked at his rags."

He hugged his knees for a few minutes. He was remembering the rags, and the fog-darkened room in the slums, and the loud, hideous laughter.

"What if you want something that will harm somebody else?" he said next. "What if you hate someone and wish you could kill him?"

"That was one of the questions my father asked that night on the ledge. The holy man said people always asked it," Marco answered. "This was the answer:

"'Let him who stretcheth forth his hand to draw the lightning to his brother recall that through his own soul and body will pass the bolt.'"

"Wonder if there's anything in it?" The Rat pondered. "It'd make a chap careful if he believed it! Revenging yourself on a man would be like holding him against a live wire to kill him and getting all the volts through yourself."

A sudden anxiety revealed itself in his face.

"Does your father believe it?" he asked. "Does he?"

"He knows it is true," Marco said.

"I'll own up," The Rat decided after further reflection—"I'll own up I'm glad that there isn't anyone left that I've a grudge against. There isn't anyone—now."

Then he fell again into silence and did not speak

until their journey was at an end. As they arrived early in the day, they had plenty of time to wander about the marvelous little old city. But through the wide streets and through the narrow ones, under the archways into the market gardens, across the bridge and into the square where the "glockenspiel" played its old tinkling tune, everywhere the Citadel looked down and always The Rat walked on in his dream.

They found the hair-dresser's shop in one of the narrow streets. There were no grand shops there, and this particular shop was a modest one. They walked past it once, and then went back. It was a shop so humble that there was nothing remarkable in two common boys going into it to have their hair cut. An old man came forward to receive them. He was evidently glad of their modest patronage. He undertook to attend to The Rat himself, but, having arranged him in a chair, he turned about and called to someone in the back room.

"Heinrich," he said.

In the slit in Marco's sleeve was the sketch of the man with smooth curled hair, who looked like a hair-dresser. They had found a corner in which to take their final look at it before they turned back to come in. Heinrich, who came forth from the small back room, had smooth curled hair. He looked extremely like a hair-dresser. He had features like those in the sketch—his nose and mouth and chin and figure were like what Marco had drawn and committed to memory. But—

He gave Marco a chair and tied the professional white covering around his neck. Marco leaned back and closed his eyes a moment.

"That is NOT the man!" he was saying to himself. "He is NOT the man."

How he knew he was not, he could not have explained, but he felt sure. It was a strong conviction. But for the sudden feeling, nothing would have been easier than to give the Sign. And if he could not give it now, where was the one to whom it must be spoken, and what would be the result if that one could not be found? And if there were two who were so much alike, how could he be sure?

Each owner of each of the pictured faces was a link

in a powerful secret chain; and if a link were missed, the chain would be broken. Each time Heinrich came within the line of his vision, he recorded every feature afresh and compared it with the remembered sketch. Each time the resemblance became more close, but each time some persistent inner conviction repeated, "No; the Sign is not for him!"

It was disturbing, also, to find that The Rat was all at once as restless as he had previously been silent and preoccupied. He moved in his chair, to the great discomfort of the old hair-dresser. He kept turning his head to talk. He asked Marco to translate divers questions he wished him to ask the two men. They were questions about the Citadel—about the Mönchsberg— the Residenz—the Glockenspiel—the mountains. He added one query to another and could not sit still.

"The young gentleman will get an ear snipped," said the old man to Marco. "And it will not be my fault."

"What shall I do?" Marco was thinking. "He is not the man."

He did not give the Sign. He must go away and

think it out, though where his thoughts would lead him he did not know. This was a more difficult problem than he had ever dreamed of facing. There was no one to ask advice of. Only himself and The Rat, who was nervously wriggling and twisting in his chair.

"You must sit still," he said to him. "The hair-dresser is afraid you will make him cut you by accident."

"But I want to know who lives at the Residenz?" said The Rat. "These men can tell us things if you ask them."

"It is done now," said the old hair-dresser with a relieved air. "Perhaps the cutting of his hair makes the young gentleman nervous. It is sometimes so."

The Rat stood close to Marco's chair and asked questions until Heinrich also had done his work. Marco could not understand his companion's change of mood. He realized that, if he had wished to give the Sign, he had been allowed no opportunity. He could not have given it. The restless questioning had so directed the older man's attention to his son and Marco that nothing could have been said to Heinrich without his observing it.

"I could not have spoken if he had been the man," Marco said to himself.

Their very exit from the shop seemed a little hurried. When they were fairly in the street, The Rat made a clutch at Marco's arm.

"You didn't give it?" he whispered breathlessly. "I kept talking and talking to prevent you."

Marco tried not to feel breathless, and he tried to speak in a low and level voice with no hint of exclamation in it.

"Why did you say that?" he asked.

The Rat drew closer to him.

"That was not the man!" he whispered. "It doesn't matter how much he looks like him, he isn't the right one."

He was pale and swinging along swiftly as if he were in a hurry.

"Let's get into a quiet place," he said. "Those strange things you've been telling me have got hold of me. How did I know? How could I know—unless it's because I've been trying to work that second Law? I've been saying to myself that we should be told the right things to do—for the game and for your father—and so that I could be the right sort of aide-de-camp. I've been working at it, and, when he came out, I knew he was not the man in spite of his looks. And I couldn't be sure you knew, and I thought, if I kept on talking and interrupting you with silly questions, you could be prevented from speaking."

"There's a place not far away where we can get a look at the mountains. Let's go there and sit down," said Marco. "I knew it was not the right one, too. It's the Help over again."

"Yes, it's the Help—it's the Help—it must be," muttered The Rat, walking fast and with a pale, set face. "It could not be anything else."

They got away from the streets and the people and reached the quiet place where they could see the mountains. There they sat down by the wayside. The Rat took off his cap and wiped his forehead, but it was not only the quick walking which had made it damp.

"The strangeness of it gave me a kind of fright," he said. "When he came out and he was near enough for me to see him, a sudden strong feeling came over me. It seemed as if I knew he wasn't the man. Then I said to myself—'but he looks like him'—and I began to get nervous. And then I was sure again—and then I wanted to try to stop you from giving him the Sign. And then it all seemed foolishness—and the next second all the things you had told me rushed back to me at once—and I remembered what I had been thinking ever since—and I said—'Perhaps it's the Law beginning to work,' and the palms of my hands got moist."

Marco was very quiet. He was looking at the farthest and highest peaks and wondering about many things.

"It was the expression of his face that was different," he said. "And his eyes. They are rather smaller than the right man's are. The light in the shop was poor, and it was not until the last time he bent over me that I found out what I had not seen before. His eyes are gray—the other ones are brown."

"Did you see that!" The Rat exclaimed. "Then we're sure! We're safe!"

"We're not safe till we've found the right man," Marco said. "Where is he? Where is he? Where is he?"

He said the words dreamily and quietly, as if he

were lost in thought—but also rather as if he expected an answer. And he still looked at the far-off peaks. The Rat, after watching him a moment or so, began to look at them also. They were like a loadstone to him too. There was something stilling about them, and when your eyes had rested upon them a few moments they did not want to move away.

"There must be a ledge up there somewhere," he said at last.

"Let's go up and look for it and sit there and think and think—about finding the right man."

There seemed nothing fantastic in this to Marco. To go into some quiet place and sit and think about the thing he wanted to remember or to find out was an old way of his. To be quiet was always the best thing, his father had taught him. It was like listening to something which could speak without words.

"There is a little train which goes up the Gaisberg," he said. "When you are at the top, a world of mountains spreads around you. Lazarus went once and told me. And we can lie out on the grass all night. Let us go, Aide-de-camp."

So they went, each one thinking the same thought, and each boy-mind holding its own vision. Marco was the calmer of the two, because his belief that there was always help to be found was an accustomed one and had ceased to seem to partake of the supernatural. He believed quite simply that it was the working of a law, not the breaking of one, which gave answer and led him in his quests. The Rat, who had known nothing of laws other than those administered by police-courts, was at once awed and fascinated by the suggestion of crossing some borderland of the Unknown. The Law of the One had baffled and overthrown him, with its sweeping away of the enmities of passions which created wars and called for armies. But the Law of Earthly Living seemed to offer practical benefits if you could hold on to yourself enough to work it.

"You wouldn't get everything for nothing, as far as I can make out," he had said to Marco. "You'd have to sweep all the rubbish out of your mind—sweep it as if you did it with a broom—and then keep on thinking straight and believing you were going to get things—and working for them—and they'd come."

Then he had laughed a short ugly laugh because he recalled something.

"There was something in the Bible that my father used to jeer about—something about a man getting what he prayed for if he believed it," he said.

"Oh, yes, it's there," said Marco. "That if a man pray believing he shall receive what he asks it shall be given him. All the books say something like it. It's been said so often it makes you believe it."

"He didn't believe it, and I didn't," said The Rat.

"Nobody does—really," answered Marco, as he had done once before. "It's because we don't know."

They went up the Gaisberg in the little train, which pushed and dragged and panted slowly upward with them. It took them with it stubbornly and gradually higher and higher until it had left Salzburg and the Citadel below and had reached the world of mountains which rose and spread and lifted great heads behind each other and beside each other and beyond each other until there seemed no other land on earth but that on mountain sides and backs and shoulders and crowns. And also one felt the absurdity of living upon flat ground, where life must be an insignificant thing.

There were only a few sight-seers in the small carriages, and they were going to look at the view from the summit. They were not in search of a ledge.

The Rat and Marco were. When the little train stopped at the top, they got out with the rest. They wandered about with them over the short grass on the treeless summit and looked out from this viewpoint and the other. The Rat grew more and more silent, and his silence was not merely a matter of speechlessness but of expression. He LOOKED silent and as if he were no longer aware of the earth. They left the sight-seers at last and wandered away by themselves. They found a ledge where they could sit or lie and where even the world of mountains seemed below them. They had brought some simple food with them, and they laid it behind a jutting bit of rock. When the sight-seers boarded the laboring little train again and were dragged back down the mountain, their night of vigil would begin.

That was what it was to be. A night of stillness on the heights, where they could wait and watch and hold themselves ready to hear any thought which spoke to them.

The Rat was so thrilled that he would not have been surprised if he had heard a voice from the place of the stars. But Marco only believed that in this great stillness and beauty, if he held his boy-soul quiet enough, he should find himself at last thinking of something that would lead him to the place which held what it was best that he should find. The people returned to the train and it set out upon its way down the steepness.

They heard it laboring on its way, as though it was forced to make as much effort to hold itself back as it had made to drag itself upward.

Then they were alone, and it was a loneness such as an eagle might feel when it held itself poised high in the curve of blue. And they sat and watched. They saw the sun go down and, shade by shade, deepen and make radiant and then draw away with it the last touches of color—rose-gold, rose-purple, and rose-gray.

One mountain-top after another held its blush a few moments and lost it. It took long to gather them all but at length they were gone and the marvel of night fell.

The breath of the forests below was sweet about them, and soundlessness enclosed them which was of unearthly peace. The stars began to show themselves, and presently the two who waited found their faces turned upward to the sky and they both were speaking in whispers.

"The stars look large here," The Rat said.

"Yes," answered Marco. "We are not as high as the holy man was, but it seems like the top of the world."

"There is a light on the side of the mountain yonder which is not a star," The Rat whispered.

"It is a light in a hut where the guides take the climbers to rest and to spend the night," answered Marco.

"It is so still," The Rat whispered again after a silence, and Marco whispered back:

"It is so still."

They had eaten their meal of black bread and cheese after the setting of the sun, and now they lay down on their backs and looked up until the first few stars had multiplied themselves into myriads. They began a little low talk, but the soundlessness was stronger than themselves.

"How am I going to hold on to that second Law?" The Rat said restlessly. "'Let pass through thy mind only the image thou wouldst see become a truth.' The things that are passing through my mind are not the things I want to come true. What if we don't find him—don't find the right one, I mean!"

"Lie still—still—and look up at the stars," whispered Marco. "They give you a SURE feeling."

There was something in the curious serenity of him which calmed even his aide-de-camp. The Rat lay still and looked—and looked—and thought. And what he thought of was the desire of his heart. The soundlessness enwrapped him and there was no world left. That there was a spark of light in the mountain-climbers' rest-hut was a thing forgotten.

They were only two boys, and they had begun their journey on the earliest train and had been walking about all day and thinking of great and anxious things.

"It is so still," The Rat whispered again at last.

"It is so still," whispered Marco.

And the mountains rising behind each other and beside each other and beyond each other in the night, and also the myriads of stars which had so multiplied themselves, looking down knew that they were asleep—as sleep the human things which do not watch forever.

"Someone is smoking," Marco found himself saying in a dream. After which he awakened and found that the smoke was not part of a dream at all. It came from the pipe of a young man who had an alpenstock and who looked as if he had climbed to see the sun rise. He wore the clothes of a climber and a green hat with a tuft at the back. He looked down at the two boys, surprised.

"Good day," he said. "Did you sleep here so that you could see the sun get up?"

"Yes," answered Marco.

"Were you cold?"

"We slept too soundly to know. And we brought our thick coats."

"I slept halfway down the mountains," said the smoker. "I am a guide in these days, but I have not been one long enough to miss a sunrise it is no work to reach. My father and brother think I am mad about such things. They would rather stay in their beds. Oh!

He is awake, is he?" turning toward The Rat, who had risen on one elbow and was staring at him. "What is the matter? You look as if you were afraid of me."

Marco did not wait for The Rat to recover his breath and speak.

"I know why he looks at you so," he answered for him. "He is startled. Yesterday we went to a hair-dresser's shop down below there, and we saw a man who was almost exactly like you—only—" he added, looking up, "his eyes were gray and yours are brown."

"He was my twin brother," said the guide, puffing at his pipe cheerfully. "My father thought he could make hair-dressers of us both, and I tried it for four years. But I always wanted to be climbing the mountains and there were not holidays enough. So I cut my hair, and washed the pomade out of it, and broke away. I don't look like a hair-dresser now, do I?"

He did not. Not at all. But Marco knew him. He was the man. There was no one on the mountain-top but themselves, and the sun was just showing a rim of gold above the farthest and highest giant's shoulders. One need not be afraid to do anything, since there was no one to see or hear. Marco slipped the sketch out of the slit in his sleeve. He looked at it and he looked at the guide, and then he showed it to him.

"That is not your brother. It is you!" he said.

The man's face changed a little—more than any other face had changed when its owner had been spoken to. On a mountain-top as the sun rises one is not afraid.

"The Lamp is lighted," said Marco. "The Lamp is lighted."

"God be thanked!" burst forth the man. And he took off his hat and bared his head. Then the rim behind the mountain's shoulder leaped forth into a golden torrent of splendor.

And The Rat stood up, resting his weight on his crutches in utter silence, and stared and stared.

"That is three!" said Marco.

23
The Silver Horn

During the next week, which they spent in journeying towards Vienna, they gave the Sign to three different persons at places which were on the way. In a village across the frontier in Bavaria they found a giant of an old man sitting on a bench under a tree before his mountain "Gasthaus" or inn; and when the four words were uttered, he stood up and bared his head as the guide had done. When Marco gave the Sign in some quiet place to a man who was alone, he noticed that they all did this and said their "God be thanked" devoutly, as if it were part of some religious ceremony. In a small town a few miles away he had to search some hours before he found a stalwart young shoemaker with bright red hair and a horseshoe-shaped scar on his forehead. He was not in his workshop when the boys first passed it, because, as they found out later, he had been climbing a mountain the day before, and had been detained in the descent because his companion had hurt himself.

When Marco went in and asked him to measure him for a pair of shoes, he was quite friendly and told them all about it.

"There are some good fellows who should not climb," he said. "When they find themselves standing on a bit of rock jutting out over emptiness, their heads begin to whirl round—and then, if they don't turn head over heels a few thousand feet, it is because some comrade is near enough to drag them back. There can be no ceremony then and they sometimes get hurt—as my friend did yesterday."

"Did you never get hurt yourself?" The Rat asked.

"When I was eight years old I did that," said the

young shoemaker, touching the scar on his forehead. "But it was not much. My father was a guide and took me with him. He wanted me to begin early. There is nothing like it—climbing. I shall be at it again. This won't do for me. I tried shoemaking because I was in love with a girl who wanted me to stay at home. She married another man. I am glad of it. Once a guide, always a guide." He knelt down to measure Marco's foot, and Marco bent a little forward.

"The Lamp is lighted," he said.

There was no one in the shop, but the door was open and people were passing in the narrow street; so the shoemaker did not lift his red head. He went on measuring.

"God be thanked!" he said, in a low voice. "Do you want these shoes really, or did you only want me to take your measure?"

"I cannot wait until they are made," Marco answered. "I must go on."

"Yes, you must go on," answered the shoemaker. "But I'll tell you what I'll do—I'll make them and keep them. Some great day might come when I shall show them to people and swagger about them." He glanced round cautiously, and then ended, still bending over his measuring. "They will be called the shoes of the Bearer of the Sign. And I shall say, 'He was only a lad. This was the size of his foot.'" Then he stood up with a great smile.

"There'll be climbing enough to be done now," he said, "and I look to see you again somewhere."

When the boys went away, they talked it over.

"The hair-dresser didn't want to be a hair-dresser, and the shoemaker didn't want to make shoes," said The Rat. "They both wanted to be mountain-climbers. There are mountains in Samavia and mountains on the way to it. You showed them to me on the map."

"Yes; and secret messengers who can climb any-where, and cross dangerous places, and reconnoiter from points no one else can reach, can find out things and give signals other men cannot," said Marco.

"That's what I thought out," The Rat answered. "That was what he meant when he said, 'There will be climbing enough to be done now.'"

Strange were the places they went to and curiously

unlike each other were the people to whom they carried their message. The most singular of all was an old woman who lived in so remote a place that the road which wound round and round the mountain, wound round it for miles and miles. It was not a bad road and it was an amazing one to travel, dragged in a small cart by a mule, when one could be dragged, and clambering slowly with rests between when one could not: the tree-covered precipices one looked down, the tossing whiteness of waterfalls, or the green foaming of rushing streams, and the immensity of farm- and village-scattered plains spreading themselves to the feet of other mountains shutting them in were breath-taking beauties to look down on, as the road mounted and wound round and round and higher and higher.

"How can anyone live higher than this?" said The Rat as they sat on the thick moss by the wayside after the mule and cart had left them. "Look at the bare crags looming up above there. Let us look at her again. Her picture looked as if she were a hundred years old."

Marco took out his hidden sketch. It seemed surely one of the strangest things in the world that a creature as old as this one seemed could reach such a place, or, having reached it, could ever descend to the world again to give aid to any person or thing.

Her old face was crossed and recrossed with a thousand wrinkles. Her profile was splendid yet and she had been a beauty in her day. Her eyes were like an eagle's—and not an old eagle's. And she had a long neck which held her old head high.

"How could she get here?" exclaimed The Rat.

"Those who sent us know, though we don't," said Marco. "Will you sit here and rest while I go on further?"

"No!" The Rat answered stubbornly. "I didn't train myself to stay behind. But we shall come to bare-rock climbing soon and then I shall be obliged to stop," and he said the last bitterly. He knew that, if Marco had come alone, he would have ridden in no cart but would have trudged upward and onward sturdily to the end of his journey.

But they did not reach the crags, as they had thought must be inevitable. Suddenly halfway to the sky, as it seemed, they came to a bend in the road and found themselves mounting into a new green world—an astonishing marvel of a world, with green velvet slopes and soft meadows and thick woodland, and cows feeding in velvet pastures, and—as if it had been snowed down from the huge bare mountain crags which still soared above into heaven—a mysterious, ancient, huddled village which, being thus snowed down, might have caught among the rocks and rested there through all time.

There it stood. There it huddled itself. And the monsters in the blue above it themselves looked down upon it as if it were an incredible thing—this ancient, steep-roofed, hanging-balconied, crumbling cluster of human nests, which seemed a thousand miles from the world. Marco and The Rat stood and stared at it. Then they sat down and stared at it.

"How did it get here?" The Rat cried.

Marco shook his head. He certainly could see no explanation of its being there. Perhaps some of the oldest villagers could tell stories of how its first chalets had gathered themselves together.

An old peasant driving a cow came down a steep

path. He looked with a dull curiosity at The Rat and his crutches; but when Marco advanced and spoke to him in German, he did not seem to understand, but shook his head saying something in a sort of dialect Marco did not know.

"If they all speak like that, we shall have to make signs when we want to ask anything," The Rat said. "What will she speak?"

"She will know the German for the Sign or we should not have been sent here," answered Marco. "Come on."

They made their way to the village, which huddled itself together evidently with the object of keeping itself warm when through the winter months the snows strove to bury it and the winds roared down from the huge mountain crags and tried to tear it from among its rocks. The doors and windows were few and small, and glimpses of the inside of the houses showed earthen floors and dark rooms. It was plain that it was counted a more comfortable thing to live without light than to let in the cold.

It was easy enough to reconnoiter. The few people

they saw were evidently not surprised that strangers who discovered their unexpected existence should be curious and want to look at them and their houses.

The boys wandered about as if they were casual explorers, who having reached the place by chance were interested in all they saw. They went into the little Gasthaus and got some black bread and sausage and some milk. The mountaineer owner was a brawny fellow who understood some German. He told them that few strangers knew of the village but that bold hunters and climbers came for sport. In the forests on the mountain sides were bears and, in the high places, chamois. Now and again, some great gentlemen came with parties of the daring kind—very great gentlemen indeed, he said, shaking his head with pride. There was one who had castles in other mountains, but he liked best to come here. Marco began to wonder if several strange things might not be true if great gentlemen sometimes climbed to the mysterious place. But he had not been sent to give the Sign to a great gentleman. He had been sent to give it to an old woman with eyes like an eagle which was young.

He had a sketch in his sleeve, with that of her face, of her steep-roofed, black-beamed, balconied house. If they walked about a little, they would be sure to come upon it in this tiny place. Then he could go in and ask her for a drink of water.

They roamed about for an hour after they left the Gasthaus. They went into the little church and looked at the graveyard and wondered if it was not buried out of all sight in the winter. After they had done this, they sauntered out and walked through the huddled clusters of houses, examining each one as they drew near it and passed.

"I see it!" The Rat exclaimed at last. "It is that very old-looking one standing a little way from the rest. It is not as tumbled down as most of them. And there are some red flowers on the balcony."

"Yes! That's it!" said Marco.

They walked up to the low black door and, as he stopped on the threshold, Marco took off his cap. He did this because, sitting in the doorway on a low wooden chair, the old, old woman with the eagle eyes was sitting knitting.

There was no one else in the room and no one any-where within sight. When the old, old woman looked up at him with her young eagle's eyes, holding her head high on her long neck, Marco knew he need not ask for water or for anything else.

"The Lamp is lighted," he said, in his low but strong and clear young voice.

She dropped her knitting upon her knees and gazed at him a moment in silence. She knew German it was clear, for it was in German she answered him.

"God be thanked!" she said. "Come in, young Bearer of the Sign, and bring your friend in with you. I live alone and not a soul is within hearing."

She was a wonderful old woman. Neither Marco nor The Rat would live long enough to forget the hours they spent in her strange dark house. She kept them and made them spend the night with her.

"It is quite safe," she said. "I live alone since my man fell into the crevasse and was killed because his rope broke when he was trying to save his comrade. So I have two rooms to spare and sometimes climbers are glad to sleep in them. Mine is a good warm house and I am well known in the village. You are very young," she added shaking her head. "You are very young. You must have good blood in your veins to be trusted with this."

"I have my father's blood," answered Marco.

"You are like someone I once saw," the old woman said, and her eagle eyes set themselves hard upon him. "Tell me your name."

There was no reason why he should not tell it to her.

"It is Marco Loristan," he said.

"What! It is that!" she cried out, not loud but low.

To Marco's amazement she got up from her chair and stood before him, showing what a tall old woman she really was. There was a startled, even an agitated, look in her face. And suddenly she actually made a sort of curtsy to him—bending her knee as peasants do when they pass a shrine.

"It is that!" she said again. "And yet they dare let you go on a journey like this! That speaks for your courage and for theirs."

But Marco did not know what she meant. Her strange obeisance made him feel awkward. He stood up because his training had told him that when a woman stands a man also rises.

"The name speaks for the courage," he said, "because it is my father's."

She watched him almost anxiously.

"You do not even know!" she breathed—and it was an exclamation and not a question.

"I know what I have been told to do," he answered. "I do not ask anything else."

"Who is that?" she asked, pointing to The Rat.

"He is the friend my father sent with me," said Marco smiling. "He called him my aide-de-camp. It was a sort of joke because we had played soldiers together."

It seemed as if she were obliged to collect her thoughts. She stood with her hand at her mouth, looking down at the earth floor.

"God guard you!" she said at last. "You are very—very young!"

"But all his years," The Rat broke in, "he has been in training for just this thing. He did not know it was training, but it was. A soldier who had been trained for thirteen years would know his work."

He was so eager that he forgot she could not understand English. Marco translated what he said into German and added: "What he says is true."

She nodded her head, still with questioning and anxious eyes.

"Yes. Yes," she muttered. "But you are very young." Then she asked in a hesitating way:

"Will you not sit down until I do?"

"No," answered Marco. "I would not sit while my mother or grandmother stood."

"Then I must sit—and forget," she said.

She passed her hand over her face as though she were sweeping away the sudden puzzled trouble in her expression. Then she sat down, as if she had obliged herself to become again the old peasant she had been when they entered.

"All the way up the mountain you wondered why an old woman should be given the Sign," she said. "You asked each other how she could be of use."

Neither Marco nor The Rat said anything.

"When I was young and fresh," she went on, "I went to a castle over the frontier to be foster-mother to a child who was born a great noble—one who was near the throne. He loved me and I loved him. He was a strong child and he grew up a great hunter and climber. When he was not ten years old, my man taught him to climb. He always loved these mountains better than his own. He comes to see me as if he were only a young mountaineer. He sleeps in the room there," with a gesture over her shoulder into the darkness. "He has great power and, if he chooses to do a thing, he will do it—just as he will attack the biggest bear or climb the most dangerous peak. He is one who can bring things about. It is very safe to talk in this room."

Then all was quite clear. Marco and The Rat understood.

No more was said about the Sign. It had been given and that was enough. The old woman told them that they must sleep in one of her bedrooms. The next morning one of her neighbors was going down to the valley with a cart and he would help them on their way. The Rat knew that she was thinking of his crutches and he became restless.

"Tell her," he said to Marco, "how I have trained

myself until I can do what anyone else can. And tell her I am growing stronger every day. Tell her I'll show her what I can do. Your father wouldn't have let me come as your aide if I hadn't proved to him that I wasn't a cripple. Tell her. She thinks I'm no use."

Marco explained and the old woman listened attentively. When The Rat got up and swung himself about up and down the steep path near her house she seemed relieved. His extraordinary dexterity and firm swiftness evidently amazed her and gave her a confidence she had not felt at first.

"If he has taught himself to be like that just for love of your father, he will go to the end," she said. "It is more than one could believe, that a pair of crutches could do such things."

The Rat was pacified and could afterwards give himself up to watching her as closely as he wished to. He was soon "working out" certain things in his mind. What he watched was her way of watching Marco. It was as if she were fascinated and could not keep her eyes from him. She told them stories about the mountains and the strangers who came to climb with guides or to hunt. She told them about the storms, which sometimes seemed about to put an end to the little world among the crags. She described the winter when the snow buried them and the strong ones were forced to dig out the weak and some lived for days under the masses of soft whiteness, glad to keep their cows or goats in their rooms that they might share the warmth of their bodies. The villages were forced to be good neighbors to each other, for the man who was not ready to dig out a hidden chimney or buried door today might be left to freeze and starve in his snow tomb next week. Through the worst part of the winter no creature from the world below could make way to them to find out whether they were all dead or alive.

While she talked, she watched Marco as if she were always asking herself some question about him. The Rat was sure that she liked him and greatly admired his strong body and good looks. It was not necessary for him to carry himself slouchingly in her presence and he looked glowing and noble. There was a sort of reverence in her manner when she spoke to him. She reminded him of Lazarus more than once. When she gave them their evening meal, she insisted on waiting on him with a certain respectful ceremony. She would not sit at table with him, and The Rat began to realize that she felt that he himself should be standing to serve him.

"She thinks I ought to stand behind your chair as Lazarus stands behind your father's," he said to Marco. "Perhaps an aide ought to do it. Shall I? I believe it would please her."

"A Bearer of the Sign is not a royal person," answered Marco. "My father would not like it—and I should not. We are only two boys."

It was very wonderful when, after their supper was over, they all three sat together before the fire.

The red glow of the bed of wood-coal and the orange-yellow of the flame from the big logs filled the room with warm light, which made a mellow background for the figure of the old woman as she sat in her low chair and told them more and more enthralling stories.

Her eagle eyes glowed and her long neck held her head splendidly high as she described great feats of courage and endurance or almost superhuman daring in aiding those in awesome peril, and, when she glowed most in the telling, they always knew that the hero of the adventure had been her foster-child who was the baby born a great noble and near the throne. To her, he was the most splendid and adorable of human beings. Almost an emperor, but so warm and tender of heart that he never forgot the long-past days when she had held him on her knee and told him tales of chamois- and bear-hunting, and of the mountain-tops in mid-winter. He was her sun-god.

"Yes! Yes!" she said. "'Good Mother,' he calls me. And I bake him a cake on the hearth, as I did when he was ten years old and my man was teaching him to climb. And when he chooses that a thing shall be done—done it is! He is a great lord."

The flames had died down and only the big bed of red coal made the room glow, and they were thinking of going to bed when the old woman started very suddenly, turning her head as if to listen.

Marco and The Rat heard nothing, but they saw that she did and they sat so still that each held his breath.

So there was utter stillness for a few moments. Utter stillness.

Then they did hear something—a clear silver sound, piercing the pure mountain air.

The old woman sprang upright with the fire of delight in her eyes.

"It is his silver horn!" she cried out striking her hands together. "It is his own call to me when he is coming. He has been hunting somewhere and wants to sleep in his good bed here. Help me to put on more fuel," to The Rat, "so that he will see the flame of them through the open door as he comes."

"Shall we be in the way?" said Marco. "We can go at once."

She was going towards the door to open it and she stopped a moment and turned.

"No, no!" she said. "He must see your face. He will want to see it. I want him to see—how young you are."

She threw the door wide open and they heard the silver horn send out its happy call again. The brush-wood and sticks The Rat had thrown on the coals crackled and sparkled and roared into fine flames, which cast their light into the road and threw out in fine relief the old figure which stood on the threshold and looked so tall.

And in but a few minutes her great lord came to her. And in his green hunting-suit with its green hat and eagle's feather he was as splendid as she had said he was. He was big and royal-looking and laughing and he bent and kissed her as if he had been her own son.

"Yes, good Mother," they heard him say. "I want my warm bed and one of your good suppers. I sent the others to the Gasthaus."

He came into the redly glowing room and his head almost touched the blackened rafters. Then he saw the two boys.

"Who are these, good Mother?" he asked.

She lifted his hand and kissed it.

"They are the Bearers of the Sign," she said rather softly. "'The Lamp is lighted.'"

Then his whole look changed. His laughing face became quite grave and for a moment looked even anxious. Marco knew it was because he was startled to find them only boys. He made a step forward to look at them more closely.

"The Lamp is lighted! And you two bear the Sign!" he exclaimed. Marco stood out in the fire glow that he might see him well. He saluted with respect.

"My name is Marco Loristan, Highness," he said. "And my father sent me."

The change which came upon his face then was even greater than at first. For a second, Marco even felt that there was a flash of alarm in it. But almost at once that passed.

"Loristan is a great man and a great patriot," he said. "If he sent you, it is because he knows you are the one safe messenger. He has worked too long for Samavia not to know what he does."

Marco saluted again. He knew what it was right to say next.

"If we have Your Highness's permission to retire," he said, "we will leave you and go to bed. We go down the mountain at sunrise."

"Where next?" asked the hunter, looking at him with curious intentness.

"To Vienna, Highness," Marco answered.

His questioner held out his hand, still with the intent interest in his eyes.

"Good night, fine lad," he said. "Samavia has need to vaunt itself on its Sign-bearer. God go with you."

He stood and watched him as he went toward the room in which he and his aide-de-camp were to sleep. The Rat followed him closely. At the little back door the old, old woman stood, having opened it for them. As Marco passed and bade her good night, he saw that she again made the strange obeisance, bending the knee as he went by.

24

"How Shall We Find Him?"

In Vienna they came upon a pageant. In celebration of a century-past victory the Emperor drove in state and ceremony to attend at the great cathedral and to do honor to the ancient banners and laurel-wreathed statue of a long-dead soldier-prince. The broad pavements of the huge chief thoroughfare were crowded with a cheering populace watching the martial pomp and splendor as it passed by with marching feet, prancing horses, and glitter of scabbard and chain, which all seemed somehow part of music in triumphant bursts.

The Rat was enormously thrilled by the magnificence of the imperial place. Its immense spaces, the squares and gardens, reigned over by statues of emperors, and warriors, and queens made him feel that all things on earth were possible. The palaces and stately piles of architecture, whose surmounting equestrian bronzes ramped high in the air clear cut and beautiful against the sky, seemed to sweep out of his world all atmosphere but that of splendid cities down whose broad avenues emperors rode with waving banners, tramping, jangling soldiery before and behind, and golden trumpets blaring forth. It seemed as if it must always be like this—that lances and cavalry and emperors would never cease to ride by. "I should like to stay here a long time," he said almost as if he were in a dream. "I should like to see it all."

He leaned on his crutches in the crowd and watched the glitter of the passing pageant. Now and then he glanced at Marco, who watched also with a steady eye which, The Rat saw, nothing would escape: How absorbed he always was in the game! How impossible it was for him to forget it or to remember it only as a boy would! Often it seemed that he was not a boy at all. And the game, The Rat knew in these days, was a game no more but a thing of deep and deadly earnest—a thing which touched kings and thrones, and concerned the ruling and swaying of great countries. And they—two lads pushed about by the crowd as they stood and stared at the soldiers—carried with them that which was even now lighting the Lamp. The blood in The Rat's veins ran quickly and made him feel hot as he remembered certain thoughts which had forced themselves into his mind during the past weeks. As his brain had the trick of "working things out," it had, during the last fortnight at least, been following a wonderful even if rather fantastic and feverish fancy. A mere trifle had set it at work, but, its labor once begun, things which might have once seemed to be trifles appeared so no longer. When Marco was asleep, The Rat lay awake through thrilled and sometimes almost breathless midnight hours, looking backward and recalling every detail of their lives since they had known each other. Sometimes it seemed to him that almost everything he remembered—the game from first to last above all—had pointed to but one thing. And then again he would all at once feel that he was a fool and had better keep his head steady. Marco, he knew, had no wild fancies. He had learned too much and his mind was too well balanced. He did not try to "work out things." He only thought of what he was under orders to do.

"But," said The Rat more than once in these midnight hours, "if it ever comes to a draw whether he is to be saved or I am, he is the one that must come to no harm. Killing can't take long—and his father sent me with him."

This thought passed through his mind as the tramping feet went by. As a sudden splendid burst of approaching music broke upon his ear, a strange look twisted his face. He realized the contrast between this day and that first morning behind the churchyard, when he had sat on his platform among the Squad and looked up and saw Marco in the arch at the end of the passage. And because he had been good-looking and had held himself so well, he had thrown a stone at him. Yes—blind fool that he'd been—his first greeting to Marco had been a stone, just because he was what he was. As they stood here in the crowd in this far-off foreign city, it did not seem as if it could be true that it was he who had done it.

He managed to work himself closer to Marco's side. "Isn't it splendid?" he said. "I wish I was an emperor myself. I'd have these fellows out like this every day." He said it only because he wanted to say something, to speak, as a reason for getting closer to him. He wanted to be near enough to touch him and feel that they were really together and that the whole thing was not a sort of magnificent dream from which he might awaken to find himself lying on his heap of rags in his corner of the room in Bone Court.

The crowd swayed forward in its eagerness to see the principal feature of the pageant—the Emperor in his carriage. The Rat swayed forward with the rest to look as it passed.

A handsome white-haired and moustached personage in splendid uniform decorated with jeweled orders and with a cascade of emerald-green plumes nodding in his military hat gravely saluted the shouting people on either side. By him sat a man uniformed, decorated, and emerald-plumed also, but many years younger.

Marco's arm touched The Rat's almost at the same moment that his own touched Marco. Under the nodding plumes each saw the rather tired and cynical pale face, a sketch of which was hidden in the slit in Marco's sleeve.

"Is the one who sits with the Emperor an Archduke?" Marco asked the man nearest to him in the crowd. The man answered amiably enough. No, he was not, but he was a certain Prince, a descendant of the one who was the hero of the day. He was a great favorite of the Emperor's and was also a great personage, whose palace contained pictures celebrated throughout Europe.

"He pretends it is only pictures he cares for," he went on, shrugging his shoulders and speaking to his wife, who had begun to listen, "but he is a clever one, who amuses himself with things he professes not to concern himself about—big things. It's his way to look bored, and interested in nothing, but it's said he's a wizard for knowing dangerous secrets."

"Does he live at the Hofburg with the Emperor?" asked the woman, craning her neck to look after the imperial carriage.

"No, but he's often there. The Emperor is lonely and bored too, no doubt, and this one has ways of making him forget his troubles. It's been told me that now and then the two dress themselves roughly, like common men, and go out into the city to see what it's like to rub shoulders with the rest of the world. I dare say it's true. I should like to try it myself once in a while, if I had to sit on a throne and wear a crown."

The two boys followed the celebration to its end. They managed to get near enough to see the entrance to the church where the service was held and to get a view of the ceremonies at the banner-draped and laurel-wreathed statue. They saw the man with the pale face several times, but he was always so enclosed that it was not possible to get within yards of him. It happened once, however, that he looked through a temporary break in the crowding people and saw a dark strong-featured and remarkably intent boy's face, whose vivid scrutiny of him caught his eye. There was something in the fixedness of its attention which caused him to look at it curiously for a few seconds, and Marco met his gaze squarely.

"Look at me! Look at me!" the boy was saying to him mentally. "I have a message for you. A message!"

The tired eyes in the pale face rested on him with a certain growing light of interest and curiosity, but the crowding people moved and the temporary break closed up, so that the two could see each other no more. Marco and The Rat were pushed backward by those taller and stronger than themselves until they were on the outskirts of the crowd.

"Let us go to the Hofburg," said Marco. "They will come back there, and we shall see him again even if we can't get near."

To the Hofburg they made their way through the less crowded streets, and there they waited as near to the great palace as they could get. They were there when, the ceremonies at an end, the imperial carriages returned, but, though they saw their man again, they were at some distance from him and he did not see them.

Then followed four singular days. They were singular days because they were full of tantalizing incidents. Nothing seemed easier than to hear talk of, and see the Emperor's favorite, but nothing was more impossible than to get near to him. He seemed rather a favorite with the populace, and the common people of the shopkeeping or laboring classes were given to talking freely of him—of where he was going and what he was doing. Tonight he would be sure to be at this great house or that, at this ball or that banquet. There was no difficulty in discovering that he would be sure to go to the opera, or the theater, or to drive to Schönbrunn with his imperial master. Marco and The Rat heard casual speech of him again and again, and from one part of the city to the other they followed and waited for him. But it was like chasing a will-o'-the-wisp. He was evidently too brilliant and important a person to be allowed to move about alone. There were always people with him who seemed absorbed in his languid cynical talk. Marco thought that he never seemed to care much for his companions, though they on their part always seemed highly entertained by what he was saying. It was noticeable that they laughed a great deal, though he himself scarcely even smiled.

"He's one of those chaps with the trick of saying witty things as if he didn't see the fun in them himself," The Rat summed him up. "Chaps like that are always cleverer than the other kind."

"He's too high in favor and too rich not to be followed about," they heard a man in a shop say one day, "but he gets tired of it. Sometimes, when he's too bored to stand it any longer, he gives it out that he's gone into the mountains somewhere, and all the time he's shut up alone with his pictures in his own palace."

That very night The Rat came into their attic looking pale and disappointed. He had been out to buy some food after a long and arduous day in which they had covered much ground, had seen their man three times, and each time under circumstances which made him more inaccessible than ever. They had come back to their poor quarters both tired and ravenously hungry.

The Rat threw his purchase onto the table and himself into a chair.

"He's gone to Budapest," he said. "NOW how shall we find him?"

Marco was rather pale also, and for a moment he looked paler. The day had been a hard one, and in their haste to reach places at a long distance from each other they had forgotten their need of food.

They sat silent for a few moments because there seemed to be nothing to say. "We are too tired and hungry to be able to think well," Marco said at last. "Let us eat our supper and then go to sleep. Until we've had a rest, we must 'let go.'"

"Yes. There's no good in talking when you're tired," The Rat answered a trifle gloomily. "You don't reason straight. We must 'let go.'"

Their meal was simple but they ate well and without words.

Even when they had finished and undressed for the night, they said very little.

"Where do our thoughts go when we are asleep?" The Rat inquired casually after he was stretched out in the darkness. "They must go somewhere. Let's send them to find out what to do next."

"It's not as still as it was on the Gaisberg. You can hear the city roaring," said Marco drowsily from his dark corner. "We must make a ledge—for ourselves."

Sleep made it for them—deep, restful, healthy sleep. If they had been more resentful of their ill luck and lost labor, it would have come less easily and have been less natural. In their talks of strange things they had learned that one great secret of strength and unflagging courage is to know how to "let go"—to cease thinking over an anxiety until the right moment comes. It was their habit to "let go" for hours sometimes, and wander about looking at places and things—galleries, museums, palaces, giving themselves up with boyish pleasure and eagerness to all they saw. Marco was too intimate with the things worth seeing, and The Rat too curious and feverishly wide-awake to allow of their missing much.

The Rat's image of the world had grown until it seemed to know no boundaries which could hold its wealth of wonders. He wanted to go on and on and see them all.

When Marco opened his eyes in the morning, he found The Rat lying looking at him. Then they both sat up in bed at the same time.

"I believe we are both thinking the same thing," Marco said.

They frequently discovered that they were thinking the same things.

"So do I," answered The Rat. "It shows how tired we were that we didn't think of it last night."

"Yes, we are thinking the same thing," said Marco. "We have both remembered what we heard about his shutting himself up alone with his pictures and making people believe he had gone away."

"He's in his palace now," The Rat announced.

"Do you feel sure of that, too?" asked Marco. "Did you wake up and feel sure of it the first thing?"

"Yes," answered The Rat. "As sure as if I'd heard him say it himself."

"So did I," said Marco.

"That's what our thoughts brought back to us," said The Rat, "when we 'let go' and sent them off last night." He sat up hugging his knees and looking straight before him for some time after this, and Marco did not interrupt his meditations.

The day was a brilliant one, and, though their attic

had only one window, the sun shone in through it as they ate their breakfast. After it, they leaned on the window's ledge and talked about the Prince's garden. They talked about it because it was a place open to the public and they had walked round it more than once. The palace, which was not a large one, stood in the midst of it. The Prince was good-natured enough to allow quiet and well-behaved people to saunter through. It was not a fashionable promenade but a pleasant retreat for people who sometimes took their work or books and sat on the seats placed here and there among the shrubs and flowers.

"When we were there the first time, I noticed two things," Marco said. "There is a stone balcony which juts out from the side of the palace which looks on the Fountain Garden. That day there were chairs on it as if the Prince and his visitors sometimes sat there. Near it, there was a very large evergreen shrub and I saw that there was a hollow place inside it. If someone wanted to stay in the gardens all night to watch the windows when they were lighted and see if anyone came out alone upon the balcony, he could hide himself in the hollow place and stay there until the morning."

"Is there room for two inside the shrub?" The Rat asked.

"No. I must go alone," said Marco.

ʚ 25 ɞ
A Voice in
the Night

ate that afternoon there wandered about the gardens two quiet, inconspicuous, rather poorly dressed boys. They looked at the palace, the shrubs, and the flower-beds, as strangers usually did, and they sat on the seats and talked as people were accustomed to seeing boys talk together. It was a sunny day and exceptionally warm, and there were more saunterers and sitters than usual, which was perhaps the reason why the *portier* at the entrance gates gave such slight notice to the pair that he did not observe that, though two boys came in, only one went out. He did not, in fact, remember, when he saw The Rat swing by on his crutches at closing-time, that he had entered in company with a dark-haired lad who walked without any aid. It happened that, when The Rat passed out, the *portier* at the entrance was much interested in the aspect of the sky, which was curiously threatening. There had been heavy clouds hanging about all day and now and then blotting out the sunshine entirely, but the sun had refused to retire altogether. Just now, however, the clouds had piled themselves in thunderous, purplish mountains, and the sun had been forced to set behind them.

"It's been a sort of battle since morning," the *portier* said. "There will be some crashes and cataracts tonight." That was what The Rat had thought when they had sat in the Fountain Garden on a seat which gave them a good view of the balcony and the big evergreen shrub, which they knew had the hollow in the middle, though its circumference was so imposing. "If there should be a big storm, the evergreen will not save you much, though it may keep off the worst," The Rat said. "I wish there was room for two."

He would have wished there was room for two if he had seen Marco marching to the stake. As the gardens emptied, the boys rose and walked round once more, as if on their way out. By the time they had sauntered toward the big evergreen, nobody was in the Fountain Garden, and the last loiterers were moving toward the arched stone entrance to the streets.

When they drew near one side of the evergreen, the two were together. When The Rat swung out on the other side of it, he was alone! No one noticed that anything had happened; no one looked back. So The Rat swung down the walks and round the flower-beds and passed into the street. And the *portier* looked at the sky and made his remark about the "crashes" and "cataracts."

As the darkness came on, the hollow in the shrub seemed a very safe place. It was not in the least likely that anyone would enter the closed gardens; and if by rare chance some servant passed through, he would not be in search of people who wished to watch all night in the middle of an evergreen instead of going to bed and to sleep. The hollow was well inclosed with greenery, and there was room to sit down when one was tired of standing.

Marco stood for a long time because, by doing so, he could see plainly the windows opening on the balcony if he gently pushed aside some flexible young boughs. He had managed to discover in his first visit to the gardens that the windows overlooking the Fountain Garden were those which belonged to the Prince's own suite of rooms. Those which opened on to the balcony lighted his favorite apartment, which contained his best-loved books and pictures and in which he spent most of his secluded leisure hours.

Marco watched these windows anxiously. If the Prince had not gone to Budapest—if he were really only in retreat, and hiding from his merry world among his treasures—he would be living in his favorite rooms and lights would show themselves. And if there were lights, he might pass before a window because, since he was inclosed in his garden, he need not fear being seen. The twilight deepened into darkness and, because of the heavy clouds, it was very dense. Faint gleams showed themselves in the lower part of the palace, but none was lighted in the windows Marco watched. He waited so long that it became evident that none was to be lighted at all. At last he loosed his hold on the young boughs and, after standing a few moments in thought, sat down upon the earth in the midst of his embowered tent. The Prince was not in his retreat; he was probably not in Vienna, and the rumor of his journey to Budapest had no doubt been true. So much time lost through making a mistake—but it was best to have made the venture. Not to have made it would have been to lose a chance. The entrance was closed for the night and there was no getting out of the gardens until they were opened for the next day. He must stay in his hiding-place until the time when people began to come and bring their books and knitting and sit on the seats. Then he could stroll out without attracting attention. But he had the night before him to spend as best he could. That would not matter at all. He could tuck his cap under his head and go to sleep on the ground. He could command himself to waken once every half-hour and look for the lights. He would not go to sleep until it was long past midnight—so long past that there would not be one chance in a hundred that anything could happen. But the clouds which made the night so dark were giving forth low rumbling growls. At intervals a threatening gleam of light shot across them and a sudden swish of wind rushed through the trees in the garden. This happened several times, and then Marco began to hear the patter of raindrops. They were heavy and big drops, but few at first, and then there was a new and more powerful rush of wind, a jagged dart of light in the sky, and a tremendous crash. After that the clouds tore themselves open and poured forth their contents in floods. After the protracted struggle of the day it all seemed to happen at once, as if a horde of huge lions had at one moment been let loose: flame after flame of lightning, roar and crash and sharp reports of thunder, shrieks of hurricane wind, torrents of rain, as if some tidal-wave of the skies had gathered and rushed and burst upon the earth. It was such a storm as people remember for a lifetime and which in few lifetimes is seen at all.

Marco stood still in the midst of the rage and flooding, blinding roar of it. After the first few minutes he knew he could do nothing to shield himself. Down the garden paths he heard cataracts rushing. He held his cap pressed against his eyes because he seemed to stand in the midst of darting flames. The crashes, cannon reports and thunderings, and the jagged streams of light came so close to one another that he seemed deafened as well as blinded. He wondered if he should ever be able to hear human voices again when it was over. That he was drenched to the skin and that the water poured from his clothes as if he were himself a cataract was so small a detail that he was scarcely aware of it. He stood still, bracing his body, and waited. If he had been a Samavian soldier in the trenches and such a storm had broken upon him and his comrades, they could only have braced themselves and waited. This was what he found himself thinking when the tumult and down-pour were at their worst. There were men who had waited in the midst of a rain of bullets.

It was not long after this thought had come to him that there occurred the first temporary lull in the storm. Its fury perhaps reached its height and broke at that moment. A yellow flame had torn its jagged way across the heavens, and an earth-rending crash had thundered itself into rumblings which actually died away before breaking forth again. Marco took his cap from his eyes and drew a long breath. He drew two long breaths. It was as he began drawing a third and realizing the strange feeling of the almost stillness about him that he heard a new kind of sound at the side of the garden nearest his hiding-place. It sounded like the creak of a door opening somewhere in the wall behind the laurel hedge. Someone was coming into the garden by a private entrance. He pushed aside the young boughs again and tried to see, but the darkness was too dense. Yet he could hear if the thunder would not break again. There was the sound of feet on the wet gravel, the footsteps of more than one person coming toward where he stood, but not as if afraid of being heard; merely as if they were at liberty to come in by what entrance they chose. Marco remained very still. A sudden hope gave him a shock of joy. If the man with the tired face chose to hide himself from his acquaintances, he might choose to go in and out by a private entrance. The footsteps drew near, crushing the wet gravel, passed by, and seemed to pause somewhere near the balcony; and then flame lit up the sky again and the thunder burst forth once more.

But this was its last great peal. The storm was at an end. Only fainter and fainter rumblings and mutterings and paler and paler darts followed. Even they were soon over, and the cataracts in the paths had rushed themselves silent. But the darkness was still deep.

It was deep to blackness in the hollow of the evergreen. Marco stood in it, streaming with rain, but feeling nothing because he was full of thought. He pushed aside his greenery and kept his eyes on the place in the blackness where the windows must be, though he could not see them. It seemed that he waited a long time, but he knew it only seemed so really. He began to breathe quickly because he was waiting for something.

Suddenly he saw exactly where the windows were— because they were all lighted!

His feeling of relief was great, but it did not last very long. It was true that something had been gained in the certainty that his man had not left Vienna. But what next? It would not be so easy to follow him if he chose only to go out secretly at night. What next? To spend the rest of the night watching a lighted window was not enough. Tomorrow night it might not be lighted. But he kept his gaze fixed upon it. He tried to fix all his will and thought-power on the person inside the room. Perhaps he could reach him and make him listen, even though he would not know that anyone was speaking to him. He knew that thoughts were strong things. If angry thoughts in one man's mind will create anger in the mind of another, why should not sane messages cross the line?

"I must speak to you. I must speak to you!" he found himself saying in a low intense voice. "I am outside here waiting. Listen! I must speak to you!"

He said it many times and kept his eyes fixed upon the window which opened on to the balcony. Once he saw a man's figure cross the room, but he could not be sure who it was. The last distant rumblings of thunder had died away and the clouds were breaking. It was not long before the dark mountainous billows broke apart, and a brilliant full moon showed herself sailing in the rift, suddenly flooding everything with light. Parts of the garden were silver-white, and the tree shadows were like black velvet. A silvery lance pierced even into the hollow of Marco's evergreen and struck across his face.

Perhaps it was this sudden change which attracted the attention of those inside the balconied room. A man's figure appeared at the long windows. Marco saw now that it was the Prince. He opened the windows and stepped out onto the balcony.

"It is all over," he said quietly. And he stood with his face lifted, looking at the great white sailing moon.

He stood very still and seemed for the moment to forget the world and himself. It was a wonderful, triumphant queen of a moon. But something brought him back to earth. A low, but strong and clear, boy-voice came up to him from the garden path below.

"The Lamp is lighted. The Lamp is lighted," it said, and the words sounded almost as if someone were uttering a prayer. They seemed to call to him, to arrest him, to draw him.

He stood still a few seconds in dead silence. Then he bent over the balustrade. The moonlight had not broken the darkness below.

"That is a boy's voice," he said in a low tone, "but I cannot see who is speaking."

"Yes, it is a boy's voice," it answered, in a way which somehow moved him, because it was so ardent. "It is the son of Stefan Loristan. The Lamp is lighted."

"Wait. I am coming down to you," the Prince said.

In a few minutes Marco heard a door open gently not far from where he stood. Then the man he had been following so many days appeared at his side.

"How long have you been here?" he asked.

"Before the gates closed. I hid myself in the hollow of the big shrub there, Highness," Marco answered.

"Then you were out in the storm?"

"Yes, Highness."

The Prince put his hand on the boy's shoulder. "I cannot see you—but it is best to stand in the shadow. You are drenched to the skin."

"I have been able to give Your Highness—the Sign," Marco whispered. "A storm is nothing."

There was a silence. Marco knew that his companion was pausing to turn something over in his mind.

"So-o?" he said slowly, at length. "The Lamp is lighted, and *you* are sent to bear the Sign." Something in his voice made Marco feel that he was smiling.

"What a family you are! What a family—you Samavian Loristans!"

He paused as if to think the thing over again.

"I want to see your face," he said next. "Here is a tree with a shaft of moonlight striking through the branches. Let us step aside and stand under it."

Marco did as he was told. The shaft of moonlight fell upon his uplifted face and showed its young strength and darkness, quite splendid for the moment in a triumphant glow of joy in obstacles overcome. Raindrops hung on his hair, but he did not look draggled, only very wet and picturesque. He had reached his man. He had given the Sign.

The Prince looked him over with interested curiosity.

"Yes," he said in his cool, rather dragging voice. "You are the son of Stefan Loristan. Also you must be taken care of. You must come with me. I have trained my household to remain in its own quarters until I require its service. I have attached to my own apartments a good safe little room where I sometimes keep people. You can dry your clothes and sleep there. When the gardens are opened again, the rest will be easy."

But though he stepped out from under the trees and began to move towards the palace in the shadow, Marco noticed that he moved hesitatingly, as if he had not quite decided what he should do. He stopped rather suddenly and turned again to Marco, who was following him.

"There is someone in the room I just now left," he said, "an old man—whom it might interest to see you. It might also be a good thing for him to feel interest in you. I choose that he shall see you—as you are."

"I am at your command, Highness," Marco answered. He knew his companion was smiling again.

"You have been in training for more centuries than you know," he said; "and your father has prepared you to encounter the unexpected without surprise."

They passed under the balcony and paused at a low stone doorway hidden behind shrubs. The door was a beautiful one, Marco saw when it was opened, and the corridor disclosed was beautiful also, though it had an air of quiet and aloofness which was not so much secret as private. A perfect though narrow staircase mounted from it to the next floor. After ascending it, the Prince led the way through a short corridor and stopped at the door at the end of it. "We are going in here," he said.

It was a wonderful room—the one which opened on to the balcony. Each piece of furniture in it, the hangings, the tapestries, and pictures on the wall were all such as might well have found themselves adorning a museum. Marco remembered the common report of his escort's favorite amusement of collecting wonders and furnishing his house with the things others exhibited only as marvels of art and handicraft. The place was rich and mellow with exquisitely chosen beauties.

In a massive chair upon the hearth sat a figure with bent head. It was a tall old man with white hair and moustache. His elbows rested upon the arm of his chair and he leaned his forehead on his hand as if he were weary.

Marco's companion crossed the room and stood beside him, speaking in a lowered voice. Marco could not at first hear what he said. He himself stood quite still, waiting. The white-haired man lifted his head and listened. It seemed as though almost at once he was singularly interested. The lowered voice was slightly raised at last and Marco heard the last two sentences:

"The only son of Stefan Loristan. Look at him."

The old man in the chair turned slowly and looked, steadily, and with questioning curiosity touched with grave surprise. He had keen and clear blue eyes.

Then Marco, still erect and silent, waited again. The Prince had merely said to him, "an old man whom it might interest to see you." He had plainly intended that, whatsoever happened, he must make no outward sign of seeing more than he had been told he would see—"an old man." It was for him to show no astonishment or recognition. He had been brought here not to see but to be seen. The power of remaining still under scrutiny, which The Rat had often envied him, stood now in good stead because he had seen the white head and tall form not many days before, surmounted by brilliant emerald plumes, hung with jeweled decorations, in the royal carriage, escorted by banners, and helmets, and following troops whose tramping feet kept time to bursts of military music while the populace bared their heads and cheered.

"He is like his father," this personage said to the Prince. "But if anyone but Loristan had sent him—His looks please me." Then suddenly to Marco, "You were waiting outside while the storm was going on?"

"Yes, sir," Marco answered.

Then the two exchanged some words still in the lowered voice.

"You read the news as you made your journey?" he was asked. "You know how Samavia stands?"

"She does not stand," said Marco. "The Iarovitch and the Maranovitch have fought as hyenas fight, until each has torn the other into fragments—and neither has blood or strength left."

The two glanced at each other.

"A good simile," said the older person. "You are right. If a strong party rose—and a greater power chose not to interfere—the country might see better days." He looked at him a few moments longer and then waved his hand kindly.

"You are a fine Samavian," he said. "I am glad of that. You may go. Good night."

Marco bowed respectfully and the man with the tired face led him out of the room.

It was just before he left him in the small quiet

chamber in which he was to sleep that the Prince gave him a final curious glance. "I remember now," he said. "In the room, when you answered the question about Samavia, I was sure that I had seen you before. It was the day of the celebration. There was a break in the crowd and I saw a boy looking at me. It was you."

"Yes," said Marco, "I have followed you each time you have gone out since then, but I could never get near enough to speak. Tonight seemed only one chance in a thousand."

"You are doing your work more like a man than a boy," was the next speech, and it was made reflectively. "No man could have behaved more perfectly than you did just now, when discretion and composure were necessary." Then, after a moment's pause, "He was deeply interested and deeply pleased. Good night."

When the gardens had been thrown open the next morning and people were passing in and out again, Marco passed out also. He was obliged to tell himself two or three times that he had not wakened from an amazing dream. He quickened his pace after he had crossed the street, because he wanted to get home to the attic and talk to The Rat. There was a narrow side street it was necessary for him to pass through if he wished to make a short cut. As he turned into it, he saw a curious figure leaning on crutches against a wall. It looked damp and forlorn, and he wondered if it could be a beggar. It was not. It was The Rat, who suddenly saw who was approaching and swung forward. His face was pale and haggard and he looked worn and frightened. He dragged off his cap and spoke in a voice which was hoarse as a crow's.

"God be thanked!" he said. "God be thanked!" as people always said it when they received the Sign, alone. But there was a kind of anguish in his voice as well as relief.

"Aide-de-camp!" Marco cried out—The Rat had begged him to call him so. "What have you been doing? How long have you been here?"

"Ever since I left you last night," said The Rat clutching tremblingly at his arm as if to make sure he was real. "If there was not room for two in the hollow, there was room for one in the street. Was it my place to go off duty and leave you alone—was it?"

"You were out in the storm?"

"Weren't you?" said The Rat fiercely. "I huddled against the wall as well as I could. What did I care? Crutches don't prevent a fellow waiting. I wouldn't have left you if you'd given me orders. And that would have been mutiny. When you did not come out as soon as the gates opened, I felt as if my head got on fire. How could I know what had happened? I've not the nerve and backbone you have. I go half mad." For a second or so Marco did not answer. But when he put his hand on the damp sleeve, The Rat actually started, because it seemed as though he were looking into the eyes of Stefan Loristan.

"You look just like your father!" he exclaimed, in spite of himself. "How tall you are!"

"When you are near me," Marco said, in Loristan's own voice, "when you are near me, I feel—I feel as if I were a royal prince attended by an army. You ARE my army." And he pulled off his cap with quick boyishness and added, "God be thanked!"

The sun was warm in the attic window when they

reached their lodging, and the two leaned on the rough sill as Marco told his story. It took some time to relate; and when he ended, he took an envelope from his pocket and showed it to The Rat. It contained a flat package of money.

"He gave it to me just before he opened the private door," Marco explained. "And he said to me, 'It will not be long now. After Samavia, go back to London as quickly as you can—AS QUICKLY AS YOU CAN!'"

"I wonder—what he meant?" The Rat said, slowly. A tremendous thought had shot through his mind. But it was not a thought he could speak of to Marco.

"I cannot tell. I thought that it was for some reason he did not expect me to know," Marco said. "We will do as he told us. As quickly as we can." They looked over the newspapers, as they did every day. All that could be gathered from any of them was that the opposing armies of Samavia seemed each to have reached the culmination of disaster and exhaustion. Which party had the power left to take any final step which could call itself a victory, it was impossible to say. Never had a country been in a more desperate case.

"It is the time!" said The Rat, glowering over his map. "If the Secret Party rises suddenly now, it can take Melzarr almost without a blow. It can sweep through the country and disarm both armies. They're weakened—they're half starved—they're bleeding to death; they WANT to be disarmed. Only the Iarovitch and the Maranovitch keep on with the struggle because each is fighting for the power to tax the people and make slaves of them. If the Secret Party does not rise, the people will, and they'll rush on the palaces and kill every Maranovitch and Iarovitch they find. And serve them right!"

"Let us spend the rest of the day in studying the road-map again," said Marco. "Tonight we must be on the way to Samavia!"

❧ 26 ❧
Across the Frontier

That one day, a week later, two tired and travel-worn boy-mendicants should drag themselves with slow and weary feet across the frontier line between Jiardasia and Samavia, was not an incident to awaken suspicion or even to attract attention. War and hunger and anguish had left the country stunned and broken. Since the worst had happened, no one was curious as to what would befall them next. If Jiardasia herself had become a foe, instead of a friendly neighbor, and had sent across the border galloping hordes of soldiery, there would only have been more shrieks, and home-burnings, and slaughter which no one dare resist. But, so far, Jiardasia had remained peaceful. The two boys—one of them on crutches—had evidently traveled far on foot. Their poor clothes were dusty and travel-stained, and they stopped and asked for water at the first hut across the line. The one who walked without crutches had some coarse bread in a bag slung over his shoulder, and they sat on the roadside and ate it as if they were hungry. The old grandmother who lived alone in the hut sat and stared at them without any curiosity. She may have vaguely wondered why anyone crossed into Samavia in these days. But she did not care to know their reason. Her big son had lived in a village which belonged to the Maranovitch and he had been called out to fight for his lords. He had not wanted to fight and had not known what the quarrel was about, but he was forced to obey. He had kissed his handsome wife and four sturdy children, blubbering aloud when he left them. His village and his good crops and his house must be left behind. Then the Iarovitch swept through the pretty little cluster of homesteads which belonged to their enemy. They were mad with rage because they had met with great losses in a battle not far away, and, as they swooped through, they burned and killed, and trampled down fields and vineyards. The old woman's son never saw either the burned walls of his house or the bodies of his wife and children, because he had been killed himself in the battle for which the Iarovitch were revenging themselves. Only the old grandmother who lived in the hut near the frontier line and stared vacantly at the passers-by remained alive. She wearily gazed at people and wondered why she did not hear news from her son and her grandchildren. But that was all.

When the boys were over the frontier and well on their way along the roads, it was not difficult to keep out of sight if it seemed necessary. The country was mountainous and there were deep and thick forests by the way—forests so far-reaching and with such thick undergrowth that full-grown men could easily have hidden themselves. It was because of this, perhaps, that this part of the country had seen little fighting. There was too great opportunity for secure ambush for a foe. As the two travelers went on, they heard of burned villages and towns destroyed, but they were towns and villages nearer Melzarr and other fortress-defended cities, or they were in the country surrounding the castles and estates of powerful nobles and leaders. It was true, as Marco had said to the white-haired personage, that the Maranovitch and Iarovitch had fought with the savageness of hyenas until at last the forces of each side lay torn and bleeding, their strength, their resources, their supplies exhausted.

Each day left them weaker and more desperate. Europe looked on with small interest in either party but with growing desire that the disorder should end and cease to interfere with commerce. All this and much more Marco and The Rat knew, but, as they made their cautious way through byways of the maimed and tortured little country, they learned other things. They learned that the stories of its beauty and fertility were not romances. Its heaven-reaching mountains, its immense plains of rich verdure on which flocks and herds might have fed by thousands, its splendor of deep forest and broad clear rushing rivers had a primeval majesty such as the first human creatures might have found on earth in the days of the Garden of Eden. The two boys traveled through forest and woodland when it was possible to leave the road. It was safe to thread a way among huge trees and tall ferns and young saplings. It was not always easy but it was safe. Sometimes they saw a charcoal-burner's hut or a shelter where a shepherd was hiding with the few sheep left to him. Each man they met wore the same look of stony suffering in his face; but, when the boys begged for bread and water, as was their habit, no one refused to share the little he had. It soon became plain to them that they were thought to be two young fugitives whose homes had probably been destroyed and who were wandering about with no thought but that of finding safety until the worst was over. That one of them traveled on crutches added to their apparent helplessness, and that he could not speak the language of the country made him more an object of pity. The peasants did not know what language he spoke. Sometimes a foreigner came to find work in this small town or that. The poor lad might have come to the country with his father and mother and then have been caught in the whirlpool of war and tossed out on the world parent-less. But no one asked questions. Even in their desolation they were silent and noble people who were too courteous for curiosity.

"In the old days they were simple and stately and kind. All doors were open to travelers. The master of the poorest hut uttered a blessing and a welcome when a stranger crossed his threshold. It was the custom of the country," Marco said. "I read about it in a book of my father's. About most of the doors the welcome was carved in stone. It was this—'The Blessing of the Son of God, and Rest within these Walls.'"

"They are big and strong," said The Rat. "And they have good faces. They carry themselves as if they had been drilled—both men and women."

It was not through the blood-drenched part of the unhappy land their way led them, but they saw hunger and dread in the villages they passed. Crops which should have fed the people had been taken from them for the use of the army; flocks and herds had been driven away, and faces were gaunt and gray. Those who had as yet only lost crops and herds knew that homes and lives might be torn from them at any moment. Only old men and women and children were left to wait for any fate which the chances of war might deal out to them.

When they were given food from some poor store, Marco would offer a little money in return. He dare not excite suspicion by offering much. He was obliged to let it be imagined that in his flight from his ruined home he had been able to snatch at and secrete some poor hoard which might save him from starvation. Often the women would not take what he offered. Their journey was a hard and hungry one. They must make it all on foot and there was little food to be found. But each of them knew how to live on scant fare. They traveled mostly by night and slept among the ferns and under-growth through the day. They drank from running brooks and bathed in them. Moss and ferns made soft and sweet-smelling beds, and trees roofed them. Some-times they lay long and talked while they rested. And at length a day came when they knew they were nearing their journey's end.

"It is nearly over now," Marco said, after they had

thrown themselves down in the forest in the early hours of one dewy morning. "He said 'After Samavia, go back to London as quickly as you can—AS QUICKLY AS YOU CAN.' He said it twice. As if—something were going to happen."

"Perhaps it will happen more suddenly than we think—the thing he meant," answered The Rat.

Suddenly he sat up on his elbow and leaned towards Marco.

"We are in Samavia!" he said "We two are in Samavia! And we are near the end!"

Marco rose on his elbow also. He was very thin as a result of hard travel and scant feeding. His thinness made his eyes look immense and black as pits. But they burned and were beautiful with their own fire.

"Yes," he said, breathing quickly. "And though we do not know what the end will be, we have obeyed orders. The Prince was next to the last one. There is only one more. The old priest."

"I have wanted to see him more than I have wanted to see any of the others," The Rat said.

"So have I," Marco answered. "His church is built

on the side of this mountain. I wonder what he will say to us."

Both had the same reason for wanting to see him. In his youth he had served in the monastery over the frontier—the one which, till it was destroyed in a revolt, had treasured the five-hundred-year-old story of the beautiful royal lad brought to be hidden among the brotherhood by the ancient shepherd. In the monastery the memory of the Lost Prince was as the memory of a saint. It had been told that one of the early brothers, who was a decorator and a painter, had made a picture of him with a faint halo shining about his head. The young acolyte who had served there must have heard wonderful legends. But the monastery had been burned, and the young acolyte had in later years crossed the frontier and become the priest of a few mountaineers whose little church clung to the mountain side. He had worked hard and faithfully and was worshipped by his people. Only the secret Forgers of the Sword knew that his most ardent worshippers were those with whom he prayed and to whom he gave blessings in dark caverns under the earth, where arms piled themselves and men with dark strong faces sat together in the dim light and laid plans and wrought schemes.

This Marco and The Rat did not know as they talked of their desire to see him.

"He may not choose to tell us anything," said Marco. "When we have given him the Sign, he may turn away and say nothing as some of the others did. He may have nothing to say which we should hear. Silence may be the order for him, too."

It would not be a long or dangerous climb to the little church on the rock. They could sleep or rest all day and begin it at twilight. So after they had talked of the old priest and had eaten their black bread, they settled themselves to sleep under cover of the thick tall ferns.

It was a long and deep sleep which nothing disturbed. So few human beings ever climbed the hill, except by the narrow rough path leading to the church, that the little wild creatures had not learned to be afraid of them. Once, during the afternoon, a hare hopping along under the ferns to make a visit stopped by Marco's head, and, after looking at him a few seconds with his lustrous eyes, began to nibble the ends of his hair. He only did it from curiosity and because he wondered if it might be a new kind of grass, but he did not like it and stopped nibbling almost at once, after which he looked at it again, moving the soft sensitive end of his nose rapidly for a second or so, and then hopped away to attend to his own affairs. A very large and handsome green stag-beetle crawled from one end of The Rat's crutches to the other, but, having done it, he went away also. Two or three times a bird, searching for his dinner under the ferns, was surprised to find the two sleeping figures, but, as they lay so quietly, there seemed nothing to be frightened about. A beautiful little field mouse running past discovered that there were crumbs lying about and ate all she could find on the moss. After that she crept into Marco's pocket and found some excellent ones and had quite a feast. But she disturbed nobody and the boys slept on.

It was a bird's evening song which awakened them both. The bird alighted on the branch of a tree near them and her trill was rippling clear and sweet. The evening air had freshened and was fragrant with hillside scents. When Marco first rolled over and opened his eyes, he thought the most delicious thing on earth was to waken from sleep on a hillside at evening and hear a bird singing. It seemed to make exquisitely real to him the fact that he was in Samavia—that the Lamp was lighted and his work was nearly done. The Rat awakened when he did, and for a few minutes both lay on their backs without speaking. At last Marco said, "The stars are coming out. We can begin to climb, Aide-de-camp."

Then they both got up and looked at each other.

"The last one!" The Rat said. "Tomorrow we shall be on our way back to London—Number 7 Philibert Place. After all the places we've been to—what will it look like?"

"It will be like wakening out of a dream," said Marco. "It's not beautiful—Philibert Place. But HE will be there." And it was as if a light lighted itself in his face and shone through the very darkness of it.

And The Rat's face lighted in almost exactly the same way. And he pulled off his cap and stood bare-headed. "We've obeyed orders," he said. "We've not forgotten one. No one has noticed us, no one has thought of us. We've blown through the countries as if we had been grains of dust."

Marco's head was bared, too, and his face was still shining. "God be thanked!" he said. "Let us begin to climb."

They pushed their way through the ferns and wandered in and out through trees until they found the little path. The hill was thickly clothed with forest and the little path was sometimes dark and steep; but they knew that, if they followed it, they would at last come out to a place where there were scarcely any trees at all, and on a crag they would find the tiny church waiting for them. The priest might not be there. They might have to wait for him, but he would be sure to come back for morning Mass and for vespers, wheresoever he wandered between times.

There were many stars in the sky when at last a turn of the path showed them the church above them. It was little and built of rough stone. It looked as if the priest himself and his scattered flock might have broken and carried or rolled bits of the hill to put it together. It had the small, round, mosque-like summit the Turks had brought into Europe in centuries past. It was so tiny that it would hold but a very small congregation—and close to it was a shed-like house, which was of course the priest's.

The two boys stopped on the path to look at it.

"There is a candle burning in one of the little windows," said Marco.

"There is a well near the door—and someone is beginning to draw water," said The Rat, next. "It is too dark to see who it is. Listen!"

They listened and heard the bucket descend on the chains, and splash in the water. Then it was drawn up, and it seemed someone drank long. Then they saw a dim figure move forward and stand still. Then they heard a voice begin to pray aloud, as if the owner, being accustomed to utter solitude, did not think of earthly hearers.

"Come," Marco said. And they went forward.

Because the stars were so many and the air so clear, the priest heard their feet on the path, and saw them almost as soon as he heard them. He ended his prayer and watched them coming. A lad on crutches, who moved as lightly and easily as a bird—and a lad who, even yards away, was noticeable for a bearing of his body which was neither haughty nor proud but set him somehow aloof from every other lad one had ever seen. A magnificent lad—though, as he drew near, the starlight showed his face thin and his eyes hollow as if with fatigue or hunger.

"And who is this one?" the old priest murmured to himself. "WHO?"

Marco drew up before him and made a respectful reverence. Then he lifted his black head, squared his shoulders and uttered his message for the last time.

"The Lamp is lighted, Father," he said. "The Lamp is lighted."

The old priest stood quite still and gazed into his face. The next moment he bent his head so that he could look at him closely. It seemed almost as if he were frightened and wanted to make sure of something. At the moment it flashed through The Rat's mind that the old, old woman on the mountain-top had looked frightened in something the same way.

"I am an old man," he said. "My eyes are not good. If I had a light"—and he glanced towards the house.

It was The Rat who, with one whirl, swung through the door and seized the candle. He guessed what he wanted. He held it himself so that the flare fell on Marco's face.

The old priest drew nearer and nearer. He gasped for breath. "You are the son of Stefan Loristan!" he cried. "It is HIS SON who brings the Sign."

He fell upon his knees and hid his face in his hands. Both the boys heard him sobbing and praying—praying and sobbing at once.

They glanced at each other. The Rat was bursting with excitement, but he felt a little awkward also and wondered what Marco would do. An old fellow on his knees, crying, made a chap feel as if he didn't know what to say. Must you comfort him or must you let him go on?

Marco only stood quite still and looked at him with understanding and gravity.

"Yes, Father," he said. "I am the son of Stefan Loristan, and I have given the Sign to all. You are the last one. The Lamp is lighted. I could weep for gladness, too."

The priest's tears and prayers ended. He rose to his feet—a rugged-faced old man with long and thick white hair which fell on his shoulders—and smiled at Marco while his eyes were still wet.

"You have passed from one country to another with the message?" he said. "You were under orders to say those four words?"

"Yes, Father," answered Marco.

"That was all? You were to say no more?"

"I know no more. Silence has been the order since I took my oath of allegiance when I was a child. I was not old enough to fight, or serve, or reason about great things. All I could do was to be silent, and to train myself to remember, and be ready when I was called. When my father saw I was ready, he trusted me to go out and give the Sign. He told me the four words. Nothing else."

The old man watched him with a wondering face.

"If Stefan Loristan does not know best," he said, "who does?"

"He always knows," answered Marco proudly. "Always." He waved his hand like a young king toward The Rat. He wanted each man they met to understand the value of The Rat. "He chose for me this companion," he added. "I have done nothing alone."

"I call myself his aide-de-camp!" burst forth The Rat. "I would be cut into inch-long strips for him."

Marco translated.

Then the priest looked at The Rat and slowly nodded his head. "Yes," he said. "He knew best. He always knows best. That I see."

"How did you know I was my father's son?" asked Marco. "You have seen him?"

"No," was the answer; "but I have seen a picture which is said to be his image—and you are the picture's self. It is, indeed, a strange thing that two of God's creatures should be so alike. There is a purpose in it." He led them into his bare small house and made them rest, and drink goat's milk, and eat food. As he moved about the hut-like place, there was a mysterious and exalted look on his face.

"You must be refreshed before we leave here," he said at last. "I am going to take you to a place hidden in the mountains where there are men whose hearts will leap at the sight of you. To see you will give them new power and courage and new resolve. Tonight they meet as they or their ancestors have met for centuries, but now they are nearing the end of their waiting. And I shall bring them the son of Stefan Loristan, who is the Bearer of the Sign!"

They ate the bread and cheese and drank the goat's milk he gave them, but Marco explained that they did not need rest as they had slept all day. They were prepared to follow him when he was ready.

The last faint hint of twilight had died into night and the stars were at their thickest when they set out together. The white-haired old man took a thick knotted staff in his hand and led the way. He knew it well, though it was a rugged and steep one with no track to mark it. Sometimes they seemed to be walking around the mountain, sometimes they were climbing, sometimes they dragged themselves over rocks or fallen trees, or struggled through almost impassable thickets; more than once they descended into ravines and, almost at the risk of their lives, clambered and drew themselves with the aid of the undergrowth up the other side. The Rat was called upon to use all his prowess, and sometimes Marco and the priest helped him across obstacles with the aid of his crutch.

"Haven't I shown tonight how much I can do?" he said once to Marco. "You can tell HIM about this, can't you? And that the crutches helped instead of being in the way?"

They had been out nearly two hours when they came to a place where the undergrowth was thick and a huge tree had fallen crashing down among it in some storm. Not far from the tree was an outcropping rock. Only the top of it was to be seen above the heavy tangle.

They had pushed their way through the jungle of bushes and young saplings, led by their companion. They did not know where they would be led next and were supposed to push forward further when the priest stopped by the outcropping rock. He stood silent a few minutes—quite motionless—as if he were listening to the forest and the night. But there was utter stillness. There was not even a breeze to stir a leaf, or a half-wakened bird to sleepily chirp.

He struck the rock with his staff—twice, and then twice again.

Marco and The Rat stood with bated breath.

They did not wait long. Presently each of them found himself leaning forward, staring with almost unbelieving eyes, not at the priest or his staff, but at THE ROCK ITSELF!

It was moving! Yes, it moved. The priest stepped aside and it slowly turned, as if worked by a lever. As it turned, it gradually revealed a chasm of darkness dimly lighted, and the priest spoke to Marco. "There are hiding-places like this all through Samavia," he said. "Patience and misery have waited long in them. They are the caverns of the Forgers of the Sword. Come!"

27

"It Is the Lost Prince! It Is Ivor!"

Many times since their journey had begun the boys had found their hearts beating with the thrill and excitement of things. The story of which their lives had been a part was a pulse-quickening experience. But as they carefully made their way down the steep steps leading seemingly into the bowels of the earth, both Marco and The Rat felt as though the old priest must hear the thudding in their young sides.

"'The Forgers of the Sword.' Remember every word

they say," The Rat whispered, "so that you can tell it to me afterwards. Don't forget anything! I wish I knew Samavian."

At the foot of the steps stood the man who was evidently the sentinel who worked the lever that turned the rock. He was a big burly peasant with a good watchful face, and the priest gave him a greeting and a blessing as he took from him the lantern he held out.

They went through a narrow and dark passage, and down some more steps, and turned a corner into another corridor cut out of rock and earth. It was a wider corridor, but still dark, so that Marco and The Rat had walked some yards before their eyes became sufficiently accustomed to the dim light to see that the walls themselves seemed made of arms stacked closely together.

"The Forgers of the Sword!" The Rat was unconsciously mumbling to himself, "The Forgers of the Sword!"

It must have taken years to cut out the rounding passage they threaded their way through, and longer years to forge the solid, bristling walls. But The

Rat remembered the story the stranger had told his drunken father, of the few mountain herdsmen who, in their grief and wrath over the loss of their prince, had banded themselves together with a solemn oath which had been handed down from generation to generation. The Samavians were a long-memoried people, and the fact that their passion must be smothered had made it burn all the more fiercely. Five hundred years ago they had first sworn their oath; and kings had come and gone, had died or been murdered, and dynasties had changed, but the Forgers of the Sword had not changed or forgotten their oath or wavered in their belief that sometime—sometime, even after the long dark years—the soul of their Lost Prince would be among them once more, and that they would kneel at the feet and kiss the hands of him for whose body that soul had been reborn. And for the last hundred years their number and power and their hiding places had so increased that Samavia was at last honeycombed with them. And they only waited, breathless—for the Lighting of the Lamp.

The old priest knew how breathlessly, and he knew

what he was bringing them. Marco and The Rat, in spite of their fond boy-imaginings, were not quite old enough to know how fierce and full of flaming eagerness the breathless waiting of full-grown men could be. But there was a tense-strung thrill in knowing that they who were being led to them were the Bearers of the Sign. The Rat went hot and cold; he gnawed his fingers as he went. He could almost have shrieked aloud, in the intensity of his excitement, when the old priest stopped before a big black door!

Marco made no sound. Excitement or danger always made him look tall and quite pale. He looked both now.

The priest touched the door, and it opened.

They were looking into an immense cavern. Its walls and roof were lined with arms—guns, swords, bayonets, javelins, daggers, pistols, every weapon a desperate man might use. The place was full of men, who turned towards the door when it opened. They all made obeisance to the priest, but Marco realized almost at the same instant that they started on seeing that he was not alone.

They were a strange and picturesque crowd as

they stood under their canopy of weapons in the lurid torchlight. Marco saw at once that they were men of all classes, though all were alike roughly dressed. They were huge mountaineers, and plainsmen young and mature in years. Some of the biggest were men with white hair but with bodies of giants, and with determination in their strong jaws. There were many of these, Marco saw, and in each man's eyes, whether he were young or old, glowed a steady unconquered flame. They had been beaten so often, they had been oppressed and robbed, but in the eyes of each one was this unconquered flame which, throughout all the long tragedy of years had been handed down from father to son. It was this which had gone on through centuries, keeping its oath and forging its swords in the caverns of the earth, and which today was—waiting.

The old priest laid his hand on Marco's shoulder, and gently pushed him before him through the crowd which parted to make way for them. He did not stop until the two stood in the very midst of the circle, which fell back gazing wonderingly. Marco looked up at the old man because for several seconds he did not speak. It was plain that he did not speak because he also was excited, and could not. He opened his lips and his voice seemed to fail him. Then he tried again and spoke so that all could hear—even the men at the back of the gazing circle.

"My children," he said, "this is the son of Stefan Loristan, and he comes to bear the Sign. My son," to Marco, "speak!"

Then Marco understood what he wished, and also what he felt. He felt it himself, that magnificent uplifting gladness, as he spoke, holding his black head high and lifting his right hand.

"The Lamp is Lighted, brothers!" he cried. "The Lamp is Lighted!"

Then The Rat, who stood apart, watching, thought that the strange world within the cavern had gone mad! Wild smothered cries broke forth, men caught each other in passionate embrace, they fell upon their knees, they clutched one another sobbing, they wrung each other's hands, they leaped into the air. It was as if they could not bear the joy of hearing that the end of their waiting had come at last. They rushed upon Marco. The Rat saw big peasants kissing his shoes, his hands, every scrap of his clothing they could seize. The wild circle swayed and closed upon him until The Rat was afraid. He did not know that, overpowered by this frenzy of emotion, his own excitement was making him shake from head to foot like a leaf, and that tears were streaming down his cheeks. The swaying crowd hid Marco from him, and he began to fight his way towards him because his excitement increased with fear. The ecstasy-frenzied crowd of men seemed for the moment to have almost ceased to be sane. Marco was only a boy. They did not know how fiercely they were pressing upon him and keeping away the very air.

"Don't kill him! Don't kill him!" yelled The Rat, struggling forward. "Stand back, you fools! I'm his aide-de-camp! Let me pass!"

And though no one understood his English, one or two suddenly remembered they had seen him enter with the priest and so gave way. But just then the old priest lifted his hand above the crowd, and spoke in a voice of stern command.

"Stand back, my children!" he cried. "Madness is not the homage you must bring to the son of Stefan Loristan.

Obey! Obey!" His voice had a power in it that penetrated even the wildest herdsmen. The frenzied mass swayed back and left space about Marco, whose face The Rat could at last see. It was very white with emotion, and in his eyes there was a look which was like awe.

The Rat pushed forward until he stood beside him. He did not know that he almost sobbed as he spoke.

"I'm your aide-de-camp," he said. "I'm going to stand here! Your father sent me! I'm under orders! I thought they'd crush you to death."

He glared at the circle about them as if, instead of allies distraught with excitement, they had been enemies. The old priest seeing him, touched Marco's arm.

"Tell him he need not fear," he said. "It was only for the first few moments. The passion of their souls drove them wild."

"Those at the back might have pushed the front ones on until they trampled you under foot in spite of themselves!" The Rat persisted.

"No," said Marco. "They would have stopped if I had spoken."

"Why didn't you speak then?" snapped The Rat.

"All they felt was for Samavia, and for my father," Marco said, "and for the Sign. I felt as they did."

The Rat was somewhat softened. It was true, after all. How could he have tried to quell the outbursts of their devotion to Loristan—to the country he was saving for them—to the Sign which called them to freedom? He could not.

Then followed a strange and picturesque ceremonial. The priest went about among the encircling crowd and spoke to one man after another—sometimes to a group. A larger circle was formed. As the pale old man moved about, The Rat felt as if some religious ceremony were going to be performed. Watching it from first to last, he was thrilled to the core.

At the end of the cavern a block of stone had been cut out to look like an altar. It was covered with white, and against the wall above it hung a large picture veiled by a curtain. From the roof there swung before it an ancient lamp of metal suspended by chains. In front of the altar was a sort of stone dais. There the priest asked Marco to stand, with his aide-de-camp on the lower level in attendance. A knot of the biggest herdsmen went out and returned. Each carried a huge sword which had perhaps been of the earliest made in the dark days gone by. The bearers formed themselves into a line on either side of Marco. They raised their swords and formed a pointed arch above his head and a passage twelve men long. When the points first clashed together The Rat struck himself hard upon his breast. His exultation was too keen to endure. He gazed at Marco standing still— in that curiously splendid way in which both he and his father COULD stand still—and wondered how he could do it. He looked as if he were prepared for any strange thing which could happen to him—because he was "under orders." The Rat knew that he was doing whatsoever he did merely for his father's sake. It was as if he felt that he was representing his father, though he was a mere boy; and that because of this, boy as he was, he must bear himself nobly and remain outwardly undisturbed.

At the end of the arch of swords, the old priest stood and gave a sign to one man after another. When the sign was given to a man he walked under the arch to the dais, and there knelt and, lifting Marco's hand to his lips, kissed it with passionate fervor. Then he returned to the place he had left. One after another passed up the aisle of swords, one after another knelt, one after the other kissed the brown young hand, rose and went away. Sometimes The Rat heard a few words which sounded almost like a murmured prayer, sometimes he heard a sob as a shaggy head bent, again and again he saw eyes wet with tears. Once or twice Marco spoke a few Samavian words, and the face of the man spoken to flamed with joy. The Rat had time to see, as Marco had seen, that many of the faces were not those of peasants. Some of them were scholars or nobles. It took a long time for them all to kneel and kiss the lad's hand, but no man omitted the ceremony; and when at last it was at an end, a strange silence filled the cavern. They stood and gazed at each other with burning eyes.

The priest moved to Marco's side, and stood near the altar. He leaned forward and took in his hand a cord which hung from the veiled picture—he drew it and the curtain fell apart. There seemed to stand gazing at them from between its folds a tall kingly youth with deep eyes in which the stars of God were stilly shining, and with a smile wonderful to behold. Around the heavy locks of his black hair the long dead painter of missals had set a faint glow of light like a halo.

"Son of Stefan Loristan," the old priest said, in a shaken voice, "it is the Lost Prince! It is Ivor!"

Then every man in the room fell on his knees. Even the men who had upheld the archway of swords dropped their weapons with a crash and knelt also. He was their saint—this boy! Dead for five hundred years, he was their saint still.

"Ivor! Ivor!" the voices broke into a heavy murmur. "Ivor! Ivor!" as if they chanted a litany.

Marco started forward, staring at the picture, his breath caught in his throat, his lips apart.

"But—but—" he stammered, "but if my father were as young as he is—he would be LIKE him!"

"When you are as old as he is, YOU will be like him—YOU!" said the priest. And he let the curtain fall.

The Rat stood staring with wide eyes from Marco to the picture and from the picture to Marco. And he breathed faster and faster and gnawed his finger ends.

But he did not utter a word. He could not have done it, if he tried.

Then Marco stepped down from the dais as if he were in a dream, and the old man followed him. The men with swords sprang to their feet and made their archway again with a new clash of steel. The old man and the boy passed under it together. Now every man's eyes were fixed on Marco. At the heavy door by which he had entered, he stopped and turned to meet their glances. He looked very young and thin and pale, but suddenly his father's smile was lighted in his face. He said a few words in Samavian clearly and gravely, saluted, and passed out.

"What did you say to them?" gasped The Rat, stumbling after him as the door closed behind them and shut in the murmur of impassioned sound.

"There was only one thing to say," was the answer. "They are men—I am only a boy. I thanked them for my father, and told them he would never—never forget."

ʕ 28 ʕ
"Extra! Extra! Extra!"

It was raining in London—pouring. It had been raining for two weeks, more or less, generally more. When the train from Dover drew in at Charing Cross, the weather seemed suddenly to have considered that it had so far been too lenient and must express itself much more vigorously. So it had gathered together its resources and poured them forth in a deluge which surprised even Londoners.

The rain so beat against and streamed down the windows of the third-class carriage in which Marco and

The Rat sat that they could not see through them.

They had made their homeward journey much more rapidly than they had made the one on which they had been outward bound. It had of course taken them some time to tramp back to the frontier, but there had been no reason for stopping anywhere after they had once reached the railroads. They had been tired sometimes, but they had slept heavily on the wooden seats of the railway carriages. Their one desire was to get home. No. 7 Philibert Place rose before them in its noisy dinginess as the one desirable spot on earth. To Marco it held his father. And it was Loristan alone that The Rat saw when he thought of it. Loristan as he would look when he saw him come into the room with Marco, and stand up and salute, and say: "I have brought him back, sir. He has carried out every single order you gave him—every single one. So have I." So he had. He had been sent as his companion and attendant, and he had been faithful in every thought. If Marco would have allowed him, he would have waited upon him like a servant, and have been proud of the service. But Marco would never let him forget that they were

only two boys and that one was of no more importance than the other. He had secretly even felt this attitude to be a sort of grievance. It would have been more
like a game if one of them had been the mere servitor
of the other, and if that other had blustered a little,
and issued commands, and demanded sacrifices. If the
faithful vassal could have been wounded or cast into a
dungeon for his young commander's sake, the adventure would have been more complete. But though their
journey had been full of wonders and rich with beauties, though the memory of it hung in The Rat's mind
like a background of tapestry embroidered in all the
hues of the earth with all the splendors of it, there had
been no dungeons and no wounds. After the adventure
in Munich their unimportant boyishness had not even
been observed by such perils as might have threatened
them. As The Rat had said, they had "blown like grains
of dust" through Europe and had been as nothing. And
this was what Loristan had planned, this was what his
grave thought had wrought out. If they had been men,
they would not have been so safe.

From the time they had left the old priest on the

hillside to begin their journey back to the frontier, they both had been given to long silences as they tramped side by side or lay on the moss in the forests. Now that their work was done, a sort of reaction had set in. There were no more plans to be made and no more uncertainties to contemplate. They were on their way back to No. 7 Philibert Place—Marco to his father, The Rat to the man he worshipped. Each of them was thinking of many things. Marco was full of longing to see his father's face and hear his voice again. He wanted to feel the pressure of his hand on his shoulder—to be sure that he was real and not a dream. This last was because during this homeward journey everything that had happened often seemed to be a dream. It had all been so wonderful—the climber standing looking down at them the morning they awakened on the Gaisberg; the mountaineer shoemaker measuring his foot in the small shop; the old, old woman and her noble lord; the Prince with his face turned upward as he stood on the balcony looking at the moon; the old priest kneeling and weeping for joy; the great cavern with the yellow light upon the crowd of passionate faces; the curtain which fell apart and showed the still eyes and the black hair with the halo about it! Now that they were left behind, they all seemed like things he had dreamed. But he had not dreamed them; he was going back to tell his father about them. And how GOOD it would be to feel his hand on his shoulder!

The Rat gnawed his finger ends a great deal. His thoughts were more wild and feverish than Marco's. They leaped forward in spite of him. It was no use to pull himself up and tell himself that he was a fool. Now that all was over, he had time to be as great a fool as he was inclined to be. But how he longed to reach London and stand face to face with Loristan! The sign was given. The Lamp was lighted. What would happen next? His crutches were under his arms before the train drew up.

"We're there! We're there!" he cried restlessly to Marco. They had no luggage to delay them. They took their bags and followed the crowd along the platform. The rain was rattling like bullets against the high glassed roof. People turned to look at Marco, seeing the glow of exultant eagerness in his face. They thought he must be some boy coming home for the holidays and going to make a visit at a place he delighted in. The rain was dancing on the pavements when they reached the entrance.

"A cab won't cost much," Marco said, "and it will take us quickly."

They called one and got into it. Each of them had flushed cheeks, and Marco's eyes looked as if he were gazing at something a long way off—gazing at it, and wondering.

"We've come back!" said The Rat, in an unsteady voice. "We've been—and we've come back!" Then suddenly turning to look at Marco, "Does it ever seem to you as if, perhaps, it—it wasn't true?"

"Yes," Marco answered, "but it was true. And it's done." Then he added after a second or so of silence, just what The Rat had said to himself, "What next?" He said it very low.

The way to Philibert Place was not long. When they turned into the roaring, untidy road, where the busses and drays and carts struggled past each other with their loads, and the tired-faced people hurried in crowds along the pavement, they looked at them all feeling that they had left their dream far behind indeed. But they were at home.

It was a good thing to see Lazarus open the door and stand waiting before they had time to get out of the cab. Cabs stopped so seldom before houses in Philibert Place that the inmates were always prompt to open their doors. When Lazarus had seen this one stop at the broken iron gate, he had known whom it brought. He had kept an eye on the windows faithfully for many a day— even when he knew that it was too soon, even if all was well, for any travelers to return.

He bore himself with an air more than usually military and his salute when Marco crossed the threshold was formal stateliness itself. But his greeting burst from his heart.

"God be thanked!" he said in his deep growl of joy. "God be thanked!"

When Marco put forth his hand, he bent his grizzled head and kissed it devoutly.

"God be thanked!" he said again.

"My father?" Marco began, "my father is out?" If

he had been in the house, he knew he would not have stayed in the back sitting-room.

"Sir," said Lazarus, "will you come with me into his room? You, too, sir," to The Rat. He had never said "sir" to him before.

He opened the door of the familiar room, and the boys entered. The room was empty.

Marco did not speak; neither did The Rat. They both stood still in the middle of the shabby carpet and looked up at the old soldier. Both had suddenly the same feeling that the earth had dropped from beneath their feet. Lazarus saw it and spoke fast and with tremor. He was almost as agitated as they were.

"He left me at your service—at your command—" he began.

"Left you?" said Marco.

"He left us, all three, under orders—to WAIT," said Lazarus. "The Master has gone."

The Rat felt something hot rush into his eyes. He brushed it away that he might look at Marco's face. The shock had changed it very much. Its glowing eager joy had died out, it had turned paler and his brows were drawn together. For a few seconds he did not speak at all, and, when he did speak, The Rat knew that his voice was steady only because he willed that it should be so.

"If he has gone," he said, "it is because he had a strong reason. It was because he also was under orders."

"He said that you would know that," Lazarus answered. "He was called in such haste that he had not a moment in which to do more than write a few words. He left them for you on his desk there."

Marco walked over to the desk and opened the envelope which was lying there. There were only a few lines on the sheet of paper inside and they had evidently been written in the greatest haste. They were these:

"The Life of my life—for Samavia."

"He was called—to Samavia," Marco said, and the thought sent his blood rushing through his veins. "He has gone to Samavia!"

Lazarus drew his hand roughly across his eyes and his voice shook and sounded hoarse.

"There has been great disaffection in the camps of the Maranovitch," he said. "The remnant of the army has gone mad. Sir, silence is still the order, but who knows—who knows? God alone."

He had not finished speaking before he turned his head as if listening to sounds in the road. They were the kind of sounds which had broken up the Squad, and sent it rushing down the passage into the street to seize on a newspaper. There was to be heard a commotion of newsboys shouting riotously some startling piece of news which had called out an "Extra."

The Rat heard it first and dashed to the front door. As he opened it a newsboy running by shouted at the topmost power of his lungs the news he had to sell: "Assassination of King Michael Maranovitch by his own soldiers! Assassination of the Maranovitch! Extra! Extra! Extra!"

When The Rat returned with a newspaper, Lazarus interposed between him and Marco with great and respectful ceremony. "Sir," he said to Marco, "I am at your command, but the Master left me with an order which I was to repeat to you. He requested you NOT to read the newspapers until he himself could see you again."

Both boys fell back.

"Not read the papers!" they exclaimed together.

Lazarus had never before been quite so reverential and ceremonious.

"Your pardon, sir," he said. "I may read them at your orders, and report such things as it is well that you should know. There have been dark tales told and there may be darker ones. He asked that you would not read for yourself. If you meet again—when you meet again"—he corrected himself hastily—"when you meet again, he says you will understand. I am your servant. I will read and answer all such questions as I can."

The Rat handed him the paper and they returned to the back room together.

"You shall tell us what he would wish us to hear," Marco said.

The news was soon told. The story was not a long one as exact details had not yet reached London. It was briefly that the head of the Maranovitch party had been put to death by infuriated soldiers of his own army. It was an army drawn chiefly from a peasantry which did not love its leaders, or wish to fight, and suffering and brutal treatment had at last roused it to furious revolt.

"What next?" said Marco.

"If I were a Samavian—" began The Rat and then he stopped.

Lazarus stood biting his lips, but staring stonily at the carpet. Not The Rat alone but Marco also noted a grim change in him. It was grim because it suggested that he was holding himself under an iron control. It was as if while tortured by anxiety he had sworn not to allow himself to look anxious and the resolve set his jaw hard and carved new lines in his rugged face. Each boy thought this in secret, but did not wish to put it into words. If he was anxious, he could only be so for one reason, and each realized what the reason must be. Loristan had gone to Samavia—to the torn and bleeding country filled with riot and danger. If he had gone, it could only have been because its danger called him and he went to face it at its worst. Lazarus had been left behind to watch over them. Silence was still the order, and what he knew he could not tell them, and perhaps he knew little more than that a great life might be lost.

Because his master was absent, the old soldier seemed

to feel that he must comfort himself with a greater ceremonial reverence than he had ever shown before. He held himself within call, and at Marco's orders, as it had been his custom to hold himself with regard to Loristan. The ceremonious service even extended itself to The Rat, who appeared to have taken a new place in his mind. He also seemed now to be a person to be waited upon and replied to with dignity and formal respect.

When the evening meal was served, Lazarus drew out Loristan's chair at the head of the table and stood behind it with a majestic air.

"Sir," he said to Marco, "the Master requested that you take his seat at the table until—while he is not with you."

Marco took the seat in silence.

At two o'clock in the morning, when the roaring road was still, the light from the street lamp, shining into the small bedroom, fell on two pale boy faces. The Rat sat up on his sofa bed in the old way with his hands clasped round his knees. Marco lay flat on his hard pillow. Neither of them had been to sleep and yet they had not talked a great deal. Each had secretly guessed a good deal of what the other did not say.

"There is one thing we must remember," Marco had said, early in the night. "We must not be afraid."

"No," answered The Rat, almost fiercely, "we must not be afraid."

"We are tired; we came back expecting to be able to tell it all to him. We have always been looking forward to that. We never thought once that he might be gone. And he WAS gone. Did you feel as if"—he turned towards the sofa—"as if something had struck you on the chest?"

"Yes," The Rat answered heavily. "Yes."

"We weren't ready," said Marco. "He had never gone before; but we ought to have known he might someday be—called. He went because he was called. He told us to wait. We don't know what we are waiting for, but we know that we must not be afraid. To let ourselves be AFRAID would be breaking the Law."

"The Law!" groaned The Rat, dropping his head on his hands, "I'd forgotten about it."

"Let us remember it," said Marco. "This is the time. 'Hate not. FEAR not!'" He repeated the last words again and again. "Fear not! Fear not," he said. "NOTHING can harm him."

The Rat lifted his head, and looked at the bed sideways.

"Did you think"—he said slowly—"did you EVER think that perhaps HE knew where the descendant of the Lost Prince was?"

Marco answered even more slowly.

"If anyone knew—surely he might. He has known so much," he said.

"Listen to this!" broke forth The Rat. "I believe he has gone to TELL the people. If he does—if he could show them—all the country would run mad with joy. It wouldn't be only the Secret Party. All Samavia would rise and follow any flag he chose to raise. They've prayed for the Lost Prince for five hundred years, and if they believed they'd got him once more, they'd fight like madmen for him. But there would not be anyone to fight. They'd ALL want the same thing! If they could see the man with Ivor's blood in his veins, they'd feel he had come back to them—risen from the dead. They'd believe it!"

He beat his fists together in his frenzy of excitement. "It's the time! It's the time!" he cried. "No man could let such a chance go by! He MUST tell them—he MUST. That MUST be what he's gone for. He knows—he knows—he's always known!" And he threw himself back on his sofa and flung his arms over his face, lying there panting.

"If it is the time," said Marco in a low, strained voice—"if it is, and he knows—he will tell them." And he threw his arms up over his own face and lay quite still.

Neither of them said another word, and the street lamp shone in on them as if it were waiting for something to happen. But nothing happened. In time they were asleep.

~ 29 ~
'Twixt Night and Morning

After this, they waited. They did not know what they waited for, nor could they guess even vaguely how the waiting would end. All that Lazarus could tell them he told. He would have been willing to stand respectfully for hours relating to Marco the story of how the period of their absence had passed for his Master and himself. He told how Loristan had spoken each day of his son, how he had often been pale with anxiousness, how in the evenings he had walked to and fro in his room, deep in thought, as he looked down unseeingly at the carpet.

"He permitted me to talk of you, sir," Lazarus said. "I saw that he wished to hear your name often. I reminded him of the times when you had been so young that most children of your age would have been in the hands of nurses, and yet you were strong and silent and sturdy and traveled with us as if you were not a child at all—never crying when you were tired and were not properly fed. As if you understood—as if you understood," he added, proudly. "If, through the power of God a creature can be a man at six years old, you were that one. Many a dark day I have looked into your solemn, watching eyes, and have been half afraid; because that a child should answer one's gaze so gravely seemed almost an unearthly thing."

"The chief thing I remember of those days," said Marco, "is that he was with me, and that whenever I was hungry or tired, I knew he must be too."

The feeling that they were "waiting" was so intense that it filled the days with strangeness. When the postman's knock was heard at the door, each of them endeavored not to start. A letter might someday come which would tell them—they did not know what. But no letters came. When they went out into the streets, they found themselves hurrying on their way back in spite of themselves. Something might have happened. Lazarus read the papers faithfully, and in the evening told Marco and The Rat all the news it was "well that they should hear." But the disorders of Samavia had ceased to occupy much space. They had become an old story, and after the excitement of the assassination of Michael Maranovitch had died out, there seemed to be a lull in events. Michael's son had not dared to try to take his father's place, and there were rumors that he also had been killed. The head of the Iarovitch had declared himself king but had not been crowned because of disorders in his own party. The country seemed existing in a nightmare of suffering, famine, and suspense.

"Samavia is 'waiting' too," The Rat broke forth one night as they talked together, "but it won't wait long—it can't. If I were a Samavian and in Samavia—"

"My father is a Samavian and he is in Samavia," Marco's grave young voice interposed.

The Rat flushed red as he realized what he had said. "What a fool I am!" he groaned. "I—I beg your pardon—sir." He stood up when he said the last words and added the "sir" as if he suddenly realized that there was a distance between them which was something akin to the distance between youth and maturity—but yet was not the same.

"You are a good Samavian but—you forget," was Marco's answer.

Lazarus' intense grimness increased with each day that passed. The ceremonious respectfulness of his manner toward Marco increased also. It seemed as if the more anxious he felt the more formal and stately his bearing became. It was as though he braced his own courage by doing the smallest things life in the back sitting-room required as if they were of the dignity of services performed in a much larger place and under much more imposing circumstances. The Rat found himself feeling almost as if he were an equerry in a court, and that dignity and ceremony were necessary on his own part. He began to experience a sense of being somehow a person of rank, for whom doors were opened grandly and who had vassals at his command. The watchful obedience of fifty vassals embodied itself in the manner of Lazarus.

"I am glad," The Rat said once, reflectively, "that, after all my father was once—different. It makes it easier to learn things perhaps. If he had not talked to me about people who—well, who had never seen places like Bone Court—this might have been harder for me to understand."

When at last they managed to call the Squad together, and went to spend a morning at the Barracks behind the churchyard, that body of armed men stared at their commander in great and amazed uncertainty. They felt that something had happened to him. They did not know what had happened, but it was some experience which had made him mysteriously different. He did not look like Marco, but in some extraordinary way he seemed more akin to him. They only knew that some necessity in Loristan's affairs had taken the two away from London and the game. Now they had come back, and they seemed older.

At first, the Squad felt awkward and shuffled its

feet uncomfortably. After the first greetings it did not know exactly what to say. It was Marco who saved the situation.

"Drill us first," he said to The Rat, "then we can talk about the game."

"'Tention!" shouted The Rat, magnificently. And then they forgot everything else and sprang into line. After the drill was ended, and they sat in a circle on the broken flags, the game became more resplendent than it had ever been.

"I've had time to read and work out new things," The Rat said. "Reading is like traveling."

Marco himself sat and listened, enthralled by the adroitness of the imagination he displayed. Without revealing a single dangerous fact he built up, of their journeyings and experiences, a totally new structure of adventures which would have fired the whole being of any group of lads. It was safe to describe places and people, and he so described them that the Squad squirmed in its delight at feeling itself marching in a procession attending the Emperor in Vienna; standing in line before palaces; climbing, with knapsacks strapped tight, up precipitous mountain roads; defending mountain-fortresses; and storming Samavian castles.

The Squad glowed and exulted. The Rat glowed and exulted himself. Marco watched his sharp-featured, burning-eyed face with wonder and admiration. This strange power of making things alive was, he knew, what his father would call "genius."

"Let's take the oath of 'legiance again," shouted Cad, when the game was over for the morning.

"The papers never said nothin' more about the Lost Prince, but we are all for him yet! Let's take it!" So they stood in line again, Marco at the head, and renewed their oath.

"The sword in my hand—for Samavia!

"The heart in my breast—for Samavia!

"The swiftness of my sight, the thought of my brain, the life of my life—for Samavia.

"Here grow twelve men—for Samavia.

"God be thanked!"

It was more solemn than it had been the first time. The Squad felt it tremendously. Both Cad and Ben were conscious that thrills ran down their spines into their boots. When Marco and The Rat left them, they first stood at salute and then broke out into a ringing cheer.

On their way home, The Rat asked Marco a question.

"Did you see Mrs. Beedle standing at the top of the basement steps and looking after us when we went out this morning?"

Mrs. Beedle was the landlady of the lodgings at No. 7 Philibert Place. She was a mysterious and dusty female, who lived in the "cellar kitchen" part of the house and was seldom seen by her lodgers.

"Yes," answered Marco, "I have seen her two or three times lately, and I do not think I ever saw her before. My father has never seen her, though Lazarus says she used to watch him round corners. Why is she suddenly so curious about us?"

"I'd like to know," said The Rat. "I've been trying to work it out. Ever since we came back, she's been peeping round the door of the kitchen stairs, or over balustrades, or through the cellar-kitchen windows. I believe she wants to speak to you, and knows Lazarus won't let her if he catches her at it. When Lazarus is about, she always darts back."

"What does she want to say?" said Marco.

"I'd like to know," said The Rat again.

When they reached No. 7 Philibert Place, they found out, because when the door opened they saw at the top of the cellar-kitchen stairs at the end of the passage, the mysterious Mrs. Beedle, in her dusty black dress and with a dusty black cap on, evidently having that minute mounted from her subterranean hiding-place. She had come up the steps so quickly that Lazarus had not yet seen her.

"Young Master Loristan!" she called out authoritatively. Lazarus wheeled about fiercely.

"Silence!" he commanded. "How dare you address the young Master?"

She snapped her fingers at him, and marched forward folding her arms tightly. "You mind your own business," she said. "It's young Master Loristan I'm speaking to, not his servant. It's time he was talked to about this."

"Silence!" shouted Lazarus.

"Let her speak," said Marco. "I want to hear. What is it you wish to say, Madam? My father is not here."

"That's just what I want to find out about," put in the woman. "When is he coming back?"

"I do not know," answered Marco.

"That's it," said Mrs. Beedle. "You're old enough to understand that two big lads and a big fellow like that can't have food and lodgin's for nothing. You may say you don't live high—and you don't—but lodgin's are lodgin's and rent is rent. If your father's coming back and you can tell me when, I mayn't be obliged to let the rooms over your heads; but I know too much about foreigners to let bills run when they are out of sight. Your father's out of sight. He," jerking her head towards Lazarus, "paid me for last week. How do I know he will pay me for this week!"

"The money is ready," roared Lazarus.

The Rat longed to burst forth. He knew what people in Bone Court said to a woman like that; he knew the exact words and phrases. But they were not words and phrases an aide-de-camp might deliver himself of in the presence of his superior officer; they were not words and phrases an equerry uses at court. He dare not ALLOW himself to burst forth. He stood with flaming eyes and a flaming face, and bit his lips till they bled. He wanted to strike with his crutches. The son of Stefan Loristan! The Bearer of the Sign! If he dared speak his mind now, he felt he could have endured it better. But being an aide-de-camp he could not.

"Do you want the money now?" asked Marco. "It is only the beginning of the week and we do not owe it to you until the week is over. Is it that you want to have it now?"

Lazarus had become deadly pale. He looked huge in his fury, and he looked dangerous.

"Young Master," he said slowly, in a voice as deadly as his pallor, and he actually spoke low, "this woman—"

Mrs. Beedle drew back towards the cellar-kitchen steps.

"There's police outside," she shrilled. "Young Master Loristan, order him to stand back."

"No one will hurt you," said Marco. "If you have

the money here, Lazarus, please give it to me."

Lazarus literally ground his teeth. But he drew himself up and saluted with ceremony. He put his hand in his breast pocket and produced an old leather wallet. There were but a few coins in it. He pointed to a gold one.

"I obey you, sir—since I must—" he said, breathing hard. "That one will pay her for the week."

Marco took out the sovereign and held it out to the woman.

"You hear what he says," he said. "At the end of this week if there is not enough to pay for the next, we will go."

Lazarus looked so like a hyena, only held back from springing by chains of steel, that the dusty Mrs. Beedle was afraid to take the money.

"If you say that I shall not lose it, I'll wait until the week's ended," she said. "You're nothing but a lad, but you're like your father. You've got a way that a body can trust. If he was here and said he hadn't the money but he'd have it in time, I'd wait if it was for a month. He'd pay it if he said he would. But he's gone; and two boys and a fellow like that one don't seem much to depend on. But I'll trust YOU."

"Be good enough to take it," said Marco. And he put the coin in her hand and turned into the back sitting-room as if he did not see her.

The Rat and Lazarus followed him.

"Is there so little money left?" said Marco. "We have always had very little. When we had less than usual, we lived in poorer places and were hungry if it was necessary. We know how to go hungry. One does not die of it."

The big eyes under Lazarus' beetling brows filled with tears.

"No, sir," he said, "one does not die of hunger. But the insult—the insult! That is not endurable."

"She would not have spoken if my father had been here," Marco said. "And it is true that boys like us have no money. Is there enough to pay for another week?"

"Yes, sir," answered Lazarus, swallowing hard as if he had a lump in his throat, "perhaps enough for two—if we eat but little. If—if the Master would accept money from those who would give it, he would always have had enough. But how could such a one as he?

How could he? When he went away, he thought—he thought that"—but there he stopped himself suddenly.

"Never mind," said Marco. "Never mind. We will go away the day we can pay no more."

"I can go out and sell newspapers," said The Rat's sharp voice.

"I've done it before. Crutches help you to sell them. The platform would sell 'em faster still. I'll go out on the platform."

"I can sell newspapers, too," said Marco.

Lazarus uttered an exclamation like a groan.

"Sir," he cried, "no, no! Am I not here to go out and look for work? I can carry loads. I can run errands."

"We will all three begin to see what we can do," Marco said.

Then—exactly as had happened on the day of their return from their journey—there arose in the road outside the sound of newsboys shouting. This time the outcry seemed even more excited than before. The boys were running and yelling and there seemed more of them than usual. And above all other words was heard "Samavia! Samavia!" But today The Rat did not rush to the door at the first cry. He stood still—for several seconds they all three stood still—listening. Afterwards each one remembered and told the others that he had stood still because some strange, strong feeling held him WAITING as if to hear some great thing.

It was Lazarus who went out of the room first and The Rat and Marco followed him.

One of the upstairs lodgers had run down in haste and opened the door to buy newspapers and ask questions. The newsboys were wild with excitement and danced about as they shouted. The piece of news they were yelling had evidently a popular quality.

The lodger bought two papers and was handing out coppers to a lad who was talking loud and fast.

"Here's a go!" he was saying. "A Secret Party's risen up and taken Samavia! 'Twixt night and mornin' they done it! That there Lost Prince descendant 'as turned up, an' they've CROWNED him—'twixt night and mornin' they done it! Clapt 'is crown on 'is 'ead, so's they'd lose no time." And off he bolted, shouting,

"'Cendant of Lost Prince! 'Cendant of Lost Prince made King of Samavia!"

It was then that Lazarus, forgetting even ceremony, bolted also. He bolted back to the sitting-room, rushed in, and the door fell to behind him.

Marco and The Rat found it shut when, having secured a newspaper, they went down the passage. At the closed door, Marco stopped. He did not turn the handle. From the inside of the room there came the sound of big convulsive sobs and passionate Samavian words of prayer and worshipping gratitude.

"Let us wait," Marco said, trembling a little. "He will not want anyone to see him. Let us wait."

His black pits of eyes looked immense, and he stood at his tallest, but he was trembling slightly from head to foot. The Rat had begun to shake, as if from an ague. His face was scarcely human in its fierce unboyish emotion.

"Marco! Marco!" his whisper was a cry. "That was what he went for—BECAUSE HE KNEW!"

"Yes," answered Marco, "that was what he went for." And his voice was unsteady, as his body was.

Presently the sobs inside the room choked themselves back suddenly. Lazarus had remembered. They had guessed he had been leaning against the wall during his outburst. Now it was evident that he stood upright, probably shocked at the forgetfulness of his frenzy.

So Marco turned the handle of the door and went into the room. He shut the door behind him, and they all three stood together.

When the Samavian gives way to his emotions, he is emotional indeed. Lazarus looked as if a storm had swept over him. He had choked back his sobs, but tears still swept down his cheeks.

"Sir," he said hoarsely, "your pardon! It was as if a convulsion seized me. I forgot everything—even my duty. Pardon, pardon!" And there on the worn carpet of the dingy back sitting-room in the Marylebone Road, he actually went on one knee and kissed the boy's hand with adoration.

"You mustn't ask pardon," said Marco. "You have waited so long, good friend. You have given your life as my father has. You have known all the suffering a boy has not lived long enough to understand. Your big heart—your faithful heart—" His voice broke and he stood and looked at him with an appeal which seemed to ask him to remember his boyhood and understand the rest.

"Don't kneel," he said next. "You mustn't kneel." And Lazarus, kissing his hand again, rose to his feet.

"Now—we shall HEAR!" said Marco. "Now the waiting will soon be over."

"Yes, sir. Now, we shall receive commands!" Lazarus answered.

The Rat held out the newspapers.

"May we read them yet?" he asked.

"Until further orders, sir," said Lazarus hurriedly and apologetically—"until further orders, it is still better that I should read them first."

ᖚ 30 ᖚ
The Game Is
at an End

So long as the history of Europe is written and read, the unparalleled story of the rising of the Secret Party in Samavia will stand out as one of its most startling and romantic records. Every detail connected with the astonishing episode, from beginning to end, was romantic even when it was most productive of realistic results. When it is related, it always begins with the story of the tall and kingly Samavian youth who walked out of the palace in the early morning sunshine singing the herdsmen's song of beauty of old days. Then comes the outbreak of the ruined and revolting populace; then the legend of the morning on the mountain side, and the old shepherd coming out of his cave and finding the apparently dead body of the beautiful young hunter. Then the secret nursing in the cavern; then the jolting cart piled with sheep-skins crossing the frontier, and ending its journey at the barred entrance of the monastery and leaving its mysterious burden behind. And then the bitter hate and struggle of dynasties, and the handful of shepherds and herdsmen meeting in their cavern and binding themselves and their unborn sons and sons' sons by an oath never to be broken. Then the passing of gen-erations and the slaughter of peoples and the chang-ing of kings—and always that oath remembered, and the Forgers of the Sword, at their secret work, hid-den in forests and caves. Then the strange story of the uncrowned kings who, wandering in other lands, lived and died in silence and seclusion, often labor-ing with their hands for their daily bread, but never forgetting that they must be kings, and ready—even though Samavia never called. Perhaps the whole story would fill too many volumes to admit of it ever being told fully.

But history makes the growing of the Secret Party clear—though it seems almost to cease to be history, in spite of its efforts to be brief and speak only of dull facts, when it is forced to deal with the Bearing of the Sign by two mere boys, who, being blown as unremarked as any two grains of dust across Europe, lit the Lamp whose flame so flared up to the high heavens that as if from the earth itself there sprang forth Samavians by the thousands ready to feed it—Iarovitch and Maranovitch swept aside forever and only Samavians remaining to cry aloud in ardent praise and worship of the God who had brought back to them their Lost Prince. The battle-cry of his name had ended every battle. Swords fell from hands because swords were not needed. The Iarovitch fled in terror and dismay; the Maranovitch were nowhere to be found. Between night and morning, as the newsboy had said, the standard of Ivor was raised and waved from palace and citadel alike. From mountain, forest and plain, from city, village and town, its followers flocked to swear allegiance; broken and wounded legions staggered along the roads to join and kneel to it; women and children followed, weeping with joy and chanting songs of praise. The Powers held out their scepters to the lately prostrate and ignored country. Train-loads of food and supplies of all things needed began to cross the frontier; the aid of nations was bestowed. Samavia, at peace to till its land, to raise its flocks, to mine its ores, would be able to pay all back. Samavia in past centuries had been rich enough to make great loans, and had stored such harvests as warring countries had been glad to call upon. The story of the crowning of the King had been the wildest of all—the multitude of ecstatic people, famished, in rags, and many of them weak with wounds, kneeling at his feet, praying, as their one salvation and security, that he would go attended by them to their bombarded and broken cathedral, and at its high altar let the crown be placed upon his head, so that even those who perhaps must die of their past sufferings would at least have paid their poor homage to the King Ivor who would rule their children and bring back to Samavia her honor and her peace.

"Ivor! Ivor!" they chanted like a prayer, "Ivor! Ivor!" in their houses, by the roadside, in the streets.

"The story of the coronation in the shattered cathedral, whose roof had been torn to fragments by bombs," said an important London paper, "reads like a legend of the Middle Ages. But, upon the whole, there is in Samavia's national character, something of the medieval, still."

Lazarus, having bought and read in his top floor room every newspaper recording the details which had reached London, returned to report almost verbatim, standing erect before Marco, the eyes under his shaggy brows sometimes flaming with exultation, sometimes filled with a rush of tears. He could not be made to sit down. His whole big body seemed to have become rigid with magnificence. Meeting Mrs. Beedle in the passage, he strode by her with an air so thunderous that she turned and scuttled back to her cellar kitchen, almost falling down the stone steps in her nervous terror. In such a mood, he was not a person to face without something like awe.

In the middle of the night, The Rat suddenly spoke to Marco as if he knew that he was awake and would hear him.

"He has given all his life to Samavia!" he said. "When you traveled from country to country, and lived in holes and corners, it was because by doing it he could escape spies, and see the people who must be made to understand. No one else could have made them listen. An emperor would have begun to listen when he had seen his face and heard his voice. And he could be silent, and wait for the right time to speak. He could keep still when other men could not. He could keep his face still—and his hands—and his eyes. Now all Samavia knows what he has done, and that he has been the greatest patriot in the world. We both saw what Samavians were like that night in the cavern. They will go mad with joy when they see his face!"

"They have seen it now," said Marco, in a low voice from his bed.

Then there was a long silence, though it was not quite silence because The Rat's breathing was so quick and hard.

"He—must have been at that coronation!" he said at last. "The King—what will the King do to—repay him?"

Marco did not answer. His breathing could be heard also. His mind was picturing that same coronation— the shattered, roofless cathedral, the ruins of the ancient and magnificent high altar, the multitude of kneeling, famine-scourged people, the battle-worn, wounded and bandaged soldiery! And the King! And his father! Where had his father stood when the King was crowned? Surely, he had stood at the King's right hand, and the people had adored and acclaimed them equally!

"King Ivor!" he murmured as if he were in a dream. "King Ivor!"

The Rat started up on his elbow.

"You will see him," he cried out. "He's not a dream any longer. The game is not a game now—and it is ended—it is won! It was real—HE was real! Marco, I don't believe you hear."

"Yes, I do," answered Marco, "but it is almost more a dream than when it was one."

"The greatest patriot in the world is like a king

himself!" raved The Rat. "If there is no bigger honor to give him, he will be made a prince—and Commander-in-Chief—and Prime Minister! Can't you hear those Samavians shouting, and singing, and praying? You'll see it all! Do you remember the mountain-climber who was going to save the shoes he made for the Bearer of the Sign? He said a great day might come when one could show them to the people. It's come! He'll show them! I know how they'll take it!" His voice suddenly dropped—as if it dropped into a pit. "You'll see it all. But I shall not."

Then Marco awoke from his dream and lifted his head. "Why not?" he demanded. It sounded like a demand.

"Because I know better than to expect it!" The Rat groaned. "You've taken me a long way, but you can't take me to the palace of a king. I'm not such a fool as to think that, even if your father—"

He broke off because Marco did more than lift his head. He sat upright.

"You bore the Sign as much as I did," he said. "We bore it together."

"Who would have listened to ME?" cried The Rat. "YOU were the son of Stefan Loristan."

"You were the friend of his son," answered Marco. "You went at the command of Stefan Loristan. You were the ARMY of the son of Stefan Loristan. That I have told you. Where I go, you will go. We will say no more of this—not one word."

And he lay down again in the silence of a prince of the blood. And The Rat knew that he meant what he said, and that Stefan Loristan also would mean it. And because he was a boy, he began to wonder what Mrs. Beedle would do when she heard what had happened— what had been happening all the time a tall, shabby "foreigner" had lived in her dingy back sitting-room, and been closely watched lest he should go away without paying his rent, as shabby foreigners sometimes did. The Rat saw himself managing to poise himself very erect on his crutches while he told her that the shabby foreigner was—well, was at least the friend of a King, and had given him his crown—and would be made a prince and a Commander-in-Chief—and a Prime Minister—because there was no higher rank or honor to give him. And his son—whom she had insulted—was Samavia's idol because he had borne the Sign. And also that if she were in Samavia, and Marco chose to do it he could batter her wretched lodging-house to the ground and put her in a prison—"and serve her jolly well right!"

The next day passed, and the next; and then there came a letter. It was from Loristan, and Marco turned pale when Lazarus handed it to him. Lazarus and The Rat went out of the room at once, and left him to read it alone. It was evidently not a long letter, because it was not many minutes before Marco called them again into the room.

"In a few days, messengers—friends of my father's—will come to take us to Samavia. You and I and Lazarus are to go," he said to The Rat.

"God be thanked!" said Lazarus. "God be thanked!"

Before the messengers came, it was the end of the week. Lazarus had packed their few belongings, and on Saturday Mrs. Beedle was to be seen hovering at the top of the cellar steps, when Marco and The Rat left the back sitting-room to go out.

"You needn't glare at me!" she said to Lazarus, who stood glowering at the door which he had opened for them. "Young Master Loristan, I want to know if you've heard when your father is coming back?"

"He will not come back," said Marco.

"He won't, won't he? Well, how about next week's rent?" said Mrs. Beedle. "Your man's been packing up, I notice. He's not got much to carry away, but it won't pass through that front door until I've got what's owing me. People that can pack easy think they can get away easy, and they'll bear watching. The week's up today."

Lazarus wheeled and faced her with a furious gesture. "Get back to your cellar, woman," he commanded. "Get back under ground and stay there. Look at what is stopping before your miserable gate."

A carriage was stopping—a very perfect carriage of dark brown. The coachman and footman wore dark brown and gold liveries, and the footman had leaped down and opened the door with respectful alacrity. "They are friends of the Master's come to pay their respects to his son," said Lazarus. "Are their eyes to be offended by the sight of you?"

"Your money is safe," said Marco. "You had better leave us."

Mrs. Beedle gave a sharp glance at the two gentlemen who had entered the broken gate. They were of an order which did not belong to Philibert Place. They looked as if the carriage and the dark brown and gold liveries were everyday affairs to them.

"At all events, they're two grown men, and not two boys without a penny," she said. "If they're your father's friends, they'll tell me whether my rent's safe or not."

The two visitors were upon the threshold. They were both men of a certain self-contained dignity of type; and when Lazarus opened wide the door, they stepped into the shabby entrance hall as if they did not see it. They looked past its dinginess, and past Lazarus, and The Rat, and Mrs. Beedle—THROUGH them, as it were—at Marco.

He advanced towards them at once.

"You come from my father!" he said, and gave his hand first to the elder man, then to the younger.

"Yes, we come from your father. I am Baron

Rastka—and this is the Count Vorversk," said the elder man, bowing.

"If they're barons and counts, and friends of your father's, they are well-to-do enough to be responsible for you," said Mrs. Beedle, rather fiercely, because she was somewhat over-awed and resented the fact. "It's a matter of next week's rent, gentlemen. I want to know where it's coming from."

The elder man looked at her with a swift cold glance. He did not speak to her, but to Lazarus. "What is she doing here?" he demanded.

Marco answered him. "She is afraid we cannot pay our rent," he said. "It is of great importance to her that she should be sure."

"Take her away," said the gentleman to Lazarus. He did not even glance at her. He drew something from his coat-pocket and handed it to the old soldier. "Take her away," he repeated. Mrs. Beedle actually shuffled down the passage to the cellar-kitchen steps. Lazarus did not leave her until he, too, had descended into the cellar kitchen, where he stood and towered above her like an infuriated giant.

"Tomorrow he will be on his way to Samavia, miserable woman!" he said. "Before he goes, it would be well for you to implore his pardon."

But Mrs. Beedle's point of view was not his. She had recovered some of her breath.

"I don't know where Samavia is," she raged, as she struggled to set her dusty, black cap straight. "I'll warrant it's one of these little foreign countries you can scarcely see on the map—and not a decent English town in it! He can go as soon as he likes, so long as he pays his rent before he does it. Samavia, indeed! You talk as if he was Buckingham Palace!"

ᔡ 31 ᔡ
"The Son of Stefan Loristan"

When a party composed of two boys attended by a big soldierly manservant and accompanied by two distinguished-looking, elderly men, of a marked foreign type, appeared on the platform of Charing Cross Station they attracted a good deal of attention. In fact, the good looks and strong, well-carried body of the handsome lad with the thick black hair would have caused eyes to turn towards him even if he had not seemed to be regarded as so special a charge by those who were with him. But in a country where people are accustomed to seeing a certain manner and certain forms observed in the case of persons—however young—who are set apart by the fortune of rank and distinction, and where the populace also rather enjoys the sight of such demeanor, it was inevitable that more than one quick-sighted looker-on should comment on the fact that this was not an ordinary group of individuals.

"See that fine, big lad over there!" said a workman, whose head, with a pipe in its mouth, stuck out of a third-class smoking carriage window. "He's some sort of a young swell, I'll lay a shillin'! Take a look at him," to his mate inside.

The mate took a look. The pair were of the decent, polytechnic-educated type, and were shrewd at observation.

"Yes, he's some sort of young swell," he summed him up. "But he's not English by a long chalk. He must be a young Turk, or Russian, sent over to be educated. His suite looks like it. All but the ferret-faced chap on crutches. Wonder what he is!"

A good-natured-looking guard was passing, and the first man hailed him.

"Have we got any swells traveling with us this morning?" he asked, jerking his head towards the group. "That looks like it. Anyone leaving Windsor or Sandringham to cross from Dover today?"

The man looked at the group curiously for a moment and then shook his head.

"They do look like something or other," he answered, "but no one knows anything about them. Everybody's safe in Buckingham Palace and Marlborough House this week. No one either going or coming."

No observer, it is true, could have mistaken Lazarus for an ordinary attendant escorting an ordinary charge. If silence had not still been strictly the order, he could not have restrained himself. As it was, he bore himself like a grenadier, and stood by Marco as if across his dead body alone could anyone approach the lad.

"Until we reach Melzarr," he had said with passion to the two gentlemen, "until I can stand before my Master and behold him embrace his son—BEHOLD him—I implore that I may not lose sight of him night or day. On my knees, I implore that I may travel, armed, at his side. I am but his servant, and have no right to occupy a place in the same carriage. But put me anywhere. I will be deaf, dumb, blind to all but himself. Only permit me to be near enough to give my life if it is needed. Let me say to my Master, 'I never left him.'"

"We will find a place for you," the elder man said, "and if you are so anxious, you may sleep across his threshold when we spend the night at a hotel."

"I will not sleep!" said Lazarus. "I will watch. Suppose there should be demons of Maranovitch loose and infuriated in Europe? Who knows!"

"The Maranovitch and Iarovitch who have not already sworn allegiance to King Ivor are dead on battlefields. The remainder are now Fedorovitch and praising God for their King," was the answer Baron Rastka made him.

But Lazarus kept his guard unbroken. When he occupied the next compartment to the one in which Marco traveled, he stood in the corridor throughout the journey. When they descended at any point to change trains, he followed close at the boy's heels, his fierce eyes on every side at once and his hand on the weapon hidden in his broad leather belt. When they stopped to rest in some city, he planted himself in a chair by the bedroom door of his charge, and if he slept he was not aware that nature had betrayed him into doing so.

If the journey made by the young Bearers of the Sign had been a strange one, this was strange by its very contrast. Throughout that pilgrimage, two uncared-for waifs in worn clothes had traveled from one place to another, sometimes in third- or fourth-class Continental railroad carriages, sometimes in jolting diligences, sometimes in peasants' carts, sometimes on foot by side roads and mountain paths, and forest ways. Now, two well-dressed boys in the charge of two men of the class whose orders are obeyed, journeyed in compartments reserved for them, their traveling appurtenances supplying every comfort that luxury could provide.

The Rat had not known that there were people who traveled in such a manner; that wants could be so perfectly foreseen; that railroad officials, porters at stations, the staff of restaurants, could be by magic transformed into active and eager servants. To lean against the upholstered back of a railway carriage and in luxurious ease look through the window at passing beauties, and then to find books at your elbow and excellent meals appearing at regular hours, these unknown perfections made it necessary for him at times to pull himself together and give all his energies to believing that he was quite awake. Awake he was, and with much on his mind "to work out"—so much, indeed, that on the first day of the journey he had decided to give up the struggle, and wait until fate made clear to him such things as he was to be allowed to understand of the mystery of Stefan Loristan.

What he realized most clearly was that the fact that the son of Stefan Loristan was being escorted in private state to the country his father had given his life's work to, was never for a moment forgotten. The Baron Rastka and Count Vorversk were of the dignity and courteous reserve which marks men of distinction. Marco was not a mere boy to them, he was the son of Stefan Loristan; and they were Samavians.

They watched over him, not as Lazarus did, but with a gravity and forethought which somehow seemed to encircle him with a rampart. Without any air of subservience, they constituted themselves his attendants. His comfort, his pleasure, even his entertainment, were their private care. The Rat felt sure they intended that, if possible, he should enjoy his journey, and that he should not be fatigued by it. They conversed with him as The Rat had not known that men ever conversed with boys—until he had met Loristan. It was plain that they knew what he would be most interested in, and that they were aware he was as familiar with the history of Samavia as they were themselves. When he showed a disposition to hear of events which had occurred, they were as prompt to follow his lead as they would have been to follow the lead of a man. That, The Rat argued with himself, was because Marco had lived so intimately with his father that his life had been more like a man's than a boy's and had trained him in mature thinking. He was very quiet during the journey, and The Rat knew he was thinking all the time.

The night before they reached Melzarr, they slept

at a town some hours distant from the capital. They arrived at midnight and went to a quiet hotel.

"Tomorrow," said Marco as The Rat was leaving him for the night, "tomorrow, we shall see him! God be thanked!"

"God be thanked!" said The Rat, also. And each saluted the other before they parted.

In the morning, Lazarus came into the bedroom with an air so solemn that it seemed as if the garments he carried in his hands were part of some religious ceremony.

"I am at your command, sir," he said. "And I bring you your uniform."

He carried, in fact, a richly decorated Samavian uniform, and the first thing Marco had seen when he entered was that Lazarus himself was in uniform also. His was the uniform of an officer of the King's Body Guard.

"The Master," he said, "asks that you wear this on your entrance to Melzarr. I have a uniform, also, for your aide-de-camp."

When Rastka and Vorversk appeared, they were

in uniforms also. It was a uniform which had a touch of Eastern design in its picturesque splendor. A short fur-bordered mantle hung by a jeweled chain from the shoulders, and there was much magnificent embroidery of color and gold.

"Sir, we must drive quickly to the station," Baron Rastka said to Marco. "These people are excitable and patriotic, and His Majesty wishes us to remain incognito, and avoid all chance of public demonstration until we reach the capital." They passed rather hurriedly through the hotel to the carriage which awaited them. The Rat saw that something unusual was happening in the place. Servants were scurrying round corners, and guests were coming out of their rooms and even hanging over the balustrades.

As Marco got into his carriage, he caught sight of a boy about his own age who was peeping from behind a bush. Suddenly he darted away, and they all saw him tearing down the street towards the station as fast as his legs would carry him.

But the horses were faster than he was. The party reached the station, and was escorted quickly to its place in a special saloon-carriage which awaited it. As the train made its way out of the station, Marco saw the boy who had run before them rush onto the platform, waving his arms and shouting something with wild delight. The people who were standing about turned to look at him, and the next instant they had all torn off their caps and thrown them up in the air and were shouting also. But it was not possible to hear what they said.

"We were only just in time," said Vorversk, and Baron Rastka nodded.

The train went swiftly, and stopped only once before they reached Melzarr. This was at a small station, on the platform of which stood peasants with big baskets of garlanded flowers and evergreens. They put them on the train, and soon both Marco and The Rat saw that something unusual was taking place. At one time, a man standing on the narrow outside platform of the carriage was plainly seen to be securing garlands and handing up flags to men who worked on the roof.

"They are doing something with Samavian flags

and a lot of flowers and green things!" cried The Rat, in excitement.

"Sir, they are decorating the outside of the carriage," Vorversk said. "The villagers on the line obtained permission from His Majesty. The son of Stefan Loristan could not be allowed to pass their homes without their doing homage."

"I understand," said Marco, his heart thumping hard against his uniform. "It is for my father's sake."

At last, embowered, garlanded, and hung with waving banners, the train drew in at the chief station at Melzarr.

"Sir," said Rastka, as they were entering, "will you stand up that the people may see you? Those on the outskirts of the crowd will have the merest glimpse, but they will never forget."

Marco stood up. The others grouped themselves behind him. There arose a roar of voices, which ended almost in a shriek of joy which was like the shriek of a tempest. Then there burst forth the blare of brazen instruments playing the National Hymn of Samavia, and mad voices joined in it.

If Marco had not been a strong boy, and long trained in self-control, what he saw and heard might have been almost too much to be borne. When the train had come to a full stop, and the door was thrown open, even Rastka's dignified voice was unsteady as he said, "Sir, lead the way. It is for us to follow."

And Marco, erect in the doorway, stood for a moment, looking out upon the roaring, acclaiming, weeping, singing and swaying multitude—and saluted just as he had saluted the Squad, looking just as much a boy, just as much a man, just as much a thrilling young human being.

Then, at the sight of him standing so, it seemed as if the crowd went mad—as the Forgers of the Sword had seemed to go mad on the night in the cavern. The tumult rose and rose, the crowd rocked, and leapt, and, in its frenzy of emotion, threatened to crush itself to death. But for the lines of soldiers, there would have seemed no chance for anyone to pass through it alive.

"I am the son of Stefan Loristan," Marco said to himself, in order to hold himself steady. "I am on my way to my father."

Afterwards, he was moving through the line of guarding soldiers to the entrance, where two great state-carriages stood; and there, outside, waited even a huger and more frenzied crowd than that left behind. He saluted there again, and again, and again, on all sides. It was what they had seen the Emperor do in Vienna. He was not an Emperor, but he was the son of Stefan Loristan who had brought back the King.

"You must salute, too," he said to The Rat, when they got into the state carriage. "Perhaps my father has told them. It seems as if they knew you."

The Rat had been placed beside him on the carriage seat. He was inwardly shuddering with a rapture of exultation which was almost anguish. The people were looking at him—shouting at him—surely it seemed like it when he looked at the faces nearest in the crowd. Perhaps Loristan—

"Listen!" said Marco suddenly, as the carriage rolled on its way. "They are shouting to us in Samavian, 'The Bearers of the Sign!' That is what they are saying now. 'The Bearers of the Sign.'"

They were being taken to the Palace. That Baron

Rastka and Count Vorversk had explained in the train. His Majesty wished to receive them. Stefan Loristan was there also.

The city had once been noble and majestic. There were domed and pillared structures of white stone and marble, there were great arches, and city gates, and churches. But many of them were half in ruins through war, and neglect, and decay. They passed the half-unroofed cathedral, standing in the sunshine in its great square, still in all its disaster one of the most beautiful structures in Europe. In the exultant crowd were still to be seen haggard faces, men with bandaged limbs and heads or hobbling on sticks and crutches. The richly colored native costumes were most of them worn to rags. But their wearers had the faces of creatures plucked from despair to be lifted to heaven.

"Ivor! Ivor!" they cried; "Ivor! Ivor!" and sobbed with rapture.

The Palace was as wonderful in its way as the white cathedral. The immensely wide steps of marble were guarded by soldiers. The huge square in which it stood was filled with people whom the soldiers held in check.

"I am his son," Marco said to himself, as he descended from the state carriage and began to walk up the steps which seemed so enormously wide that they appeared almost like a street. Up he mounted, step by step, The Rat following him. And as he turned from side to side, to salute those who made deep obeisance as he passed, he began to realize that he had seen their faces before.

"These who are guarding the steps," he said, quickly under his breath to The Rat, "are the Forgers of the Sword!"

There were rich uniforms everywhere when he entered the palace, and people who bowed almost to the ground as he passed. He was very young to be confronted with such an adoring adulation and royal ceremony; but he hoped it would not last too long, and that after he had knelt to the King and kissed his hand, he would see his father and hear his voice. Just to hear his voice again, and feel his hand on his shoulder!

Through the vaulted corridors, to the wide-opened doors of a magnificent room he was led at last. The end of it seemed a long way off as he entered. There were many richly dressed people who stood in line as he passed up toward the canopied dais. He felt that he had grown pale with the strain of excitement, and he had begun to feel that he must be walking in a dream, as on each side people bowed low and curtsied to the ground.

He realized vaguely that the King himself was standing, awaiting his approach. But as he advanced, each step bearing him nearer to the throne, the light and color about him, the strangeness and magnificence, the wildly joyous acclamation of the populace outside the palace, made him feel rather dazzled, and he did not clearly see any one single face or thing.

"His Majesty awaits you," said a voice behind him which seemed to be Baron Rastka's. "Are you faint, sir? You look pale."

He drew himself together, and lifted his eyes. For one full moment, after he had so lifted them, he stood quite still and straight, looking into the deep beauty of the royal face. Then he knelt and kissed the hands held out to him—kissed them both with a passion of boy love and worship.

The King had the eyes he had longed to see— the King's hands were those he had longed to feel again upon his shoulder—the King was his father! The "Stefan Loristan" who had been the last of those who had waited and labored for Samavia through five hundred years, and who had lived and died kings, though none of them till now had worn a crown!

His father was the King!

It was not that night, nor the next, nor for many nights that the telling of the story was completed. The people knew that their King and his son were rarely separated from each other; that the Prince's suite of apartments were connected by a private passage with his father's. The two were bound together by an affection of singular strength and meaning, and their love for their people added to their feeling for each other. In the history of what their past had been, there was a romance which swelled the emotional Samavian heart near to bursting. By mountain fires, in huts, under the stars, in fields and in forests, all that was known of their story was told and retold a thousand times, with sobs of joy and prayer breaking in upon the tale.

But none knew it as it was told in a certain quiet but stately room in the palace, where the man once known only as "Stefan Loristan," but whom history would call the first King Ivor of Samavia, told his share of it to the boy whom Samavians had a strange and superstitious worship for, because he seemed so surely their Lost Prince restored in body and soul—almost the kingly lad in the ancient portrait—some of them half believed when he stood in the sunshine, with the halo about his head.

It was a wonderful and intense story, that of the long wanderings and the close hiding of the dangerous secret. Among all those who had known that a man who was an impassioned patriot was laboring for Samavia, and using all the power of a great mind and the delicate ingenuity of a great genius to gain friends and favor for his unhappy country, there had been but one who had known that Stefan Loristan had a claim to the Samavian throne. He had made no claim, he had sought—not a crown—but the final freedom of the nation for which his love had been a religion.

"Not the crown!" he said to the two young Bearers of the Sign as they sat at his feet like schoolboys. "Not a throne. 'The Life of my life—for Samavia.' That was what I worked for—what we have all worked for. If there had risen a wiser man in Samavia's time of need, it would not have been for me to remind them of their Lost Prince. I could have stood aside. But no man arose. The crucial moment came—and the one man who knew the secret, revealed it. Then—Samavia called, and I answered."

He put his hand on the thick, black hair of his boy's head.

"There was a thing we never spoke of together," he said. "I believed always that your mother died of her bitter fears for me and the unending strain of them. She was very young and loving, and knew that there was no day when we parted that we were sure of seeing each other alive again. When she died, she begged me to promise that your boyhood and youth should not be burdened by the knowledge she had found it so terrible to bear. I should have kept the secret from you, even if she had not so implored me. I had never meant that you should know the truth until you were a man. If I had died, a certain document would have been sent to you which would have left my task in your hands and made my plans clear. You would have known then that you also were a Prince Ivor, who must take up his country's burden and be ready when Samavia called. I tried to help you to train yourself for any task. You never failed me."

"Your Majesty," said The Rat, "I began to work it out, and think it must be true that night when we were with the old woman on the top of the mountain. It was the way she looked at—at His Highness."

"Say 'Marco,'" threw in Prince Ivor. "It's easier. He was my army, Father."

Stefan Loristan's grave eyes melted.

"Say 'Marco,'" he said. "You were his army—and more—when we both needed one. It was you who invented the game!"

"Thanks, Your Majesty," said The Rat, reddening scarlet. "You do me great honor! But he would never let me wait on him when we were traveling. He said we were nothing but two boys. I suppose that's why it's hard to remember, at first. But my mind went on working until sometimes I was afraid I might let something out at the wrong time. When we went down into the cavern, and I saw the Forgers of the Sword go mad over him—I KNEW it must be true. But I didn't dare to speak. I knew you meant us to wait; so I waited."

"You are a faithful friend," said the King, "and you have always obeyed orders!"

A great moon was sailing in the sky that night—just such a moon as had sailed among the torn rifts of storm clouds when the Prince at Vienna had come out upon the balcony and the boyish voice had startled him from the darkness of the garden below. The clearer light of this night's splendor drew them out on a balcony also—a broad balcony of white marble which looked like snow. The pure radiance fell upon all they saw spread before them—the lovely but half-ruined city, the great palace square with its broken statues and arches, the splendid ghost of the unroofed cathedral whose High Altar was bare to the sky.

They stood and looked at it. There was a stillness in which all the world might have ceased breathing.

"What next?" said Prince Ivor, at last speaking quietly and low. "What next, Father?"

"Great things which will come, one by one," said the King, "if we hold ourselves ready."

DEDICATION

MY MOM, CLAUDETTE WALKER THIS ONE IS FOR YOU.

ACKNOWLEDGMENTS

First of all, I want to thank God for all that he has instilled in me. Thank you for my gift to pen all these books that my readers enjoy. To my kids all I do is for you. My grandkids Kyleigh Michelle and Grayson Kyrie, just know the world is yours.

RECAP OF PART ONE

"What the hell is going on here?" My eyes opened at the sound of Patrice's voice.

"What are you doing here?" I asked her as I got up to go hug her and Amber. I never got around to calling them, but I needed my friends right now. I noticed Patrice was standoffish.

"What's wrong with you?" She was breathing all hard and her chest was moving up and down at a faster pace than normal. I knew that she was mad. Then I noticed she was staring a hole in Taymon.

"What the fuck, Nevaeh?"

"Gone head with that shit, Patrice. She doesn't even know what's going on."

"Yes, the fuck she does. You mean to tell me this the nigga you been bragging about for months?"

"Didn't I say leave her out of this shit? Don't come in here with your bullshit. My brother in there fighting for his life, and we ain't about to get put out because of you."

"Patrice, just come on. I honestly don't think Nevaeh knows. She wouldn't do you like that," Kam told her. She had been standing there the whole time, not saying anything.

"Wait a minute, can somebody please tell me what the hell is going

1

on?" I was starting to get a weird feeling, and I didn't like this shit. It was like everyone in the room knew what was going on but me. I hated being in the unknown.

"Everybody talking about me, like I ain't standing right here. The only thing is, I am in the blind. What did I or didn't I know?"

"Oh, you really gonna stand there and act like you didn't know shit?"

"Patrice, we are better than this. We have all been friends for as long as I can remember. I don't have a clue what you are talking about. You need to start talking before you say some shit we can't come back from."

"Bitch, you knew you were fucking my ex," she said as she football tackled my ass to the floor. Hearing that news knocked more wind from me than the actual push she gave my ass. The whole room spun before I passed out.

CHAPTER ONE

NEVAEH

*W*hen my eyes opened, people were standing around me. I wasn't in a hospital bed or anything, so I wasn't sure what had happened. "What's going on?" I asked as I leaned my head back against the wall. I was sitting in a chair in the waiting room.

"You had an anxiety attack," Kam told me. I noticed Patrice wasn't there. I remembered her ass pushing me, and she got me fucked up if she thought I wasn't gonna get my lick back.

Being that Kam was there, it let me know she wasn't taking sides. I looked over at Taymon and he couldn't even look at me. "Taymon, what the fuck is Patrice talking about? Did you know we were friends?"

I didn't even know why I asked him that question. Of course, he knew. If he didn't know, he would have told her I didn't have anything to do with this. "When did y'all date, I guess is the question I should ask?"

"That is T," Kam informed me as she stood there with her arms crossed under her breasts. "Are you serious?" It hit me like a ton of bricks. Now the conversations we had came rushing back to me.

"I knew you didn't know, Nevaeh. You ain't that type of friend. They were dating while you were away at school. You never even met that nigga. Now, him, on the other hand..." She pointed at Taymon. "That nigga knew who you were. I don't give a damn what he says. Your name ain't that damn common. That's fucked up, T," she told him.

"Oh, and what Patrice did ain't fucked up?"

"Typical nigga, want to place blame somewhere else. Yes, what Patrice did is fucked up. It is worse than you if you ask me. She didn't even give Nevaeh a chance to explain shit, and she know that girl wouldn't do that to her. I am going to get in her shit, too, but right now, I am getting in yours."

"Taymon, when you met me, did you know I was Patrice's friend?" I was trying to give him the benefit of the doubt, but he was making this shit hard.

"Not at first, but it didn't take me long to figure it out."

"When were you planning on telling me?"

"Listen, Nevaeh, I never meant to hurt you. Yes, I should have told you. I like you. I more than like you, I love you. I need you. I ain't never felt what I feel for you for another woman, not even Patrice. Sorry, Kam, but it's the truth."

"You don't have to apologize to me about your feelings, T. I can't make you feel something for my aunt you didn't feel. My problem with you is how you handled it. Nevaeh wouldn't have ever talked to you had she known the truth."

I looked over at Kam. "Am I wrong because I love him, too?" I had tears in my eyes because I knew I couldn't continue this relationship. The first man I ever fell in love with was my best friend's ex-boyfriend. This one right here was one for the books.

"No, you ain't wrong, Nevaeh. I know you have feelings for him. We all do. We have heard you talk about him; you just never mentioned his name. I am here, so you can see I ain't taking Patrice side. Aunt or no aunt, she is wrong as hell for putting her hands on you, and over a nigga at that. We are better than that. We have all been friends since forever. She should have just talked to you like a civilized person. I pray y'all can get around this."

4

"I don't know, Kam. I will try. For right now, I am done with this situation. My sister is in the hospital, too. My daddy waiting on me to get back."

"What's wrong with Kayla, and why you didn't say anything?"

"Whew, it is a long story. I meant to call y'all. If you want to come and see her, I will explain it on the way." I walked over to Taymon and slapped the dog shit out of him. "Don't you ever fucking play on my top again, nigga. I don't know what the fuck you thought this was. Yes, I love your ass, but it is over. Don't you ever call my fucking phone again."

"Ew, she is cussing," Kam said as she started laughing. She knew I was pissed the fuck off, being that I was not a big curser. You had to really piss me off for me to curse at you.

"Let's go," I told her, trying to hold back my tears.

"I thought you got lost," my daddy said when I walked back in the room with Kam in tow. "Hey, Kam, I didn't know you were coming up here.

"Hey, Mr. Price. How are you holding up?"

"I am alright, considering." He pointed at my sister. "You know how I am about my girls."

"Yes, sir, I do."

"Daddy, you can go ahead and go now. Me and Kam will be here."

"What's wrong with you?" my daddy asked me as I tried to avoid his stare. My daddy could read me like a book. Now I was kicking my own ass for coming straight in here. I should have gotten myself together first. I didn't want to upset him more than he already was.

"Nothing, I am fine. Tired, that's all."

"You don't look like you're fine, but if you say so."

"I am alright, daddy, for real."

"All right, call me if you need anything."

"How are you for real?" Kam asked me as soon as the door slammed behind my daddy.

"Not good. I feel like somebody has walked all over my heart. I love him, but I can't be with him. Have you ever loved someone you know you can't be with?"

5

"Chingy's ass!" she yelled out, causing me to laugh, which was something I needed at the time.

"His ass doesn't count."

"Why he don't?" she asked as she sat back in her chair and crossed her legs.

"You can be with him, that's why."

"No, I can't be with his lying, cheating ass. Do you know that nigga was waiting in my driveway for me last night when I got off work?"

"I ain't surprised. Did you let him in?"

"I did let him in. I needed some closure. He stayed the night because I ended up falling asleep."

"You shouldn't have done that. You know you led him on with that. Now he is going to think he has a chance."

"I know, because when we woke up, he wanted to finish our talk. I told him I had something to do and put his ass out."

"You put him out?" I asked her again for clarification because I was laughing like hell.

"Yes, I did. I told him thanks for the money and food, but he could leave now."

"Money and food?"

"Yes, he ruined my food, so he had to buy me some more. He gave me a band for the food, but I know it was a sorry gift. I can't be bought, though. Fuck that nigga."

"I feel you on that," I told her as I remembered I still had Taymon's black card in my purse.

"What are y'all doing here?" We both turned to look at my sister as her groggy voice questioned us.

"You really don't know what happened to you, huh?" I asked her.

"No, what is going on? Where is Tylan?"

Kam looked over at me because I had already filled her in on everything that was going on. "Why are you looking at her?" Kayla asked Kam. "What is going on?"

"Tylan was murdered."

"What! Oh my God!" She let out a blood-curdling scream, causing the medical staff and the police that had been lingering around to rush in the room.

6

"What's going on?" one police officer asked as he looked around the room like he was looking for someone.

"Nothing, she just woke up," I answered him. The nurse checked her vital signs, trying to ignore what was going on in the room.

"Ms. Price, do you mind if I ask you a few questions?"

"Not right now," her doctor said as he came into the room and walked towards my sister's bed. "She just woke up. Let me make sure my patient is all right first. Y'all be killing me with that. She can't help you solve not one case if she ain't together." He continued to examine my sister while the detective stood there, looking dumb as hell.

"Do you think I should call my daddy?" I asked Kam. He had just left, so I knew he couldn't be too far.

"I know he would want you to call him. He is going to be mad if you don't." There was so much shit going on at one time, I didn't know if I was coming or going. Taymon was blowing my phone up, but I couldn't deal with this shit with him right now.

I was mad and sad at the same time if that even made any sense. Patrice had me fucked up if she thought for a minute, I wasn't gonna get my lick back. It was on sight when I saw her ass. I wasn't asking questions.

She should have known I would never backstab her. I loved her ass like a sister. We grew up together. I would never put a nigga in front of what we had. For her to show her ass on me like this, I didn't even know if we could come back from this.

"Hello," my daddy said, snapping me from my trance.

"My fault, daddy."

"I said hello three times. Are you sure you're alright? I just left, but I can come back."

"I am all right. Kayla has woken up and the police are everywhere."

"I am turning around now. Tell her not to say shit until I get there."

"Alright, daddy." I ended the call.

"Kayla, Daddy said wait on him before you talk to the police."

"She is well over eighteen. She can talk to us if she pleases," one of the officers said with a nasty attitude.

"I know how old my sister is. I have known her longer than you. Like I said, Kayla, wait on Daddy. If they want to get technical, then

7

tell them you will wait on your lawyer. That way they can't ask you shit else." I matched his attitude. I swear I hated cops.

"I will wait on my daddy or my lawyer. I don't even know what's going on. Soon as I woke up, you were in my face, grilling me."

"We will be outside your room, Ms. Price," they told her and walked out the door.

"I swear the police irk my nerves," Kam said, shaking her head at the same time.

"Yeah, mine, too." I leaned back in my chair and looked at my sister. She looked fragile, and I was really worried about her mindset right now. "You alright?" I asked her.

"No, not really. I honestly don't remember much."

"Do you remember talking to Daddy about paying your car payment?" I only asked her because I was trying to piece some things together. Now I was wondering if she was even in her right mind when she made that phone call to him.

"Tylan paid my car payment already, so I didn't need Daddy to pay it." Hearing her say that, confirmed she was more than likely forced to call him.

"What did you and Tylan have going on, Kayla?" She didn't answer right away. She put her head down and sobbed. I got up from my seat, along with Kam, and we wrapped our arms around her.

"What's going on?" my daddy asked as he walked into the room. The way Kayla was sobbing, and we were hovering around her, I could see the reason for his question.

"Tylan robbed someone. That's all I can really remember."

"Was it the same guy that was in your house?" my daddy asked her. He didn't know my sister couldn't remember everything that had happened.

"Who was in my house, daddy?" He never got to answer her because the detective walked back in the room.

"Are you ready to talk now, Ms. Price? We found two bodies in your home. This is profoundly serious."

"No, you found one body. We called you about the second body." My daddy interrupted him. "If we had to be technical, you didn't find that body, either, we did."

"Well, anyway..." The detective continued what he was saying. You could tell he was annoyed with my daddy. I burst out laughing and Kam followed suit. We had been friends for so long, we could always pick up on each other vibes.

I needed these laughs, I swear. Deep down inside, I was fuming. I wanted to be here for my sister, hence the reason I was still here, but I had all kinds of thoughts running through my mind right now.

"Could you tell us what happened, Ms. Price? We know you didn't kill your boyfriend. We already know who killed him, we just don't know why."

"Well, if you know who killed him, why are you in here asking me these questions? You need to be questioning them."

"It ain't that simple."

"Why not?"

"Your daddy killed him." He slammed his hand down on the table, startling Kayla." That got a reaction from my daddy.

"Hold up now. My daughter is in a very fragile state right now. Nobody, and I do mean nobody, is gonna come in here, trying to handle her like that. I don't care who you are. I will protect my kids and I don't care how old they are. You just said you know she didn't kill Tylan, so what is all the hostility about? I know I ain't under arrest either because it was self-defense."

"Oh, really?"

"Yes, really," my daddy said while staring him in his eyes. "Now, Kayla, tell this man whatever it is you remember so he can get the hell up outta here."

"All I remember is I was about to walk out my door when some man pushed me back in the door. He kept asking me where Tylan was at, and I kept telling him I didn't know, because I didn't. Tylan hadn't been home all day. We had gotten in an argument earlier and he told me he needed to clear his head."

"Is that normal for him?" the detective asked.

"Is what normal?" Kayla wanted to know.

"For him to be gone all day to clear his head?"

"Yes. After an argument, he normally left to clear his head, then we talked once he comes back home."

"Alright, we'll finish your story then."

"Like I was saying, I kept telling him, I didn't know. He made me call Tylan, and that alone alerted Tylan."

"Why do you say that alerted Tylan?" the detective asked as he wrote on a tablet.

"I never bother him after an argument. Like I said, after he cools off, he normally comes back home so we can talk about it."

"What was the argument about, if you don't mind me asking."

"His ex-girlfriend had been texting him and he was entertaining it." I was catching on to the fact that Kayla was not letting him know what she had just told us about him robbing someone. I mean, I ain't mad at her. I already knew that was the reason dude was in their house.

I mean, it wasn't a secret. Tylan was a robber, everyone knew that. He just robbed the wrong nigga this time. I hated the fact it fell on my sister's plate, though. The doctor had already told us she was raped multiple times. He tested her for every STD but only time would tell if she had HIV or not, because it could show up later.

"Alright, so what happened after you called Tylan?"

"He asked me was I all right and I told him no. That is when the guy smacked me across my face with the butt of his gun. He said he didn't tell me to say all of that. That was when Tylan told him he was on his way and not to hurt me. That was all I remembered. I don't remember anything else."

"Alright, thank you for your time." He then looked over at me. "What exactly did you witness when you walked in the door?" Before I could answer him, Amber burst through the door.

"Why in the hell didn't you call me?"

"Amber..." My daddy called her name in a stern tone.

"My fault, Unk. I didn't even see you. You know I wouldn't have cursed if I had seen you."

"Oh, but you still would have cursed. Just not in front of me."

"Yep," she said as we all laughed. "Seriously, though. What is going on?"

"Hey, Amber," Kayla said.

"Aunt Beck told me you were in the hospital, but what is going on?

Who the hell are you?" She pointed at the detective. This damn girl didn't give two fucks about anything.

"He's the police," I told her.

"Why are the police here? Girl, what the hell have you done?" She plopped her ass on the side of Kayla's bed. "Scoot over so I can sit down. So, what are you here for, Mr. Policeman?"

"Well, actually, I was just leaving."

"Yeah, you do that." He looked a little uncomfortable, and that confused me. He was just about to question me again, but changed his mind.

"Kayla, are you alright?"

"Yes, Daddy, I am fine. Thank you to everyone that is here. I have to process all of this. My best friend is gone. I know his family is going to hate me."

"Fuck them people. Excuse my language, Unk, but fuck them, for real." We all just laughed, because Amber would apologize about something but still do or say what she was apologizing about. "Why would they be mad at you? Wait, a damn minute. Who is gone? That flew over my head. What the hell did I miss?"

Not only did I need this laugh, but Kayla did as well. She was laughing so hard, she was bent over. "Somebody get Amber's behind. She get on my darn nerves."

"Nah, for real, though, who gone?"

"Tylan was killed."

"Oh no, Suga foot, I'm so sorry to hear that." She reached over and gave Kayla a hug, and she cried on Amber's shoulder. "I'm not gonna say the typical thing everyone always says: it's gonna be alright. It ain't gonna be alright for a long time."

Next thing I knew, we were all crying. We really had a *Waiting to Exhale* moment while my daddy just looked on. "Look, I'm gonna give y'all a few moments. I will be back in a few." My daddy walked out the door.

After about an hour, Amber and Kam had left. "Once Daddy gets back, I'm gonna head on home for a few. Your lil sister is tired," I said as I stretched my arms. I hadn't had a decent night of sleep in a few days. Honestly, I didn't know how much I was going to get tonight either.

This shit with Taymon and Patrice had me all over the place. Amber still didn't know what had happened, so I knew I had to call her later and let her know what was going on. "I see y'all have cleared the room out," my daddy said as he walked back in the room.

"Yeah, it's getting a little late. Amber got work in the morning and Kam said she had a few early clients. Do you mind if I leave? I'm tired."

"No, I don't mind. I got your sister."

"Well, call me if you need anything."

"I will," he said as I walked out the door.

CHAPTER TWO

PATRICE

$\mathcal{I}$ was mad and hurt at the same damn time. I can't believe how Nevaeh and T played me. I hated the fact I couldn't get her how I wanted to. I only got one damn lick in. It's on sight when I saw the bitch. Laughing in my motherfucking face and fucking my nigga behind my back.

That bitch just wanted my whole damn life. "What's wrong with you?" my sister asked me as she walked in the door of our parents' house.

"Nothing," I told her as I continued to pace the floor. I was wearing the carpet out on the floor; I had been pacing it since I got here.

"Well, it doesn't look like nothing to me. It's written all over your face. You looking like you just lost your best friend."

"I did."

"You did, what?" she asked while standing there with one hand on her damn hip. She was talking about me looking crazy. I burst out laughing as she stood there with hair rollers in her head. They were all colors and sizes. "What is so funny, Patrice?"

"You are funny. Why did you come outside looking like you looking?"

"Girl, hush. I ain't looking no type of way. I ain't trying to impress these people, I got a man."

"That's who you need to be worried about impressing, shoot. You gotta always look good for your man," I told her.

"Yeah, whatever," she said as she waved her hand at me. "Now, what you mean by you just lost your best friend? What's going on with you and Nevaeh?" All four of us hang together, but Nevaeh was my best friend, and it was known.

"That bitch is sleeping with T. Can you believe that?"

"Whoa, wait a minute. What you mean, she is sleeping with T?" I laughed at the fact my sister was doing everything to avoid cursing. She was in the church and doesn't curse. "That doesn't even sound like something she would do. Are you sure about this?"

"Yes, I'm sure she is sleeping with him."

"How could you be so sure, Patrice? She is your friend."

"Correction, she was my friend. That bitch ain't no friend of mine. With friends like her, I don't need any enemies."

"Lord, let me sit down. I gotta hear the whole story first."

"I just told you the story. What do you mean, you gotta hear the whole story? I just told you."

"Well, it's two sides to a story, Patrice."

"I mean, whose sister are you?"

"I'm your sister, but you know I stand for what's right. If you didn't want to hear the truth, then you shouldn't have said nothing to me."

"I didn't say anything to you. You asked, remember?" I said as I stuck my tongue out at her.

"Girl, you ain't too big for me to give you a whooping. Now, what happened? I refuse to believe Nevaeh would do that to you. Wait a minute. Do Nevaeh even know T?"

"Listen, all I know is when I got to the hospital to check on Antwan, she was there with T."

"What you mean, check on Antwan? What's going on with him? It's too much going on for me. You skipping too much of this story."

"He was shot."

"Is he alright?"

"Last I heard, he wasn't okay. That is why I went there. When I walked in the waiting room, T was hugged up with Nevaeh's ass. I knocked the shit out of her ass, too. T had the nerve to say don't be mad at her because she didn't know. That bitch knew and I ain't fucking with her no damn more."

"First of all, I can't believe you put your hands on Nevaeh. What in the world was you thinking? He told you she didn't know, and I believe him."

"Why do you believe him? How could she not know? She is my friend." I pointed to my chest.

"He wouldn't have said it if it wasn't true. You told me out your own mouth that even if it hurt, T never lied to you. That darn girl wasn't even around when y'all was dating. I remember when she used to say how crazy it was that she never met him and y'all had been dating for a while. You talking about you ain't messing with her no more; you better pray she still wants to be your friend. You straight tried her over a man. He did all the lying and you ain't even mad at him. You're mad at her, and for what?"

I was furious. I didn't want to hear shit my sister was talking about. She was supposed to be on my side, but here she was, taking up for T and Nevaeh. "I am mad at her because she is sleeping with T. What do you mean? I am trying to figure out why you can't see it my way."

"You don't have a way, Patrice. You're dead wrong for putting your hands on that darn girl."

"This conversation is over. I don't want to talk to you anymore."

"You just mad because I ain't marching to the beat of your drum. I'm on the side of right, and right about now, you're wrong."

"Yeah, whatever," I told her. I walked off and left her standing there, looking crazy, hair rollers and all. "Hello?" I answered my ringing phone as it rang in my back pocket.

"Patrice, you wrong as hell." What was this, double team Patrice day? First, it was my sister, now it was her damn daughter.

15

"Kam, I don't want to hear shit you gotta say. You and your mama getting on my damn nerves. How am I so wrong? Nevaeh is the one sleeping with my man, and I'm wrong?"

"Correction, he ain't even your nigga now, for real. You mad at Nevaeh, for what? You know good and damn well that girl didn't know who T was. I think your ass living in La-La Land or something, talking about your man. That nigga been put your ass out."

"Who the fuck you talking to?" I said to her because she had me all the way fucked up. I checked my watch and realized I had time today.

"I'm talking to your ass. I didn't stutter, not one damn time. You gotta make this right."

"Why do everyone keep screaming I gotta make this right when Nevaeh is the one sleeping with my nigga?"

"Something is seriously wrong with you, Patrice. You keep screaming your nigga; Taymon is not your nigga, he is Nevaeh's nigga." I couldn't even lie, when she said T belonged to Nevaeh, that shit stung.

I knew I did him wrong when we were together, but I was still in love with him. That was the real reason I hadn't seriously dated anybody else since we broke up. I was hoping he would forgive me and take me back.

Now all my people must be crazy if they think I was going to let Nevaeh have him. "Ain't nothing wrong with me. Something is wrong with y'all asses. I can't believe you taking her side in real life."

"This ain't even about sides, Patrice. Now, I love you and all, but you're wrong. I can't stand behind you on this one. Nevaeh got a heart of gold, and you know that. She is feeling fucked up about this shit right now."

"And how do you know how she is feeling?"

"I talked to her. I been around her since you pulled that punk ass move."

"How was that a punk move?"

"You know good and damn well that girl didn't know you was about to swing on her. You better watch your back, too."

"I ain't watching nothing. I ain't thinking about her ass."

"Well, you better. You already know she ain't gonna let that shit

16

go." After she said that, she hung the phone up on me, not even giving me a chance to respond.

* * *

NEVAEH

A Week Later

J was glad school was out because I could mope around in peace. It had been a week since I had talked to Taymon or Patrice. Taymon, or T, whatever he was calling himself these days, had been blowing my phone up.

People had been sending me screenshots of Patrice's Facebook posts, asking me what was going on with her. She never said my name, so they didn't have a clue she was talking about me. Only the people who knew the situation knew she was talking about me.

I couldn't believe she had taken our problems to The Book. She was the one who put her hands on me, so I didn't know what she was mad at me for. I didn't know Taymon was her ex, therefore, as far as I was concerned, I hadn't done shit to her.

I still hadn't told Amber yet. She was going to be thirty-eight hot when she found out. My sister had been discharged from the hospital, and she had been staying with our daddy. He had been taking her to her rehab sessions. Since she hadn't voluntarily taken the drugs, they decided she should do outpatient. They just wanted to make sure her body didn't crave it. Other than that, she was doing all right.

I missed Taymon like crazy, I wasn't even going to lie. I was in love with this man. My first time being in love, and it was with my best friend's ex. I swear life was a bitch.

"Hello?" I answered my phone for Amber's ass.

"Why the fuck didn't you tell me you and Patrice got into it? What the hell is going on?"

"I was going to tell you."

"When? I mean, because from what I was told, this shit happened about a week ago."

"Well, who told you, then?"

"Kam."

"Kam talks too damn much."

"In her defense, she didn't even know she was telling it. She thought I knew, which I should have."

"Yeah, you should have. My mind been so boggled. Like, I love this man, for real, and can't even be with him."

"Why you can't be with him?"

"He is Patrice's ex, that's why."

"Fuck Patrice. I can't even believe she did that shit to you. She should know better than that. She knows you would never do no shit like that on purpose. What does Taymon have to say about all of this?"

"I don't know."

"What you mean, you don't know? Y'all ain't talked about this shit?"

"No, because I won't give him a chance to talk. I don't have shit to say to no damn Taymon."

"Why not?"

"Because he lied. What kind of question is that?"

"Well, technically, he didn't lie, he just withheld information." She started laughing at her own joke, but I didn't see shit funny.

"Same damn thing. Quit taking up for that nigga."

"I ain't taking up for no-damn-body. Don't let Patrice stop your happiness. This is the first time I have ever seen you this happy. You been glowing and shit. I mean, you didn't do anything behind her back, Nevaeh. You ain't never met that nigga. Shit, I was right here and only saw him a handful of times when she was dating him. You were in Raleigh, so I know good and damn well you didn't have a clue who he was."

"You mean to tell me, you wouldn't look at me funny if I stayed with him?"

"No, and Kam wouldn't, either. We already talked about it. Truthfully, it doesn't matter what we think, anyway. This is your life. You deserve to be happy, and that man makes you happy. Every time you talk about him, your whole face lights up. I ain't never seen that on Patrice when she used to talk about him. She doesn't want him, for real. She just wants what he used to do for her, and that's take care of her ass."

"I hear you."

"No, you don't, but for real, I only knew him by T as well. That's why I never put it together. Now, if you had mentioned it to Kam, then she would have known, but you never said his name around them. You only mentioned his name to me and that was in the beginning of y'all's relationship."

"I just don't know, Amber. I mean, I feel like I'm in a twilight zone."

"I know you do. You should at least talk to him. I don't think you should just give up on y'all. It was fucked up how he played it; I can't and won't downplay that. The moment he figured shit out, he should have told your ass."

"Now you see why I'm so mad."

"I never said I didn't. You have every right to be mad. I heard you slapped the shit out of that nigga, though."

"Yeah, but it still didn't make me feel any better. I want to go slap his ass again."

"As you should. Girl, I knew I raised you right."

"Oh, you raised me?" I burst out laughing because my cousin didn't have anybody's sense.

"You already know who raised you. Girl, do not play. Now, what are you going to do about Patrice?"

"What you mean, what I'm gonna do? I'm gonna beat her ass. It's on sight. I mean that shit on our granddaddy. I'm going to her ass."

"As you should," she said again. "She already knows you on her ass, though. Kam already told her. If she thought you weren't, then she doesn't know you very well."

"Oh, that bitch knows. She knows how I roll, that's why she played it like that."

"I ain't gonna tell your ass no more to call that man. Kam also told me Patrice is walking around here like they still in a relationship or some shit."

"What? You got to be kidding me."

"I wish I were. It's sad, I almost feel sorry for her. Kam said she is walking around mad at the world. I told Kam shit the world ain't done nothing to Patrice. She caused all that shit on herself. Like I said, I wouldn't look at you sideways for staying with that man. It's your life, though, so do what you wanna do."

Amber had given me a lot to think about, I just didn't have anything to say to Taymon right now. "Well, Amber, I'm going to get off this phone. I will call you later." I hung up. I had a headache from hell.

I really wanted to dial Taymon's number. *Shit!* I said to myself. I picked up my phone and blocked my number. "Hello?" I didn't say anything. "Hello?" he said again. Still, I said nothing. "Patrice, stop playing on my motherfucking phone."

Hearing him say that broke my heart in two. All I wanted to do was hear his voice and now I felt like I had lost mine. I hated I even called. Now he just reminded me of all the reasons I couldn't be with him.

"No...no, this ain't Patrice," I managed to get out.

"Nevaeh, baby, I'm—" I hung up before he could get the rest of his sentence out. Of course, he called me back a few times, but I didn't answer. I cried myself to sleep.

* * *

TAYMON

"Fuck!" I yelled aloud. I couldn't believe I said Patrice's name and it was Nevaeh. In my defense, though, I really thought it was Patrice. She had been calling my phone like crazy since that day at the hospital. When I wouldn't answer, she started calling me private.

I was stressed the hell out. My brother was still fucked up, and I was missing the hell out of Nevaeh. I heard it in her voice, I'd hurt her feelings. I had to fix this shit. I had to get her back. I knew I should have told her when I first figured this shit out, but I didn't want to lose her. Look at me now, I had lost her anyway.

"Mom, I will be back," I told her as I rubbed my hand down my face. I knew I had grown a few gray hairs since last week.

"You alright, son?"

"No, I'm not, but I will be."

"Son..." She touched my leg, letting me know she wanted me to listen to her. I stopped for a moment so I could hear what she had to say. "I know you got a lot going on, but I have to say this. I like Patrice and all, but I know where your heart is. I didn't see this glow on your face with Patrice that I see with Nevaeh. Yes, you should have told Nevaeh, but don't give up. Go get your woman."

"I know, Ma. I should have told her, but I ain't giving up. I love her too much to give up on us. That's why I'm leaving. I'm going to her house."

"See you when you get back, son," my daddy said, and my mom just smiled. "I will see y'all later!" I yelled over my shoulder. I started Googling flower shops as I walked to my car. I remembered her saying something about daisies being her favorite flower, so I wanted to buy her some.

I pressed the phone number to the nearest shop I found. I wanted to make sure they had the flowers before I went there. "Hello, thank you for calling Fulton's Flower Shop. This is Lasharra, how can I help you?"

"Yes, do you have any daisies in?"

"We do."

"Can I get three dozen? Do y'all sell edible bouquets as well?"

"Yes, sir, we do."

"Let me add that on, too. How soon can you have it ready?"

"How soon do you need it?"

"Yesterday," I told her. We both laughed, but I was dead serious.

"I can make that happen for you. What time will you be by?"

"I'm actually not too far from you. Can you have it ready by then?"

"Give me about thirty minutes, and it will be ready."

"Alright, thank you." We hung up. According to my phone, I was only like fifteen minutes away, but I headed on over there, anyway. I didn't have shit else to do, because I was not showing up to her house empty-handed.

Once I pulled in the parking lot, I gave Patrice a call. I wanted to nip this shit in the bud. I didn't want any more mishaps. She was wrong as hell for the shit she pulled with Nevaeh.

"Hello?" She answered the phone and the sound of her voice irritated my soul.

"I just called to tell you not to contact me anymore. This shit is ridiculous."

"You the one fucking my friend and I'm the one being ridiculous?"

"Girl, something is seriously wrong with you. You know good and damn well that girl didn't know anything about us. I ain't never meet her when we were dating, and you know that."

"You knew, though," she emphasized.

"Well, if I'm the one that knew, why you mad at her, then?"

"You are off limits, and she knew that."

"Didn't you just admit I was the one that knew?"

"She knew that shit, too. I know you told her."

"I'm done with this conversation. Apparently, it ain't no getting through to you."

"When I see Nevaeh, I am going to get her ass again." I laughed at her antics.

"What is so damn funny?" she asked.

"You want to fight your friend so bad. That is what is so funny. She didn't know shit about me and you, yet and still, you're so quick to want to get back with me. If anybody betrayed you, as you say, it was me. You ain't trying to hear none of that, though. Ain't no way in the hell I would lose my A1 over somebody that doesn't even want me."

"Whatever, T, you know you want me."

"Patrice, I really don't want you. That's on my parents, I don't want you. Let me ask you a question."

"What?" She said it with so much attitude, but I didn't give two fucks. I knew what I was about to ask her, she was not even going to know the answer to. Her answer was going to determine a lot about our past relationship.

"What is my favorite color?"

"What?"

"You heard me the first time, but since you act like you didn't, I will ask you again. What is my favorite color?"

"What kind of question is that? Your favorite color is blue." I laughed in her face.

"How in the hell were you with me for all those years and don't know my favorite color? Your favorite color is green. Bitch, bye. If you touch Nevaeh, I will kill you," I told her before I hung the phone up on her dumb ass.

I walked in the flower shop. "Hey, I just called an order in about thirty minutes or so ago."

"Yes, the guy that needed them like yesterday," she said with a smile.

"That would be me."

"Give me a few minutes. I am packaging up your items now. How would you like to pay?"

"Do y'all take cash?"

"We sure do. She is a special lady," she told me. "I wish someone would do something like that for me."

"How much do I owe you?" I asked, totally ignoring what she had just said. I knew she was trying to flirt with me, and I was unsure why. Women killed the hell out of me. I guess they didn't mind being side pieces. It was clear I was buying flowers for a woman.

"The total came out to be two hundred and thirty-two dollars."

I placed two hundred and fifty dollars in her hand. "Keep the change and buy you something nice with it." A few moments later, someone walked from the back and handed me my package.

* * *

I was sweating bullets as I pulled up to Nevaeh's house. I was wishing upon a damn star right now, because I didn't even know if she was going to let me in. I sat there for a minute before I got out of my car. I had to get my thoughts together.

Finally, I was out of the car and walking towards her door. I already knew she could see me through her doorbell camera, but I rang her doorbell, anyway. "What do you want, Taymon?" I could tell I had awakened her from her sleep. She sounded groggy.

"Open the door, Nevaeh. You already know why I am here."

"I don't have anything to say to you, Taymon. I told you not to play

23

with me, and what did you do? Not only did you play with me, but you played me, too."

"I did not play you. Just let me in, so I can explain." She got silent for a moment, but I heard her unlocking the door. That caused me to smile. I handed her the flowers, along with the edible fruit bouquet.

"What is this for?" she asked as she put her nose to the flowers to sniff them.

"Just because I felt you deserved something nice." I followed her to the kitchen.

"Would you like something to eat?" she asked as she started pulling food from her refrigerator. Instantly, my mouth watered because she was a hell of a cook. I had been missing her food as well.

"Yeah, let me go to the bathroom and wash my hands."

When I walked back in the kitchen, she had my plate on the table. She had fried barbecue ribs, macaroni and cheese, greens, cornbread, and potato salad. My stomach started growling, causing me to realize I really hadn't eaten anything in a couple of weeks.

My appetite was gone, but it was back now. I sat down and dug right in. "I see someone is hungry," she said with a laugh.

"Yep, you see I'm fucking this food up." She laughed as she shook her head, placing her own food in her mouth.

"So, what's up?" she finally asked.

"Listen, when I first approached you, I had no idea you were Patrice's friend. I mean, no, you don't have a common name, but I still had never met you. She talked about you a lot, though."

"When did you figure it out?"

"A week later. I was already kind of putting it together, but I still wasn't sure. It wasn't until y'all had that fight and you showed me the video. Once I saw it, I knew for sure who you were."

"You didn't think you were supposed to tell me?"

"Yes, I knew I should have, but I couldn't. I knew you weren't going to fuck with me anymore once I told you that shit."

"It still should have been my choice, Taymon. I mean, what else are you lying about?"

"I ain't lying about nothing."

"How am I supposed to know that?" I leaned back in my chair before I answered her question.

"I pray you can just trust me when I tell you that. I know it is hard, considering what we are going through now, but I feel something different for you. I ain't never felt this way before about Patrice or another woman. It is something about you."

"Oh, really? Taymon, this is a lot to process. Right now, I just don't know what I want to do. I mean, you are my best friend's ex-boyfriend. This is going against the girl code. How can I face her, knowing I am sleeping with you?"

"Fuck Patrice, you gotta worry about your own happiness."

"It ain't that simple, Taymon."

"Honestly, Nevaeh, you didn't know. You're not going behind her back. Do I make you happy?" She shook her head yes as she bit her bottom lip, causing my dick to rise. Every time she did that, she caused my dick to rise. I always found it sexy.

"What is the problem, then?"

"The problem is you lied."

"I understand, and I was wrong. I apologize for that. I don't want your friend, though."

"It ain't really about if you want her or not, Taymon. Shit, if I had to tell myself the truth, I know you don't want her."

I got up and grabbed her from behind because she was still sitting in her seat. I placed a kiss on her forehead. She relaxed, so I grabbed her hand and led her to her bedroom. "I can't do this, Taymon." She managed to get it out of her mouth before I kissed her.

"What can't you do?" I asked in between kisses, already knowing her answer. The way her body was reacting to my kisses let me know she wanted it just as bad as I did.

I started trailing kisses down her neck and gently removed the cami she had on. All she was wearing was a cami and a pair of panties.

Normally, she either slept in that or her birthday suit. I mean, I don't mind the birthday suit. I ripped her panties off her. "Those are Victoria's Secret."

"So, I will buy you some more," I told her as I eased my dick in her, not giving a damn about a condom.

25

"Tay-mon, you forgot to put on." I hushed her up by sticking my tongue in her mouth.

"I will give you the money to get a Plan B in the morning." I told her that, but in the back of my mind, I knew I was not going to give her any money. I was ready to start a family, and I was ready to start a family with her.

I climbed on top of her and spread her legs as wide as she would allow me to. "Aw," she moaned, causing me to speed up because her pussy was soaking wet. It was so wet, you could hear it gushing.

"I missed this," I whispered in her ear. She grabbed my neck and started kissing me all over, causing me to moan in her ear. For the next twenty minutes, all you could hear were the sounds of our lovemaking.

* * *

The next day, I woke up to the ringing of my cell phone. I didn't even remember falling asleep. "Hello?" I answered for my mom in a groggy voice.

"Son, I didn't mean to wake you up. I was a little worried when I didn't hear from you."

"You alright, I need to get back up there, anyway. I don't even remember falling asleep." I looked over at Nevaeh, and she was sprawled out across the bed. I watched as her chest heaved up and down, as she snored lightly. I wish I could just lay with her here all day.

I wonder where we stand. I ain't the person thinks sex can fix everything. I knew she was horny, just like me. "Take your time, son. Me and your daddy are here with your brother. We will call you if anything changes."

"I am going home to shower and check on my crib. Then, after, I will check on Junior."

"Yeah, Maria stopped by here earlier."

"She did?" I asked, no longer lying down. "What did she want?"

"She wanted to know how Antwan was doing and she stated Junior was stable and needed his daddy to pull through." I chuckled at my mom's statement. In our heart, that was my brother's son. I swear hoes were grimy. I was so glad I didn't have those problems.

That was why, when Patrice told me she was pregnant, I took her to the abortion clinic myself. Not only did I take her, but I stayed with her until the procedure was done. Not that I didn't want kids, I just wanted to make sure I had them with the right person.

"Well, we need him to pull through, too. I am happy to hear Junior is stable. Antwan will be happy to hear that once he wakes up."

"I went to see him. Regardless of everything that went on, he is still my grandson." I heard the hint of sadness in her voice.

"I will be there in a few."

"See you when you get here." I disconnected the call. I felt Nevaeh staring at me, so I turned around to face her.

"What's up?" I asked as I headed to the bathroom to take a piss.

"What your mama say?"

"She told me Maria came by to check on my brother and that my nephew was stable."

"Well, that is good news."

"Yes, it is."

"Look—" We both said something at the same time.

"You can go first," I told her.

"Last night was just sex. Nothing more, nothing less," she told me, causing a lump to form in my throat. I mean, I was expecting it, but that ain't what I wanted to hear. This girl was my world, whether she knew it or not.

"Nevaeh, don't do this."

"Don't do what? I know you didn't think us having sex was going to instantly fix all of our problems. I mean, I can get sex from anywhere."

"Don't say that," I told her. My heart was crushed from hearing her speak those words. "Don't say you can get sex from anywhere. Do not make me go to jail for murder one."

"I mean, I'm just saying. It ain't that I want to have sex with anyone else, I was just making a statement. I fell hard for you, but I can't be with nobody who feels the need to lie to me. I have been friends with Patrice forever. You have cost me my friendship."

"She couldn't have been that much of a friend if she bailed out on you like that." She got quiet for a minute. I wasn't trying to add insult

27

to injury, but it was the truth. A real friend would have at least heard her side of the story before she pulled the move Patrice made.

Shit, she committed the ultimate no-no. She put her hands on her. The whole thing was crazy if you asked me. "I just don't know what her problem is. She doesn't even talk about you anymore. I mean, yes, she has every right to be upset, but not with me. I didn't do anything to her."

In real life, I wanted to tell her all the things Patrice used to say about her, but I didn't want to seem like a hater. I mean, I knew all of Nevaeh's business because she used to tell me. For some reason, Patrice was jealous of her. Hell, she was jealous of her whole clique. She had talked shit about them all.

She used to say they thought they were better than people. I knew why she was saying those things, though. They were bettering themselves, and she wasn't doing anything but the same thing. Her niece, Kam, was doing her own thing. She even had celebrity clients. Amber was doing something in the medical field, then here goes Nevaeh. She went away to college.

I used to tell Patrice all the time to go back to school. I was even going to pay for it. All she wanted to do was lie around the house all day and shop. Let me not forget how much she liked to shop.

"I don't know, Nevaeh. She got her own demons, is all I can say. Again, I am sorry. I wasn't trying to make y'all fall out."

"I know that was not your intention, but look at us now. She put her hands on me. I bet not catch her ass in the streets or I am going to punish her, and she knows it, too." If it had been anyone else, I would have loved to see that fight. I wanted to see if Patrice could fight, for real. She already be popping off at the mouth like she can beat the entire world or something.

I didn't want to see the two of them go at it, though. I grabbed her hand and kissed it. "I am sorry."

"Can I think about this, please?" she asked as she got up from the bed. I watched her ass jiggle as she walked into the bathroom. That sight made my dick hard, but I knew now was not a good time.

I followed her to the bathroom. I had clothes here, or I hoped I still had clothes here, so I might as well take a shower here. "Hey, you didn't burn my clothes, did you?" She let out a laugh, causing me to playfully nudge her head. Not that I couldn't buy more, but it was the principle. "Don't play with me, woman."

"I didn't burn them, but um..." She laughed again.

"But um, what? You play too much." I started laughing.

"Man, ain't nobody done nothing to your clothes. I ain't that type of person. I don't damage people's stuff."

"Shit, the way you slapped my ass, I don't know what you may do."

"Oh, you didn't deserve that slap?"

"Okay, I will let you have that one."

"Oh, I already know you will."

"What are your plans for today?"

"I am going to the mall on you today. Since somebody thought it was cool to rip my panties off, I gotta go buy me some more."

"I only ripped one pair, so get you one pair." She looked at me and stuck her tongue out at me.

"Whatever, me and my sister going shopping on this black card today. I am about to call and tell her to get ready."

I fell out laughing. "You can't be doing what you want to do with my card, woman."

"I can, and I am. I will call you once we are done, so I can meet you somewhere to get your card." I was just messing with her about my card. I didn't care what she spent on that card.

"I will get it. You don't have to call me to come get it." I wanted her to keep the card. To me, it was a given that as long as she had my card, I would see her again.

"You sure?" she asked me with raised eyebrows.

"Yes, I am sure." I didn't say anything else, just hopped in the shower, told her goodbye, and headed to the hospital.

CHAPTER THREE

NEVAEH

Once Taymon walked out the door, I picked up my phone and called my sister. It had been a while since we spent time together. After everything that happened, though, she promised me she would do better.

"Hey, Vaeh," was how she answered the phone. I heard my daddy in the background, so they must have been already in conversation or something.

"Hey, Kayla. Tell Daddy I said hey as well."

"Vaeh said hey, Daddy."

"I was calling to see if you wanted to go to the mall."

"I don't have any money."

"I didn't ask you all that." I started laughing, and so did she. It felt so good to hear her laugh again.

"I mean, I am just saying. You can't go shopping with no money, and your sister don't do the window-shopping thing. I miss my dude. I didn't have to worry about this shit with him."

"Like I said, I didn't ask you all of that. I got Taymon's black card."

"Oh, shucks now. Yes, I am down with a shopping trip. What time do I need to be ready?"

"Now that is what I wanted to hear. I will be there in about an hour. Be ready, Kayla."

"I will be ready."

"We all know what you're ready is, though." She burst out laughing.

"I will be ready, I promise."

"Yeah, okay. I will see you in an hour." I pressed the end button on my phone and continued to get dressed.

A little after an hour later, I pulled into my daddy's driveway. He stood on his porch, smoking a blunt. All I could do was shake my head. My daddy said when he dies, bury him with it.

"Hey, Daddy." I spoke to him as soon as my foot hit the pavement.

"What's up? Why didn't you invite me to shop? Shit, I like to shop with other people's money, too." We both laughed because we knew my daddy didn't need a thing from anyone. He was a real OG out here in these streets.

"I mean, you can pass your black card along to if you want to."

"Black card? What's that? I don't know anything about no black card."

"Daddy, you know good and well you got a black card. I don't know why you trying to play on my top."

"Whatever, you don't know what I got. Quit trying to count my pockets."

"Old man, ain't nobody counting your pockets."

"Where your mama at?"

"Don't be asking about my mama. I know you still in love with her. Let me find out you want that old thang back."

"Don't nobody want your mama, girl."

"Yeah, whatever," I told him as I playfully waved him off. "Where is Kayla at? She better be ready, too. Don't nobody got all day to be waiting for her."

"Don't be talking about me like I can't hear you. I am ready. Dang, it be your own sister," she said as she walked towards me.

"Yep, it sure does be your own sister. Now, come on, girl, don't nobody got time to be fooling with you all day."

"Don't forget who called who," she said playfully.

"Whatever, girl, come on. See you later, Daddy."

"Here you go," he told me as he placed some money in my hand. "This is for you and your sister." I didn't even count it, I just placed it in my pocket. I was going to put whatever he gave us in my bank account. I was spending Taymon's money today.

"How much did Daddy give us?" my sister asked as soon as I got in the car.

"I don't know because I didn't count it."

"Well, what you waiting for?" I didn't even respond, I just pulled the money out so I could count it before we pulled out the driveway.

"He gave us fifteen hundred apiece," I told her as I her half to her.

"Whew, thank you, Daddy. I needed this."

"I just told you shopping was on me."

"Yeah, I know that, but I still needed this. I got bills to pay." Nothing else was said as I backed out of the driveway.

* * *

"$\mathcal{J}$ am hungry and tired," Kayla said after we walked out of Gucci. We had been at the mall for almost three hours. I had to admit, the feeling was mutual.

"What do you want to eat? Right now, I don't even care." I didn't even finish what I was about to say because I could have sworn I spotted Patrice's ass. For her sake, she better hope not.

I was probably going to jail today if it was her. I meant everything I said. It was on sight with her. "What caught your eye, sis?"

"I thought I saw Patrice, but I don't see her anymore."

"Well, you know I am down with whatever," Kayla said as she cracked her knuckles, causing me to laugh.

"Oh, hell nah, I want that hoe to myself. I am going to punish her. She didn't put her hands on you, she put her hands on me. This shit right here is personal."

"I ain't never seen you this hype about a fight. I mean, I know you will fight, but I mean, you are ready. Pop your shit, sis."

"Just come and get me out."

"What about your job?"

"I have thought about all of that, trust me, but I can't let her get away with putting her hands on me."

"Let me fight her, sis."

"Nah, I can't do that. I don't need any help."

"She ain't worth your career, though. We all know that hoe is garbage. She doesn't have anything, and she don't want anything."

"I hear you, and I am going to get her." I dropped the subject and headed to the food court. Like I said, I wasn't even sure if it was her or not. "What do you have a taste for?"

"Jake's," my sister said as she scrunched up her nose like something was stinking.

"What are you scrunching your nose up for?"

"I want some wings from Jake's and some loaded fries, that's why."

"So, you snarling your nose up for that? Girl, let's go." I grabbed her hand and we headed towards my car.

* * *

"*T*his place stays packed," Kayla said as I made my way around the parking lot for the second time, looking for a place to park my car. Little did she know, I only circled the parking lot a second time because I was sure this time that I saw Patrice's car. I knew I could get away with whooping her ass in here.

"There goes a parking space," Kayla said, pointing at the same time. "Shit, you out here playing, and I am hungry in real life."

"Girl, ain't nobody playing." I grabbed a ponytail holder from off my gear shift and put my hair in a ponytail.

"What are you doing all of that for?" I didn't even answer her. I didn't want her to try to talk me out of it.

As soon as we walked into Jake's, we were greeted by his wife, Monae. She always comes in to be a greeter. I guess she doesn't have anything else to do. Hell, her man is swimming in money.

"Hey, how are you ladies doing today?" she asked us.

"We are good, thanks for asking."

"I sat Patrice over by the bar. Do you want to join her?" Kayla's eyes got big as she looked at me. Monae didn't have a clue what she had just done. All she knew was that we were friends. She didn't know anything about the fallout.

I honestly didn't want anyone in our business, either, but Patrice was on one on social media. I knew no one had a clue what she was talking about, but I did. I said it was on sight, so I had to keep my word.

"She at the bar," I said, more as a confirmation than a question.

"Yes, she is right over there." She pointed in her direction. Patrice's back was turned. I wasn't going to sneak her like she snuck me. I wanted that bitch to see me coming because I wanted a fair fight.

"Thank you, Monae. I will talk to you later."

"You gonna do it here?" Kayla asked as she pulled her hair back behind her ears.

"I said on sight, and I may never get another opportunity." I walked towards Patrice, and she had a smirk on her face when she saw me. That let me know the bitch wasn't sorry about shit she had done.

Boom! I pushed her ass out of her seat, causing her drink to spill all over her and the person beside her, too. I didn't give a damn. She tried to fight me back, but I was so damn angry, she was only swinging at the air. Patrice was a fighter now, so I was shocked she hadn't landed one punch.

"Don't nobody put their hands on my motherfucking sister while she is kicking big ass," I heard Kayla say. Bap! Bap! Bap! I rained blow after blow on her face, causing her to hold her hands up to protect it.

It was like now, she wasn't even trying to fight back. She looked defeated. I almost wanted to stop, but I kicked her ass in the face. "Bitch, don't you ever in your fucking life try me about a nigga again. You got me fucked up," I told her as I backed away from her.

I felt a hand on my shoulder, and I knew it was my sister, so I didn't even try to resist. "That's enough," she told me. "I think she got the picture." I looked over at the crowd standing there. I knew they were shocked. I saw the confused expression on Monae's face and knew she was trying to figure this out. Everyone was, but I didn't give a damn anymore. Patrice wanted the smoke, so I brought it to her. We had been friends too long and she let a misunderstanding come in between us.

Now I was about to let everyone there know why I had just whooped my best friend's ass. I didn't want any controversy if I stayed with Taymon. I knew how Patrice loved to twist a story around to make herself look good, but not today.

"While you're on Facebook making all those posts, you need to be telling them the truth. Patrice was dating a man I never met while I was away at college. Fast forward, I started dating him and didn't have a clue he was her ex, and she knew it. She pulled a bitch ass move and put her hands on me over a nigga that don't even want her ass. I pray you know what you're doing because this friendship is over." I walked away and didn't even look back.

I knew my sister was behind me because I heard her footsteps. "Damn, you could have at least let me order my food," she said as we got in the car. I knew she was joking, but I wasn't in a joking mood right now.

More than anything, my feelings were hurt. I couldn't believe all of those years of friendship came down to this. Patrice was really selfish. She didn't even want Taymon for real. I hadn't heard her say that nigga's name in years. She had been sack chasing since I'd been back in Charlotte, so fuck Patrice, as far as I was concerned.

I hopped in my car and skid from the parking lot. I was done with that bitch. She was never my friend to begin with.

* * *

AMBER

I had just watched my cousin Nevaeh beat Patrice's ass on Facebook live. I saw the look on Nevaeh's face, though. I knew that shit hurt her to her heart. One thing about Nevaeh, she loved hard. She could either be your best friend or your best enemy. I preferred not to be on her bad side.

I mean, the whole thing was crazy to me. Yes, Patrice needed her ass beat, so don't get me wrong, I just hated the whole thing had to gone down at all. Now it was going to seem awkward when we got together because one of them wasn't coming.

I dialed Nevaeh's number, and just like I expected, it went straight to voicemail. I knew she was alright, though, so I would just wait on her to call me.

"You ready to go?" I looked at my man of three months and gave him a response.

"Yes, Mr. Detective, I am ready to go." Yep, you heard it right. I was dating the detective from the hospital. Nobody knew about it because I wanted to make sure it was real. I loved his white tail and I didn't care what anybody thought. The only reason I didn't say anything at the hospital was because I wanted him to be my little secret just a little while longer.

Don't get me wrong, I love my Black men, so me dating him had nothing to do with me saying I was tired of Black men because I was not. I just love the way Trent makes me feel. He was always attentive to my needs.

He makes sure I eat every day and sends me flowers to my job. I wasn't sure how long this ride was going to last, but I would ride with him until the wheels fell off. I met him at Food Lion when my battery died in my car. I was waiting on triple A, and he was a good Samaritan. We exchanged numbers and it was on from there.

They say white men can't jump, but Woody Harrelson proved them wrong in the movie. I said all that to say this—my man was packing in that department, and he knew how to work it, too. When I was with him, I didn't even look at color. All I see is him.

He gave me a sloppy kiss and we made our way out the door.

"You okay, baby?" I asked him once we were in the car.

"Yes and no," he told me.

"Well, start with why you ain't okay first, then."

"I just keep thinking about that day you came to the hospital."

"What about it?"

"I mean, we never talked about it."

"I mean, what is there to talk about?"

"Who are those people to you?"

"That is my family. The girl that was in the hospital and her sister are my cousins. Why? What's up all of a sudden?"

"Why did you act like you didn't know me? Are you ashamed of the fact I'm white?"

"No, I am ashamed of the fact you are a cop," I told him as I stuck my tongue out at him, letting him know I was joking. "You were working, so I didn't feel like it was appropriate to be telling people, by the way, I am fucking this man."

"I mean, I see your point, but I guess it was how you said it."

"What you mean, how I said it?"

"Have you ever heard of the saying, it ain't what you say, but how you say it?"

"Yes, I have."

"Well, it was one of those situations. You walked in and was like, *who is this,* like you didn't know who I was. You could have just spoke and kept it moving."

"Look, I wasn't trying to offend you. If you were, then I apologize. I like you in real life, Trent. No, I ain't never dated a white man before you, but I like it." He grabbed my hand and kissed it, causing me to blush.

See, it was those gestures right there that had me falling for him. "I am going to introduce you to my family in due time. One thing about me, I have always dated who I wanted to date. I never cared who liked or didn't like them. Long as I liked them, that is all that mattered."

"I like you, too. Seeing you in rare form at the hospital had me turned on, too. I was like, look at my baby. You just don't know how bad I wanted to bend you over and fuck the shit out of you."

"Oh, yeah?" I said as I glanced over at him.

"Yep, sure did."

"What was the yes, you are okay part?"

"Huh?"

"When I asked if you were you okay, you said yes and no. What is making you okay?"

"Oh, the yes was that I am in your presence now, and that is all that matters to me."

"I can dig that. Where are we heading?"

"I wanted to take you to Steak 48 if that is alright with you?"

"Hell, you know I like to eat. You know I ain't against food." We both fell out laughing.

Once we pulled into the restaurant, we both got out while they valet parked his car. When we walked into the place, it was not what I expected. I wasn't talking about the food because we hadn't gotten far. I was talking about the actual restaurant itself.

The whole city had been hyping this place up, so I was expecting something extraordinary. I know one damn thing, the food better be good, or I was going to talk big boy shit on Facebook.

The waitress showed us to our table. "Can I get you something to drink?"

"Just bring me a water for now because I am not sure what I want to drink. Do you recommend anything?"

"Do you like wine?"

"I do."

"Well, the Pieropan Soave is a favorite here."

"I will try that, then. I still want my water, too, though."

"I will put that in, along with it. And for you, sir?"

"I will try the same."

"Alright, I will be right back with your drink orders." He walked away and I continued to look at the menu.

"Do you know what you want to eat?" Trent asked as he sat back in his chair.

"I have an idea. Everything sounds good, so it better be good, or I am going to talk about their ass on Facebook."

"You are a mess, woman."

"I know I am."

"Here are your drinks," our waiter said as he walked back to our table and set our drink orders down. "Are you ready to order, or do you need more time?" I was ready to order. *I want everything in real life,* I thought to myself.

"I am ready, but I am not sure if he is." I pointed towards Trent.

"Nah, I am ready. I want the prime steakhouse meatballs."

"And you, ma'am?"

"I want the crispy shrimp, along with the whipped praline sweet potatoes. I also want to add asparagus fries. You don't want any sides?" I looked at Trent.

"Oh yeah, add some asparagus fries to my order as well."

"Will that be all?" the waiter asked us.

"Yes, for now, it will be," I told him.

"I will be back shortly with your order." We made small talk while we waited on our food.

"Have you ever thought about going back to school?" I thought about his question, because going back to school had been on my mind lately. I wanted to take my medical career a little further. Right now, though, I just didn't have the motivation.

"I have thought about it. I have actually been thinking about it recently. I want to become a registered nurse. I am a medical assistant and my nurse friends always be laughing at me."

"Why do they be laughing at you?" I noticed how his face scrunched up. "They think they're better than you or something?"

"No, nothing like that. They be laughing at me because I always say a medical assistant ain't nothing but a low budget nurse."

"Why do you feel like that?"

"It is, that's why. A medical assistant does everything a nurse can do. Even the doctor I work for says they should start us off with more. Most doctors hire a medical assistant, so they don't have to pay for a registered nurse. They give injections, I give injections. Like I said, they don't do anything I don't do."

"I got you. What's keeping you from going back to school right now?"

"Laziness, I guess. I mean, I like—no, I love what I do. If I would have known then when I was in school to be a medical assistant what I know now, I would have just become a registered nurse. I was just trying to be on the fast track."

"Well, I think you should go back."

"Here you go." The waiter started putting our food on the table. It smelled good, causing my stomach to growl. "Someone is hungry, I see," the waiter said, causing us to laugh.

"I am fat, phat; I am always hungry." I caused another laugh.

"I hope y'all enjoy," he told us as he walked away from our table.

"Back to this school thing," Trent said as he placed asparagus into his mouth. I laughed a little at how persistent he was. I was not going to bring it back up, but I see he was not dropping it. I was not upset or anything. It felt good to have a man pushing you to do better.

"I am not sure yet. I will think about it. Is that fair enough?"

"I will drop it for now. Know this, though, we will revisit this conversation in the near future." We ate the rest of our food with casual conversation.

* * *

TAYMON

A Month Later

I hadn't talked to Nevaeh since the day I left her house. She sent me a text message, telling me I could get my card anytime I wanted it. I had seen the fight with her and Patrice. It was all over Facebook, so there was no way I could miss it.

Even if it wasn't on Facebook, which was all everyone was talking about, considering the fact they used to be friends, they wanted to know what the fight was about, and of course, everyone had their own speculations on the situation.

The rumors were already starting to fly. Some people were saying Nevaeh was wrong for talking to me, but how could she be wrong, though? She didn't know anything about me. Then you had others who said Patrice was wrong. Either way, I didn't give a damn. I felt as if it was our life, and we should be happy.

I was lying in my bed on my back with my hands behind my head. The television was playing *The First Purge*. It was more so watching me, though. I had already seen this movie a thousand and one times. I just had the television on for background noise.

In real life, I didn't think Nevaeh was fucking with me. Like I said, she only said something about my card. Other than that, she had left me on read. I really was contemplating on telling her I wanted my card back just to see her. I wasn't a petty nigga, though, and I knew she would see right through that. She would give me my card back, though, even though I didn't want it. A part of me wanted to just let her hold on to it because I knew I had access to her. *Fuck it*, I thought as I picked my phone up to call her.

I didn't know what type of spell this woman had on me. It was like her pussy had some voodoo shit on it. I was hooked and being without her had me sick. There was no way in this world I could lose her. I was glad I wasn't foolish enough to think that just because we had sex, everything was going to be all right.

I knew even if she took me back, we had a long way to go. I was going to spend the rest of my life making it up to her if she gave me the opportunity to. Yes, I could have told her. I put myself in this predicament.

The way I feel about her, I have never felt this way before about a woman. With Patrice, yes, I loved her, but I am realizing now I was not in love with her and there is a substantial difference. Patrice was not in love with me, either. She was in love with what I could do for her.

I would never wife a bitch who couldn't hold her own. If I got popped, I needed to make sure we were still good. She didn't want shit in life. All she ever had was her damn hand out. When I met her, it should have been a red flag, then. She didn't have a job. Even before I moved her in, she still wasn't trying to get one. I used to talk to her all the time about what she wanted to do. She talked about going to cosmetology school, and I told her I would pay for it. Of course, she never took it a step further. The crazy part was, she could actually do hair. She and Maria talked about opening a shop together. Me and my brother had no problem with paying for it since we needed to wash our money, anyway. Honestly, Maria could have still done it because she had her license, but since she'd had my nephew, she hadn't been doing shit, either.

The ringing of my phone brought me from out of my thoughts. I was supposed to had been calling Nevaeh but got caught up in my thoughts.

"Hello?" I answered the phone for my mom.

"He woke up," she said with so much excitement in her voice. I heard what she was saying, but it wasn't processing.

"Who woke up?" I had sat up in my bed by this time and ran my hand down my face.

"Your brother, he woke up. You need to get to the hospital now." I jumped up out of my bed and ran to the bathroom to get my hygiene together.

"I will be there shortly." I hung up. Yes, I could walk and chew bubble gum, but talking on the phone slowed me down.

After I was done getting my life together, I hopped in my car and sped to the hospital. I knew I had broken so many traffic laws on my way, but I didn't give a damn. My mama said my brother had woken up, and that was all that was on my mind at the time.

When I walked into my brother's room, my parents, along with Maria's bitch ass, were standing over his hospital bed. I wanted to curse Maria's ass slap out and ask her what the fuck she was doing there, but I didn't. There was a time and place for everything, and now was not the time nor the place. I had other things to be thankful for, and my brother waking up was one of them.

My brother looked around and he didn't seem to mind that she was there, so who the fuck was I to say something if he didn't?

"Hey, bro." I walked over to his bed and started bogarting. I lightly pushed Maria out of the way. She looked at me all crazy, but she knew better than to say anything to me or I would kindly take her ass outside.

"What's up?" he said to me, but his voice sounded weak as hell. I mean, I didn't know what to expect, being that he had been in a coma for over a month. I reached out to dap him up, and again, that was weak as well. I cried real tears. They were tears of joy, though. I had cried enough sorrow. *I guess God really do love a nigga*, I thought. "Oh no, nigga, don't come in with that sappy shit," he told me with a big ass Kool-Aid smile plastered across his face.

"I thought I lost you, bro. I don't know what I would have done if something would have happened to you."

"Well, they can't kill a real nigga. I am here. We ain't gonna think like that." I hugged him tight.

"I love you, nigga," I told him as I whispered in his ear. "I took care of that nigga that shot you. You ain't got to worry about his bitch ass no more." He shook his head, letting me know he understood everything I had just said. He looked over at Maria, and I could sense how his mood shifted.

She looked everywhere but at him. She knew she had messed up with my brother. She also knew that other nigga was dead. My brother was her lifeline, and he had cut her water off now. I knew he would continue to take care of his son, though, so she didn't have to worry about that.

"What are you doing here?" he asked her, and it was like suddenly, he found his strength.

"What do you mean, why am I here? Why wouldn't I be here?"

"You know I ain't fucking with you."

"Antwan, I am sorry. I—" He threw his hands up, cutting her off. She had a look of defeat on her face, but I knew that look. She was just like Patrice. She knew her water was about to be cut off. She didn't really give a damn about losing my brother.

"I am going to need you to leave, Maria," my mom told her.

"Mrs. Jackson..." Maria looked at my mom with tears in her eyes. I knew those tears didn't move my mom when it came to her kids. Antwan was her baby boy; she wasn't about to play the radio about him.

"You can take my son to my mom. I will raise him. Hell, I been raising him, anyway."

"You ain't taking my son anywhere." She emphasized the word *my son,* causing my brother to rise in the bed. You could tell it took a lot for him to do that, because he was holding himself like he was in pain.

"You aight, bro?"

"Yeah, I am good. Maria, don't play with me. I don't give a damn what that blood test says. That is my motherfucking son. I don't care if not one drop of my blood flows through his veins, he belongs to me. He is my namesake. Bitch, I will kill your motherfucking ass. Now try me if you want to."

"He is my son, Antwan. Why would you try to take him from me?"

"You can still see him, I just want full custody of him. I don't trust you with him. Your hoe ass couldn't even watch him. You were too busy in a nigga's face that you let him get hit by a car. Do you really want to fight me on this?"

"I make one mistake and now I am the worst mother. Nigga, you ain't father of the year. Yes, we can go to court. I will go in there and tell them all types of shit. Do you really think once I tell them you're a drug dealer and a killer, they will give you full custody?"

"Bitch, prove that shit. You really on one today, Maria. I am telling you now, my son better be at my mama's house once I am discharged, or I am coming for your ass. That ain't a threat, either, it is a promise. Now, bitch, get the fuck out of my room."

"Aight, Maria, that is enough," I told her. My mama had already told her as well. She would not be told again. She was getting my brother worked up, causing his blood pressure to rise. The nurse had just walked in to check on him.

"What is going on? Mr. Jackson, are you alright?" She looked at him, then at Maria. I knew she was looking at her because she was the only other person outside of Antwan was fuming.

"He good," I told her as I grabbed Maria by her arm and pushed her ass out the door.

"Well, whatever is causing your blood pressure to rise, I am going to need you to calm down. We can't have that. You just woke up today."

"It won't happen again. When do you think the doctor will discharge me?"

"I am not sure. I know it will not be today, though." She continued to check the rest of his vitals, and then she left the room.

"Ma, please get my son from her."

"How am I going to do that, Antwan? It was just proven he is not yours."

"I am on his birth certificate, therefore, he is mine."

"I don't trust that girl. She may try to call the police and say I kidnapped that child."

"I will kill that bitch."

"I will get him before you come home, son, just calm down," my daddy told him.

"You good for real, bro?" I asked him as I took a seat in one of the chairs they had in the room. I was trying to change the subject.

"Yeah, I'm good. What's been going on with you?" I leaned back in my chair and pulled my phone out of my pocket before I answered his question. I shot Nevaeh a quick text message, letting her know Antwan had woken up. I prayed she responded because that was going to tell me something else about her.

People being mad, I get it. You don't want to be bothered with someone you are mad at. Mad or not, though, if someone you love needs you, you come running. I put my phone in my lap and told my brother about all the drama that unfolded between Nevaeh and Patrice, including the fight, and how Patrice pushed Nevaeh on the floor.

"Man, I am glad she beat Patrice's ass. You know I never cared for her." He started laughing.

"I never knew that. Why you didn't tell me you didn't like her? Shit, you see I don't hesitate about telling you I don't like Maria's ass."

"I haven't always disliked her, that's why. She be doing the most, which is why I stopped liking her ass. Every time I see her out and about, she be like, hey, brother-in-law. I told her the last time she said that shit, how am I your brother-in-law with no brother?"

I fell out laughing. "What did she say when you told her that?"

"She was like, what do you mean, with no brother?" He mimicked her to the T. "She had her hands on her hips and everything, bro. It was hilarious. You know me being me, said it in front of everybody, too. I was like, you ain't even with my brother, and ain't been with him in a while. Shit, if you want to be technical, y'all wasn't together when you were together."

My brother had me rolling. This was what I missed the whole time he was in a coma. There was no way I could have lost my brother. I didn't know what I would have done. Glad I never had to find out.

"That bitch garbage, bro."

"Watch your mouth, Antwan," my mama spoke up, causing us both to look over at her. We were so deep into our conversation, we had forgotten our parents were even in the room.

"My fault, Ma, but you know I am right." I looked down at my phone because it had alerted me I had a text message. My smile grew wide when I saw Nevaeh had responded. That brought joy to my heart because it let me know she really cared about a nigga.

She didn't let whatever we were going through get in the way of what was going on with my brother.

Nevaeh: OMG, I was praying he pulled through. What are the doctors saying? Like I ain't a medical person lol but is he going to be alright?

Me: Nigga ok thanks for asking. He in here telling jokes like ain't nothing happened.

Nevaeh: I'm super geeked for y'all right now. Do y'all need anything?

I knew I was about to try my luck with this next text message, but I had to say it. I needed her right now. This woman had a spell on me. "What you over there grinning about?" my brother asked, catching me off guard. I didn't even realize I was still grinning.

"Huh?" I said like I hadn't heard him the first time.

"Don't huh me. You know what Daddy always said when we were growing up. If you can say huh, you can hear."

"Nigga, I know," I said to him with a smile on my face. "I was texting Nevaeh."

"She good?" he asked with a raise of his eyebrows.

"Yeah, nigga, and what was you gonna do if she wasn't? You a few hours out of a coma and want all the smoke."

"You already know I do."

Me: I need you. That's all I need. I held my breath as I pressed send.

"I was telling her you were out of your coma, that's all."

"You seem so happy to be talking about her."

"I just told him that," my mom chimed in. "I ain't never seen that look on him when he was with Patrice or any other female."

"Bro, if that's what you want—excuse my language, Ma—fuck Patrice. You deserve to be happy."

"I know that, but can you convince Nevaeh the same thing? She loves me, that I know, because she told me she did. In her mind, though, she is doing Patrice wrong."

"Bro, she has a valid point."

"I ain't saying she doesn't have a point. I feel where she is coming from. In my mind, I want to just let her go and be happy, but my heart won't let her go, though. I love that woman."

Bing. I got a text message alert on my phone. I knew it was Nevaeh and I prayed it was her, anyway. I let out a sigh of relief.

Nevaeh: Sure, I will come. Just give me about an hour.

Me: I will be waiting for you.

That was all I wanted to hear. "She is coming, bro."

"Who coming?" He looked at me with a confused look on his face.

"Nevaeh, nigga, who else?"

"Shit, you tell me. I didn't know." We continued the conversation, and I didn't even realize how much time had passed when Nevaeh knocked on the door, then came into the room.

* * *

NEVAEH

When I walked into the room, it was like time stood still. Whatever they were in here talking about, the conversation stopped, and all eyes were on me. "Hello, everyone," I said as I made my way into the room. Taymon was sitting in a chair against the wall and his parents were sitting on either side of him. The only time I'd met his brother was when his son got hit by a car, and that was briefly.

It was so much going on that day, he might not have even remembered me being there. "I'm Nevaeh." I spoke up because it seemed as if Taymon wasn't going to say anything.

"My fault," he finally spoke up. "You already met everyone, though."

"Things were crazy that day, though. I was trying to do a formal introduction."

"You're so right, and I am Antwan. It is finally nice to meet the woman that got that bright ass smile on my brother's face." I looked over at Taymon when his brother said that. He avoided looking at me.

If only he knew I wanted him just as bad as he wanted me. I just wished he hadn't lied to me. Granted, I wouldn't have continued to talk to him. I don't go behind my friends. I wasn't that hard up for a nigga that I had to fuck behind my friends.

I mean, I couldn't unfuck him. It wasn't like I could get my sex back. I guess it depended on where we were at in our relationship. We all could have talked about it. I should have never found out the way I found out.

"I got you smiling?" I asked as I grabbed his hand. I wanted him to look me in my eyes. It was a different feeling when a person was not ashamed to tell you how they felt in front of other people.

"You already know that. I love you, Nevaeh. I don't want to lose you." I squeezed his hand before I walked to the empty seat. I didn't respond to what he said. I was here because he asked me to be here for him, so that alone should tell him something.

"I dreamed of fish last night," his mom blurted out. I turned to look at her, wondering what she was telling me for.

"Ma, gone head with that," Antwan said. "The last time you said that, Maria was pregnant, and the baby not even mine. Well, he is mine, but you know what I'm saying."

"The point is, someone was pregnant, though," she said as she ran her hands through her hair. I just looked back and forth between them, not saying a word. Honestly, I was confused, and my facial expression showed it.

"Who pregnant?" I finally broke my silence.

"You sure it ain't you?" his mom asked as she looked at me up and down.

"Yeah, I'm sure it ain't me."

"How can you be so sure?" Now this old lady was starting to piss me off. I was trying to be respectful, but I was like two seconds from cursing her ass out. I didn't want to disrespect her, so I decided it was time for me to leave.

"Um, Taymon, I think I am going to get ready to go." I could tell from the look on his face, he wasn't too happy with what I had just said.

"You alright?" I shook my head yes in response to his question. There was no way I was about to tell him his mom was the reason I was leaving. Not that she had disrespected me or anything like that. It was her line of questioning I was not too fond of.

"Ma, you just don't know when to be quiet." Without me even saying anything, he already knew it was because of what she had said. I assumed this wasn't the first time. I knew Antwan had said she mentioned it when Maria was pregnant, but it was a little deeper than that. She had to have said it to him before, too. I made a mental note to ask him about that.

"Nah, she good." I tried to play it off. She was good, though, because I wasn't mad. I just didn't want what she was saying to be true. I didn't want any kids right now. That would be like the perfect storm. I would probably have to fight Patrice every damn time I saw her if I were pregnant. Nah, I didn't want to even think about that.

"For real, I know your mom is just being a mom. That is what her generation does. I ain't upset. I never planned on staying long." That part was the truth. I came here with the intentions of only staying about an hour.

"Well, let me at least walk you down. Y'all, I will be right back."

"I really didn't mean any harm, Nevaeh. I like you."

"I know you didn't," I told her with my hand on the door handle. "It was nice to officially meet y'all." They cracked a smile because they knew why I'd said that.

"The feeling is mutual," they said at the same time.

"I really hope my mom ain't the reason you're leaving," Taymon said to me once we were downstairs.

"Why would I be upset by anything she said? I ain't the one pregnant. I know she didn't mean any harm. I have heard my grandma say the same thing a million times."

"How do you know?"

"How do I know what?" I already knew what he was asking. He sounded like a damn broken record, repeating what his mom had just said. I just wanted to hear him say it in its full entirety.

"How do you know it ain't you that's pregnant? It ain't like we used a condom the last time we had sex." I swallowed the lump that had formed in my throat. For the first time, I was at a loss for words.

I had a flashback of that night. I remembered saying something to him about not using protection, but we both were so caught up in the moment, protecting ourselves didn't cross our minds. Well, it didn't cross mine. My judgement was cloudy, and I didn't think about it until afterwards.

I meant to get a Plan B the next day, but it slipped my mind. I had been so stressed out, I couldn't even remember if I had gotten my period or not. School was starting back in two weeks, and I didn't have time for this right now.

"Cat got your tongue?" I guess I had been quiet too long for him.

"I just know I ain't. I can't be." I saw how his demeanor changed once I said that.

"Damn, is it such a bad thing if you were pregnant by a nigga?"

"No. I mean, yes. Look, I don't know, Taymon. Maybe in another lifetime, I would have been hyped the fuck up. I love you, I just don't want to be fighting this damn girl every time I see her. You know she would never forgive me."

"Fuck that bitch. I don't know why you so worried about her any-damn-way. As you can see, she doesn't give a damn about y'all's friendship."

"I ain't worried about her. Look, it don't matter, anyway. I ain't pregnant no damn way. I will talk to you later." I reached out and tried to hug him, but he blocked me from it. I didn't know why, but I had a feeling this would be the last time Taymon reached out to me.

"Nah, I'm good on a hug from you, Nevaeh. I wish you well." He turned and walked away without saying anything else.

"Taymon." I called his name, but all I got was his back. He never turned around to acknowledge he heard me calling him. I walked away with my heart broken. I felt worse than I felt the day I found out he was Patrice's ex-boyfriend.

* * *

*I*t was the first day of school and I hadn't had any sleep. My stomach was turning, and I had a headache from vomiting off and on all night. I laughed when I thought about finding out where Taymon's mama lived just so I could beat her ass.

I felt as if she had cursed me. No, I hadn't taken anybody's pregnancy test, but deep in my heart, I knew I was pregnant. That day after I left the hospital, I went home and checked my pad supply. It hadn't been touched.

I had been waiting for my period just like an inmate waiting to get released and it hadn't happened yet. I honestly didn't know how I was going to get through today with no sleep and feeling like I felt.

The first person I saw when I got out of my car was Ashley. We hadn't talked over the summer like we normally did. During the week we were here before school started, I barely saw her. When she locked eyes with me, I could tell she felt some type of way towards me. She had called me a few times, but I hadn't answered and never returned her phone calls. It wasn't on purpose, I just had a lot going on.

"I see you been busy this summer," she said, finally breaking the silence.

"What do you mean by that?"

"I saw quite a few live videos where you were the star." She had a smirk on her face, which led me to believe she wasn't too mad at me. "I called you, too, and never, and I do mean never, got a call back. I knew you were still breathing, though." She grabbed me and gave me a hug.

"I just thought you could use a friend, considering all you were going through." A lone tear escaped my eye, but I wiped it away before she could see it. I had also been emotional lately.

"Thanks, Ashley. That means a lot. I didn't mean any harm; you know you're my girl."

"Yeah, I know. You better not let it happen again, though." We laughed and she walked towards her classroom, and I did the same.

I looked at my watch and I swear this day was dragging. I felt terrible all day and we were only in third block. I couldn't wait for the day to be over. I was going to the CVS around the corner as soon as we got released from here. The principal had already told us he wanted to do a fifteen-minute meeting after school.

I wondered if he had a sign-in sheet because I was not feeling this meeting today. I wanted to skip out on it. *I mean, who holds a meeting on the first day of school?* I thought.

One good thing about this year was I had the same planning block as Ashley, which was second block. I spent all of last block, catching her up on the damn reality TV show I called life.

I had done a getting to know me assignment with my students and they enjoyed that. I told them they better enjoy it, because on

Wednesday, it was on. We had our first assignment, and their first read was *Beowulf*.

I laughed when they asked me what made me choose him as their first read. I told them his story was interesting and promised them they would enjoy it. While I was waiting for the bell to ring, I emailed my principal.

I was going to let him know I wasn't feeling my best and ask if he minded if I didn't make the meeting. I just couldn't today. To be honest, even if he did mind, I wasn't staying. I was also eager to get this pregnancy test over with.

I hadn't even talked to Taymon since the day he turned his back on me at the hospital. He hadn't reached out to me, and I hadn't reached out to him, either. Yes, I missed him, but I guess he was letting me feel how he had been feeling.

All that played through my head was, *what if I am pregnant?* I was really about to be a single parent out here. Lord knows that wasn't what I wanted for myself. I was about to potentially bring a baby into this world by a man I didn't even talk to. This just couldn't be my life.

As soon as the bell rang, I received a response from my principal. He told me that was my one pass, and I was starting off badly. I knew he was joking, though, because he had typed lol, along with what he had written.

That was a relief. Now all I had to do was get through fourth block and I would be free. "Hey, Ms. Price," one of my students said as they walked into my classroom. "I was so happy when I got my schedule and saw I had you for my English teacher."

"I'm glad you feel this way, Yolanda."

"You know you're the best, "she said as she walked past me and took a seat.

The rest of the block went by smoothly. Once the bell rang, I grabbed my purse and other items so I could leave when my students left. I ran into Ashley on the way to my car.

"Steve said you could leave?" she asked, referring to the principal. It was funny because we always called him by his first name, just not to his face.

He was not much older than us, which was why we initially started calling him that. We knew it was a respect thing, but I literally didn't see myself calling him Mr. Owens. "Yeah, he said I could leave. I told him I wasn't feeling too well. I mean, it is only a briefing of today and it ain't like he's not gonna email it to us, anyway."

"Now that is true. Call me once you find out. I ain't playing with you, Nevaeh. Don't have me waiting for you all night. I don't want to come knocking on your door." I laughed because I knew she would come and knock on my door just like she said.

"I will call you. I will talk to you later," I told her as I headed to my car. If I was gonna stand there and talk to her, then I might as well stay for the meeting. Lord knows Ashley could talk, and she would have if I had let her.

I walked in CVS and went straight to the aisle where the pregnancy tests were. I was familiar with this store because it was right by my job, so I always stopped there. I looked over the different tests they had. I wasn't sure which one to choose from because this was my first time taking a pregnancy test.

I purchased two of them because I wanted to be sure. Before I could leave the aisle, I felt someone staring at me. When I turned around, I saw a light-skinned girl. She was thick in all the right places. She wasn't a runway model, but she was cute. She threw me for a loop because she had a smirk on her face.

I was about to ask her what it was about, but she beat me to it. "Nevaeh, right?" she stated, catching me off guard because she knew my name. I blew air from my lungs. I really was not in the mood for any more foolery. My life had been a whirlwind lately.

Instead of answering her question, I asked her one. "Who are you?"

"Are you pregnant by Lamar?" she asked another question.

"Alright, this is not what we are about to do. I don't even know you, so you have a good day, Ms. Whoever You Are." I threw my hand up in the air and walked away.

"Gia," she said, barely above a whisper.

"What?" I turned around to ask her.

"My name is Gia." I walked closer to her because I didn't want to cause a scene.

"Why are you questioning me, though? I don't even know you."

"I don't know you either, per se, but I know Lamar is in love with you."

"Lamar?" I had to ask her slowly because that was a name I hadn't heard in months.

"Yes, Lamar."

"I am still confused, though. Why are you questioning me about Lamar? Who are you to him?" Lamar hadn't called me in a minute, and here this girl was, standing here talking about some damn Lamar. All I wanted to do was go home. I swear these people wouldn't let me be great.

"I ain't nothing to him. I mean, I want to be, but he so in love with you, he just cut me off like I ain't nothing."

"Listen, lady, I don't know you, and I haven't dealt with Lamar in months. I know this, though. One thing for certain and two things for sure, I would not be around here, moping about a man that don't want me. You stepping to me for what? Excuse me, but I am tired, and all I want to do is go home. Why does it even matter if he still messes with me or if I am pregnant by him or not? What does me being pregnant have to do with you? We ain't friends. Then you had the nerve to say, 'Nevaeh, right?' Bitch, stop playing. You know my first and last name, plus my twitter and Instagram name, too."

I walked away without saying another word to her. I couldn't believe these women. First, it was Patrice, which I could understand, to a certain extent. Now this Gia chick. I paid for my stuff and walked to my car. I couldn't wait to call Lamar's ass.

As soon as I cranked my car up, I dialed his number, but he didn't answer, which was cool with me. I honestly didn't know what he had going on. He could be in a relationship with someone. Like I stated earlier, I hadn't talked to him in months.

Once I was home, I went straight to my master bathroom. I wanted to get this pregnancy test over with. I read the directions on both tests and pissed on the sticks. It said within minutes, I would have my results.

One test was a plus sign and the other was two solid pink lines. I slid down to the floor after seeing that. The tears rolled down my face.

How was I supposed to tell this man I was pregnant, and we weren't even fucking with each other?

Maybe I could just raise the baby by myself. I mean, it ain't like he would know, I thought. I grabbed my phone and took a picture of both tests. I made a group message and included Ashley in the message. I left Patrice out of it, though.

Within seconds, my phone rang. It was my cousin Amber. "Hello?" I answered, sounding all dry.

"Bitch, Patrice is going to commit suicide when she finds out. You know she ain't gonna like this shit."

"Fuck Patrice," I told her.

"Oh shit, now. This is the first time I have heard you say that about her. You must be fed up with her ass."

"And is," I said, finally smiling about the whole situation. I was tired of her. I was tired of worrying about her feelings when it was clear she didn't care anything about mine.

"Well, what are you going to do, cuzzo?"

"What do you mean, what am I going to do?"

"I mean, are you going to keep it?"

"Grandma will kill me. You know we don't believe in abortions."

"Shit, how in the hell is Grandma going to know?"

"You know that ole lady be finding out everything. Don't do Grandma." We both started laughing because she knew I was right. My grandmother knew everything, and I do mean everything.

"Yeah, Grandma definitely be on one for sure. That ole lady swears she be knowing, too. When are you going to tell Taymon? I need to meet this nigga, too. He around here causing all this commotion and shit, and ain't nobody ever met his ass. All I know is he better be real."

"So, I made myself pregnant?" I asked her, all smiles. I swear my cousin always knew how to make me smile. She had jokes for days. "Girl, he is real."

"Shit, heffa, I don't know what you did. Nah, but on a serious tip. How do you feel?" I was about to answer her when my phone vibrated in my ear. I knew it was a text message because, so far, Amber was the only one out of the four people in the group message who had said anything.

I was still waiting for my sister, Kam, and Ashley to respond. When I looked at my phone, it was Kam.

Kam: Honestly, I am happy for you. Now I don't know what this is going to do to my aunt. No hard feelings, I still love you.

I knew Kam more than likely felt like shit. She didn't want to take sides because, in reality, I didn't do anything. I was going to try my best not to involve her in anything dealing with Patrice.

"That was Kam texting me."

"What did she say?"

"She told me she was happy for me and basically, she didn't want to get in it, which I understand fully. Trust me, I do. She also said she didn't know what me being pregnant was going to do to Patrice."

"I already told you what it was going to do to her. That damn girl is going to have a heart attack. Watch what I tell you."

"Well, enough about her. I am trying to figure out how I am going to tell my baby daddy," I said as I smiled. I never thought 'my baby daddy' would be part of my vocabulary.

"It really ain't nothing to say but to tell him, shit. He knows he was nutting all in your ass raw and shit."

"His mama said a couple of weeks ago when I went to the hospital that she had dreamed of fish."

"Are you serious?"

"Yes, girl, and I hightailed it right on out of there. I wasn't trying to hear none of what she was saying."

"I bet your butt wasn't. Oh well, looks like she was right, though."

"Yeah, she was. I ain't gonna tell him today because we need to meet in person. I mean, that ain't something you just tell someone over the phone."

"Shit, if it was me, I would shoot that nigga a text message."

"Girl, I ain't messing with you today."

"I bet you ain't. Well, call me if you need me. I was just checking on you."

"I am great, thank you for checking up on me. You just don't know how much I needed that." We got off the phone.

CHAPTER FOUR

TAYMON

The Next Day

J looked at the time on my eleven-thousand-dollar Rolex; it was eleven in the morning. I had just got a text message from Nevaeh saying she wanted to meet with me in person. I hadn't talked to her since that day at the hospital.

Did I miss her? Yes, I missed her, but I wasn't kissing anybody's ass. I didn't even attempt to call her. Now I was sitting here trying to rack my brain on what she could want from me.

I contemplated on whether I wanted to even text her back. The love I had for her was the part I wanted to respond to her with. The other part of my heart didn't know if it was ready to hear whatever she had to say.

I wish she would have just texted me what she wanted to talk about. In fact, I might just text her that. I knew she was at work.

Me: You can't just text me what you want with me?

Nevaeh: It is really important. I would rather talk to you face to face.

Me: Just text it to me Nevaeh. I really ain't fucking with you right now. You be leading me on and shit. Either text it to me or don't text me at all.

Nevaeh: Really T?"

I laughed when she called me T because I knew she was being funny. She had never called me that before. She didn't even know about my nickname that was T.

Me: Yes, really. You the one made it like this. Now you either tell me or don't hit my line until you are ready to tell me.

Nevaeh: Alright baby daddy.

Alright baby daddy played in my mind after reading her text message. I reread it quite a few times just to make sure my eyes weren't playing tricks on me. I dialed her number, because now she was playing. She wouldn't even pick the phone up for my ass.

I called and texted, then it clicked in my head that she might be at work. I knew she was laughing at me right now.

Me: I will be at your house later on today.

Nevaeh: Oh, now you want to talk? Nah, we good baby daddy. You will not be getting in my house.

Me: Like I said I will be by there later.

Nevaeh: Like I said, you won't be getting in.

I texted her a few more times, but she didn't respond. I knew she wouldn't, but I wasn't worried about it. Like I said, I would be by her house later. She had me all the way fucked up if she thought she wasn't going to talk to me today.

I thought back to the day at the hospital when my mom stated she had dreamed of fish. Nevaeh acted like her world would be over if she were pregnant by me. I wasn't worried about her getting an abortion or anything like that. If those were her plans, she wouldn't have even told me she was pregnant.

My mom was going to be happy to have another grandbaby on the way. I was going to wait to tell her, though. I already knew we both had to get ready for the drama with Patrice. I wasn't really concerned about it, but I knew how Patrice could get.

On everything I loved, though, if she touched Nevaeh while she was pregnant, or even attempted to bring her any harm, I was going to get her.

I picked my phone up to call my brother. He had been home for two days now and back to his normal self. As promised, my mom had his son when he got out of the hospital. Of course, Maria was mad, but one thing for certain, two things for sure, she was not going to buck my mama.

For some reason, the women we talk to act like they're scared of my mama. I laugh because my mama was only five feet even, but her little, short self still tried to run shit. Like, woman, have several seats. "Yo," he said as he picked the phone up.

"What you up to?"

"Not shit, just lying here, chilling."

"Yo, guess what?"

"Nigga, I ain't about to play no guessing games, just tell me."

"Why did Nevaeh text me and tell me she was pregnant?"

"Yeah, I know, Kam told me."

"Huh?" I asked because I needed clarification. What did he mean, Kam told him?

"My fault. Shit, we grown." I knew he wasn't talking to me because I heard Kam talking in the background. I started laughing because I didn't think she wanted me to know she was with him.

"Why are you with Kam? Chingy gonna fuck both of y'all up." I fell out laughing because I knew my brother was about to say something stupid.

"Chingy gonna fuck who up?"

"Fuck Chingy, by this time," Kam said in the background.

"Oh, it's fuck him, huh? Y'all crazy, but um, when did this happen?"

"None of your business, nigga, but um, I'm happy for you. Did you tell Ma yet?"

"Nah, I want to wait and tell her. Shit, I just found out. I told her I would be over there later, but she told me not to come to her house."

"Nevaeh is stubborn," Kam said, loud enough for me to hear her. "I hate this whole situation, but it is what it is. She is a good woman, though, and when she loves, she loves hard. In a way, and I hate to say this, but I wish you would have met her first."

"Hell, I wish I would have met her first, too. Kam, I didn't mean to cause all this confusion. I honestly didn't know when I first met her, but yes, I should have said something once I found out. I knew she wasn't gonna fuck with a nigga anymore once she found out, though. What I feel for her, I never felt that shit for your aunt. I mean—" she cut me off.

"You don't have to explain anything to me. I know my aunt can be a handful, but she is my aunt and I love her. Do I agree with what she is doing? No, I don't, and I have told her that. I am not going to down talk her, though. Nevaeh deserves to be happy, and I have told her that. This whole situation is killing Nevaeh, trust me, I know her. She wouldn't have dared talked to you had she known."

"I know that," I told her.

"Nothing really matters now, though, because y'all have a child on the way, and everyone is gonna have to accept the situation and move on. I mean, she can't unfuck you, so in my opinion, y'all might as well just be together."

It felt good to hear Kam say that. She was friends with Nevaeh and Patrice's niece. She knew both very well, and she was not taking sides. "I want this, I just have to convince Nevaeh it's alright."

"She will come around, just give her some time. Like I said, she is pregnant now, so y'all are tied together for life. I want to say the worst has happened, but the baby is a blessing, so I'm not gonna say that. I will handle Patrice and Nevaeh. I honestly don't think Patrice will bother her while she is pregnant."

"She doesn't need to bother her at all, because she didn't do anything."

"True, but we all know that ain't gonna happen because, in her mind, this is all Nevaeh's fault."

"Well, let me let y'all two love birds gone about y'all business since y'all so secretive and shit."

"That ain't me, that's her. You know I don't give a damn."

"Yeah, we know," we both said. I got off the phone so I could be left alone with my thoughts.

A few hours later, I rang Nevaeh's doorbell. I knew her ass was there, but she wasn't coming to the door. I pulled my phone from my pocket and dialed her number. "Hello?" I couldn't do anything but laugh because I couldn't with this damn girl.

"So, you didn't just hear me? Forget hear me because I know you're looking at your doorbell camera."

"Yes, and I told you not to come. You are so hardheaded."

"You know we need to talk about this."

"Well, when I told you to come by so we could talk, you told me no."

"I didn't know you were going to say you were pregnant."

"Well, you didn't know what I was going to say. I wasn't fucking with you when Antwan was in the hospital, but I still came. Do you want to know why? Because you needed me, that's why." I got quiet after hearing her say that because she was right.

"Just open the door." A few seconds later, I heard her unlocking the door. "Thank you," I told her as I leaned in and kissed her on the forehead. She tried to move away, but I was too quick for her. "You a mess."

"Whatever, just follow me to my room." I stopped at her room, but she went to her bathroom. When she walked back in her room, she handed me two pregnancy tests. I looked at them both for a few moments, like the results were going to change.

I walked over to her bed and sat down. "So, it's real, huh?"

"Yep," she said, sitting down beside me. "Look, I ain't trying to trap you. I have no problem with raising this baby by myself." I looked at her like she was crazy.

"Girl, Taymon is not a dead beat. I already know you ain't trying to trap me. If anything, I was trying to trap your ass."

"What do you mean, you were trying to trap me?" I took a deep breath before I responded to her question. I didn't want any more lies and secrets between us. I was trying to get her back, and I had already put it out there, anyway.

"The last time we had sex, I didn't intentionally go in you raw, but once we were having sex, I knew I wasn't going to pull out. I don't want kids with anyone else. Even if you don't come back to me, I guess this will be my only child."

"Why would you say that? Don't let me keep you from having more kids."

"You ain't keeping me, but I ain't about to have three and four baby mamas, either." She nodded her head, letting me know she understood.

"I would never keep our baby from you."

"I already know that." I reached over and rubbed her belly.

"You know you're not going to feel anything, right?"

"I still want to feel, though. Have you made a doctor's appointment yet?"

"No, I wanted to talk to you about it first. I honestly didn't want to take that from you."

"Go ahead and make one for tomorrow. Just keep me updated on the time."

"I will. You know Patrice is going to be a problem, don't you?"

"If she touches you while you're carrying my baby, I will kill that bitch."

"I ain't worried about her touching me. I just know how drama filled she is."

"Now that I know all too well. I ain't gonna keep you up, though. I know you got work in the morning. How is this year going so far?"

"So far, so good. You know all the students love me."

"I love you, too." I gave her a peck on the lips, and to my surprise, she didn't push me away. "Call me tomorrow."

"I will." She got up with me so she could walk me to the door. "Have a safe ride home," she told me as I was getting in my car. I watched her shut the door before I pulled off.

* * *

LAMAR

A Week Later

J had yet to call Nevaeh back. I was about to call her phone when I noticed the missed call. Before I could call her back, though, Gia ended up calling me. Once she told me about what happened at CVS, I already knew why Nevaeh was calling me.

I cursed Gia's ass out like a dog. She had some nerve to be upset about the things Nevaeh said to her. People trip me out, starting shit with people, then wanting to play victim. Then when she told me Nevaeh was buying a pregnancy test, that pissed me off even more.

I cursed her out worse. I already knew I was taking it out on her, but oh well. She shouldn't have come for me. She wanted to know if the baby was mine. I didn't even answer her question. I knew her baby wasn't mine, but I wasn't going to tell her that. I hadn't slept with her in months and I did mean months. I prayed she wasn't pregnant, though.

* * *

KAM

"Oh my God, what are you doing here?" I asked Chingy as my hand went to my chest. He had startled me. I had just walked out my door and he was standing on my porch. I was about to check my mailbox; I wasn't expecting company.

"I didn't know I had to have permission to come to your house."

"Why would you think you don't have to have permission to come to my house, Chingy? We ain't together. I meant what I said when I said I wasn't fucking with you."

"Who you fucking with then? Antwan?" He caught me off guard when he said that, but I tried to play it off so he wouldn't catch it. He caught it, though. Chingy wasn't a dumb nigga, so I should have known better. "Oh, you are fucking with that nigga. I thought it was just a damn rumor. Well, I was hoping it was, anyway."

"Who I'm fucking with ain't none of your damn business. I ain't worried about who you sticking your little ass dick in."

"Oh, ain't nothing little about my dick and you know it." In light of the situation, I couldn't help but laugh because he was right. There wasn't anything small about his dick. You know people say anything when they're mad.

"Whatever," I said, waving him off.

"I ain't sticking my dick in nobody if it ain't you."

"You should have thought about all of that before you stuck my so-called dick in your nasty ass baby mama. I would never fuck you again after you fucked that bitch. I ain't one of these insecure ass little girls that's hard up for a nigga."

"What are you talking about? What does you being insecure have to do with this conversation?"

"Insecure ass women keep taking their nigga back after they repeatedly cheat on them."

"I ain't repeatedly cheat on you, though. A nigga made one mistake and you won't let me live it down."

"I watched my mama keep taking my daddy back when I was younger. She acted as if she couldn't live without that man. I thought she was pathetic and weak. I hate to say that about my mama because I love her dearly, but it's the truth. When she finally walked away, I knew it took courage for her to do that, and I started looking at her different. She made that nigga miss her ass, and now you can't pay that nigga to cheat. He be groveling at her damn feet. I mean, I love my daddy, God knows I do, but at one point in my life, I hated that nigga. I hated him for hurting my mama and making her cry. Now I know hate is a strong word, but that was a dark moment in my life because I really had hate in my heart."

I sobbed, something I didn't want to do in front of him, but he had opened my floodgates. He grabbed me in for a hug. "I'm sorry, Kam. I never knew you were holding all of this inside."

I didn't even pull away from him. It felt so good to finally let that out. This was the first time I had ever admitted it to anyone. I didn't know why I chose him to release it to. Maybe it was because he was the one who had hurt me. He was my first heartbreak. I didn't like this feeling.

I now knew what my mom felt inside. She probably wanted to leave a million times, but the love she had for my dad had a hold on her. The heart is funny. Your mind tells you to leave, but your heart tells you to stay.

"You hurt me, Chingy. You hurt me bad."

"I know I did, and I am sorry. I don't want to lose you, Kam." I didn't say anything, just stood there and let him hold me. I didn't know what me and Antwan were doing, but I wasn't going to let him get close to my heart. I honestly didn't know when another nigga would get that close to me again.

I knew I shouldn't be in Chingy's arms, thinking about another nigga, but I was. He was the one who brought us to this point. I loved this nigga, and he took my heart and crushed it like it was nothing. Now I was about to be Beyoncé in these streets. When she wrote that song "If I Were a Boy", she wrote it just for me. That was exactly how I felt right now.

"Can we go inside and talk?"

"No," I told him while I shook my head. "I have already said too much."

"Why do you feel you've said too much?"

"I just told you things I ain't ever told anyone, not even my damn aunt, and you know how close we are. I'm racking my brain, trying to figure out why I even told you. I know why, though."

"Why?" he asked with a raise of his eyebrows.

"I wanted you to feel my pain. I need you to know how I felt and the reason I felt that way. When a man cheats, the other woman always feels like she won if the other woman walks away. In reality, she didn't win shit but a lifetime of heartache and pain. It takes a real woman to walk away. Now that, my friend, is strength. That is why I said when my mom finally left, I looked at her in a whole different light. She finally found her courage. She walked away from my daddy with her pride. For three years, we stayed with my grand-parents. That nigga realized the grass ain't always greener on the other side."

"I understand that, Kam. I never thought it was. I had a moment, but it will never happen again."

"How can you be so sure?" He didn't even have time to respond to my question because my eyes got big as saucers. Not that I was in a relationship with anyone, because I could do what I wanted to do, but I didn't like drama, which was another part of the reason I was leaving him alone.

I knew this situation was about to get messy. It was like something got caught in my throat, and I couldn't speak. What was today? Was it pop up at Kam's crib day? I didn't discuss with anybody about coming to my house today, but yet and still, here people were, popping up like they paid bills at my crib.

I got an instant headache. I raised my hand to my head to rub my temples. Chingy followed my gaze until his eyes landed on what I had been looking at for what seemed like forever.

I was so glad I wasn't hugged up with Chingy anymore. Even though the hug was innocent, to the naked eye, it didn't look that way. I had told Antwan I was done with Chingy, which I was, so I didn't want to seem like I was lying about the situation.

You know how people swear they're not doing anything, but they really be doing everything they claim they are not. Like Chingy, for example. He knew he had cheated on me with his ugly ass baby mama. I just didn't want to seem like that person.

"Oh, this nigga," Chingy said with a smirk on his face. Chingy was a real street nigga, just like Antwan. I got scared because Antwan had just gotten shot, but he thought he was 50 Cent.

"Chingy, don't you say nothing. I mean it. I am single and I can do whatever I want to do."

"I am a grown ass man. Don't nobody tell me what to do." I ran my hand down my face and stood in front of Chingy. In my mind, they wouldn't go around me. Neither one of them had a reason to even dislike the other one. I guess it was an ego thing.

"What's up, Kam?" Antwan said once he made it towards us. He had the sexiest grin on his face, I swear. It had been so long since I'd had sex. My panties got wet. He licked his lips. He knew what he was doing. When I was at his house the other day, we came close to having sex, but I stopped him.

No, I didn't want to have anything to do with Chingy, but I wanted him completely out of my system. Having sex with Antwan would have only been revenge sex, and that wasn't what I wanted.

"Nigga, what you doing at my girl's house?" Chingy had a mean mug on his face as he stared at Antwan.

"Don't be asking me no damn questions like we on *The First 48*, nigga. I can come and go anywhere I damn well please. What the fuck you gone do to me?"

"I ain't with all that talking, nigga."

"Yeah, me either. I didn't even come over here for you. What you got going on, Kam?"

I felt like it was time for me to intervene. "I'm gonna have to ask you both to leave. Nobody asked me if they could come to my house. I came outside to check my mailbox and both of you pulled up. This is where I lay my head and I want it to remain peaceful. I don't even know what the animosity is between y'all two, but I know it ain't me. This ain't just start; it's way deeper than me."

Neither one of them said anything, they just looked at each other. "You're right, Nevaeh. I ain't gonna disrespect your crib like that, my fault," Antwan said, as he walked backward, toward his car. "Nigga, I will see you." He hopped in his car and pulled off so fast, he left skid marks in front of my house.

I pray this didn't escalate into something. Like I told them both, this was bigger than me. I was about to ask Chingy to leave as well, but I decided against it. I wanted to know, no, I needed to know what the beef was about. It hadn't always been this way, so I knew it had to possibly have something to do with Antwan getting shot.

"What was that about?" I asked as I stood with my hands on my hip, tapping my right foot. He knew when I did that, I was serious, and he better not lie.

"His bitch ass brother killed my motherfucking cousin."

"Huh?" I asked because now I was confused. "Antwan don't got but one brother."

"I know that. Taymon killed my damn cousin."

"Well, if Taymon killed your cousin, that means your cousin is the one that shot Antwan."

"And?" he asked. His whole demeanor had changed. Normally, I knew how to choose my battles, but I couldn't drop this.

"And what, nigga? Taymon was protecting his brother; he did what he had to do. The same way you feel about your little sisters is the way he feels about his little brother. If it had been one of them, you would have killed him, too."

I stood there, waiting for him to respond, still tapping my right foot. He had pissed me off. "From what I was told, Antwan went over there starting shit over that hoe. He was mad my cousin fucked that nasty ass bitch. If he wouldn't have gone, his ass wouldn't have gotten shot."

I was quiet as I listened to him talk. I knew they had gotten in a fight, but I didn't know it was over Maria's ass. Hell, you find out new shit every day. "They were fighting over Maria?" I finally asked.

"That and the fact Antwan's baby belonged to my cousin."

"What the fuck!" I said aloud. Antwan didn't tell me all of that when we were talking about what had happened to him. I mean, not that he had to, but I mean, we were already talking, so why keep it a secret?"

"Now the last part about his son, I'm not sure about that. That's just what I heard. Now don't go around here spreading rumors and shit. You know I don't like a messy ass shit. I ain't a bitch ass nigga."

"When have you ever known me to pull a hoe move like that? All those damn pillow talks we have had. If I were bitter, I would have been blown your damn spot up. You know I know some shit, too."

He got quiet because he knew I was telling the truth. Chingy had done some shit, and I had never told a soul about it. When I say he had done some shit, I mean jail time, people would kill him type of shit. I didn't fall out with people and start telling their business, though.

I knew plenty of niggas fucked up to this day behind a bitter ass woman. She got mad at her nigga and told some shit she didn't have any business telling. Then, after she had calmed down, she regretted the shit. It was too late then, though.

"Nah, but I'm saying, though."

"Chingy, you ain't saying shit. As a matter of fact, I'm still waiting on your ass to speak. You mad at that nigga for damn what? That's how the game go. You either kill or be killed. I don't know nan nigga that's gonna let another nigga kill them, including your ass."

"Are you done or are you fucking done?" he asked, shooting daggers at my ass like I was supposed to be scared or something.

"Yeah, I'm fucking done, and I do mean done. Don't bring your ass by my house anymore and don't call my damn phone."

"I know all this ain't behind that bitch ass nigga."

Now it was my turn to shoot daggers at his ass. "Nigga, you just don't have a clue, do you? Before Antwan even brought his ass over here, I told you I was done. Did you forget about that? Maybe I need to tell your ass in Spanish because you don't seem to comprehend the English version. Ya no te estoy jodiendo (I ain't fucking with you no more)." I didn't even check my mailbox. I walked back in my house and slammed the damn door.

* * *

NEVAEH

A Week Later

It was an optional teacher workday today, and I opted to stay my ass home. I was waiting on Taymon to pull up and get me. Today was our first doctor's appointment. I was nervous but excited at the same time. I told him I could just meet him there, but he insisted on us going together.

"Hello?" I answered the phone for Taymon. "You better be on your way. I gotta be there in thirty minutes, Taymon. If you ain't, I'm gonna take myself. I was planning on doing that, anyway."

"Girl, hush, and come on out the door. I'm outside." I pressed the end button and walked out the door. As he stated, he was sitting there, waiting for me. "You always got something to say, girl."

"Shoot, I just didn't want to be late and miss my appointment. You know they only give you like a fifteen-minute grace period, then they try to make you reschedule."

"I wouldn't miss this appointment for nothing in this world. I got you, but most importantly, I got y'all." He grabbed my hand and kissed it while he continued to drive. I didn't say anything else for the rest of the ride. I grabbed his phone and put it on Pandora.

I started crying when New Edition started blasting through his radio. *Still in love. Still in love baby. Listen. Oh, what can I do girl? So much in love girl, but your friends got you thinking and it's affecting you. What can I do girl? So, in love girl. And I don't know what to do, cause I don't want to lose you. No, what would I do without your love? Baby its heaven sent from above. So, you don't believe what your friends tell you 'bout me.*

I was crying because he started singing the song to me. As he was driving, he would glance at me, then back at the road. My emotions were all over the place. I knew he was a good man, I just couldn't get past the fact he was Patrice's ex-boyfriend. Even though I knew we were about to bring a baby into this world. I had every right to talk to this man because I was stuck with him for life, whether I wanted to be or not. She was going to have to get over it, eventually.

I mean, right now, I didn't care if she did or didn't. Our friendship was over, if you wanted to even call it that. If we were really friends, she would have heard me out, and she would have never put her hands on me in the first place.

A part of me believed she'd been wanting to do that, she just never had a reason to until then. Even now, she still didn't have a reason to, but I was going to give her that. "What you thinking about?" Antwan asked as he turned the music down. The song had just ended.

"We about to be somebody's parents, and whether I want to or not, we are tied together for life. Patrice is not gonna like it, but I don't give a damn anymore. I don't know how these family functions and church functions gonna work out, though."

He smiled as he squeezed my hand. I still didn't tell him we were going to be together, but oh well. We pulled up to the doctor's office and he got out to open my door. I laughed at his antics. "What's so funny?" he asked.

"You didn't open my door when I first got in here."

"That's because your ass always be talking shit. Like now, I can't even do nothing nice for you." He playfully mushed me in the back of my head as I got out of the car.

"You better gone head now," I told him while I laughed.

"What you gone do?"

"Nothing. I ain't gonna do nothing."

"Hello, welcome to Mecklenburg OB. Who are you here to see today?" the receptionist asked us as soon as we walked through the door.

"Um, hello, I am here to see Dr. Walls. I am a new patient."

"Here." She handed me an iPad. "Fill out all your information and give your electronic signature." I grabbed it from her hand and went to have a seat.

"This your first time here?"

"Ain't that what I just said?"

"I mean, I thought maybe you would have already had a, you know, a woman doctor." I fell out laughing.

"Do you mean a gynecologist?"

"Yeah, one of them."

"My primary doctor normally handles my pap smears. He can't handle my pregnancy, though. If I like this new doctor, I might just let them handle everything on that end from here on out." I finished filling out my information and pulled my insurance card from my purse to hand everything back to the lady at the desk.

"Here you go," I told her as I handed her back the iPad. I also handed her my insurance card so she could scan it in their system. I tried to look at her badge so I could catch her name, but it was flipped over.

"The nurse will call you back shortly," she told me as she handed my insurance card back to me. I was so glad I always picked the good health insurance plan. One of my cousins told me when I was still in high school to never slight myself when it comes to my health insurance. She said I never knew what type of curve ball life would throw my way. Look at me now, pregnant.

The other plans were garbage, and I would have been coming out of pocket for a lot of money if I hadn't picked the plan I chose. "You good?" Taymon asked as I sat back down beside him.

"Yeah, of course. I'm just a little nervous."

"That's to be expected. If I had to be honest, I am a little nervous, too." He squeezed my knee.

"Nevaeh Price." The nurse came to the door and called my name. We both stood up to follow her to the back. "I like to see when both parents come to the doctor. That shows the support system the mom has."

"I am going to be at every visit."

"You know you're going to have to fight Amber's ass."

"Well, she better get ready for me then." I laughed at his antics, but I loved it.

"They can both come if you would like them to."

"Well, I already know my mom will not be in the delivery room. She is too scary for that. She will more than likely be in the waiting room, along with my daddy and everyone else."

"Right this way," the nurse said as she led us into the examining room. "Here is a gown. Take your clothes off from the waist down and I will be right back." She closed the door behind herself, and I undressed. A few minutes later, she returned to the room with the ultrasound machine.

"I am going to do an ultrasound on you first, then the doctor will be in to examine you. Now, lay back for me." I did as I was told, and she placed the warm gel on my tummy. As soon as I heard my baby's heartbeat, the tears rolled down my face. The smile that had appeared upon my face was wiped away when I saw the look on her face.

"What's wrong with you?" The tone in my voice alerted Taymon, causing him to look up at the nurse.

"Is everything alright?" he asked her.

"Oh my, let me get the doctor in here."

"Nah, tell us what's going on. We ain't got time for you to be running to get no-motherfucking-body."

"Sir, I will be right back." She rushed out of the room, totally ignoring what he had just said. I looked up at Taymon, wanting him to fix whatever caused her to rush up out of here.

"Try not to think the worst," he told me. A few moments later, even though it seemed like forever, the nurse came back in the room, along with the doctor.

"Hello, Ms. Price and..." She looked at Taymon, waiting for him to tell her his name.

"Just call me Taymon. But forget all of that, what is going on that caused her to run up out of here?"

"Well, we are about to find out." She rolled her sleeves up and sanitized her hands. After she placed gloves on her hands, she picked the ultrasound probe up and moved it around on my stomach. The suspense was killing me.

"Alright, Ms. Price, there seems to be a bit of a surprise here." She had a smile on her face, so now I knew whatever was going on may not have been as bad as I thought.

"Dr. Walls, can you please tell us what is going on? My mind is all over the place."

"I'm so sorry. My nurse got me because she thought she heard three heartbeats. She wanted me to confirm it, which is why she didn't say anything to you. She is right, though; I hear three heartbeats as well."

"What you mean by three heartbeats?" Taymon asked. I was glad he asked because I couldn't seem to find my voice to ask her what in the hell she was talking about. There was no damn way this lady was telling me I was pregnant with three damn kids at the same damn time.

How in the hell was I supposed to carry three babies in me? I was going to be miserable. Taymon was trying to register this shit, too. I could see it on his face, even after he asked the question.

"It means she is carrying triplets." She had the biggest damn smile on her face.

"Well, I'm glad someone is happy, because I damn sure ain't," I told her.

"Yes, I am excited. You're the first patient I have ever had to get pregnant with triplets on her own."

"What you mean, on her own? I think I may have something to do with this as well," Taymon told us, causing us to laugh.

"No, I mean without going through IVF."

"Gotcha," we both said in sync.

"Damn," Taymon said as he kissed me on the lips. "I shot three babies in your ass. I'm a bad man." I was not happy at all about any of this. No way in the world I was or would ever be prepared for three babies at the same damn time.

"It's a set of twins and a single baby," she said as she kept moving the probe. In about another three weeks, you can take a blood test to find out what sex you're having. You're ten weeks pregnant." She printed the pictures and handed them to Taymon. I think she could tell I wasn't happy about it. I hadn't said two words.

She finished her exam and wrote a prescription for prenatal vitamins. Being pregnant with three babies, he told me I was high risk, so I would have to come in more frequently than most women. All that shit went through one ear and out the other one. I knew this was going to have to grow on me, because as of right now, all I wanted to do was crawl up in a ball and cry my eyes out.

"God knew what He was doing," Taymon said to me as soon as we got in the car.

"And what's that?" I looked at him sideways because I was not feeling this at all. I didn't feel like joking.

"I said if me and you didn't work out, I wasn't having any more kids and he gave me three at one time. I don't want a bunch of baby mamas. That shit is for the birds."

"Hmm," was all I said as I laid back in my seat. I didn't say anything else on the way back to my house.

CHAPTER FIVE

The Next Day

My heart was broken in a million pieces as I read Taymon's Facebook status. I knew I shouldn't have even been on his page, but hey, his post was public. The way I see it, when you make public statuses, you want people to see it.

He had an ultrasound picture posted, talking about he put three in her. He tagged Nevaeh in the post, even though she didn't comment. I wasn't too sure about what he meant by saying he put three in her, but the fact remained the same: she was pregnant. I picked my phone up to call my niece.

"Grandma's house better be on fucking fire since you calling me at seven in the damn morning. My first client doesn't come in until eleven and I was planning on sleeping until at least nine-thirty."

"Why didn't you tell me Nevaeh was pregnant? I know you knew." I was hysterical, and I knew you could hear it in my voice.

"Bitch, I know good and damn well you didn't wake me up out of my sleep for this bullshit. How in the hell do you even know she is pregnant any-damn-way?"

"I saw it on Taymon's Facebook. He made a post and tagged her in it, talking about he shot three in her, whatever that means." She laughed, causing me to get even more upset than I already was. "What's so damn funny?" I asked, because maybe I wanted to laugh, too.

"Your ass is funny. Stay off that man's Facebook page, hurting your own damn feelings."

"How am I hurting my own feelings?"

"If you weren't on his page, we wouldn't even be on this phone. Do you want to know why we wouldn't be on this phone? You wouldn't have known she was pregnant."

"So, she is pregnant?"

"Patrice, you saw the shit with your own two eyes. I'm confused why you are calling me. When I answered the phone, you asked me why I didn't tell you. Yes, to confirm what you already know, I guess, she is pregnant. She is pregnant with triplets."

"Why didn't you tell me? I shouldn't have had to find out from Facebook."

"You and that girl ain't friends no more, so it ain't my place to be telling you her business. Like I said, if you weren't lurking, you wouldn't have found out on Facebook. You and Taymon ain't even friends on Facebook. They got three kids on the way. Either way it goes, they are gonna be around each other. Please drop this mess. You messed up your friendship for what?"

"What do you mean, for what? Why does everyone keep saying that? I guess y'all don't see anything wrong with my best friend having a baby by my ex?"

She let out a deep breath before she spoke. "Yes, in a normal world, there is something wrong with it. It goes against the girl code."

"Thank you."

"Nah, hold up, I'm not finished talking yet." I shut up and let her talk. I couldn't believe I shut up, but I did.

"Key word, I said was normally. Nevaeh didn't know he was your ex, so that's when it becomes not a normal situation. Listen, you are my aunt and it ain't about sides; it's about right and wrong. You're wrong in this situation. Nevaeh ain't done nothing to me, so I ain't about to stop talking to her and being around her. That's your loss. You the one couldn't see past this façade you got up. Take some time to see how she feels. She is the only one that didn't have a clue who Taymon was. I talked to Taymon."

"You did?"

"Yes, I did. I told him he was wrong for not telling her when he first discovered who she was. Either way, the damage was already done, but we could have avoided this. Then again, I don't know. You still would have blamed Nevaeh. Can I ask you something?"

"I mean, either way it goes, you're gonna ask me, anyway."

"Yeah, you're right. Why are you so mad at Nevaeh, but you ain't mad at Taymon at all? He's the one you should be mad at. You still trying to get back with him after you know he is in love with that girl. If you ask me, you're the one that's shiesty."

"How am I the one being shiesty? I had him first."

"Did she know you had him first? I'm gonna answer the question for you, because you're not gonna tell the truth. No, she didn't know, but you know now that she is with him. You're going behind her back and you know she was with him. Girl, I'm about to get off this phone. You going outside. When my real aunt, the one I grew up with, shows up, call me back then. Until she does, I ain't got nothing to say to you. This is pathetic and nerve wrecking. You draining my energy."

She didn't even give me a chance to respond. She hung the phone up in my face. "What's wrong with you?" My mom had walked up, and I hadn't even heard her. She was always up early, fixing my daddy some breakfast.

"Your granddaughter."

"Which one?" She had a smirk on her face because she knew which one. Yes, she had a few granddaughters, but only one was my age. Even though I wasn't in the playing mood, I knew better than to get smart with Carrie Ann Jones. Baby, she would smack the taste out of my mouth.

"What did Kam do?" I told her everything that happened. I needed my mama on my side. I felt as if the entire world was against me right now. I didn't see why they didn't feel as if Nevaeh was wrong.

"So, what are you mad at Kam and Nevaeh for?" my mom asked as she sat on the couch across from me. I blew air from my mouth. She hadn't said anything for twenty minutes. She sat right there and let me vent the entire time. Once I was done, that was all she had to say.

"Ma, did you not hear anything I said?"

"I heard everything you said. I don't think you heard what you said. Now you know I'm not about to sugarcoat nothing for you. You're my daughter and I always got your back, but you're wrong in this situation. If you're gonna be mad at anyone, then you need to be mad at Taymon. Nevaeh was innocent in this whole situation."

"Agh, why does everyone keep saying that?"

"Because she was. Your friendship may never be the same with Nevaeh, but you owe her an apology."

"I'm not apologizing to that girl." My mama looked at me for a moment before she spoke again.

"Now I know I raised you better than that. Just think about what I said. Now I like Nevaeh, been knowing that girl her whole life. I really hate y'all's friendship has come down to this. Do the right thing. If you're going to be mad at her, then be mad at him, too. I never understood y'all young girls."

"What you talking about, Ma?"

"Y'all be mad at the woman, but let the man off scot-free. It wouldn't be me. Let your Daddy had pulled something like that back in the day. I would have gone upside his head so fast."

"So, you mean to tell me you wouldn't have done nothing to the lady?"

"Do something to her for what? I ain't marry her, I married him. He is the one that stepped out on me."

"What if it was Sister Sarah?" Sister Sarah was my mama's best friend. I knew that would get a spark from my mama.

"I would kill both of them. Sarah knows I'm married to your daddy, though. She wouldn't get a pass. Nevaeh didn't know, that's the only reason she gets a pass. If she knew, I would have nothing to say to you."

My mom got up from her seat, leaving me still sitting in my thoughts. I heard her in the kitchen, humming, which meant she had already started cooking breakfast for my daddy. I was glad I had this talk with my mama. I had a lot to think about.

Normally, when my mom said something, I listened to her. That was one person, without a shadow of a doubt, I knew always wanted what was best for me.

* * *

NEVAEH

It had been two weeks since I found out I was pregnant with triplets. I was slipping more and more into a depression. Everyone around me was happy except me. I mean, I wanted to be happy, but I was still trying to process it all.

Three babies was a lot, especially at one time. Three kids were a lot, period. Now look at me. All I could do was shake my damn head. I looked down at my ringing phone. To my surprise, it was Lamar. He never called me back from when I called him about a month ago, so I was curious about what he wanted now.

"Hello?" I finally answered the phone.

"What's up with you?"

"Not much, just lying around my house. I called you about a month ago and you just now calling me back?"

"I meant to call you back, but it slipped my mind. What's up, though? I'm on the phone now."

"Well, honestly, I'm over it now. Your lil girlfriend, Gia, or whatever she said her name was, called herself stepping to me about you."

"Oh yeah, I heard about that." He laughed a little. "I cursed her ass out for that, too. I told her don't be asking you shit about me."

"Yeah, I told her the same thing. Like I said, I'm over it now. I don't think she will try me ever again."

"So, is it true?"

"Is what true?"

"Are you pregnant?"

"Yes, I'm pregnant."

"That's crazy how we were fucking for two years, and you never once let me go up in you raw. Every time I asked you, you always shut me down. Now this nigga you have only known for six months got you pregnant. Make that make sense, Nevaeh. What is it?"

I took a deep breath before I spoke. "I don't think we were meant to be, Lamar. I mean, it was fun while it lasted. Did I want more from you? Yes, I did. But it never happened. I take responsibility for my part in it because I should have told you. I'm pregnant with not one but three babies. No, I'm not with Taymon, but if it ain't with him, I don't want to be with nobody else."

"So, you don't even be thinking about me?"

"Honestly, I don't be thinking about nobody. I just told you I was pregnant with triplets. Right now, that is the only thing on my mind. We will always be friends, and you will always have a place in my heart."

"You know what, I'm gonna have to respect that. I don't want to because I was feeling you for real. I should have been a man and made you mine. You are too good of a woman to be what we were to each other."

"Thank you, Lamar. That means a lot coming from you. Now find Gia and make her your woman before I gotta kill her."

"I still don't want that girl. She a good woman and all, but when she stepped to you, that killed any chances she had with me."

"Why, though?"

"I don't want a woman that thinks it is cool to be confronting people about me. She gotta trust me and what I say."

"I feel you on that. Well, you take care, Lamar."

"You do the same. Let me know what you're having, and I will buy you a gift."

"Thanks," I told him before I ended the call. Truthfully, I already knew what I was having, I just didn't tell him . Not that I was hiding it, but I just felt like I would disrespect Taymon by accepting a gift from him.

At one point, I was fucking that man. They were both in the streets. Not saying Lamar would, but I didn't even want to give him the opportunity to tell people he bought something for his kids. Taymon was more than capable of providing for his kids.

My twins were girls, and the other one was a boy. So, I was having identical girls. Lord, be with me. Even though everyone was trying to get me to do a gender reveal, I declined. I already knew money wasn't an object because everyone was trying to pay for it.

Now, I wasn't turning down a baby shower. I would rather the money go on that. My baby shower was about to be over the top. That was the only highlight of my pregnancy. My daddy and baby daddy told me not to worry about the cost. They messed up telling me that. Normally, I was a simple person, but baby, this baby shower was already at ten thousand dollars. I was going over the top with my baby shower because I wasn't having any more kids. I got all my kids with one pregnancy. If I had to be real with myself, I didn't want multiple baby daddies, either. I was cool with just one baby daddy. I had a cousin who had three kids and three baby daddies and none of them do anything for their kids.

At least I didn't have to worry about that with Taymon because his mom would kill him. Between her and my mama, I knew these kids were going to be spoiled. They were already trying to take over the planning of my baby shower. As long as they implemented the things I wanted, I didn't care what they did.

I looked down at my swollen feet and they looked like little piglets. My doctor had already told me I was not going to go full term, so she was setting me up for a cesarean. I had no problem with that.

Taymon was starting to grow on me. I mean, yes, he had lied to me, or should I say, he kept a secret from me, but overall, he was a good man. I was really thinking about giving in before he said fuck it and moved on. I mean, people make mistakes every day, including me, and I had already forgiven him.

My face lit up when I saw Taymon was calling my phone. He checked on me all day, every day, asking me if I was good and if I needed anything. "Hello?"

"How are you and my babies doing?"

"We over here managing. My feet are swollen."

"Do you want me to come and rub them for you?"

"Sure, I would like that."

"Let me drop something off right quick and I'm on my way. Are you hungry?"

"I'm always hungry. Shit, thanks to you, I'm eating for four people."

"Yeah, I think I gotta agree with you on that one. What do you got a taste for?"

"Do you feel like stopping by Jake's?"

"Do I feel like it? No. I asked you, though, so I will. Just call it in for me and I will stop by there and get it."

"Alright, bet." I hung the phone up and dialed Jakes. I already knew what I wanted.

"Thank you for calling Jakes. How may I help you?"

"I would like to place an order, please."

"Do you know what you want?"

"Yeah, can I get the Monae special?" The Monae special was ten wings, chili cheese fries, along with a drink. Pacino, the owner, who was also her husband, named it after her. He said she ate it so much when she was pregnant with their first child, he started calling it that. Next thing he knew, he had added it to the menu.

"Will that be all for you?"

"Yes..." I drug it out because I wasn't sure if that was all I wanted. I forgot to ask Taymon if he wanted me to order him something as well. "Could you hold on for a second? I want to check and see if my baby daddy wants something to eat as well."

"Sure," she said as I clicked over to call him back.

"Yo," he answered the phone, sounding all sexy like. His voice kind of remind me of singer Michael McCary from that group Boyz II Men. My mom used to listen to them all the time when I was younger, that's how I know who they are.

"I got the girl from Jakes on the other line. Did you want me to order you something?"

"What did you order?"

"The Monae special."

"Yeah, get me one, too."

"What do you want to drink?"

"A fruit punch."

"Alright." I clicked back over. "Can you add another Monae special with a fruit punch? As a matter of fact, make that two fruit punches. Can you also add ranch and blue cheese?"

"I sure can. Will that be all?"

"Yes, for real this time."

"Can I have a name for your order, please?"

"Nevaeh."

"Oh, hey, Nevaeh. This is Gia."

I blew air from my lungs because now I didn't even want the food anymore. I didn't know why this damn girl thought we were friends or something, the way she kept saying my name like she knew me. I was not about to eat anything she had something to do with.

"You know what, cancel my order."

"I wouldn't do anything to your food, Nevaeh. I am not even like that. I don't even fix the food, I work at the desk."

"Is Monae there?" I asked because I really wanted those wings.

"Yes, she is here. Would you like to speak with her?"

"Yes, I would."

"Hold on, let me get her for you." Monae was a little older than me, but we were from the same hood. We both grew up in Dalton Village. They tore Dalton Village down, though. My mom ended up finishing school and getting a better job that allowed her to buy a house. It worked out perfectly because the neighborhood got torn down around the same time. I was always the little girl from around the way. I knew her husband as well.

"Hello?" Monae answered after holding about five minutes.

"Hey, girl, this is Nevaeh."

"Hey, what's up with you? Word on the streets is you are having triplets."

"Yes, girl, I am so overwhelmed."

"Well, congratulations are in order. Keep me posted on the baby shower. You know I will be there, and I am bringing Pacino, too. What can I help you with today, though? Gia said you wanted to speak with me."

"Yes, and I ain't trying to get her in trouble because she hasn't done anything to me, per se. We had a little run-in about a month back, and I just wanted to make sure she was not touching my food."

"Oh, girl, you never have to worry about that here. I got you. I understand your concern, though. I wouldn't want anyone I had words with fixing my food, either. She only works at the front desk, though. Not sure what y'all altercation was about, and I am not asking, but she ain't like that. But again, people never seem to surprise me. I am about to put your order in myself. Did you need anything else from me?"

"No, I am good. Taymon is coming to pick up the food, though."

"That's cool, you take care now. Don't forget, I want an invitation to the baby shower."

"You know I got you. I would be honored to have you and Pacino at my shower. You have always been good to me. I admire your strength, for real. I will let you get back to doing whatever you were doing. Have a good rest of your day."

"You do the same." We hung the phone up.

I was watching *The Black Hamptons* by Carl Weber when my phone rang. I knew it was Taymon. I didn't even bother to answer it, I just went to open the door. "Delivery for..." was all I remembered.

* * *

"What are you doing? Why did you snatch me? Can't you see I am pregnant?" I asked question after question, not even giving him the opportunity to respond to the first question. The crazy part was, I knew who had grabbed me.

Yes, he had a mask on and everything, but you couldn't hide your demeanor. I didn't even care how he tried to disguise his voice, I still knew it was him. I didn't want to let on that I knew who he was, though. I didn't want him to kill me.

All this time, I was depressed about having triplets, but not now. Now I was in survival mode. I knew I had to protect my kids. I hated that I didn't look at my phone and answer it. I just assumed it was Taymon. That was the biggest mistake of my life.

The thing was, what did I do to this person? I didn't even know we had bad blood until now. "Bitch, this ain't got shit to do with you."

"Well, if it doesn't have anything to do with me, why did you snatch me?"

"Yo' nigga know what's up." Now I was more confused than ever.

"I don't have a nigga."

"Well, your baby daddy. Quit trying to be so damn smart before I knock all your teeth out of your mouth." I knew how to pick my battles, so I was quiet. I didn't know what in the world Taymon had done, but I knew I was not going out without a fight.

As soon as I got a chance, I was getting away from here. He better pray I didn't get the opportunity. Taymon nor my daddy were going to get a chance to do anything to him because I was going to kill this bastard myself with my bare hands.

He had me all the way fucked up. I didn't know why everyone underestimated Nevaeh, but they better learn how to count, trying to count me out.

* * *

TAYMON

Where in the hell is Nevaeh? I asked myself because something wasn't right. I had called her phone to tell her I was on my way, but she never answered the phone. Then when I got here, she was gone, but her phone was lying on her bed. Not to mention, her door was wide open, which was something she would never do.

I ran my hand down my face, my mind racing. Something was wrong, I could feel it in my heart. I picked her phone up, trying to think what her passcode could be. I wanted to look at her cameras and I knew she had the app on her phone.

I typed her due date, but it didn't budge. "Fuck!" I yelled out loud. *Who would know her password?* Kam crossed my mind, but more than likely, it was probably her cousin, Amber. The only damn thing was, I didn't know Amber's number.

I called my brother and prayed he picked up. "Yo," he answered, sounding just like a mini me.

"Call Kam for me."

"What's wrong, bro?" I knew he was asking because he heard the panic in my voice.

"I will explain to you both at the same time. Please call her for me." He didn't ask any more questions, he did exactly what I had asked him to do.

"I didn't think I would hear from you."

"You probably still wouldn't be if my brother didn't want me to call you." I didn't even have time to try to figure out what they had going on. I put it in my mental Rolodex to ask him later what that was all about.

"Kam, I think something has happened to Nevaeh."

"Wayment, what?" they both asked at the same time.

"This some serious shit right here, bro. What the fuck is going on? Why do you think something has happened to her?"

"When I got to her house, her door was wide open, her car was still here, and her phone was lying on her bed."

"Nevaeh would never leave her door wide open," Kam said.

"Yeah, I know that. I need to get in her phone so I can look at her door cam app. Can you give me Amber's number? I'm sure she probably has it."

"I will still call Amber, but I got the code. We all have each other's code just in case something like this happens."

"Good, what is it?"

"It's zero six, two six, ninety-nine."

"What kind of number is that?" I asked while I typed the number in the phone.

"We had a friend get killed when we were younger. That's her birthday."

"I never knew that," I said while I tried the number again because it wasn't working. I repeated the number back to her for confirmation. "Shit, it ain't working."

"Shit, she must have changed it, then."

"Is there any other number you can think of that she may use?"

"This is weird to me because all of us use that number for everything. I don't know. Let me call Amber. I'm gonna conference her in, too." She clicked over.

"What's up, Kam?"

"Are you sitting down? If not, you need to be."

"Girl, what the hell is going on? You scaring me, and you know I ain't scared of shit."

"Taymon is on the phone, and he thinks something has happened to Nevaeh."

"Something like what? Where you at, Taymon? You need to start damn talking." I told her what I discovered. "I'm about to call her parents and we're on the way to you. If the code Kam gave you ain't working, I'm with her; I don't know what it could be."

"I'm on my way, too, bro."

"Yeah, I'm about to be on my way as well," Kam chimed in. I got off the phone with them and paced the floor. Whoever did this shit better count their motherfucking days. She was pregnant with my kids, too.

I see motherfuckers wanted to go to war. Behind Nevaeh and my kids, I would turn this bitch into Afghanistan. I tried her phone again, but I stopped because I didn't want to lock it up.

My brother was the first one to the house, and her daddy pulled up right behind him. Her daddy hopped out of the car so fast. "Taymon, please tell me Amber is over-exaggerating and my daughter ain't missing."

"I wish this was one of those times Amber was cutting up, but she ain't." Everyone knew Amber was a clown in real life. She was always on joke time.

"What do you know?"

"I don't know anything. I been trying to get in her phone so I can pull the footage from her cameras. I know her cameras had to have caught something." I noticed my brother hadn't said two words since he got out of his car. He just listened to our conversation.

"Are you beefing with anyone?"

"No, are you?" He gave me a stern look. I meant what I said, but I didn't mean for it to come out like that. I mean, he may not be in the streets now, but he was in the streets. Just because he retired didn't mean other people did, too.

"What's going on with my baby?" Her mom burst through the door all hysterical. Not saying she wasn't supposed to, but still. I remember Nevaeh saying how her mom was always extra. I had only met her a few times, but of course, it was under normal circumstances.

"Tell me something, Taymon. My niece called and said you was the last person to see her."

"No—" Before I could finish my sentence, Amber burst through the door.

"Auntie, I swear you will mix a story up. I did not say that man was the last one to see her. He was on his way to see her. He was bringing her food. That is why he was here. Other than that, we all know Nevaeh ain't fucking with this nigga."

I was about to check her for her comment, but I decided against it. Like I said, we all knew how Amber and her mouth was. I knew we could be in here arguing for the rest of the night, and that wasn't going to help us find Nevaeh.

She was probably playing, but I didn't feel like playing. "I'm just messing with you, Taymon. Don't get your panties all in a bunch," she said before I could even put more thought into it. "I actually like you for my cousin."

"Same thing I said," Kam said as she walked in the door. If it had been a different situation, I would be laughing. It was crazy how everyone was walking in, picking up on conversations.

"Does anyone know what her password could be?" I didn't give a damn who liked what; I needed her back here with me. As far as I was concerned, all that shit they were talking about was irrelevant.

"Try my birthday!" her daddy yelled.

"What's your birthday?" He gave it to me, and I punched it in the phone. Just like I figured, that didn't work, either. "I ain't trying no more. I don't want to lock her phone up. Shit, we all know how iPhones are."

About an hour later, my phone rang, and it was from an unknown number. Something told me this call was about to be some bullshit. "Yo," I answered with a pause.

"I got your bitch." I threw the phone on speaker.

"Who the fuck is this?"

"Nigga, don't worry about who this is. Just know I got your bitch."

Bad as I wanted to act bad, right now, I knew I couldn't. He held the fate of Nevaeh's life in the palm of his hands.

"That voice sounds so familiar, I just can't place it right now." Kam whispered so the so-called kidnapper wouldn't know he had an audience. "Keep him talking while I record him."

"What do you want from me?" Kam held her phone up and started recording our conversation.

"I want your life, nigga. You took something from me that can't be replaced."

"What exactly did I take from you?"

"I am the one doing all the talking right now. I want a life for a life." It didn't take a rocket science to figure out it had to have been over Malik. Little did the dude on the other end of the phone know, that was my first body. Now Antwan, on the other hand, had caught plenty of bodies. We were two totally different people. It was obvious I would pull the trigger, but Antwan was the craziest one out of the two of us. I was the brain whereas he was the hothead. We couldn't have two hotheads because we would make no money.

I know they say you should feel some type of way when you catch your first body, but I didn't. It could be because I was protecting my little brother. There was no way in hell I could have gone home and looked my parents in the face, knowing I hadn't tried to save my little brother.

All I had to do was figure out who Malik's people were, and I should have Nevaeh home in no time. "A life for a life, huh?"

"That's what I just said, nigga. I want your head on a mother-fucking platter."

"So, where you want to meet at?"

"Shit, you tell me."

"This is your plan. You're supposed to be calling all the shots."

"I will call you back with a location." I could tell I had hit a nerve with that statement. He hung the phone up in my ear.

"I know that damn voice," Kam said again once we got off the phone. Only this time, she voiced it to everyone in the room.

"Who do you think it is?"

"I got an eerie feeling. I am so serious, I know that voice, I just can't pinpoint it right now. Trust me, I am going to get to the bottom of this once I get by myself and can really analyze this."

"Y'all don't think Patrice would stoop this low, do you?" Nevaeh's mom asked.

I was the first to speak. I watched how Kam got agitated after hearing her say that, but I could understand her reason for asking. She was agitated with what she said, but she didn't speak on it.

"Nah, I don't see Patrice stooping that low. She may be capable of a lot of things, but kidnapping ain't one of them. She does a lot of petty shit, that nobody in here would approve of. At the end of the day, though, she doesn't want anything like that to happen to Nevaeh."

"I ain't her best friend right now, either, Auntie, but I am going to have to agree with Taymon."

"Well, all right, if y'all say so."

"Come, Ms. Price, you been knowing Patrice all her life. I can't believe you even asked that question."

"Kam, I have known a lot of killers and drug dealers all of their lives. What is that supposed to mean? My own child did stuff I never would have thought she would do, so I really don't understand why you said that." There was a moment of silence.

"Alright with all of this unnecessary talking. None of what y'all is saying is going to bring my daughter home. If you ain't serious about helping, then you can leave." After Mr. Price said what he had to say, all the side bar conversations ceased.

* * *

KAM

It had been three days since Nevaeh had been officially missing. Nobody—well, Taymon and her daddy—didn't want the police involved. I guess since they were street niggas, they wanted to keep it in the streets. I mean, I wasn't a huge fan of the police myself, but I didn't agree with their decision. I felt like they should have been involved.

Taymon and Antwan had Belem combing the streets, along with her daddy, day in and day out. Everyone knew she was missing, except the damn police. Being that she was pregnant, I felt like the police should have been called. I was worried about her. Even though Patrice was on her bullshit, I still called and told her about what was going on with Nevaeh.

She was concerned as well. I mean, you couldn't just stop loving a person because you were mad at them. I had played that video repeatedly. As a matter of fact, I had just finished listening to it again. Even though they used a machine to disguise their voice, there were a few things they said that stood out.

"*I want your head on a motherfucking platter.*" I replayed that part. My heart broke in two at the thought of who could have possibly made that phone call. I picked my phone up to call Chingy.

"What the hell do you want?" was how he answered the phone. I pulled the phone away from my ear to look at who I had called. I had to make sure I had called the right person. Lamar had me fucked up. He had never talked to me like that before.

"Excuse you," I said, matching his tone. "What the hell is wrong with you?"

"Ain't nothing wrong with me. What's wrong with you? You the one told me you weren't fucking with me no more, now you calling a nigga? So, yeah, what the fuck do you want?"

"You know what, never mind. I don't want shit. I hate I even called your motherfucking ass." I didn't want shit, for real, I was just trying to feel his temperature. I hung the phone up on his ass. Fuck that nigga, and if what I thought was right, I prayed Taymon murk nigga. As a matter of fact, I forgot to tell Antwan how greasy that nigga was talking.

Not that I was trying to be messy, I just didn't want Antwan to get hurt. Chingy had a secret beef with him he knew nothing about. Yes, I knew Antwan could hold his own, but I also knew a person couldn't protect themselves if they didn't know what was coming.

"Yo," he answered the phone, sounding just like his damn big brother.

"I got something to tell you."

"Meet me at your girl's house. Amber said she may have a way to help us find Nevaeh."

"Alright, bet. I will be on my way over there then." I hung up with him and threw on some tights and a Nike pull over. I slipped a pair of socks on along with my Crocs. I grabbed my keys along with my purse and walked to my garage. Once inside my car, I pulled off.

When I pulled up to Nevaeh's house, there were quite a few cars already outside. I recognized a few of them, but there was one that stood out. I wondered who it was, but I knew I was soon to find out.

I walked into the living room, and there was a white man standing there. Not just any man, but the same detective from when Kayla was in the hospital. I guess they called the police after all.

"I'm glad y'all finally listened to me."

"What do you mean, we finally listened to you?" Antwan asked. "What did we listen to you about?"

I did a head nod in the detective's direction. "Oh, that's Amber's new boo," he said with a chuckle. I knew he found that shit funny as hell. Amber, with a white boy? I never thought I would see the day.

"Her new boo?" I asked with a raise of an eyebrow. "When in the hell did this happen? I mean, did y'all exchange numbers at the hospital or some shit? I ain't ever think I would see you with a white boy. No offense, dude, but I'm just saying."

"None taking. She told me all of her friends were very outspoken."

"She's probably over-exaggerating because that's what she does. For real, though, what did I miss? When did this happen?"

"Girl, mind your damn business."

"And ain't." I stuck my tongue out at her.

"We already knew each other when all that stuff went on at the hospital. We were dating then." The detective spoke up. I still didn't know his damn name.

"You sneaky bitch," I told her while laughing. "Well, anyway, what is he doing here if y'all didn't want the police involved? He is still the damn police at the end of the day. I pray y'all can trust his ass."

"We trust Amber," Mr. Price spoke up.

"We are good. I already told him what's going on. Him being on the police force gives us connections. We need to give him Nevaeh's phone, so he can take it in. We are sure someone at the station can unlock it for us."

Just as she finished talking, someone rang the doorbell. "I will get it," I told them. There was an older Black lady, standing on the porch. By her demeanor, you could tell she was older, not by her looks. She didn't look a day over forty.

She had a streak of blonde across the front of her hair. The front of her hair was in a swoop, while the rest of her hair was in loose curls. She stood about five foot seven and she had some hips on her. I could tell she used to turn heads back in her day.

"How can I help you?"

"I stay across the street." Now that she'd that, I remembered seeing her a few times when I was over at the house.

"Um, Nevaeh is not here."

"Yes, I kind of figured that. I haven't seen her in a few days, actually, but that ain't why I am here. I was supposed to have a package delivered the other day, but it never came." I blew air from my mouth. Now this damn old lady was about to get on my nerves.

I had just told her Nevaeh wasn't here. She even agreed with me, so why was she standing on the porch, talking about a damn package? She knows good and damn well if Nevaeh hadn't been here, then she didn't know anything about her package.

"Well, like I said, and you agreed, Nevaeh ain't here and ain't been here, so I'm sure she ain't seen your package."

"I'm well aware of that," she said as I was about to shut the door in her face.

"Well, I'm confused why you're here then."

"Kam, who at the door?" Taymon had walked to the door by this time to see what was going on. I knew his mind was all over the place when I didn't return right away.

"Like I was telling this young lady, I stay across the street. When my package said delivered, but never showed up, I pulled my cameras."

"You did?" we both said as realization kicked in that this lady may be on to something."

"Yes, I did. From the looks on you guys' faces, I assume you both know why I'm here. I saw some very disturbing footage and I was going to call the police, but I decided against it. I saw too many cars over here, so I came here first."

"Ma'am, thank you so much," I told her. "Can we view it?"

"Of course, you can. Can I have your email and I will send you the link to view it? I'm sure you would want to have your own copy so you can view it at your leisure." She pulled out her cell phone, and I rattled off my email address.

"Thank you again," I told her as she walked off the porch.

"No problem." She waved and headed across the street.

"We might not need your white boy," I announced as I walked back into the living room.

"And why not?" Amber wanted to know.

"That was Nevaeh's neighbor."

"Okay, and what did she want?"

"She actually just emailed me the footage from her camera."

"Well, what in the hell are you waiting for to play it?" Mr. Price snatched my phone from my hand. I didn't get upset, though, because I knew he was upset. Everyone who knew him, knew he didn't play about his girls.

"I gotta pull it up, Mr. Price." He handed me my phone back so I could do just that.

"Nah, cast it to her television," her sister Kayla said.

"Yeah, good thinking," I told her. We needed it to be blown up. I walked over towards her television, which was more for show than anything. My reason for saying that was because it may be the second or third time it had ever been on.

I was with her when she bought it. She was so excited, and we both laughed when I asked her what she was going to do with an eighty-inch television. She told me she was going to put it in her living room.

I remembered asking her for what because she didn't even like people in her living room. She stuck her tongue out at me and told me so it would still look good in there. I prayed my friend was all right. I didn't know how I would take losing another friend.

We were sixteen when we lost our friend, Apryl. She was dating an older man she never even told us about. When I say older, I mean married with kids older. He lied and told her he was twenty-one. I had to admit, though; he looked younger. I would have never thought he was damn near thirty if the news wouldn't have given his age up.

The same time she found out she was pregnant was the same time she found out he had a wife and three children already. When we found out about the man, she was pregnant and didn't have a choice but to tell her best friends she was pregnant because she was scared.

We were all raised in the same church, but her mom was worse than ours religion-wise. I mean, we grew up holy, skirt wearing and all. In high school, our parents had eased up some. By easing up, I mean, they would let us do things normal high school students did, like going to football games and movies, stuff like that. Not her mama, though.

She couldn't go anywhere, so of course, she snuck and did it. That was the reason she told us she was pregnant; she knew her mom was going to disown her. Not literally, but yes. there were definitely going to be some problems.

She wanted us to go with her to let the dude know, and to also support her when she told her mom. We actually found out about the dude's wife and kids together. When she told him she was pregnant, he told her about them.

He wanted her to get an abortion because he didn't want his wife to find out he had been having an affair. Not only had he been having an affair, but with a teenager at that. We didn't believe in abortions, and neither did her mom. Upset and all, her mom would have made her keep her baby.

About a week later, he called her to meet with him. He told her he wanted to talk about the situation. Unbeknownst to him, she was on the phone with Nevaeh and told her she was waiting for him. Once he arrived, she hung up with her, or so she thought.

He was relying on her keeping him from us, he didn't even think the plan through. Nevaeh was the last one to talk to her, so she took it the hardest. She told the police she was with him because she heard her talking to him. Nevaeh said once the conversation got heated, she recorded the conversation.

She heard him kill our friend. They gave that bastard life without parole. That's what he gets, and I prayed he rotted in hell for taking her life at such a youthful age. She didn't deserve that. He was the one who knew he was married, not her.

"Kam." Antwan called my name, snapping me from thoughts. I was so caught up in them, I had forgotten the task at hand. Once I had my phone connected to the television, I hit play. We couldn't see the guy's face from the camera. His back was turned.

I didn't need to see his face, though. I already knew who it was. I had been sleeping with this man for two years. I knew the way he walked and talked. That was why I was trying to call him over to my house earlier.

"That's Chingy!" I blurted, causing everyone to turn my way.

"Are you sure?" Antwan asked.

"Yes, I am sure. I don't know why he would grab Nevaeh, though. That is what I had to tell you, too, Antwan. Do you remember the day at my house when y'all had a few words?"

"Yeah, I remember," he said as his brother looked at us, all confused. I assumed he never told Taymon about what happened at my house. Here I go with my big ass mouth again.

"Well, he was talking greasy after you left."

"What did he say?"

"He was talking about how your brother killed his cousin. I was like he doesn't have but one brother, and he was like he already knew that."

"Now it all makes sense," Taymon finally spoke up. "When we were on the phone a few days ago, he said I took something from him and how he wanted my head on a platter. This is about me killing his cousin, Malik."

"Yeah, he also told me if Antwan wouldn't have come over there starting shit about Maria, none of this would have happened."

"I wasn't fighting his ass over no damn Maria. Fuck that bitch. I was fighting him for my son. I told him to stay away from my son. He was with him and Maria the day he got hit by that car. That's neither here nor there, though. Where does that nigga stay so we can get my sister-in-law back?"

"Well, we got to come up with a plan," Mr. Price said.

CHAPTER SIX

NEVAEH

I kind of lost track of how many days this nigga had me captive against my will. I was tired and hungry. He was barely feeding me, like I wasn't eating for four damn people. He was only feeding me once a day, and sometimes, not at all.

I had been wrecking my brain, trying to figure out what I had ever done to his ass. As far as I was concerned, I had never even rolled my eyes at him. Whatever he had going on with Kam or Taymon, I wished he would have just left me out of it. The other day, I thought I heard him on the phone with Taymon, but I hadn't heard anything else since then.

I smelled because I hadn't had a bath in days. My hair was sweated out and I only had one eyelash on because the other one fell off yesterday. It looked like a little spider sitting on the floor. This house he had me in seemed as if it had been here forever.

My body shivered as a gust of wind blew through the room. It didn't help any that my body was already soaking wet. I knew I was more than likely going to end up being sick. Cobwebs were in every corner of the room. A big web hung from the ceiling and the window had a crack going straight down the middle. The paint on the walls was peeling and I wondered how long it had been since someone had actually stayed here.

Chingy had been gone all day. He doesn't really be here like that. He comes in and peeks at me and gives me food. The last time he came, I wanted to yell out so badly, *Chingy, I know it's you*, but I decided against it.

Like I said before, I didn't want to give him a reason to kill me. I heard the door squeaking, so I knew it was him coming. I prayed he brought me something to eat because I was more than hungry; I was starving.

My eyes lit up when I saw a McDonald's bag in his hand. "Bitch, this ain't for you," he told me. He started pulling the food from the bag.

"I know you see I am pregnant. How can you be so heartless? I ain't done nothing to you." I wanted to cry, but I refused to let him see one tear fall from my eyes. He walked over and pushed some fries into my mouth. I guess what I said kind of struck a nerve.

He untied one of my hands. He had me tied with zip ties, so they were hard to break free. "Now, if you try anything funny, you won't be getting anything to eat tomorrow. I ain't your baby daddy. It doesn't matter to me whether you eat or not." I didn't say anything else, just grabbed the fries from him and stuffed them into my mouth. I ate those fries like it was my last meal because, in reality, it could have been.

I had to figure out a way to escape. This shit was for the birds. I honestly didn't know why he thought he was doing an excellent job at disguising himself. He had on one of those clear masks like the girls had on in the movie *Set it Off*. To me, all a mask does was smash your face in. He was also using a voice box to disguise his voice, which wasn't working, either.

"Thank you for the fries," I told him. I prayed being nice to him would get me some food tomorrow. He nodded without responding to what I had just said. In a sense, I didn't care either way.

It was really at that moment, I realized all the anger I had towards

Taymon was petty. Life was too short to let life pass you by. Then we had Patrice. I really didn't think I could forgive her for treating me the way she had since all of this shit went down. I wasn't raised that way, though.

If I could forgive Taymon, then I definitely could forgive her. If I didn't forgive her, then I was no better than she was. Although things would never be the same between us, I missed the closeness we once shared. I still felt like she had some growing bitterness towards me, though.

I mean, why else would she act like that? Even if I knew about her and Taymon, she didn't even like that nigga like that. I thought back over the years, trying to remember if I ever saw any signs and I couldn't come up with one.

Now I was sitting here, looking at this nigga with disgust. I blew out a noisy breath as my eyes scanned the room, looking for an escape route. I knew my blood pressure was through the roof, and I had more than me to think about right now. I was responsible for three other people who couldn't protect themselves.

Lord, if You're punishing me for not being grateful for my kids, I apologize. Just help me get out of this mess, please, and I won't ever be ungrateful again. That was the prayer I sent up. I knew it had been a few months since I went to church, but I also knew God didn't forget about His child.

"You finished yet?" he asked as I offered a fake smile. He walked back to tie my hand back up when his phone rang. "What do this bitch want now?" he said, more to himself than to me. When he answered the phone, he didn't use the voice box, which gave me more confirmation that it was indeed Chingy. Not that I didn't already think that, but he just made it clearer.

"I'm still trying to figure out what you want. I mean, this the second time you have called me since you told me you weren't fucking with a nigga no more." From the sound of his conversation, I could tell he was talking to Kam. That made me smile because I knew my friend. If she was calling him, that meant she was on his ass.

I needed her to keep him talking because I was looking for something, anything to cut this zip tie on my left wrist. I was glad he never got the chance to put the other one on. My eyes landed on his bag he had from McDonald's. His plastic silverware was hanging out of the bag.

Yes, the knife was plastic, but hell, I had to try. I stretched my leg out so I could try to reach it, and that was when he walked back in the room. I was slipping. I hadn't even heard his conversation end. "Bitch, what the fuck are you doing?"

He walked in and stomped on my leg, causing a jolt of pain to shoot through my body. If I weren't already lying down, he would have brought me to my knees with that kick. I was trying to scoot back into the position I was in when he kicked me in my ass.

"Bitch, thanks to your dumb ass friend, I know you figured out who I am by now. Since she called, now I gotta kill you. I can't leave any witnesses. I want your bitch ass nigga to watch you suffer, though, so I'm gonna wait on him before I kill your ass."

"Honestly," I spoke, all choked up because I was in so much pain. "I already knew who you were. I knew the moment you brought me here. "Since he already knew I knew and he was gonna kill me anyway, I felt like, what the hell? He must be going to shoot me because if he didn't, he was in for a fight.

"Chingy, I ain't ever done shit to you. Why did you snatch me up?"

"Your bitch ass nigga killed my cousin. Now I'm gonna kill you."

"Nigga, you ain't gonna kill nothing. Shit, you can't even kill time." I knew that nigga was mad because I was trying his manhood, but I didn't give two fucks. His lips were pressed tightly together as if he were thinking of a comeback.

Bam! My head hit the wall. He kicked me in my face and blood ran down my face. I knew my lip was busted and my nose was probably broken as well. "Bitch, shut the fuck up, talking to me all sideways. You don't fucking know me like that. As a matter of fact, I wonder what that pregnant pussy feels like."

Suddenly, I heard my heart beating outside of my chest. I was just talking big boy shit a few moments ago, but now I was hushed mouth. *Lord, please don't let this man rape me.* "No, Chingy, that ain't what you want to do. I ain't never known for you to just take sex from a woman."

"Bitch, didn't I tell you to shut the fuck up? Don't talk unless I tell you to." He walked over and grabbed my leg and I started kicking him in his face, trying to fight him off me. I still had one hand zip tied while I swung with my free hand.

I stunk, so I didn't understand why he would even want to hunch on me with me smelling so bad. This couldn't be my life right now. My head was pounding from being kicked in the head. Not to mention, my back and legs. I hadn't even felt my babies move all day.

I couldn't have been that bad of a person for all of this to transpire in my life. I needed a miracle right now, so I sent up a silent prayer. Not for me, but for my kids.

* * *

PATRICE

Contrary to popular belief, I love Nevaeh. My mom and my niece had been keeping me updated on what was going on with her. Like I said, we had all been tight since we were babies. Our mamas had been friends long before we were even thought of.

It could have been me in her situation if I were still with Taymon. I hate it was her, but at the same time, I thank God for small favors. I had been praying for her day in and day out. The last conversation I had with my mama about our friendship had been weighing heavy on my mind. It was hard for me to admit when I was wrong.

I knew it wasn't a good trait to have, but at least I was honest enough to admit it. I was wrong for how I handled our situation. I acted out of anger and not hurt. I wasn't hurt when I found out her new man was Taymon. I had no reason to be hurt. I honestly didn't give two fucks about Taymon when I was with him. Yeah, I liked what he could do for me, but that was about all. I had to admit that to myself.

He only knows about the one time I cheated, but honestly, I was cheating on him just about the whole time. I lost respect for him when he made me get that abortion. I told him how I felt about abortions, and he didn't give two fucks. Nobody even knew I had one because we didn't believe in them.

To this day, I was still dealing with that. It still weighed heavily on my mind and my heart. When I saw him post those ultrasound pictures on Facebook, it was like an instant rage shot through my body. Like what made her better than me? He was so happy about her pregnancy, but he was angry when I told him I was pregnant.

I had to be honest with myself about a lot of shit. I felt as if Nevaeh was always winning. She went off to college after we graduated high school, leaving me here. Even Amber went to school to be a medical assistant, but she didn't count. To me, since she was still here in Charlotte, it wasn't that big of a deal.

Nevaeh would always come home with one of her college friends, and I would feel left out. She never made me feel left out, though; all of that was on me. She would even invite me up to her campus on the weekends, and homecoming was always a blast.

I didn't know why or when I felt like the two of us were in competition. She always got good grades in school because becoming a teacher was all she talked about. I, on the other hand, only did enough in school to get by.

When I met Taymon, it was an achievement to me. I mean, yes, I should have had bigger dreams, but I had a man taking care of me. I knew Nevaeh was going to have to work to get the things she wanted in life, and I didn't have to do any of that.

I was staying in a nice house, driving a decent car. My man did all that for me, so I felt like I had one up on her. Everything I was trying to achieve with this man, here she comes like a thief in the night and snatched his heart.

I wasn't saying Taymon never loved me because I was sure he did, he just didn't love me like he loved her. It was a proven fact. It was written all over his face. My mom was right. Not just my mom, but my niece, along with other people. I had no reason to be mad at Nevaeh. Now, I had possibly lost a good friend.

These hoes I'd been hanging with lately weren't loyal worth a damn. They all talked about each other, then were all up in each other's faces. I wasn't used to that shit. My girls didn't do that. If Nevaeh made it up out of this mess, I was going to apologize to her.

Not to mention, that ass whooping she gave me at Jake's. I was more embarrassed than anything. That was my first loss, and at first, I wanted to get my lick back, but for what? I'd started this shit, so I was just going to leave well enough alone.

"Patrice." I looked over at my daddy as he called my name. It wasn't the fact he was calling my name; it was how he called my name that alarmed me. It was like something was wrong, and my heartbeat immediately sped up.

The first thought that went through my mind was Nevaeh. "What's up, Daddy?" I was almost too afraid to ask.

"We need to talk." Now my antennas went up. What in the world did we need to talk about? "I don't know where I went wrong with you. Well, I do, but I pray it ain't too late for change."

"What are you talking about, Daddy? What do you mean, you don't know where you went wrong with me?"

"You're spoiled rotten, and a lot of that is my fault. You're my baby girl. Your mom and I didn't even think we could have any more kids after trying for years, we had finally given up. As you can see, there are twenty years between you and your sister."

"Yes, I know that."

"Let me finish. When your mom told me she was pregnant with you, I couldn't have been happier. When I should have made you get a job like everyone else did, I didn't. I told myself you had all your life to work. Not making you get a job and at least paying your own phone bill was a big mistake. Do you know why?"

"No," I said to him, trying to figure out where all of this was going.

"I am still paying your phone bill till this day, Patrice. You are twenty-five years old. Yes, I know I set the bar high when it comes to men in your life, but don't you want your own things? When you were with Taymon, he took good care of you. That was the perfect time for you to go back to school and make something of yourself. As your daddy, I am telling you it is time for a change. What do you want to do with your life?"

I held my head down. I honestly didn't know what to say. My daddy always made me feel like I was still his little girl. I didn't like getting tongue lashes from my daddy. "Nah, hold your head up. What have I always told you about holding your head down?"

"You said to always hold my head up. No matter what I got going on, always be proud of who I am."

"Now answer my question. What are you planning on doing with the rest of your life? I want the best for you. I will help you do whatever it is you want to do. If it's a business you want to start up, just say the word."

"You ain't gonna think it's dumb, are you?"

"No, of course not. I told you to just say the word and I got you."

"I want to be an event planner."

"An event planner?" He scrunched his nose up.

"See, Daddy, you said you wasn't gonna laugh."

"I ain't laughing at you, baby girl. I just don't know what all they do."

"Daddy, you getting old."

"I may be. Now, tell me what an event planner does."

"They plan and decorate events. They do stuff like personalize stuff. Like, say for instance, I do a birthday party. I would personalize their drink bottles and chip bags stuff like that."

"Oh, okay, I get it now." I went to Facebook and pulled up a few pictures to show him. Even though he said he got it, I knew my daddy.

"Look at these pictures." I handed him my phone. My daddy wasn't getting an argument from me. Just like him, I wasn't happy with my life, either. I knew I had to make some changes because I wanted my own crib. I had never had one before. That was Taymon's crib, I was just living in it.

"So, how do they personalize these things?"

"They use a machine called a Cricut."

"How much does something like this cost?"

"Well, it depends on what kind of machine you buy. I am gonna need it all, though. I wanna be a one stop shop."

"What's a one stop shop? I mean, I know what a one stop shop is, but coming from your lane, what does it entail?"

"I want to do all the personalization. The balloons, the backdrop, I want to do it all." I went through Facebook and pulled up some more pictures. Shoot, I was getting excited just having this conversation with my daddy. "Look at these pictures."

"So, you can personalize wine glasses and stuff, too?"

"Yes, that's something I can do just because, though. Like, I can make T-shirts and stuff, too."

"I can dig it. So, you're gonna need a heat pressed, too?"

"Yep," I told him, nodding my head up and down like a kid in a candy store.

"Well, research everything for me. Once you have priced everything, we will sit down together and come up with a plan and I will buy everything you need."

"Aw, thank you so much, Daddy." I grabbed his neck and hugged him, and he hugged me back.

"You're welcome. And another thing." I let out a deep breath.

"Yes, Daddy?"

"Whatever you got going on with Nevaeh, you need to dead that. Now, this is coming from a man. Don't be chasing behind a nigga that don't want you. Your last name is Wright. Always remember you are the prize. If he doesn't want you, that's his loss, not yours. You know better than that. I know your feelings are more than likely hurt. You know I stay out of a lot of things that go on around here, but this one, I couldn't hold my peace on."

"Daddy, I'm over it. That's what I was just sitting here thinking about right before you came in here. I'm your child, so you know I don't like to be wrong. I was just mad."

"Mad at who, though?" I got quiet for a moment. I knew I had to be honest with myself again.

"I was mad at Nevaeh. I felt like she had won again."

"What you mean, she had won again? What did she win? I'm confused by that statement." I was about to put my head down again, but I caught myself. I was ashamed to tell my daddy I was low key jealous of my own friend. I had opened that can of worms, though.

"I just felt like she was always beating me at life."

"How is that?"

"She went off to college, got a decent career, and she was the first one to buy a house. Now she got Taymon, who I had first, and he's a good man."

"You could have had all of those things, too, but you never applied yourself. Now that's one thing I stayed on you about. I always told you to do good in school."

"Yes, you did."

"And if I ain't mistaken, you're the one that messed your relationship with Taymon up, not him. I remember when you came crying to me, asking me how to fix it. If you wanted to be mad at anybody, you should have been mad at yourself. Try looking in the mirror first, sweetheart."

"I know, Daddy. At the time, I didn't think anything I was doing was wrong. Now that all of this stuff is going on with Nevaeh, I've been sitting back, analyzing my life, and I want more for myself. Even Kam got her own things going on."

"I didn't come in here to bash you."

"I already know that, Daddy. You ain't gotta tell me that. I don't ever remember you putting me down."

"I just want to help you. I knew you would understand it better coming from me. I don't think Nevaeh is the only one you owe an apology, too, though."

"Who else I owe one to?"

"My other daughter. She felt some type of way after she got on you about your actions. You know she thinks she is your other mama. She feels like you disrespected her."

"I wouldn't never disrespect her, she tripping."

"Well, try telling her that." He threw his hands in the air. "I swear the saying is true. The messenger is always the one to get shot." We both fell out laughing. "You know me and your mama's anniversary coming up."

"Daddy, I ain't got no money. Didn't you just tell me you paying my phone bill?"

"Now that I do." He laughed. "That ain't what I'm talking about, though. I want to have a party this year. It will be our fiftieth anniversary. Let that be your first party. That way, you can start getting your name out there."

"Really, Daddy? That's a great idea. I got so many plans for you and Mama. Let me get to planning. I will apologize to your daughter."

"Thank you, that's all I wanted." He walked out of my room, smiling.

* * *

TAYMON

Boom! Me and my brother, along with Nevaeh's daddy, kicked the door in. We had a bounty on his head since we'd learned it was him who snatched her. When Kam first suspected it was him, she should have said something then, and I told her that.

She stated she wasn't sure, but in situations like this, you have to eliminate the suspects. You can't eliminate them if you don't even know they are one. We could have been brought her home.

One of the hoes I served called and told me she saw Chingy's car. She said it stood out like a sore thumb. For one, the house it was parked in front of had been empty for years. Two, it had been there for hours. Chingy didn't have a normal paint job, either. He was in a car club and his car was painted the color of the Carolina Panthers. He even had a panther on the hood of his car.

I didn't know what this nigga was on that he would drive around in his own car. Even when we looked at the video, he was driving a different car. "No, no, please stop!" We heard Nevaeh's cries as we stormed through the door.

The scene in front of me, I was not expecting at all. I mean, this nigga was actually taking pussy. I didn't even know he got down like that. The rage that came over me, I couldn't even explain it.

I football tackled that nigga, and he fell face first. I hopped up like we were on the football field for real and kicked that nigga in his head like I was kicking a field goal and his head was the ball. Buah! I kicked his ass again because I wasn't satisfied with the first kick, causing blood to squirt from his mouth.

My brother and her dad pulled her up and blood was everywhere. My anger multiplied as I thought of my unborn kids possibly not making it into this world. Oh, I was going to kill this nigga, but I was going to make him suffer first.

I grabbed the nigga and flipped him over as I grabbed my pistol from my waistline. "Oh, you like to rape women, huh?" I hit him in the face with the butt of my gun. Pow! I shot that nigga in his dick.

"Wait, wait, wait, don't take my manhood." He had thrown his hands up in a defensive mode.

"Nigga, you did this to yourself. You took away your own manhood when you raped Nevaeh. Do you know what they do to rapists in prison?" His eyes got big as hell. "You ain't got to worry about that, though. No need to get alarmed." He released the breath he was holding.

"Oh, no need to be relieved, either. You ain't gonna make it to jail. I'm gonna send your ass to hell." Pow! I shot his ass again, and this time, both his hands went to try to cover his dick. In front of his pants was a pool of blood.

"Kill this nigga so we can go. We gotta get Nevaeh to the hospital," my brother came in and told me. I didn't want to be done torturing this nigga, but Antwan was right. Nevaeh needed medical attention, and that alone outweighed his ass. Pow! I let one off in his dome. "You go ahead to the hospital and I will take care of this." Antwan took the gun from my hand and I ran to the car where a shaking, bloody Nevaeh was waiting for me, along with her daddy. She was sitting in the back seat with her head on his shoulder.

I hopped in the driver's seat and sped off. I looked in the rear-view mirror at her. This shit had me heated. I wanted to kill that nigga again.

I pulled in front of Atrium Health's main hospital on two wheels, drawing the attention of the security guards, causing them to rush to the car. When they saw all the blood, they yelled for a nurse. Next thing I knew, a nurse snatched my backdoor open, and along with Mr. Price, they placed her in a wheelchair. "What happened to her?" she frantically asked no one in particular.

"She is pregnant, and she was raped."

"Oh, my God. What kind of monster would do something like this?" She didn't ask or say anything else as she rushed Nevaeh through the door.

"Fuck!" I yelled as I punched the steering wheel with my fists. I felt as if I had failed her. I wasn't there to protect her. If it weren't for me, she wouldn't have even been in this situation.

"Go ahead and park." Her daddy came back to the car to tell me. The front of his shirt was drenched in blood. "They have taken her back to treat her. I called her mama, because I know more than anything, she is going to need her."

"What are they saying about my babies?"

"They ain't said nothing yet. When they took her back, I came out here to check on you. Listen, we can beat ourselves up all day, but it ain't nothing we could have done to prevent this."

"This is my fault. He only took her because I killed his cousin."

"Wasn't you protecting your brother?"

"Yes," I said, bobbing my head up and down.

"He is a sick individual. The whole time I was in the streets, women and kids was off limits. This is a new breed coming up. The men back in my day would never. Just park your car. I will be inside waiting on you."

"Yo." I answered for my brother as I pulled off, looking for a parking space.

"I took care of everything. I will meet you at the hospital in a few. Take care of my sister-in-law. I like her for you." I didn't even get a chance to say anything before he hung up.

Once I walked back toward the hospital, I saw Patrice making her way through the door. I blew air from my mouth. I swear I wasn't up for her shit today. She better come in here acting like she got some damn sense, or I was going to carry her ass right on up out of here.

I slowed down a little and let her make her way into the hospital. When I finally made my way through the door, she looked up at me, then turned her attention back to her phone.

I shook my head as she rose from her seat and headed my way. "Hey, Taymon." I looked at her, but didn't say anything. It was the way she said my name that made me look at her differently at this moment. She sounded genuine.

"What's up, Patrice?" I asked as I sat back in my chair with my arms folded across my chest. I swear I had spent so much time at this hospital in the last few months than I had in my life.

I knew the emergency staff was familiar with us by now. "I just wanted to apologize to you about how I acted. I was wrong all the way around the board."

"Come again?" I said because I couldn't believe she was standing in front of me, apologizing.

"I said I wanted to apologize," I cut her off.

"I heard you the first time, I am just shocked to hear you say that. You don't owe me an apology, though." Since she had come to me correct, I had to man up to my shit too. I was wrong in this situation as well. "I owe you an apology, too."

"You do?" she asked with a shocked expression on her face. I could understand her confusion. The whole time everyone was coming for her, and I was to blame as well. The only innocent person in this situation was Nevaeh.

"Yeah, I do. I am the one that made all this mess awkward. You came in blindsided. When you saw me hugged up with Nevaeh, I know it hurt your feelings. It should have, she was your best friend. Where you became wrong was when you put your hands on her. You should have kept it with me. You know your friend, so you know she would never do you like that."

"I overreacted. That is why I am here. I owe her an apology as well. I prayed for her the whole time she was missing. I never thought Chingy had it in him. What are they saying? Is she okay?"

I hesitated at first because I was not sure if I should tell her what I was about to say. I knew she was going to find out anyway because their families were close knit as well. "She was raped."

"Oh my God." Her hand went to cover her mouth. "Did Chingy rape her?"

"Yep," I said as I shook my head.

"I honestly don't even know what to say about that." She didn't say anything else to me as she went and sat back in her seat. She was still trying to process what I had just said. As soon as she sat down, everyone started coming in.

Her mama ran straight to Mr. Price. An elderly lady walked in with her mama. I had never met Nevaeh's grandma before, but I assumed this had to be her. I could see the family resemblance. The mama looked just like the grandma.

I saw Patrice talking to the elderly lady, then she pointed at me. Once she headed my way, I knew my theory was more than likely right. "Hello, young man. I am Pastor Mckinnley, also Nevaeh's grandma." She stuck her hand out for me to shake.

"Hello, ma'am, nice to meet you."

"The feeling is mutual. I would love to see you at church."

"I will get by there. I have heard so much about you. I am sure you will baptize my babies."

"I am sure I will, too."

"The family of Nevaeh Price." We all looked towards the lady who had just walked in and called us. I forgot all about the conversation I was having with her grandmother as I walked towards the lady.

"Hi, my name is Taymon. I am the daddy of the unborn kids. Is everything alright?"

"Well, I am Doctor Turner. We did a rape kit on her, and the babies are safe. The blood y'all saw was mostly from tearing of her vaginal area. She has some abrasions and trauma from the blows to her face and head. We are monitoring the babies' heartbeats. After she gets some rest, she should be fine physically. Now, the emotional trauma is a different story. The police has a few questions."

"We already figured that." Her daddy stepped forward and spoke. "Where are they?"

"They should walk in here shortly." We already had our story together. We brought her phone with us and planted it on her, saying we tracked her location. She does share her location with her girls. We were going to tell them she wasn't missing twenty-four hours, so that was why we didn't contact them.

Being missing for twenty-four hours was their rule, not ours, so what could they say? We were worried about her, and when we tracked her down, that was how we found her. That way, they won't question us about a suspect.

Just like Doctor Turner stated, the police waltzed through the door. I was tired of dealing with their asses. I didn't like them all up in my business. As of late, I felt like my life was a reality television show.

"Hello, I am Detective Gill, and this is my partner, Detective Monroe. We are here to question the rape and assault on a Ms. Nevaeh Price. Do we know who did this to her and how it happened?"

"We know what y'all know." Her daddy stepped up and started doing the talking. "Nobody had heard from her all day, so her boyfriend right here"—he pointed to me—"went by her house to check on her. When he got there, he noticed her door was open."

"Okay, so what is your name, Mr. Boyfriend?" Detective Gill turned towards me and reached his hand out for me to shake.

"Taymon," I told him as I shook his hand.

"Why didn't you call us when you noticed her door open?"

"Y'all said y'all have a twenty-four-hour missing person's policy. I figured y'all wasn't going to do anything. Everything that he just said was true. After a few hours, we tracked her phone and that's when we found her."

"Did you see anybody other than her?"

"No, she was lying there, covered in blood. Honestly, my main focus was to get her some help."

"Alright, thank you. We don't have any further questions. If we think of anything else, we will reach out to one of you." They walked off and I walked off behind them and headed to the desk. I had to see her.

"How can I help you, sir?"

"Can you ask the doctor if Nevaeh Price can receive visitors yet?"

"Yes, can you give me a moment to find out?" She picked the phone up, I am assuming to call to the back. I shook my head; she acted like I had a choice. After a few minutes, even though it seemed like forever, she hung the phone up and gave me her undivided attention. "She can see two at a time," she told me.

"Thank you, I will let everyone know." I walked back towards the crowd. "Yo, they said two people can go back and see her at a time."

"Well, I am going first," Amber told us.

"No, you ain't. How do you figure you can go first?" Kam asked her. I noticed Patrice hadn't said anything.

"Let Taymon go first, and Von, you can go with him. I spent time with her in the car on the way here. I know she needs her mama, so I ain't selfish. Those are Taymon's kids, so he needs to speak with her as well." I walked off with her mom right beside me.

The lady at the front desk got up from her seat and took us to the back. Once we were in the room, all I heard were my babies' heartbeats echoing in the background. Just like the doctor said, they were monitoring their hearts.

Nevaeh's face was swollen, and her head was wrapped in gauze. She looked pitiful. "Hey, mama," she said above a whisper.

"Hey, baby," her mom said back as she walked closer to the bed. She brushed her hair out of her face.

"You think I am ugly now, don't you? I know you don't look at me the same way." I knew she was talking to me because she looked my way.

"Don't you ever think that. You will always be beautiful to me." I placed a soft kiss on her forehead. "I ain't going nowhere." A pool of tears formed in the corners of her eyes. I reached over and wiped them away.

"The storm is over now, baby. I am sorry for not being able to protect you. I had one job to do, and I failed."

"No, it is not your fault. When I saw you calling me, I assumed you were outside. I didn't even bother to answer the phone, I just went straight to the door. That was the biggest mistake of my life. I will never do that again."

I pulled a chair up and laid my head on her pillow. Her mom followed suit. We stayed that way for a while with nobody saying anything.

* * *

NEVAEH

Two Months Later

*J*t was the day of my baby shower, and I couldn't have been happier. So much money had been spent on this day.

Between my daddy and Taymon, they made sure this baby shower was everything I wanted and then some.

Patrice had apologized to me, and because of my upbringing, you know I forgave her. Truth be told, I had already forgiven her, I just wasn't going to fuck with her again. We could still be cordial, but we would never be as close as we once were.

She had started her party planning company, so I let her do my baby shower. She told me her first event was supposed to be her parents' anniversary party. She said she would be honored to do this event for me. I was a little skeptical at first, though; I wasn't going to lie. I wasn't sure if she was going to try to sabotage my event because she was still in her feelings.

Kam had just finished my eyelashes and eyebrows, and I was checking myself out in the mirror.

"Girl, you look the fuck good," she told me. "I already know you and Taymon about to bring the whole city out. Patrice sent me some pictures of the event. It looks good. She actually did an excellent job."

"Yeah, I saw the pictures. She sent them to me as well."

"I am so glad she found her niche, because baby, I thought I was gonna have to kill my own aunt." We both started laughing. "You don't know how big of a relief it is that y'all are back talking. Shit, me and Amber hated being in the middle of y'all's shit."

"Speaking of Amber," I told her, changing the subject. I didn't want to talk about Patrice's ass right now.

"What about her?"

"Um, when did white boy come into play? I met him the other day for the first time. I feel like I know him from somewhere, though, I just can't put my finger on it."

"You really don't know, huh?" she asked as she laughed at me.

"What don't I know?"

"That is the detective dude."

"What detective dude? I am lost in the sauce, baby."

"The one from your sister's case. He was the one in the room, asking all those damn questions."

"Oh, so when did they exchange numbers? I could have sworn when he left, she was still there."

"Oh, she was. You're going to get her when I give you the tea on those two."

"Oh, Lord. I guess it's a good thing I am sitting down, then."

"Yes, because we were all shocked. We found out about him when you got kidnapped. When I got to your house, he was already there. So, you know me and my big ass mouth. I was like, I thought y'all didn't want to call the police, and they were like, we don't. I was like, well, what is he doing here then? Antwan was like, oh, that's Amber's new boo."

"Wait a minute, what?"

"Yeah, girl, same thing I said. To sum it all up, that day at the hospital, they already knew each other."

"You mean to tell me Amber sat in that hospital room and acted like she didn't even know that man?"

"Girl, yes. Ain't no way a nigga would have done that to me."

"This is crazy. I didn't know all of that. Wait until I talk to her. You mean to tell me I just found out about him the other day? I was thinking all of this was new. I didn't have a clue she'd been talking to him. As a matter of fact, I am about to get her on the line now."

I picked my phone up and dialed Amber's ass on speaker. "Hello?" She sounded like she was in the car.

"You an ole sneaky hoe," I said to her and me and Kam both burst into laughter.

"What the hell I do?"

"You introduced me to white boy like y'all had just started kicking it or something. I am over here talking to Kam, and she tells me this shit been going on. Alright, I see how we do."

"Girl, gone head with that. And Kam, you talk too damn much." We all laughed.

"Nah, because when I said she talked too much for telling you my business, you took up for her. Now she talks too much because she is telling your business."

"Oh, so y'all just gonna sit here and talk about me in my face like I ain't standing right here?"

"Yep," we both said and shared a laugh. Kam knew she was our girl, but we all knew, just like she knew, she talked too damn much.

115

"Y'all ain't finished yet?"

"Yeah, she just finished. I am about to get dressed. She came to my house to hook her girl up. I will see you shortly." We hung up.

"I am about to go in your hallway bathroom and take a shower. What time is Taymon coming to pick you up?"

"He should be on his way. The baby shower starts at three and it is a little after one."

"Well, take your shower, and I will help you put your tiara on and stuff." I thanked her and got in the shower. We were going to walk in together, wearing white. I had a dress code. I wanted the women in pink to represent my girls and the men to wear blue to represent my son. Our theme was teddy bears.

* * *

I walked into Jake's, holding Taymon's hand, and my mouth fell open. The pictures Patrice had sent me for my baby shower had nothing on the real-life version. This was absolutely beautiful. She had really found her mark.

She had a pink and blue balloon arch with a teddy bear hanging from a swing. The tables were pink and blue, but she did every other one with an assorted color. The blue tables had pink chairs and the pink tables had blue chairs. The backdrop had a picture of a bear hanging from balloons and it said, *we can bearly wait*.

At the entrance, she had a picture up of me and Taymon from our maternity shoot. He was on one knee, kissing my belly. Then she had our kids' names lit up in different areas around the room. The thing that got me was the two thrones. I didn't care about anything else, but I wanted my thrones.

They were in the front of the room with parents-to-be hanging from the ceiling. There was a teddy bear attached to the sign, one on each side. I walked over to the candy table and was incredibly pleased there as well, too.

The chip bags had our theme and, 'welcome', with each one of the kids' names on it. We had cake pops, lollipops, juice boxes, water, and even the sodas had our theme on it.

"Do you like it?" Patrice walked over to us and asked.

"Yeah, you did a good job," Taymon told her as he ran his hand down his face. He was against me letting her do our baby shower. Like I said, I was against it in the beginning, too, but I could tell how serious she was about it.

"Yeah, girl, you found your niche. You should have started this a long time ago, but that's neither here nor there. Like I said, you did an excellent job." I reached out and hugged her as much as my pregnant belly would allow me to.

Taymon grabbed my hand and helped me sit on my throne. As soon as I was situated, he went and sat on his. Shortly after, people came in. Everyone who walked in the door walked over to greet us, then set their gift on the table.

Truthfully, it was not about the gifts, I just wanted to be around people I loved and who loved me back. Taymon had already brought everything our kids were going to need. I mean, we were having triplets, so I knew we could never really have enough.

My house went from two empty rooms to all three of my bedrooms being full. While they were small, we were putting all three of them in the same room. We were going to separate them once they got a little older.

We gave our kids Biblical names. The girls' names were going to be Adah, which meant adornment, and Areli, which meant golden, and of course, our son's name was Amos. His name meant to carry, borne by God. My triple A's was what I called them.

I no longer walked around here sad and feeling some type of way about being pregnant with triplets. My kids were a blessing from God. Just to think, I almost lost them. I would never take my pregnancy for granted again.

A lot of Taymon's friends and family showed up as well. Kam and Amber were my hostess. Of course, I had had them both be hostess because they weren't having it any other way. They said Patrice did the whole baby shower by herself and didn't let them help, so this was their way of being a part of my day. Hey, who was I to argue with them? My sister said she didn't care one way or the other.

If you ask me, though, Patrice did this more out of guilt than anything else. Even though I paid her, she said she would do it for no charge. I wasn't going for that, though. Once a person shows you who they really are, believe them. Like I said, I forgave her, but we would never be as close as we once were.

"Here you go." Amber handed me my plate first, then handed Taymon his plate. I sat around and watched everyone enjoying themselves.

"I see you're happy," Taymon whispered in my ear.

"I am. I just love this whole vibe."

"I am glad you are." He got up and walked over to the DJ booth. I saw him talking to the DJ, but I didn't know what they were talking about. Next thing I knew, Taymon had the microphone in his hand.

The music went low, and he talked. "Excuse me, may I have everyone's attention?" Everyone who was talking stopped their conversation and turned their attention towards him. He then walked over towards me and helped me from my seat. He held my hand until we were in the middle of the floor. Now all eyes were on us.

"First off, I want to thank everyone for coming out to show us some love. You don't know how much this means to Neveah and me. I couldn't believe I was about to be somebody's daddy, y'all." When he said that, I looked over at Patrice. To my surprise, she was smiling. Maybe she was over us being together. I mean, who knows. If she wasn't, she damn sure deserves an academy award.

"Nevaeh, thank you for everything. I couldn't have asked for a better half. We ain't known each other that long, but when it is right, it's right." He then went down in his all-white and got on one knee. My tears fell because I already knew what was coming next.

"Oh, my God!" I screamed, causing my guests to laugh at me.

"Calm down, he ain't asked you nothing yet," my mama told me as I waved her off with my hand. I wasn't thinking about her.

"Will you marry me?" I stuck my hand out so he could put the diamond on my finger. It was absolutely beautiful. It was white gold. I softly punched him.

"What was that for?"

"You asked me a few weeks ago if I preferred white gold or just gold. I didn't think anything of it." I grabbed him around his neck as he got up and stuck my tongue in his mouth in front of everyone as they yelled and clapped.

I didn't give a damn who knew. This was my man. I had a good one and I wasn't letting him go. His parents came over and congratulated us. I looked over at my sister and my girls and couldn't believe this was happening to me.

"Y'all knew, didn't y'all?" They all shook their heads yes.

"That's why I wasn't too pressed about helping with the baby shower. I was given the honor of helping pick out the ring. I was at the house the day he came and asked Daddy if he could marry you. He then asked me if I would help him with the ring." I grabbed my girls as best as I could.

"I am getting married, y'all."

"Oh, yes, we got a wedding to plan!" Amber yelled.

The rest of the baby shower went off smoothly. We had so much stuff, we were going to have to put a lot in the storage house I had in the back of my house.

EPILOGUE

I was exhausted. I had just delivered my babies from my scheduled caesarean. I had been nervous for the last few days. I kept questioning myself, wondering if I was really ready to be someone's mama. I guess, ready or not, I had to get ready. My babies were here, ready or not. The doctor had told me I could only have two people in the delivery room, but I convinced her to let me have three.

I had to have both of my parents, along with Taymon, with me. My heart filled with joy as I watched Taymon trying to juggle all three babies. I told him we should take turns with the babies doing skin to skin, but he insisted he do all three babies together. I mean, who was going to argue with a man about his own kids? My girls weighed four pounds and nine ounces and my son weighed five pounds and three ounces. The girls were seventeen inches long and my son was nineteen inches long.

He was going to be tall like his daddy. My kids, all three of them, looked just like that man. God, you gave me three; I couldn't get one who looked like me? I laughed to myself at the thought.

We got married because I wanted to be married before my babies were born. We had a small ceremony and only invited our close friends and family. We were going to do a big reception once I was healed from having my babies.

Taymon moved me out of my house, and into a bigger house. We had a five bedroom, three and a half bathroom house. I couldn't be happier. We agreed I was going to take a year off from teaching. Taymon said he didn't feel comfortable putting our kids in daycare until they were at least one-year-old. Well, he said two, but I convinced him to let them go at one.

I still had nightmares about what happened with Chingy, but I didn't tell Taymon. This was a situation he couldn't do anything about, so I just kept it to myself. Patrice, well, let's just say she had come a long way. Her business had been booming since she had my baby shower. Everyone talked about how well it was put together and they wanted to know who did it. We weren't close like we were, and we didn't even talk every day, but we talked.

Amber and the detective were holding it down. I think my cousin may be in love with him. I never thought it would be with a white man, but hey, to each their own. I was so happy for her.

As for Kam and Antwan, those two were crazy, and I really wished they would get it together. Those were two people who love each other, and everyone knows it, they just don't want to do right. They were fucking, and everyone knew that, but that was all they were on these days.

AJ, Antwan's son, was staying with him. He meant what he said when he made it clear that was still his son. As far as Maria goes, we hadn't heard from her. She didn't even call and check on her son. Now that I was a mother, I didn't know how you could just walk away from something you birthed.

"Thank you, baby." The nurse had just walked into the room to take our children to the nursery.

"What are you thanking me for?" He kissed me softly on the lips.

"Everything. My beautiful family and just for being you. I love you."

"I love you, too."

THE END

ABOUT THE AUTHOR

Shmel Carter, born Shmel Walker, is a native of Charlotte, NC. Ms. Carter has been struggling with diabetes since the age of eighteen. She graduated from North Mecklenburg Senior High School in Huntersville, NC, and Shaw University in Raleigh, NC. She is the mother of three kids who she loves very dearly. She has five siblings. She has a passion for writing has been writing since she was twelve. She is currently working her way to the top.

Join her on Facebook under Shmel Carter.

Follow her on Twitter @author_scarter

Like her author page on Facebook https://www.facebook.com/#!/pages/Author-Shmel-Carters-Passion/225439567664185

Instagram @author_shmel_carter or email her at authorshmelcarter49@gmail.com

ALSO BY SHMEL CARTER

An ATL Love Story: Tone & Khandi

All the way from the Queen City to the grimy streets of Atlanta, Tone and Kandi have enemies and exes coming from everywhere. From secrets, lies, and murders, this couple doesn't know where to turn. Tone is holding a devastating secret from Kandi, but unbeknownst to him, she is holding a few of her own. Kandi just may not be the good girl Tone thinks she is. Will this couple survive everything is thrown their way?

A Hood Affair

Take a ride down the streets of Charlotte, NC, better known as the Queen City as Shaneice, bka Neicee and her boyfriend, Quentin, known as Q, take you on a whirlwind of surprises. Q loves Neicee with everything in him, but he can't remain faithful. Neicee is from the hood, and she grew up the only girl of six children. She is determined to never have to go back to the hood. Despite where she is from, she graduated from law school and has built the reputation as the baddest hood lawyer to ever grace the streets of Charlotte. Now, someone is out to kill Neicee. Could it be one of Q's sideline hoes? Unbeknownst to Q, Neicee has her own secret. Will Q lose Neicee, or will she remain his ride or die chick?

If It Isn't Love: Duke and Myesha

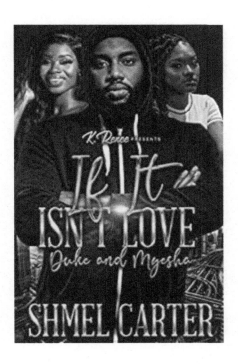

Falling in love was never on Myesha's agenda until she met Duke. She fell hard for Duke, only for him to turn around and break her heart. Once she found out about Duke's big secret, she just could not let it go. Unbeknownst to Myesha, Duke is holding on to another secret. To get over Duke, Myesha starts seeing Zeke, but does Zeke have her best interest at heart?

Duke fell in love with Myesha at first sight. He knows how Myesha feels about secrets and lies, but in his mind, he is protecting her. He feels as if telling her his secrets would bring more harm than good. He can't stand to see Myesha with another man, and he refuses to let what they have go.

All types of drama have been going on around Myesha and she doesn't know which way to turn or who she can trust. Will Duke become truthful about all his lies before Myesha finds out about them? Will she take Duke back after finding out? You don't want to miss this banger as these characters show you how it goes down in the Queen City.

Certified: A ride or die love story

Shenika was young and in love. She was madly in love with the infamous Junior, and she has proven it on many occasions. She does not care what anyone has to say about it, including her own mother. Shenika thought Junior loved her back until he did the unthinkable. Shenika just knew taking his charge would prove her loyalty to her man, but it didn't.

Junior left Shenika for dead when she got sentenced to 10 years in a State prison for a crime he committed. After Shenika is released from prison, Junior just knew she was the same young, dumb girl she was before she got locked up. After seeing her at the club one day, he knew then he had to have her back. Shenika has clearly earned the title of being Certified. Will she take Junior back or will she make him regret the day he ever did her dirty?

Made in the USA
Monee, IL
23 May 2023

34383057R00080